DEVIL'S OWN DAUGHTER

A feature on Old Wives' Tales is not exactly the assignment to make Kate Mallory's pulse race. She fancies herself an investigative journalist and crime reporter, and when her research throws up a vital clue to the series of arson attacks and gruesome murders that is baffling the Darlaston police, she teams up with Richard Torrey, an enigmatic man with intuitive psychic powers, on the trail of a story too good to miss. It leads her into a deadly encounter with a ruthless woman, a coven of Satanists – and Evil incarnate.

DEVIL'S OWN DAUGHTER

DEVIL'S OWN DAUGHTER

by

Meg Hutchinson
writing as Margaret Astbury

Magna Large Print Books
Long Preston, North Yorkshire,
BD23 4ND, England.

British Library Cataloguing in Publication Data.

Hutchinson, Meg writing as Astbury, Margaret
     Devil's own daughter.

     A catalogue record of this book is
     available from the British Library

     ISBN   978-0-7505-2697-5

First published in Great Britain in 2005 by Hodder & Stoughton
A division of Hodder Headline

Cover illustration © Larry Rostant by arrangement with
Hodder & Stoughton Ltd.

Published in Large Print 2007 by arrangement with
Hodder & Stoughton Ltd.

Magna Large Print is an imprint of Library Magna Books Ltd.

Printed and bound in Great Britain by
T.J. (International) Ltd., Cornwall, PL28 8RW

1

Soft, sibilant, the swish of curtains undulated like some giant black snake crossing walls and windows, secreting the room from the evening light, closing away the pale cream of wallpaper, enveloping the whole in a shroud of darkness.

Within the doorway two figures moved forward, carrying between them a roll of cloth. Watching as it was set down, Venetia Pascal felt a tremor run through her. Not fear; she had witnessed the Offering before; no, what she felt was excitement, the heady anticipation of taking part in something in which she delighted ... the joy of serving the All Powerful, the Prince of Darkness.

Slowly, with painstaking care, every crease and wrinkle smoothed, the cloth was spread in the centre of a floor muted by overhead lighting; light which caressed rather than revealed a painted design. Bold against a stark black background, a double-rimmed circle of gold banded a series of letters whilst the inner circle encased a great five-pointed golden star.

The Pentagram!

Venetia Pascal's veins fluttered again.

The symbol of protection, but would that protection prove sufficient guard against the force soon to be called forth, Belial, Servant of the High Throne, Belial, Destroyer of life? There was an element of danger in every act of worship no matter how insignificant the Coven; a wrong word when summoning, a wrong move whilst the Presence was among them and everyone in this room, even the Magus himself, could be snatched into purgatory.

All, that was, except Venetia Pascal!

A smile touching her mouth, she looked down at the black and gold cloth stretched across the floor. The overhead lighting had been extinguished and now it seemed to move and writhe like a living, breathing thing beneath the flickering flame of freshly lit black candles, their tall wooden sconces marking the four points of the compass.

In the cloying silence Venetia watched as a table draped in black silk was set within the Pentacle, then a knife and bronze bowl placed upon it.

It was time!

Her own head unbowed, her eyes following the movement of Theo Vail as he stepped to the table, Venetia's nerves tautened. Theo Vail, Magus of the High Coven, master of magic, was a man with aspirations, and he saw this night as another step on the road to fulfilling them.

'We are of one mind?'

Vail's voice was velvet soft, yet the half-circle of worshippers trembled visibly as they replied.

'We are of one mind.'

It would make no difference should they not be! Venetia smiled to herself. Whether they knew it or not, from the moment of entering this house, each was given to the Master, albeit they had not as yet performed the ritual of Offering. They could refuse to go through with that, they could withdraw from the Coven, but death would find them ... the Coven would be protected and the Lord of Darkness would have his sacrifice of souls.

'In Nomine Satanum.'

The tones of the leader of the Coven rose as his hands lifted shoulder high.

'To him who was before time we do homage.'

To each side the initiates knelt and it seemed to Venetia she could feel the vibrations emanating from them. They were nervous now ... in a few minutes they would be terrified!

'Great One ... Lord of the Dark Realms...'

Theo Vail called again.

'...on this Night of Dedication we bring new souls to your service. Send forth your envoy that he might accept them onto The Path, command him in your name.'

Beyond the flickering candle light, sound crept from the corners of the room, moving along its walls like the slither of some huge reptile.

Standing within the Pentacle, hands still raised, Theo Vail's blond head arched on his neck, his eyes closing, his tone now soft as though speaking to a lover.

'Lucifer, Lord of the Earth, hear your servant; accept the gift he makes to your Glory.'

The slithering sound ceased. A stillness that could almost be touched lowered over the room, a stifling nerve-shattering stillness that grabbed the brain, holding it in a vice-like grip and Venetia heard the gasps of the kneeling group, the sob of a woman. Then within that awesome stillness, from its very centre, came a rustle, a whisper of breath that moved and spread, fingering along the curtained walls, circling the Pentagram.

Answer had been given!

Familiar as she was with evenings such as this, excitement mingled with trepidation caught in Venetia Pascal's throat. She must remain absolutely still; to move could be fatal; though unseen the emissary of Satan was in the room.

Slowly, Theo Vail's hands lowered to his sides, his hair gleaming in the light of the candles as he straightened his neck.

He was so sure of himself. From her position a little apart from the newly selected, those chosen by Vail to become novitiates of several other covens, Venetia saw the gleam in his eyes as they opened. He was so certain of his standing with the Master, so confident of his own powers as a Magus. But power was that which the Master allowed ... and it could be taken as easily as it was given.

'All High...'

Theo Vail spoke again, rapture throbbing in every word.

'...Lord of the World, make known your will.'

Sound which until now had been soft began to build, whirling and crashing, a maelstrom of soundless noise, then, as though turned off by a switch, it dropped once more to mind-gripping stillness.

Among the half-circle a woman's sob spilled. Would she move ... rise to her feet and run from the room? Venetia's glance rested a moment on the bent head. It would be a pity if fear drove her to that for she would be dead before she reached the street.

12

'Angel of the High Throne, Messenger of the Prince of Darkness, pass beyond The Gates.'

As if in answer to Vail's soft call the candle flames flickered and lowered, leaving the room in almost total darkness, then just on the point of dying they flared upward, the light from each spearing to a point above the table, joining light into light, coalescing into a pool of brilliance.

For a moment it hovered and in those brief seconds Venetia saw fear. Reflected by the glow of the being he had summoned, Theo Vail's belief in himself showed its cracks; though never admitting it, he knew his fallibility, knew that he, as everyone in this room, stood in mortal danger.

Above his head, losing none of its brightness, the spread of light spiralled into a column which, as it slowed, separated into spindrifts, forming torso, arms, legs, limbs of golden flame, and lastly a head, the face of which seemed made of beaten bronze while the eyes were crimson fire.

Looking at it, Venetia felt a wild exultation sweep her veins. This was what she longed for, power not just to call the demons of hell but to dominate them, to have them do her bidding, to stand before the Master, to be supreme leader of the High Coven.

'Those who choose to become servants of the Master come into the circle.'

Vail had picked up the knife and as the first novitiate stepped within the Pentacle, he asked in ringing tone, 'Do you accept the Prince of Darkness as your Lord, your Master in all things?'

Floating inches above them the glowing figure waited, its glistening fiery eyes fastening on the man reaching a hand to Theo Vail, while he answered quietly, 'With this, my blood, I pledge life and soul to Lucifer, Lord of the Earth.'

The reply had been given. A rapid flick of the knife nicked the skin above the man's wrist and as several scarlet drops fell into the bronze bowl an arm of diaphanous golden mist lifted and from a finger a dart of violet flame touched the cut, leaving it healed without blemish.

The gift had been accepted!

A smile curving his handsome mouth, Theo Vail glanced at Venetia.

A smile of triumph or of mockery? Her own gaze portrayed none of the bitterness raging inside her, the dislike she held for the leader of the High Coven, the venom she could almost taste. That, like her own aspirations must, for the moment, be kept hidden.

One by one the initiates entered the Pentacle, repeating the ritual whereby they offered life and soul to the Devil. In return for what? Venetia's glance returned to the group. What had each of these people asked in exchange?

A sob cutting off the thought, she watched the one woman among the rest. Terror was stamped clear on a face as pale as a corpse while eyes stretched wide with panic stared at the floating, amorphous figure.

'I ... I...'

The woman stammered as Vail called her forward.

'I ... I...'

She had reached the rim of the Pentacle.

Enhanced by the blackness surrounding it, the

gleaming figure too watched the woman, its terrible eyes twin furnaces of living fire.

'I...' Abject with fear, her words refusing to come, the woman halted and in that moment the finger of violet flame which had touched the wrist of the others stabbed against the pale forehead.

Rejection! Venetia watched the slight figure crumple and fold like some paper doll. Fear had bound the woman's tongue as it would have kept her from serving the Master. Fear had brought its reward. The envoy of the All Powerful had taken her life. Satan had no place on the earthly plane for those attempting to leave his service, but hell was filled with their souls.

Floating in dark-filled space the fiery eyes turned from the woman fallen to the floor. Beneath the lambent figure the bronze dish shone in the reflected light, the contents glistening like a sea of rubies.

No one moved. A sharp shake of Theo Vail's head warned against it, and all the time the being from the Dark Regions watched.

How long would it remain, unmoving, its gaze fastened on those afraid almost to breathe? Would it withdraw with only one life, would the woman be alone in her death? Her own breathing even, though slower than she would wish, Venetia watched the devil's intermediary.

Theo Vail too was wondering. Had he made some mistake? Had the Ritual of Dedication been wrongly performed? It was a justifiable fear.

The Master tolerated no mishap! A trickle of cold perspiration ran the length of his spine.

It was then a great golden arm lifted, a glittering hand outstretched over the bowl.

Beneath it the bronze dish glistened in the reflected glow; then, of itself, the collected blood of the newly inducted Followers rose in a carmine column to become absorbed into the spindrift hand, into arms, legs, torso, until the whole body was one throbbing, pulsing mass of blood from which a face stared. Sound without sound, wind that held no air roared around the room, the ferocity of it seeming to rock the walls, to shake the foundations while within it all the envoy of Lucifer erupted into spirals of flame; violet, scarlet, gold, they spumed upward into the darkness of shadow then curved inward, drawn back into the heaving mass; only the golden face showing what it had been, a face that smiled as the spectre faded to nothingness.

'Call just come in, looks like we might have another one.'

'Christ!' Detective Inspector Bruce Daniels slammed his half-eaten sandwich on to the plate set amid the paper jungle that was the surface of his desk. 'Not another bloody bonfire?'

'Seems like it.' Sergeant David Farnell looked ruefully at the plate now cracked right across. That would be the third this week to come out of the Inspector's office ... better order plastic next time.

'Where?' Daniels' question came through half-chewed bread and corned beef.

'Station Street, paint factory, quite a blaze by all account, took the crew of a couple of fire

16

engines to bring it under control, early report says it could be arson.'

Could be arson! Bruce Daniels' lips clamped against a surge of stomach acid. It could also be flying pigs shittin' firecrackers – of course it was bloody arson, factories didn't set themselves on fire.

Watching him pop an antacid tablet on to his tongue, the station sergeant guessed the thoughts pushing their way about his colleague's mind. They had both joined the Darlaston force at roughly the same time and over the years he had come to know Bruce Daniels well enough to recognise the 'surly copper' bit paid off. The local low life knew he made no empty threats, that he was as good as his word; there were a few in Winson Green would find no argument with that.

Seeing him touch a hand to the pocket of his jacket, David Farnell had the good sense to keep the ensuing smile to himself. Checking car keys and antacid tablets was another of Bruce Daniels' little idiosyncrasies; the car-key check was understandable ... but the eternal tablets? That brief stay in hospital a couple of years back had done nothing except recommend surgery to relieve a stomach ulcer. They could have suggested a trip to the moon, it would have met with the same response; Daniels wanted none of it! But just how long could he go on sucking antacid tablets, how long before that ulcer burst? Have that happen and Detective Inspector Daniels would be finished for good.

'Should anybody ask, you know where I am...' at the rear entrance of Darlaston Police Station

17

Daniels paused, '...anybody except them from the *"Star"*.'

They would be here with noses sharper than the points on their pencils. Newshounds! He sniffed ruefully. Bloodhounds would be a more apt description, especially Kate Mallory; that one would sniff a story out of stone.

He unlocked the door of the blue Ford Fiesta and eased his five foot eleven into the driving seat. Pity his wife didn't have another relative to leave her another inheritance, for that was how they had come to buy this car and seeing the way his luck went they were not likely to buy another.

Detective Chief Inspector! The engine idling, he stared unseeingly at the yard filled with other cars. Detective Chief Inspector; the gold braid he could do without but the salary was nice. In the end he had got neither. *He* had brought in those counterfeit plates, thus averting a crisis that would have had the whole of the Middle East in flames, *he* it had been who had cracked that case involving the importing and selling of heroin, but he had *not* reaped the reward; Bruce Daniels had not been promoted to Chief Inspector. That tit-bit had gone to somebody else, leaving Bruce Daniels to do what he had done for years – scrape the shit from Darlaston's streets!

Acid reared into Daniels' throat.

Connor, whose arse had never left his chair except for that one time... Connor hadn't sweated and worried, he hadn't dealt with Echo Sounder, the little canary who had been made to sing of a deal going down at a factory unit for freezing poultry; Connor hadn't sat for hours cooped up in a car waiting for things to break, but *he* had come sweeping into that yard just as half a million pounds' worth of heroin had been pulled from the arses of dead chickens. 'I'll take things from here.' That was what Connor had said, and with the case he had taken the glory ... and the promotion!

Connor had gone up the ladder sharper than a ferret down a rabbit hole; Chief Superintendent of Police! Daniels swallowed hard. Nice work if you got it... only he never got any, not even after nabbing the boss of that printing works. Julian Crowley was counterfeiting every major currency of the Middle East; he was printing war! But even bringing him home to roost had sewn no gold braid to Bruce Daniels' uniform, for Connor's rapid departure from Darlaston had been filled by an equally smart-arsed git, one as quick to grab the credit as Connor had been.

Martin Quinto! Touching the accelerator pedal, Daniels guided the car into the street. That one wouldn't mind how many arses he climbed up so long as there was a bit of gold braid to be pulled out of 'em!

Turning the corner of Victoria Road he hit the horn and swore to himself as a lanky teenager grinned, gave the 'V' sign and raced into the park. Bloody kids, he knew what he'd do with the lot of 'em; no doubt it was kids set fire to that paint factory, but fat lot of use it would prove nabbing them, they'd just be told by magistrates to behave better in the future.

Future! He pressed harder on the pedal, shooting the small car forward. The only future

19

kids like that deserved was a few years in the Army – and no bloody Member of Parliament allowed to bail them out!

Rounding the bend into Station Street he brought the car to a halt then glanced at the shell of a building, its charred timbers standing like blackened ribs.

Fair was fair. Kate Mallory had been of some help in bringing that heroin bust, and a little also in breaking that counterfeit racket. Yes, fair was fair. He swallowed the last of the tablet. She could have this story; after all there was nothing exactly mind-blowing about a tuppenny-ha'penny factory being set ablaze by bloody loony kids!

2

'Are you serious?'

'No time to be otherwise, Kate, and neither have you if you intend having copy ready before we put the baby to bed; however, if the assignment is too much...'

David Anscott, editor of the *Star* newspaper, kept his eyes on the piece he was reading; he didn't need to look at Kate Mallory to sense the disgust registered on that tilted mouth, or into the brown eyes he knew at this moment were filled with the same; her mild explosion at being given that assignment told him all of that. 'If it's too much...' he went on, pen slashing viciously through carefully typed script, replacing words, discarding phrases until the paper lying on a desk hidden beneath layers of the same read to his very particular satisfaction, '...then I can put one of the juniors on to it.'

That was where rubbish such as this should be parked, on the desk of the youngest junior, they would be more used to fairytales! The words were fire on her tongue but Kate Mallory, journalist on the same newspaper, forced every last red-hot syllable to remain there. Allowing them to spew like a stream of molten lava would be to have Scottie set her a truly exciting assignment, like writing up the damn weather forecast!

Making no effort to disguise the irritation chorusing in every vein, she stomped back to her seat and grabbed the large leather bag from the floor beside it. Banging it on to the desk, her fingers rummaging in its vast chaotic depths, she heard the chuckle from a few yards away.

'Scottie living up to expectations is he?'

Kate didn't want to answer, didn't want the anger inside to explode.

'Don't let the bastard get you down.'

It was meant as encouragement but, Kate noted, the blaspheming of the office Almighty had been said with no more sound than a whisper, and even so the speaker glanced towards the inner sanctum as he uttered it.

'Easy to say, hard to do.' Kate's fingers continued their in-depth search.

Long legs swinging from the edge of his own desk, Philip Jackson, known more familiarly as 'Red' due to a mane of bright auburn hair, nodded.

21

'Happens to us all, kid, just got to go with the flow.'

Go with the flow! Fingers screwing together inside the bag, Kate bit hard on the answer she wanted to scream. Go with the bloody flow! So how many flows had he gone with!

'Another supermarket "do" is it? Covering the opening of Asda's new place along of King Street, are we?' Philip Jackson grinned.

Discarding further exploration of her bag, Kate lifted it to her shoulder, hoping the acid of her feelings would not scorch her tongue.

'Nothing so important, he's keeping that scoop for someone else. My advice is keep your head down or the someone might turn out to be you.'

'No fears on that score.' The liberally freckled face grinned again. 'Got the Wolves' match to write up, our Lord and Master won't risk having that delayed; after all it's the sports page sells this newspaper.'

He was waiting for the usual debate that followed such claims but today Kate declined the invitation; the way she was feeling right now the precious sports columnist could well find himself blasted into orbit. Biting down on the hard core of cynicism sitting in her throat she forced a smile which could only be written in the book of the Recording Angel as unmitigated deceit and therefore warranting a stay in hotter climes. Just as well she had no beliefs in crap of that kind! Just for a second it seemed something touched the heat inside her, something so cold the fires of anger paled at its coming, a whisper like an icicle in her brain ... remember Monkswell ...

remember Asmodai!

Monkswell ... the ghost of a murdered hitch hiker ... all those horrible deaths, revenge killings from beyond the grave, and Torrey offering his soul in exchange for that of a young priest.

She had come to know that man was no fool. Richard Torrey was not one to see little green men from Mars watching from behind every bush ... nor one to believe in Satan and all his demons, yet he had sat beside her that afternoon relating all that had happened, it was clear he believed something was not quite your everyday happening.

He had talked quietly, no dramatic overtones adding colour. At first she had found it hard not to laugh, an ex-commando tough as bullets claiming he had been haunted by a dead lover! Lord, who wouldn't have laughed? But as he had gone on she had felt what she was hearing was no dupe, no story told to catch an inquisitive journalist by the nose, but the solid unadorned truth.

A shiver trickled coldly along Kate's spine, preceding a name that came on spindrifts of memory, tendrils of mist wrapping her mind, cold fingers squeezing away common sense.

Anna...

So real were the memories, so clear the voice in her head, she drew a sharp breath, her glance raking the busy room and seeking refuge in the familiar, but the familiar was gone and she was in Victoria Park sharing a bench with Richard Torrey, the cigarette between her fingers forgotten as he told her of the struggle that had taken place in a small cottage in the sleepy village of Monkswell; of himself and an older woman, protected

23

only by a ring of salt, confronting a figure fashioned of living flame, a column of glittering fire which slowly changed, separating then re-forming until the slender shape of a girl floated where it had been; a smiling, hyacinth-eyed girl, the Anna he had loved, Anna whose apparition had promised that same love, promised eternity together.

Running like some video in fast-forward mode, pictures raced unopposed through Kate's mind, and then as if some invisible button had been pressed the picture slowed, showing a face half shot away, the charred edges of a raw black hole twitching, a grotesque mouth screaming in soundless agony. Then came the words, the words with which Richard Torrey had made the bargain for the priest's immortal soul and offered his own.

'...*a man's life is not enough to satisfy you is it, Anna? You want his soul along with it. Well, you can have mine, it's no more than I deserve ... but it will be exchanged ... for that of the priest...*'

'I'd like that copy sometime this year ... that's if I'm not hurrying you!'

The editor's irate blast cut through the fog holding her mind and Kate convulsively gripped the handle of her bag.

'Make you jump did he, Kate?' Jackson laughed, a blue pen twisting acrobatically between his fingers. 'He's very good at scaring lady journalists, keeps them on their toes.'

The last trace of mist gone completely, Kate Mallory's brain kicked once more into gear. Throwing a glance towards the freckle-covered face, she adopted a knowing smile. 'I hear he's not bad at putting the wind up male journalists either ... the way Wolves are playing this last couple of seasons must be the reason for his decision.'

'Decision?'

The pen paused in mid-turn and Kate felt a surge of satisfaction. That had pricked his balloon. Brown eyes widening just enough, allowing exactly the right modicum of surprise to colour her voice, she pretended surprise. 'You mean he hasn't told you yet? Oh Lord, me and my big mouth!'

'Told?' Philip Jackson's brows came together. 'Told what?'

Two shakes of her head gave Kate time to force the invading grin back beyond her teeth and her quick surreptitious look towards the editor's office brought the response she had aimed for. It didn't take much to rattle Philip Jackson's cage ... and today the bars would sing.

'I ... I think it best Scottie tell you himself.' She had almost whispered the words but a gun going off next to his ear couldn't have produced the same effect. He had jumped off that desk so quick the cheeks of his backside were aflame.

'Kate...' As he stepped in front of her as she made to leave, Jackson's face was shades paler than full-cream milk. 'Kate ... what hasn't he told me?'

'I shouldn't...' Another glance towards the inner sanctum to lend drama, Kate spoke in a hurried whisper, 'We, both you and I, are not bringing in the goods so Scottie says, he thinks the paper needs a fillip, one that might appeal to women, that's why he has given us each new assignments. Mine is to ferret out any myths and legends associated with the local area. Scottie already has the heading. "Myths, Legends and Old Wives' Tales".'

Easing the strap of her bag more comfortably on her shoulder, Kate had not needed to look at Jackson to see the Adam's apple shoot up and down his neck like a test-your-strength machine at the fair. The mere thought of penning anything other than who scored which goal was enough to bring him to mild apoplexy.

'Old Wives' ... bloody hell!'

Jackson's swallow, loud and distinct, brought glances from the office junior but Kate remained undeterred. She really shouldn't do this, but then why not? She needed to scratch her irritation against a stump and Jackson would do as well as any tree.

'Bloody hell was my thought when Scottie told me what was to be the basis of my new column,' she murmured, 'but then seeing what he had lined up for you I realised I had the lesser evil.'

'Christ!' Freckles dancing, Jackson's face contorted. 'Old Wives' Tales the lesser evil? Then what the hell does he have in mind for me?'

'Kate! Is it going to need my boot against your backside to get you through that door!' David Anscott's voice blasted again.

'Her master's voice, how it charms the maiden's ear.' Kate grinned while the office junior bent his head so low it almost brushed the paper he was supposed to be correcting.

'Wait!' Jackson caught her arm. 'You have to tell

me what my column is to be about.'

'Oh, I think you'll like it.' Kate shook off his hold. 'You are getting an agony slot. Scottie has the heading for that too; he's calling it "Red's Letter Day". Apt, isn't it?'

'By, lass, but you'll be gettin' wronged for tellin' such lies.' Walking towards the stop where she could get a bus to the Bull Stake, Kate heard the words in her mind. How often had her mother repeated them, warning her that lying would have her tongue covered in painful ulcers the very next morning. But the threat had never materialised ... well, almost never ... and neither had she learned to heed her mother's warning.

But Jackson was so smug! He needed knocking from his perch ... and she had enjoyed giving the push. But would the enjoyment still be there if Scottie called her to book?

As she waited at the bus stop, several enquiring looks directed at her bag made Kate realise her hand was once more rummaging in its depths. Conscientiously drawing out a paper handkerchief she touched it to her nose. She had been feeling for a tab, one that might miraculously be there in the bottom of her bag, one she had overlooked ... one lone cigarette. But there wasn't one. Pushing the paper handkerchief into the pocket of her coat, she let her fingers explore the corners. There was no cigarette there either, not even a half-smoked one.

Lord! Inside the pocket her fingers clenched. Why had she listened to Torrey ... if he needed to play the saviour why didn't he start with his own faults first!

And he had them! She passed coins viciously into the ticket machine aboard the bus and snatched the ticket before sliding bad temperedly into a rear seat.

Yes, you've got 'em Torrey, you might close your eyes to 'em but you've got 'em all right! Venting her displeasure by short breaths in and out of flared nostrils, Kate ignored curious glances from other passengers. Coffin nails, Torrey had called her tabs, warning of the danger to her health each time she lit up, but it was *her* health and if she wanted to endanger it then that was her prerogative ... wasn't it?

'Yes.' Richard Torrey had nodded when she had thrown that self-same indictment but there had been no smile in his dark eyes, no hint of sympathy to say he understood how difficult it was to break the addiction. But then nothing was difficult for Richard Torrey; Kate's thoughts were sour. Nothing came hard to that man; Torrey the commando! Torrey the hard man! Assailants, black magicians, demons from Hell, he had seen them all off in his time ... but what was a demon compared to the devil sitting on her shoulder ... the torment dragging at her, the longing to smoke a cigarette?

Alighting from the bus Kate ground her frustration between clenched teeth. Bruce Willis, Jean-Claude Van Damme, Steven Seagal, Torrey was all of them rolled into one ... or at least *he* thought he was.

Now you stop right there, Kate Mallory!

The abruptness of the thought brought her up

sharp. Kate halted in mid-step.

Richard Torrey had more guts than any celluloid superman, there was more courage in his little finger than in the whole bodies of the sham Hollywood super-troopers! Torrey had lived the horrors they were only acting out, he had faced the terrors ... and not on any cinema screen but in the cottage of an old woman, and in a cellar beneath the print room of Darlaston Printers, stood eyeball to eyeball in a situation no imagining could conjure; like the challenge he had thrown at Julian Crowley, a Black Magician, a Magus so hungry for power he had sacrificed a young girl, offering her life to the god he worshipped.

Even thinking of it caused her veins to clog and the mist that had enmeshed her brain while in that cellar seemed once more to shroud her senses.

Julian Crowley had stabbed his victim through the heart, a cold, deliberate killing and had been eager to do the same with herself, to offer her also to his satanic lord.

Her mind gripped by the horrors of that night, Kate was oblivious of the irritated tutting of passengers whose path she blocked.

Crowley had intended her for a victim, had tried to accomplish it! Trapped by fear she had stood, only Torrey and a ring of salt between her and the viciously smiling worshipper of the Devil.

He had spoken words she could not understand, phrases that, while unintelligible, had turned her spine to ice-water, and in response to his incantations had come something he had entitled the Messenger, Keeper of the Great Seal,

29

Asmodai, High Angel of the Dark Lord. It had materialised out of thin air, floated before them golden and beautiful and she had been so seduced by the beauty of that demon she had wanted nothing more than to go to it, to be drawn with it into the realms of Hell and but for the courage and will of Richard Torrey she would have been.

The shove of an irate passerby pushed her to the kerb where the broad black and white markings of a Panda crossing striped the busy junction that was the Bull Stake, but caught in the net of memory Kate continued to stand.

How many men would have done what Torrey had done? How many would have shown the grit, the pure bulldog determination it had taken to defeat the Messenger of Satan?

The blare of a car horn dispelling the cloud from her brain, Kate glanced toward the windscreen of a vehicle, the glower of its driver speaking volumes none of which would ever find a place in her mother's favourite Catherine Cookson novels ... the *Star* maybe ... but not Cookson. A second bellow of the horn was no polite request for her to use the crossing or move away. Kate smiled, then lips pursed in a mock kiss, one finger raised in acid salute, she stepped on to the crossing. White-van syndrome, that driver had overdosed!

Recollections that had pulsed moments ago faded as she reached the opposite side of the road. In front of her sharply pointed gables surmounting the windows of the recently built public library seemed strange and out of place, lacing as they did a row of sadly neglected shops that might have stepped right out of Dickens.

'Good shops they be, same as was them they pulled down to mek way for that thing!'

Kate smiled, this time a genuine, affectionate smile, as her landlady's condemnation of the building echoed in her mind.

'...and look at what be left.'

Annie's disapproval had allowed no margin of doubt of her opinion of those responsible for the showy new edifice.

'Lettin' 'em tumble down ... why couldn't the Council 'ave done them up instead of wastin' folks' money on some high falutin building which holds naught 'cept books when shops be what be needed, places where folks can get groceries an' such! Them there councillors should be throwed out, they don't know "A" from a bull's foot about what folks need.'

A conviction held by many! Annie's chagrin had not been eased by the construction of an Asda supermarket.

'...sprawled itself over half of King Street an' down into Pinfold Street...'

The lament which had found a chorus in a bevy of Annie's friends mourned afresh in Kate's mind.

'...be like some bloody great vulture a'swallowing of businesses been in them streets from afore I were born ... the town don't be same no more, it's a'lost of its character!'

As she climbed the broad steps leading to the doors of the library, Kate Mallory's smile widened. Darlaston would never lose its character while it held people like Annie Price with her

31

forthright ways... and you could find them on almost every street corner, people like the ferret-sharp finger in every pie, 'Echo' Sounder, a race track devotee expert in learning the private affairs of everybody else and singing them ... for a fee! Then there were the real sleazy types such as Philip Bartley, smart arse and dope peddler who had got himself thrown out of a window by a ghost – and of course the inimitable Detective Inspector Bruce Daniels! He would never have believed the ghost of a hitch-hiker had claimed the life of Philip Bartley and the rest of his heroin-dealing associates and as for asking him to believe the doings of Julian Crowley and his satanic cult, the calling forth of Asmodai, Highest of the Dark Angels, and the Seal, that tattoo which had marked a young girl as the Devil's own, her soul claimed by that deity had it not been for Torrey... Daniels would have bust a gut laughing at that!

Inside the library Kate ascended the stairs leading to the reference section. Yes, Darlaston had its characters, and for a time it had held a few most of its inhabitants would never know of.

Selecting a table devoid as yet of other users, she deposited her bag on its empty surface, her lips pursing as she surveyed the book-lined shelves and carousels. Where would she find Myths and Legends? Was there a section on Old Wives' Tales?

It could take the rest of the day and knowing her talent she would still not come up with the necessary!

Deciding against a search she reasoned was destined for failure, Kate assumed what she hoped was an engaging smile ... that should bring home the bacon!

Approaching what might almost be termed a barrier, she gleamed at the young man sat behind a semi-circular desk hosting a pair of computers. He could well need its protection should Annie decide to take up reading!

Hiding the thought behind the glassy smile, she asked her question then waited while the young man tapped a keyboard. She really ought to master the art herself, but technology had never been her strong suit, her time as a student at Lord Lawson High School painfully proving the fact, and even now that particular skill remained low on her list of must haves.

'Sorry.' The young man tapped one last time, his glance running swiftly over the monitor screen and absorbing the information on it before he looked at Kate.

'Sorry.' He shook a mane of hair reminiscent of a floor mop. 'We have no information on the subject of Old Wives' Tales. There are, however, several titles dealing with Myth and Legend, you'll find them downstairs in the section headed Mythology.'

Returning once more to the ground floor, the longing for a cigarette hit like a fist in her chest. One tab, one miserable little tab was all she asked … but thanks to Torrey one tab was all she didn't have!

After selecting a couple of volumes from the section pointed out by yet another member of the library staff, she sank dejectedly into a chair strategically positioned beside a table covered with a selection of daily newspapers. Her voluminous bag cut a swathe through them.

Myths, Legends. She stared at the books she had dumped beside the bag. She could find an item or two in them that might conceivably satisfy her complacent editor ... and a pig with a jet engine in its derrière might fly! Scottie was never easily pleased and handing him copy dealing with only half of what he asked could have him handing her her cards. But where the hell was she supposed to find information when the library didn't have it!

Myths, Legends and Old Wives' Tales! The words spit in her mind. Unlike Julian Crowley, Richard Torrey had not died that evening in the cellar of Darlaston Printers; Asmodai, Messenger of Satan, had failed to take his life ... but Torrey would kill himself laughing over this.

Damn Scottie! Vexation reclaiming lost territory, she flipped open the first of the books. And damn his bloody newspaper!

3

'He's given you what?'

Richard Torrey laughed, the short breath of it whipping most of the frothy head from his glass of Banks' Best Bitter.

'I knew that would be your response!' Kate's brown eyes gleamed their warning.

'Well, come on, wouldn't you laugh if you were in my shoes?'

Seizing a chance she might not get again all evening. Kate retorted acidly, 'Were I in your shoes I would be more mindful of other people... their feelings as well as their noses!'

'Oh, now *that!* You being mindful of other peoples' feelings ... *that* is a bigger joke than Scottie having you chase up any old wife's tale.' Torrey grinned over his glass. 'And anyway what is this about people's noses, are you inferring my feet smell?'

'Are you claiming they don't?'

'Well, maybe just a little ... but they would improve if you washed my socks.'

'Dream on, Torrey.' Kate swung her bag on to the table and the weight of it set both glasses rattling.

'The pay is good.' Torrey's grin widened as he watched her scrabble about in the depths of a bag he reckoned would hold a year's groceries and still leave room for half a sheep.

'It would have to be phenomenal!' Kate's retort was sharp, the ferreting in her bag adding acerbity.

'As much as that?' Torrey pursed his lips wryly. Dark eyes twinkling, he watched sherry-coloured curls dance with impatience as they almost touched the bag. Kate had at last given up cigarettes but had they given up on her? Not as yet, he decided as a curt 'sod it!' snapped seemingly from the bag's interior. There was some way to go yet before the hold of tobacco was given the final push. He could make light of her search, try some amusing remark, but instinct warned Kate Mallory would be anything but amused.

'Why do I damn well listen to other people?' A frown, dark thunder sitting above her brown eyes, Kate almost threw the bag aside. 'I should bloody well tell 'em to mind their own business!'

A swallow of cold beer helping to drown the rising chuckle, Torrey answered, 'You do, Kate ... maybe not so gently, but you do it nonetheless, though what comes after the telling ... the following or otherwise of advice ... that is your doing entirely, nobody takes you by the throat and chokes you into agreeing to what they say.'

He was right of course. Kate glanced into eyes of midnight darkness, eyes she knew could suddenly turn to hardened steel. But right now they were soft, a humorous smile lurking in their black depths.

'Tell me,' she sipped her lager and lime, 'how does it feel being a contender for MENSA?'

'Pretty good.' Torrey's smile became a grin. 'It feels pretty good.'

'Smart arse!' Kate lifted her glass, her laugh gurgling over its top.

'That's better.' Torrey eased his six foot plus – the curved seating of the lounge bar of the Frying Pan pub always left him feeling like a banana – 'Now what's this you say Scottie has you working on?'

Pretending to work on! Guilt at her half-hearted research at the library took the smile from Kate's mouth.

Waiting for an answer and getting none he tried again. 'Has Scottie really set you that project or are you winding my spring?'

'He's really set it,' the answer was dour, 'he says

it will grab a larger share of female readership ... female readership ... the *Star*. I ask you!'

He knew what she meant. The local newspaper was no *Hello!* magazine; apart from sports coverage and the eternal reports of some teenage thuggery it held little of interest ... and that not often in the female department.

'You must admit it's different.' Torrey tried appeasement.

'Different yes, but of interest to whom ... apart from your grandmother!'

'I don't have a grandmother; should I try rent-a-grannie?'

Kate's laugh bubbled. 'Maybe we both should, if they took the *Star* it would double the sales.'

'Now, Kate, let's not be vicious.'

'I feel like being vicious!' Kate attacked the lager and lime. 'I feel like telling Scottie to shove his brainchild where the sun don't shine. Myths, Legends and Old Wives' Tales! Where the hell am I supposed to find them? Not in the library, that's for sure ... they had virtually nowt on the subject and were no help in telling me where I might find some relevant information; but then none of that matters, does it, not to his holiness the Editor, his is the word and yours the deed, you do it or else!'

David Anscott was a fair man and a good editor, Kate had said so herself many times, and he congratulated her on a job well done, even though he knew it would feed her ambition to work for one of the nationals... and she might well have been taken on by one of them following her write-up of the Philip Bartley case. Bartley had been owner of the supermarket that had graced King Street before the Asda takeover; he had also been a heroin dealer and a lover of boys. But not only boys. Torrey felt the old anger and hate tighten his throat. Bartley had also loved Anna, but not with his heart and soul as he, Torrey, had loved her, but only with his body; he and his fancy friends had raped her, one after the other they had taken his lovely Anna and when they were done they had had her murdered, that beautiful face half blown away with a shotgun. And it had been Anna, the ghost of Anna, who in revenge had taken their lives. But Kate Mallory had not written of that, had made no mention of his own haunting, of his own narrow escape from death at the ghostly hands of that unearthly hitch-hiker.

Why hadn't she? And why had she not made report of that other happening, of the part black magic had played in the case of that counterfeiting scam? Julian Crowley had been a Satanist, a follower of the Black Arts, a worshipper of the Devil, his business merely a cover for what he truly was about, the destruction of the entire Middle East. Having them at each other's throats over payments made with fake money would take attention from the real aim of his Master, a world war that would make the last one seem like nursery games. And the Devil had almost won. Crowley had conjured what he termed the Messenger. Despite the warmth of the room Torrey shivered. Crowley had called and the Lord of Hell had answered. Asmodai, Highest of the Princes of the Throne, Archangel of Vengeance, Keeper of the Great Seal, golden and handsome, had come to his bidding, come to take the life of Kate Mallory and Richard Torrey, to suck both of them into the regions of the damned. But Kate had written of none of this, nothing of the terror played out in the cellar of Darlaston Printers. It had been more than a fight for life, it had been a struggle for the soul.

Thinking of it now, months after the event, brought a touch of cold fear. He tightened his fingers on his glass to prevent the shake he felt coming to his hands. He'd had shit scares during his time in the Army but even the worst couldn't come within shouting distance of what had happened that night. Now to have read that in the *Star!* 'Ex Commando, terrified of Bogeyman.' There were more than a few in Darlaston would relish that, including the three yobbos he had laid out in the yard of the Bird-in-Hand; yes, there were men would revel in reading what they hadn't the balls to set their tongues to: but no copy containing any of it had been handed to Scottie. Not that he would have printed it; his scorn would have been as brittle as the rest. But there was no room for scorn in Richard Torrey's mind, he knew what had taken place, known the danger to himself and to Kate and it was something he never wanted to witness again. He had fought not only with Julian Crowley, the servant of Lucifer on earth, but also with the Devil's prime emissary.

How the hell had they survived? Despite the tingle that memory jangled along his nerves, a grim smile flashed somewhere deep inside ... it certainly was no thanks to hell!

39

They had had no more to aid them than a thin ring of salt, a candle and a few drops of water he had stolen from a church. Salt, candle and water ... to fight the bloody Devil! The grim smile dropped away. Christ, what a night! It had been no imagination, no figment of a mind over-wrought or otherwise; demon, creature of the night, Old Nick's right-hand man, call it what-ever you liked, it had been no illusion, no hallucination, not even that which he had told Kate it was, Crowley's hypnotism; no, whatever had answered the invocation of that black magician it had been real, real and so damned beautiful Kate had tried to claw free of that barrier of salt to reach it, to throw herself into those gleaming lambent arms. And the creature had smiled as it called to her in a voice of pure music, called to Kate to join him in hell.

It had been all he could do to hold her back. A swallow of beer did not wash away the stricture about Torrey's throat or the memories from his mind. Had Kate touched that ring of salt, broken even the smallest space in it, the creature would have succeeded; it would have placed the mark upon them both, that same mark the ghost of young Penny Smith carried. The Seal of Asmodai, the mark of eternal damnation. Yet it had not been his own strength that had saved them. The Messenger of Satan would have claimed his prize had not a greater power intervened.

But Kate Mallory's pen had written none of it. Why?

Looking deep into his glass he searched for answers, hoping to see them in the creamy froth.

Was it Kate's own reputation as a serious journalist she had wanted to protect? Or could it have been feelings for Richard Torrey? Had she aimed to keep him from the fights, the jeers and snide remarks that story would have inevitably had him caught up in? Maybe, there was no telling with Kate, but he was grateful just the same.

'Well?'

Loud and none too pleased, Kate's demand cut through the reverie. Glancing up, Torrey could not entirely quell the thought racing into his head. If only she had bawled like that at the Devil's Messenger it would have gone bounding back to hell as if its handsome arse had been on fire!

'Well what?' He cocked an eyebrow.

'I might have known! You haven't heard a word I've said have you? I could get more response from Echo Sounder than I'm getting from you!'

Time to make a strategic withdrawal. Torrey picked up both glasses and took them to the waist-high bar, its dark wood frame gleaming in the light of green-shaded wall lamps. Gave himself time to plan his action while the opposition twiddled its thumbs ... that was if Kate Mallory ever twiddled her thumbs, which he doubted.

'You still here?' He placed a fresh lager and lime in front of Kate. 'I thought you said something about going to see Sounder.'

'Keep trying!' Sarcasm being the first weapon to hand, Kate used it liberally. 'Who knows, one of these days you might come up with a funny – though I'll not hold my breath!' But talking to Echo Sounder might not be such a bad idea, could be he knew of a few tales appertaining to Darlaston.

Sounder, the town's canary! Torrey took refuge in a long swallow of cool ale. What that scruffy little toerag didn't know of Darlaston wasn't worth knowing; but his tales wouldn't be those told by old wives, and as for myths and legends, if they were not about horses and the race track then Sounder didn't know any.

'He might at that.' Deciding against contradiction, Torrey set his own glass on the table. 'I know a few myself, let's see,' he mused a moment, 'what was it my mother used to say ... never put new shoes on the table, no knitting on a Sunday, don't cut your nails on the Sabbath, hide all cutlery and turn mirrors to the wall during a thunderstorm ... and what was the one about Good Friday? Oh yes, never let dirty water run from the sink on Good Friday.'

'What!' In the muted lighting Kate's eyes sparked anger. 'Look, Torrey, I'm being serious!'

Benign in the face of impending fury Torrey answered, 'So am I.'

'But no water to drain from the sink...'

'Ask any of these.' Torrey waved a hand to indicate the people sat in the various alcoves which, like their own, comprised curved bench-like seating faced with a table and stools. 'Ask the older ones anyway, they'll tell you the same as my mother told me, to throw dirty water down the sink on Good Friday was to throw it in the face of the Lord...'

'I don't believe it!' Kate snorted. 'How did she reckon that?'

42

A smile evident now in coal-dark eyes, Torrey regarded those staring threateningly at him. 'Don't know, I never asked. There were some things you thought twice about before challenging that sort of old wife's tale, in fact there were many things a lad didn't question his mother about, not unless he wanted his ears to ring for a few hours.'

'It was the same in the North East.' Kate's eyes softened. 'If it were something me mam couldn't explain she would go all huffy and shoo me from the room saying, *away with you now, hinny, I divna ha' the time to stand bletherin'* ... though I often wondered why that didn't apply when it were neighbours she was talking with.'

'But you never asked why?'

Kate laughed, a soft 'I remember' sort of laugh and her voice was hushed when she replied, 'Not me, I was too canny for that; like you I didn't want my ears set to ringing.'

Wrapped in the solitude of memory they sat for several minutes in silence, each locked in their own private world of childhood.

'Either of you seen Sounder?'

The abrupt demand shattered the fragile realms of yesterday, the shades of its being fading back into their dim half-forgotten world as both Kate and Torrey looked at the man settling on to a stool at their table.

'Do join us, Inspector.'

Impervious to the tone which clearly stated that was the last thing Kate Mallory wanted him to do, Bruce Daniels sat himself on the stool.

Legs splayed one to each side of a seat lost beneath an irritably shifting bottom, Daniels glanced at both faces before repeating, 'Either of you seen Sounder?'

'Many times.' Kate's syrupy answer had a stubby-fingered hand reach into the pocket of a worn tweed jacket to emerge with a flat pack of indigestion tablets.

'Had a complaint lodged today.' Detective Inspector Bruce Daniels flipped a small white tablet on to his tongue with the dexterity of long-established practice. 'Seems a certain woman journalist was harassing a member of the public. Could be I'll 'ave to look into it.'

Point taken! Kate watched the yellow and blue cardboard container of Bi-So-Dol returned to the pocket. Daniels was in his usual pleasant mood, the one which said smart alec answers resulted in trumped-up charges.

'I take it Sounder is not in the bar.'

Bless you! Kate's unspoken gratitude for Torrey's intervention showed in her glance.

'Ain't in this one nor that of the Knot.'

So Daniels had looked for Echo Sounder in the Staffordshire Knot! Kate's journalist nose twitched. He must want the town's crier pretty badly, but for what? She had heard nothing except for the usual breaking and entering; but would the Inspector bother himself to find Sounder to question him on that? No ... she lifted her glass ... that line of enquiry would be taken by a constable, which meant Daniels was after something else altogether.

'He's probably still at the track, the racing doesn't finish until nine.'

But Sounder will run faster than any greyhound if he finds you waiting for him! Kate hid the thought and the smile it gave birth to.

Glancing at the clock set to one side of the various optics cradling bottles of vodka, whisky, brandy and gin, then checking the time with the watch fastened by a dark leather strap to his wrist, the Inspector nodded once, a brief jerk of the head as abrupt as the words he had thrown at them while settling at the table.

'More than likely you're right,' Daniels swallowed, sending the residue of the tablet into the inferno that was his chest, 'still ten minutes to go.'

'Time for a drink?'

There was no syrup sweetening Kate's invitation, but innocent as she tried to make the accompanying smile Torrey recognised the undercurrent; it was already beginning to flow. Kate Mallory smelled a story.

4

Another act of vandalism!

Tapping sheets of A4 paper into a neat bundle, Kate Mallory hesitated. She had twice written a report of the fire which had gutted that paint factory, adding a line, replacing a phrase, and still it read like some police report.

Wasn't that what it was? She tapped the papers again, watching them slide into place.

The factory had been a smouldering ruin by

the time she had been allowed anywhere near. None of the fire fighters dousing the smoking timbers would commit themselves to an opinion as to the cause of the blaze, the chief officer saying only it was too early yet to arrive at any conclusion. Which was his way of saying bugger off and let us get on with the job!

'Other folk have jobs too,' Kate muttered crossly.

'Phases of the moon?' Philip Jackson's flame-red hair flopped over one eye as he looked up from his own desk.

'Nothing to do with the moon!'

'I see.' He grinned at the snap. 'Not PMT, just the T. I suffer from it myself … not the menstrual bit I'm thankful to add, just the tension.'

He should be thankful! Kate banged the sheets of copy yet again. If there was such a being as God then He was certainly male or why differentiate between genders? Why was it men had the best deal in everything while women…? Don't go down that street! Sixth sense warned against the train of thought stirring in her mind. Go that way and she might just throw that copy across the desk of the omnipotent and tell him to rake the ashes of any other damned fire for himself!

Well, one thing was certain, editor or not, Scottie could not have made a better job of covering that little episode of Darlaston's teenage hooliganism; like herself he would have only the crumbs thrown by Detective Inspector Daniels. Let Scottie try making a literary meal out of that.

'*Bloody kids!*' Daniels had spat as if the words were the bitter aloes her mother had rubbed on her fingers to stop her chewing her nails. *'A few strokes of the "cat" would soon have 'em finding better things to do with their time than setting fires! It's the bloody do-gooders of the world be to blame, they don't seem to realise the pattern they be setting for kids, that they can do just whatever it pleases 'em to do and no retribution; you mustn't blame them, it's a cry for help: it would be a cry for help they'd be giving if I had my way. They wouldn't see no streets for a very long time.'*

Some of what he had said made sense, Kate had thought while waiting for the tirade to evaporate. 'No punishment be no way of teaching bairns right from wrong, they needs to be given boundaries, they needs to be shown that wrongdoing brings its own rewards.' That had been the philosophy of her grandmother and her mother, and it had done their children no harm. Indeed it had taught them to recognise the values and rights of others as well as themselves; so what had happened to yesterday ... where had those mores gone? What was it had turned the country's thinking on its head?

'Are you going to take that to the Pope?' Philip Jackson grinned again though his voice lowered significantly as he used his term for the *Star*'s editor. 'Or is it your Last Will and Testament you've spent the last hour musing over?'

It might well have been; in fact a few more weeks of Myths, Legends and Old Wives' Tales could see her suicidal.

'Just about to approach the deity now, can I take your copy for "Red's Letter Day" in for you?'

It was vindictiveness but Kate felt no remorse as the grin faded from the freckled face. She felt like playing the bitch!

'Does'na tell a lot!' David Anscott had read quickly through the handwritten sheets and now looked at the young woman standing waiting for his verdict. Beneath the short sherry-coloured hair bright brown eyes regarded him, and they hinted rebellion. This girl from Tyne and Wear was intelligent, and moreover she was dedicated to her job ... but jobs could be changed, loyalties transferred, and Kate Mallory was restless, the call of the nationals still echoing in her journalist blood. She was a first-class reporter, that heroin piece and the one on that counterfeiting racket going on at Darlaston Printers had proved that beyond doubt, and the nationals had come sniffing... so why hadn't she taken their offers? But more concerning was how long would she settle for reporting the mindless acts of this town's vandals?

'I've told what there was!'

It was abrupt, a take-it-or-leave-it tone. Deciding an equally abrupt rejoinder would have his best reporter walk out, David Anscott read on calmly.

'You should try asking detectives for information,' Kate rasped irritably. 'Especially try asking Detective Inspector Bruce Daniels, could be you might learn a thing or two.'

Shuffling together the pages she had handed him a minute or so before, David Anscott set them before him on his chaotic desk.

'I'm not above learning, Kate...'

48

He had smiled! Against all the odds he had smiled! Kate stared unbelievingly. She had expected a bawling out but he had smiled!

'And I am not above remembering what it's like to be given an assignment you wouldn't even want to wipe your bottom on; but I canna give you what just isn't there.'

'I know.' Brilliant in their apology the brown eyes glinted. 'I'm sorry, I didn't mean to raim on.'

'To what?'

It was Kate's turn to smile. 'It's something me mam would say whenever I got to being uppity. She would just flap a hand and say, "Raim on, hinny, you sound like a chicken with its feathers plucked and you're mekin' no more of an impression." It always stopped me dead in my tracks.'

'That's another feeling I remember.'

For a moment it seemed he would say more, speak of a childhood Kate had never heard him mention to anyone, but in an instant the promise was gone and he was bending to some other copy being prepared for the print room.

Well done, Kate. You made a decent job out of nothing, Kate! Would it really have choked him to say just one of those things? Probably yes! Deciding against putting theory to the test, Kate left the small cluttered room. 'Div'nt put the blazer to a burning fire', had been another of her mother's choice epithets, and it was one that right this minute was well worth observing. Scottie had not flared at the paucity of content in her report of that fire and it would serve no purpose to fan that well-known volatility of temper into a blaze

49

for the sake of some smart-sounding remark.

Sparing a glance at Jackson as the editor's bark summoned, Kate felt a momentary touch of sympathy. 'Red's Letter Day!' She cringed at the thought. It was worse even than Myths, Legends and Old Wives' Tales.

'Kids?'

He had read the report submitted by the Chief Fire Officer. Detective Inspector Bruce Daniels sat up, the two front legs of his chair hitting smartly against the linoleum-tiled floor of his cramped office.

'Who knows!' Sergeant David Farnell shrugged his shoulders. 'Things some of 'em get up to these days are enough to make you cry.'

'Just let me get hold of the little varmints, I promise you they'll do more than cry.'

'Don't work like that, Bruce, not outside of films.'

'It's films be to blame for much of juvenile crime, things like *this!*' Daniels dropped a clenched hand on to the fawn-coloured folder holding the fire department report. 'They see gunfights, murder, arson and any other crap them film folk can dream up and 'cos the main character gets away with no more than a cut lip they think they can do the same.'

Rescuing the file the Sergeant smiled as he registered a faint echo of the past. 'So did we, Bruce.'

'Yes, so did we!' Retaliation bringing acid to his throat, Daniels reached for the remedy and threw a tablet on to his tongue. 'But we had sense enough to realise what we saw was make-believe, we didn't see ourselves as Superman.'

'Maybe not you, but some of us did.' The Sergeant's grin widened. 'There was many a time I imagined myself to be Steed, you know the posh character in "The Avengers" ... but the nearest I ever got was this. Desk sergeant at the Darlaston nick; bit of a let-down, wouldn't you say?'

The grin had died before the words. Daniels stared at the door which had closed behind his colleague. There had been more than disappointment in that final sentence, there had been heartache. Like himself, David Farnell had striven to rise in the ranks, been a bloody good copper; but good coppers were kept where the shit was while the men whose only merit was the ability to speak as if they had a plum in their mouth glided through the ranks to find a chair at the top without their feet ever touching a street: just like Quinto, and like Connor before him. Both had stepped in at the last minute, both had taken credit for a sting neither had had the least part in bringing off, and both had reaped the reward. Connor had risen rapidly, first a Chief Superintendent's chair, then his arse had settled nicely into that of Deputy Commissioner – until a broken saw had sliced his head from his neck while opening a work experience centre; but the vacancy left by Connor ... that hadn't been offered to Bruce Daniels.

Nor is it ever likely to be. Rising from his seat the Inspector kicked savagely against a leg of the desk. Bruce Daniels is a good cop, he can shit miracles ... but leave him to shovel it from the streets! That had been the attitude each time he had come before the Commissioning Board. Oh true, they had never voiced the words but he'd heard them clearly enough. Bruce Daniels was not of the right school, Bruce Daniels would never fit in.

And now he'd been handed the shovel again!

Outside in the yard he paused, the keys to the Fiesta dangling from his fingers.

The Chief Fire Officer's report had contained more than suspicion of arson; that, it seemed, was a proven fact. Christ only knew how they had arrived at that, but that wasn't Bruce Daniels' department ... but a body in that burned-out building was.

'Nothing left but bits of charred bone...'

He set the key in the lock.

'That had gone to Forensics ... results would be passed to him in due course.'

In due course! Tongue probing the residue of bismuth from the back of his teeth, he turned the key. How bloody long would that be? Meantime he was supposed to find out the whys and wherefores!

Ignoring the painful creak of the car door he had snatched open, he stared across its blue roof.

Arson? That, it seemed, was proven.

Kids? Maybe.

A body? Definitely!

Accident? A possibility.

Starting the engine, the throb of it making no inroads on the string of thoughts, he guided the car out on to Victoria Road.

Murder? That was the shit he had to shovel.

'I told ya all I knows, Mr Daniels.' Hands it seemed couldn't have touched soap since the Coronation clutched tight about a half-empty pint glass, Echo Sounder mumbled resentment. 'I told ya yesterday, I don't know nothin' about that fire.'

Summat goes down in this town without Sounder having some knowledge of it? He could believe in little green men from Mars sooner than believe that. Daniels swallowed from his own glass.

'That was yesterday.' He wiped his mouth with the back of his hand. 'Twenty-four hours ago, twenty-four hours I gave you to jog your memory...' he paused and in that fraction of time it seemed the scruffy little man shrank further into the seat in a corner of the Frying Pan bar room, '...of course I could always jog you along to the nick if that would help.'

'You can't arrest a man for not knowin' anythin'.'

'No,' Inspector Bruce Daniels agreed with deceptive amiability. 'But I can arrest him for obstructing a police officer in the line of duty.'

'Obstructin'!' Green-gold eyes as slantingly narrow as a sleepy cat's fastened momentarily upon brown ones. 'I ain't runnin' nobody to the fence.'

'Cut the racing crap!' There was no deception now in Daniels' tone, and definitely no amiability. 'Keep the horse-racing lingo for the track, that is supposing you want to see a race track some time within...' he paused again, '...shall we say five years!'

'Five!' Sharp ferret features paled visibly and the fingers clutching the glass twitched convulsively, 'That ... that be hoss shit you be talkin' and you knows it, you don't got nothin' on me, Mr Daniels, nothin'!'

The back of Daniels' throat had already begun to burn. The swallow of beer or talking to this scruffy little parasite? Both gave him acid!

Reaching for the salvation of the tablets that he carried at all times he tossed one on to his tongue, his glance never wavering from those closed ferret features.

To one side of the smoke-hazed bar the strike of a cue separated the triangle of neatly racked coloured balls, sending them skittering across the green-baized pool table.

'Nothing on you?' Daniels half shook his head, a pensive, thought-filled movement deceptive as had been his amiability. 'You be a betting man, Sounder, would you like to place a small one on that, say a score? I'll give you a hundred to one.'

'That ... that be bloody blackmail!'

'Call it what colour you like.' The blue and yellow pack already back in his pocket, Daniels glanced towards the two men intent on their game of pool. 'But the colour of the bedroom you will share for the next "X" number of years will be grey.'

'That don't be fair, Mr Daniels.' Sounder's wheeze was lost in his half-full glass.

Daniels rose abruptly, a thrust of his legs pushing the stool backwards from the table. 'Tell me about it ... on the way to the nick!'

Kate had been furious. Climbing hand over hand, Richard Torrey hauled himself up the loosely hanging climbing ropes of the gym. Myths, Legends and Old Wives' Tales, she had almost spat the words, and he had almost choked laughing over them. Where in creation had her editor dreamed that one up? Lord, they would be running a fashion and hair care column in the *Sports Argus* next. Catching the rope between the soles of trainers that had seen better days, he slid downward, feeling the heat of friction bite through his leather handguards. That method of descent was frowned on but the attendant turned a blind eye. Not only did this client behave responsibly, never using the equipment in that way when young lads were present, but watching him in action had warned he was not someone you picked an argument with.

Mind – he smiled inwardly as his feet touched the ground – fashion and hair care on the pages of the local sports paper might not be as outrageous as it seemed, judging by some prima donnas of the football field or the centre court at Wimbledon, plus a racing driver or two; it was more than likely they were already avid readers, and dedicated followers of that type of publication.

Switching the flow of the shower from hot to cold, Torrey caught his breath as lancets of icy water stung his skin.

'Red's Letter Day.' He turned, letting the water stream over every part of his body. That could be followed by 'Fashion and Beauty, Hints for the Discerning Sportsman.' Maybe he should mention the idea to Kate...

Stepping from the shower, he grabbed a towel and rubbed it briskly over a frame as hard and honed as it had been during service with the commandos.

But then again maybe not. Philip Jackson had never done anything against him so why add to the man's misfortunes, not to mention Kate Mallory's possible enjoyment of it.

But Kate was not like that. He laid the towel aside and reached for his clothes from a locker. She had smiled when telling him of the assignment dropped on the desk of the sports reporter but there had been no malice behind it; she had been as crestfallen for Jackson as she had been for herself.

Myths and Legends. He slipped a T-shirt over still-damp hair. They had been told several while at school, but literature, especially of the ancient or classical, had never grasped him by the throat, and as for old wives' tales... T-shirt pulled over the waistband of well-washed jeans, he caught up the rucksack stuffed with his damp towel and the underwear he had replaced with fresh ones ... he couldn't recall having heard many of them; his mother had been too knocked out working all hours in order to clothe and feed the two of them after his father had walked out on them. Torrey frowned viciously. He had never enquired as to the reason his father left and his mother had never volunteered the information; but, God! Torrey swallowed hard ... by God, if he ever discovered the bastard he'd ask for reasons second; first he would break the man's back!

Clear of the gym and breaking into a jog he thought would clear the bitter taste of childhood memories from his brain, he found only that it didn't, for the tired face of his mother forced itself into his consciousness, her unhappy eyes staring back at him. Old wives' tales! He swallowed again. His mother had not been given the years to become an old wife; she hadn't been given time enough for either.

5

'Somebody should shoot that bloody ref, if he 'adn't give that free kick we would 'ave gone forward to the next round, the bastard be in need of glasses!'

'Ain't glasses he'd be needin' if I 'ad five minutes with 'im, he'd be needin' a bloody wheelchair.'

Sitting at the wheel of the dark blue Hyundai that a win on the lottery had paid for, Richard Torrey smiled to himself. The gloom and despair of fans pouring from the grounds of Bescot football stadium was real and their loudly voiced wishes for personal revenge fervent, though this was mostly a letting-off of steam. But not always; there were a few local tough guys ready to slake their resentment on the next man to cross their path. Sport! The inner smile faded. Some folk had never learned the meaning of the word.

'The Saddlers should 'ave been three up easy, I reckon that ref must be fuckin' that Rangers striker, be the only explanation ... anybody could see them last two goals was off side!'

'Well, they best tek him away in a 'elicopter, for so sure he tries comin' outta the gates there won't be enough of 'im left to fuck anybody, he'll go 'ome with his balls in a bag an' his dick in his mouth.'

So much for sportsmanship! Torrey watched a thick-set man and his slighter companion walk past the car, then in the driving mirror saw them turn and walk back.

'You free, mate?'

Snatching open the rear door, the thick-set man glared challengingly as Torrey turned to look over his shoulder.

'...'cos if you ain't then that's tough on the other bloke!'

He could drag macho man out of the car, kick his arse up into his neck, smack his 'girl' friend on the wrist before chucking them both back into the gutter. For a moment Torrey played with the thought then threw it aside. To do that would teach them a lesson in good manners but what would it do for him except bring him to that same yobbo level?

'I've got no pick up.' Torrey decided against giving a free lesson in social graces, then regretted it as the heavyweight laughed.

'Would 'ave med no difference if yoh 'ad, this 'ere taxi be our ride, that's right ain't it, Batesey?'

'Too fuckin' right!'

Bouncing into the rear of the car the heavier man laid a hand on the back of the empty front seat. Fingers curling to a fist he looked menacingly at Torrey. 'You turn round and drive, that be if ya likes the face yoh got now. O'course I can change it for ya an' then yoh can still drive we to the Staffordshire Knot!'

Throw them out, do what every instinct urged! Torrey's hands tightened on the wheel. But in the skirmish one at least might have the opportunity to damage the car, maybe slash the seats and if that happened his own livelihood would be on hold. That lottery win had bought the car, licensed it as a private hire vehicle, but that had been it, there was nothing left over to pay for repairs and as yet he was taking just enough in fares to buy a meal and keep a roof over his head.

'Staffordshire Knot.' He repeated the destination, his blood tingling as both passengers sniggered. They were already tanked up, beer obviously constituting their last few meals, and now they were about to visit the next 'restaurant'.

Torrey eased the car into the stream of traffic. Ignoring the advice from the rear telling him to 'shove the bastards outta the way', he fought the growing compulsion to swivel around and serve his thick-set passenger a swift hors d'oeuvres of teeth. It was ordinarily just a few minutes' drive to Catherine's Cross, a few minutes only of suffering the sniggering pair before dropping them off at the Staffordshire Knot. But home matches meant there was no such thing as ordinary, and certainly not traffic.

Foot easing first down and then up off the

accelerator had the Sonata's engine throb like the pulse of a hundred metre runner waiting for the starter signal.

'Hey, shitface!'

The heavyweight leaned over the front seat, his leering mouth spread in a grin.

'This don't be no bloody hearse. Shift the pile o' crap or I'll shift it for ya.'

'Yea, you drive, Pete, show him how it's really done.' Thin and high-pitched, the voice was perfectly matched to the slighter man's frame.

Change! Teeth clamping, Torrey willed the lights to change and allow the stationary vehicles to move more than a few yards. Change before I put that pipsqueak through the window and his bully boy mate with him.

As if in answer to his silent request, the cars ahead moved. Green... Torrey eased into first, his bumper almost kissing that of the car in front. Green ... it was still green ... go, mate, move it! One hand on the wheel, the other shifting gear into second, his thoughts urging the drivers ahead to move, he watched the colourful display of traffic lights. Christ, it had flicked to amber! A few seconds and it would go to red, but a few seconds more of listening to Rambo in the back could see him facing a charge of GBH.

As if snatching away the blessing which had answered his silent prayers of three minutes before, the signal switched to the halt sign but Torrey kept the bumpers together and followed arse-tight on the car in front. That could be a fine and three penalty points on his licence. Glancing in the rear-view mirror Torrey saw a yellow-jacketed policeman shake his head. 'Maybe the copper had an understanding heart.' He could almost hear Kate Mallory's reply should he tell her of jumping the lights. Understanding heart or just too much paperwork? Either way he hoped the uniform thought to let things pass.

'Put your foot down, arsehole, I need to tek me a leak!'

Once this car came to a halt he might just be tempted to put his foot down, but it would be down his passenger's throat!

Guiding the vehicle along Bescot Crescent then left on to Wednesbury Road, aware all the time of the sneering remarks of one and the mouse-squeak giggles of the other, Torrey tried to curb the irritation steadily rising in his stomach. He would make this his last trip, go back to the flat, take a shower and have an early night.

'Staffordshire Knot.' He called the arrival, waiting while the pair hauled themselves from the car.

What was the mouth doing? Glancing into the wing mirror Torrey saw the thick-set figure step closer to the rear of the car.

'I thought you was burstin' forra leak.'

'Ya thought right...'

Loud in his reply the man laughed, thick ham-bone hands fumbling with the zip of his jeans. 'And that be what I'm tekin', this bloody banger could do wi' a wash, I'm doin' it for free.'

'You always docs leave a good tip...'

The last word was still in the smaller man's mouth when Torrey's hand caught his throat, the other a ball of steel landing a blow on his face

61

that threw him to the ground like some empty paper bag.

'What the–'

Urine spurting upward caught the evening breeze and sprayed into the heavy spluttering face as Torrey jerked the second man backward.

'Put it away!'

Headlights of traffic moving both ways along Pinfold Street flashed like those on Christmas trees, their drivers passing resolutely, each blind to whatever might have caught their eye. A post-football match fracas was the last thing any of them fancied being caught up in.

'Put it away!'

His own mind impervious to the consequence of a mobile phone summoning the blues, Torrey breathed the instruction again, his eyes blazing cold fury as he looked at the second figure sprawled on the ground.

'I wouldn't want to deprive our friend there of his night-time comfort much as I feel I want to rip it off and shove it in your own mouth ... seems you're not past the suckling stage yourself so p'raps a dummy–'

'Why, you smart-mouthed bastard!'

The man was on his feet, trousers open, large flabby organ hanging like he was a bull in heat.

A bull or Ronald Webster?

A scene he had thought gone from memory for good flashed brilliantly across Torrey's inner vision.

Fifteen years old, six foot tall with an ego the same size, the figure that had terrified so many years of his childhood leered from the past. He'd been no more than a kid himself, Torrey felt the old fear jolt his nerves; he couldn't be blamed for being scared, nor could he be blamed for what happened when Webster and his thugs had tried to rape him.

'*Witness my protection.*'

Words he thought equally forgotten ripped across the open fields of memory.

Those had been the words he had heard above the frightened thunder of his own heart as he was thrown face down across a workbench in Webster's father's shed.

'*Witness my protection.*'

With the soft whisper had begun the vibration, shaking the ground, the shed rocking as if caught in the throes of an earthquake while a screaming wind howled from every side. But it had not been the all. Shadows, dark and looming, had crept from the shuddering wood of the walls, shadows which had combined, drawing together to stand floor to ceiling in a cloud of darkness. But it had been a cloud which breathed; a cloud from which snake-like tendrils whiplashed, coiling around one of the fleeing lads, throwing him aside.

Once more the twelve year old, Torrey watched the silent picture show.

Webster had stood, his Fair Isle jumper short of covering his genitals, but now he wasn't the bullying leader of a gang but a terrified boy screaming his fear while a quicksilver touch of shadow tendril scorched away the lips of another to leave a charred blackened gash. Then the tendril had reached for Webster, curling itself about the semi-naked body leaving trails of smoking flesh behind each caress.

But no tendril had reached for Torrey, no whip-lash of shadow, no burning flesh. The darkness that filled the shed had thinned to grey mist that receded into the walls and as the last vestige dissolved he had heard the words again. '*Witness my protection.*'

But he was not twelve years old any more ... no frightened lad scared witless by bully boys or by words he imagined himself to have heard, and he certainly wasn't scared of the lump of flesh facing him now ... he needed no protection given by Julian Crowley ... nor by anybody!

Bringing his back against the wall of the pub, Torrey adopted the stance he had adopted years after the episode of Webster. Now he stood as he had in the yard of another pub not five hundred yards from this one. Three of the same ilk, yobbos each of them, they had taunted him over the affair of Anna, his beautiful Anna who had walked out on him. But they had chosen badly; not only was the evening wrong but they had picked on the wrong guy – only they hadn't known that. Sure of themselves, hunting only in a pack, they had followed outside and there in the yard of the Bird-in-Hand, lit only by one dim bulb, they had thought to take him.

Thought! Torrey smiled. Just as this one thought to take him; but like the three before him this lout was due for a little old-fashioned night-school education. Those others, they still walked like cripples – and avoided all contact with Rich-ard Torrey.

Zip fastened, the beefy figure glanced once at

his companion lying stunned, then eyes half closed with rage he glared at Torrey.

'I'm gonna break your fuckin' back then snap your 'ead off and stuff it up your arse.'

Would he snort before he attacked? Paw the ground and bellow before he hurled himself forward? The notion of an enraged bull returned to Torrey's mind but didn't hold his attention; that was concentrated upon himself.

Stay sharp, place your weight evenly on both feet! Methods of unarmed combat learned during commando training and kept sharp by his joining the local T.A. unit spoke silent words. The man would come from the front, he thought weight and size to be enough to down any opponent. Arms loose at his sides, fingers curved inward, Torrey waited. Any moment now one more of Darlaston's self-designated invincibles would realise the truth of folly.

'Did you hear me, arsehole, I'm gonna–'

'Didn't your father tell you never to leave a sentence unfinished... Oh, I forgot! Your mother never did know your father!' Torrey looked into the face he had smashed against the wall.

The attack had come as he guessed, a full frontal. Ready for it, quick as lightning in the execution, he had stepped aside, grabbing the head as his attacker kissed the wall. He had hit the brow twice against the brickwork then before the man could realise what had happened he had both his arms twisted upward into his shoulder blades; gelled spiked hair was grasped tortuously between steel fingers, and he was being propelled to where his urine shone damp on the boot of the car.

'It was nice of you to try washing the car but I have to tell you I'm not satisfied.' Torrey yanked him to a halt.

Moaning with the pain of a twisted arm and his head snatched back on his neck, the man dribbled spit and blood from lips already swelling to twice their normal size.

'I'm going to ask you do it again, and this time you'll do it my way.'

Across the street several passersby had stopped to watch, women murmuring someone should stop what was happening, but nobody moved.

His opponent between himself and the car, Torrey forced the man's head downward. 'Now...' he grated, '...lick it!'

Beneath his hand the head jerked backward but was no match for the strength pressing his bleeding mouth against the still-wet metal. Torrey felt a grim smile touch his own lips.

'I said lick it, or I'll use your entrails for a wash rag!'

Breath easy and controlled flowed into Torrey's lungs, but his grip didn't lessen. A dog cocked its leg where it ought not and it got its nose rubbed in the mess. That had been the way of folk in Dangerfield Lane and it would be as effective now as then. This was one dog would learn not to piss on anyone else's ground!

'I've tried the library, they have nothing relating to old wives' tales.' Kate Mallory's sherry-brown head tipped to rest against the back of her landlady's sofa, eyelids closing over bronze coloured eyes.

66

'Did you ask upstairs? You knows ... the part as don't let you take books out.'

'The reference section,' Kate's eyelids didn't lift, 'yes, I asked there but the answer was the same, nothing on old wives' tales.'

'Be a fancy building, but it's no use to folk!' A snort of derision finishing the sentence for her, Annie Price picked up the cup she had filled with hot tea.

Kate suppressed a smile. Unforgiving of any of her beloved town being robbed of its old buildings, Annie decried any value of the new. Just what she thought now those old places on the opposite side of the road from the library were being demolished was best not touched upon. Annie had bristled when the bulldozer had toppled the first wall. 'They should 'ave bin given one o' them what you call 'em ... them protection orders ... but them along of the council, they'd see 'em gone and one o' them square boxes put up in place!'

But the library was not a square box, and despite Annie's deprecation it was used extensively by old and young and boasted a wide range of books and pamphlets. Kate picked up her own cup. Why then did it have nothing on old wives' tales?

''Ave you told that there editor there be nothing?'

Kate's hair caught the light from Annie's chandelier, an inheritance of her mother and each crystal dropper cared for as tenderly as a child.

'Scottie would never accept it. He reckons whatever it is you need is out there somewhere, you just need to look hard enough.'

'Hmmh!' Annie snorted again. 'That be just like one not given the task of looking 'imself.'

'They had a fair selection of books dealing with Myths and Legends.' Kate decided not to follow the track her landlady's feet had started upon.

'Be them two different sorts o' tale?'

'I must admit I've never been too sure myself, I had to look up both in the dictionary.'

'So, be they the same thing called by two labels?' Annie replenished the cups.

'I wrote the definitions down 'cos I knew the minute I stepped from the library I'd have forgotten.' Scrabbling in the bag set on the carpet at her feet Kate extricated a small blue-covered notebook.

'Legend,' she read, 'a story handed down for generations and popularly believed to have a historical basis; Myth, a traditional story of unknown authorship, serving usually to explain customs, religious rites or beliefs.'

'Don't sound to be different to me. If a story be 'anded one generation to another then that be tradition; one be written down by nobody knows who, while the other is only *believed* to 'ave a historical basis ... so who's to say what be what?' This being a deduction she could not argue with, Kate kept her counsel.

'But if stories told mother to daughter be of any use then there be one I can tell of that could be called an old wife's tale, couldn't it?'

Let it be yes, please let it be yes! Kate's plea rose on silent wings.

'Torrey said to ask you, he said you would

68

maybe have known some of the local tales, p'raps could remember some your mother might have told.'

'Richard be a nice lad.' Annie kept stubbornly to her preferred use of Christian name; speaking to or of a person using just the surname smacked too much of her school days and teachers who thought themselves superior to the people whose children they taught.

Don't let her go off on a tangent ... please! Kate prayed again.

'He be right in what he said about Mother, her 'ad plenty of them tales, one in particular...'

Her second prayer answered, Kate breathed in relief; maybe she was at last going to get something she could write about.

'Yes, one in particular, I remembers it 'cos it scared me so when I were a little 'un...'

The rattling of Annie's cup as she rested it in its saucer brought a tiny frown to Kate's brow. Could she still be scared after so many years?

'Ar, it 'ad me frightened in them days,' Annie went on, the smile coming to her lips thin and uncertain, 'it were to do with the daughter of Jacob Corby, so my mother's mother told, he were master of Glebe Metalworks, it be gone now but the 'ouse he lived in, Butcroft House, still stands close by the Bull Stake. Well, it seemed he got religion, traipsed his wife and only child near round God's world a thumpin' of the Bible. When he died in Russia ... least Grandmother maintained that were so ... died of the terrible cold while his wife ... her were a Bedworth ... well, it were said the wolves took her, pulled her from one of them sledges, though that might 'ave been a bit of dressin' to the story...'

Where was the old wife's tale in this? Kate wanted to ask yet was somehow reluctant. Maybe it was the older woman's face, tight now where normally it was relaxed.

'Anyway the daughter returned to Darlaston with a child in her belly and no ring to her finger...'

'Does the child have descendents living in Darlaston?' A means of corroborating the story tempered Kate's reticence.

'Not that one.' Annie's head swung with sympathy. 'Never lived to see its first birthday ... there be older folk in this town who still believes t'were the sister of Jacob Corby done the little soul in ... poison so my grandmother 'eld. But were not the child her carried back be the core of the tale, it were what her carried along of Bentley Hall, what her took to the master there and what it was killed 'im.'

That was a bit of a let down! What could Scottie expect her to build out of that? Local girl becomes pregnant during trip abroad? Lord, it happened a dozen times a day!

'Sir Corbett Foley, he it was owned Bentley Hall ... he died of a 'eart attack.'

I knew it! Kate felt the brick drop in her stomach, I knew I shouldn't have let my hopes rise! Bastard child ... heart attack ... so what else was new!

'That were the cause so folk were wanted to believe, but that weren't the truth, it were a cover for what were in the box delivered to him by

Anne Corby.'

'Which was?'

'That were never rightly knowed for it were seen by nobody save Foley.'

'The girl, Anne Corby ... she surely must have looked in that box?'

'Times were different then to what they be now, a body made a promise then that promise were kept, least they was by God-fearing folk, and for sure the Corby wench 'ad a Christian upbringing.'

'So how–?'

'If you could just set a bridle to that tongue o' your'n then mebbe I could tell you!'

Annie set cup and saucer aside. A quick move designed to mask swift irritation ... or was it something other had her landlady unusually sharp? Chastened, Kate glanced at the notebook in which she had as yet written nothing.

'Call it one of them myths or legends if you will, for folk 'ave whispered of it ever since,' Annie resumed her story, ''tis said Foley knew what it were in that box, that it were the evil of it struck out at him, snatched the very life from his body. That it were the Devil's Talisman.'

6

'The Devil's Talisman? Never heard of it!'

'Neither had I until Annie told me of it.'

'Annie...' Richard Torrey's dark eyes gleamed their humour, 'you're sure she isn't winding your spring?'

Although every sense told her there was no contempt for Annie behind his words, Kate Mallory's defences sprang into action. Eyes shooting particles of brown ice, tone hard as the brickwork surrounding them her tilted mouth firmed. 'Annie would not deliberately mislead me, unlike a certain man...'

'All right ... all right, apology given. You know I love Annie as a mother.'

'You could have fooled me!' Ill temper blurted the response and immediately Kate was repentant. Torrey did think the world of the woman and she of him. They were easy together, each enjoying the other's company and there could be little doubt any man giving her grief would answer to him.

'So what was this Talisman?'

Momentary as it had been, Kate was relieved the tension was gone. 'The whole story is a bit far-fetched, even I thought that as I listened, but Annie appeared to believe every word.'

'Always believe what your mother tells you.' The quip had gone down like a lead balloon! A few minutes' conversation with the barmaid was intended to give time for Kate to cool down but when Torrey returned with both glasses replenished he was greeted with Kate's frosty retort.

'You listen without interruption ... 'cos with the next clever remark you get that beer all over you.'

'Lord, Kate, you'd do that to a man? You should have worked for the Borgias, your talent is wasted where it is.'

'Oh, that would be nobbut friendly act, hinny...' Kate's smile was brown sugar, '...I wouldn't advise you go for the warning.'

Point taken. Torrey watched the hand stray unconsciously to the leather bag feeling for cigarettes she no longer used. A day at a time, breaking the habit took one day at a time. He should know, he'd done the same after joining the Army. Lungs furred with tobacco were no asset to commando training.

'The Talisman,' Kate went on, her search abandoned, 'was a piece of jewellery, a sort of seal, at least that is what I got from Annie's story. She seems to have been taught by her grandmother that each Archangel had some badge of office and that Satan's was a jewelled piece worn about the neck. It was broken away and lost during his struggle with the Archangel Michael who threw him out of heaven.'

'So what you're saying is, this Seal or Talisman was in the package Anne...?'

'Corby.'

'...Anne Corby delivered to Bentley Hall.'

'What Annie's grandmother said,' Kate corrected.

73

'And that anyone touching it dies a violent death...'

'It happened to Rasputin and to the Russian royal family, and don't forget Sir Corbett Foley, he was okay one minute and dead the next.'

'Also,' Torrey went on as though she hadn't spoken, 'we are to believe that bringing the piece into the open causes all kinds of havoc and disasters to happen, floods, plagues, both world wars? Sorry, Kate, but I think Annie has confused her old wife's tale with the legend of Pandora and her box of tricks.'

She had thought the same. Kate kept that admittance strictly to herself.

'This Talisman,' Torrey asked at her silence, 'what happened to it, where is it now?'

'Nobody knows. The grandmother was of the opinion that the manservant who found Foley dead also found the box ... you've no need to ask the rest.'

'Spirited away!'

'Well, I'm glad that remark amused somebody, even if it was only yourself!'

A school-boy grin refusing to leave his mouth, Torrey shook his head. 'Sorry again, but you were not far from wrong when you said this was one old wife's tale I would find hard to believe, especially as it gives no explanation of why Old Nick didn't take his property back.'

Sipping lager and lime, Kate glanced around the lounge bar of the Frying Pan. How many of the people sitting in this pub knew the story Annie Price had related. How many believed it if they did?

'You haven't heard the all of it.' She returned to Torrey. 'According to the tale, the Talisman was cut away by a stroke of the Archangel Michael's fiery sword and as Satan reached to retrieve it the Almighty stayed his hand, saying that it was to be given into the keeping of mankind, that Satan would possess it only if it were given voluntarily by a mortal. With that the devil cursed it. It would bring hate, malice and affliction of an intensity that would end only with the destruction of the world. And *that* part of the story seems to prove ever more true; unrest and violence is today's menu in almost every country.'

'Give me a week and I might find a counter argument to that,' Torrey answered, attempting to hide the bitterness of truth beneath the veneer of a smile. 'But more important is Scottie's argument, did he hand you your cards there and then or is he posting them on to you?'

Across the room a man's low-pitched laugh was joined by a woman's lighter one. Kate waited for it to fade before answering. 'Neither.'

'Don't tell me he swallowed that tripe!'

Meeting the disbelief so evident in those dark eyes, Kate luxuriated in a moment of triumph. 'He said it was ... now what was the way he put it? A canny piece.'

'Now it's you winding the spring!'

The slight tilt of her mouth emphasised by a supercilious clamp of the lips, Kate answered with galling quietness. 'I'm doing no such thing. Read tomorrow's *Star* and see for yourself.'

'Lord, Kate!' Bemusement showed in the shake of Torrey's dark head. 'How did you pull that off?

75

I mean, Scottie of all people falling for—'

'For an old wife's tale?' Kate's smile broke through. 'He swallowed it 'cos I sweetened it up before giving it to him.'

'You sugared the pill? Careful, Kate, playing doctor can bring dire results … such as signing on at the dole office once a week.'

'Well, it was the only damn tale I got!' Mutiny threatened as it had when writing her copy. 'It was alter it a little or get bawled out for having nothing ready; that man thinks you can grab a story out of thin air.'

'So how much is a little? C'mon, confess; just what have you done with Annie's reminiscences?'

'Turned them around, but not that much.'

His steady look asking 'How much', Kate explained. 'Like you said, Scottie would not have accepted the story as Annie told it so I simply made it a "do you recall" piece. I didn't say where the item had come from, neither could I name the Corby or the Foley link – there are too many people ready to jump on the litigation bandwagon – so I simply asked did readers think it was myth or legend, did they place any truth on it, had anyone memories of being told about the Devil's Talisman. Scottie thought it might provide a "letters to the Editor" column, but guess who will finish up answering any letters that might come in?'

'Talking of what might come in,' Torrey nodded towards the street entrance, 'look who just walked through the door.'

The woman had fallen gently.

Venetia Pascal stared from the window of her superbly appointed office.

There had been no scream, no cry. She had left this world in silence, dropping to the floor of that room with no more sound than spent petals dropping from a flower's stem. Belial, that great golden emissary of Lucifer, that glittering beautiful envoy of the Master had taken more than the blood of offering Theo Vail had drawn with the Athame, the knife of sacrifice; it had taken a life.

And Theo Vail had smiled!

Staring across the sprawl of Birmingham's heart, Venctia felt the sting of distaste wash against her throat.

Vail had smiled!

In the terrified throb of silence that had followed the departure of that golden demon, she had watched Vail's face.

It had glowed with rapture, there was no other word could fully describe a look that was pure bliss; in his mind Vail had seen the death of that woman as the sign he so earnestly desired. The Prince of Darkness had accepted his sacrifice. In return he would bestow the ultimate gift; to him, Vail, would be given all power on earth.

But the woman's death had not been by the Athame.

Below, in the choked streets of the country's second city, traffic jostled noisily for supremacy; but Venetia neither heard nor saw.

No blood of the woman had been drawn by the sacrificial knife. No scarlet drops of life had dripped into that bronze bowl, no offering had been made. There had been no sacrifice!

77

Magus, Priest of the High Coven, Vail should have recognised the fact.

Instead he had smiled.

Venetia's nostrils flared elegant derision.

Blinded by his own conceit, his arrogant sense of superiority, an undeniable belief in himself as the Chosen, the first earthly lord of Lucifer, he had seen the death of that woman as being a gift to the Master, an offering given by his word, by his hand.

But it had not!

Venetia Pascal's mouth curved in a smile of pure satisfaction.

The great Theo Vail had made a mistake. The Lord of Darkness did not suffer mistakes and certainly he did not allow them to go unpunished, that much had been made only too obvious when another over-confident High Priest had made his mistake; Julian Crowley had paid, not with his life though he must wish that had been the punishment decreed: but it had been a far more terrible sentence the Master of Hell had ordained. Julian Crowley had paid with his sanity.

Behind her the desk intercom shrilled. Thought severed as with the incision of a scalpel, she turned to answer its demand.

'Thank you, please ask him to come in.'

A perfectly manicured finger depressed a button and the intercom returned to its 'off' position.

'Mr Vail...' Distaste hidden, a skill acquired by the years of practice during association with Julian Crowley, she smiled as the tall figure of Vail was shown into the room.

The swagger of confidence that success and wealth had imbued emphasised an air of condescension in the man smiling at the pretty brunette who blushed beneath a murmured word.

'The venue is arranged?' Vail asked first, scanning the intercom to assure himself the transmit button was in the 'off' position.

'As you asked,' Venetia answered.

'Good.' Vail sank easily into pale blue leather. 'The invitations have been despatched?'

Irritation sharp and quick stabbed beneath the façade of a smile. She was a disciple of Satan, a devotee of the Left Hand Path and more than this man's equal in brains! But not in power, not yet. But circumstances could be made to improve; one day Theo Vail would realise he could not treat her like a glorified secretary! Forcing a degree of pleasantness that was in total opposition to the feeling coursing in every vein, Venetia Pascal nodded.

'Each sent and each answered.'

'The replies ... they have been destroyed?'

Annoyance throwing aside the smile, Venetia Pascal's expertly painted lips tautened. Green eyes hardened to malachite as she stared with frigid indifference.

'Unlike yourself, Theo, I observe every care in any arrangement I make, especially when those arrangements concern the worship of the Master.'

From the vastness of the blue leather couch Theo Vail, Magus of the High Coven, tensed. This was not the first imputation Venetia Pascal had made, not the first reproach against him and his method of serving their Lord and Master. A long breath not fully restoring the feel-good factor of a moment ago, he looked at the beautiful face regarding him with ill-concealed contempt. Yes, she was beautiful, her features exquisitely formed beneath a flawless skin; one might almost think that face and body a sculpture crafted by … the devil? Involuntary breath caught in his throat. Every Follower was given his or her most desired gift in exchange for their soul. Had physical beauty been the price Venetia Pascal had demanded, or had it been something else? From her first joining the coven he had sensed a difference in her, a self assurance none of the others possessed; could it be her pact was an immunity of sorts; was Satan's promise a safe-guarding against something she had feared? But here on earth she should fear nothing more than the High Priest of the First Coven; it was he had the Master's full approval, he who held the power, Venetia Pascal would learn that, maybe very soon.

A palliative to his own irritation the thought calmed, only the twitch of one eyebrow belying the fact it had been there at all.

'Meaning?' His voice arched to match the eyebrow.

The cobra rears! Venetia met the look which despite all effort hid none of its origin. Like Julian Crowley before him, Theo Vail enjoyed the trappings of wealth, exulted in the powers his position as first disciple of Lucifer afforded him, but he had those same failings. She had watched that other priest of Satan grow in arrogance, seen that confidence in the supremacy of self erase common sense, and now she was seeing it again.

'Meaning it was a mistake to leave the woman's body in that building.'

'Mistake?'

And now the *hiss* of the cobra! Venetia kept her ground as Vail rose from the couch.

'That is what I said and that is what I think. The body should have been removed before we left. There should have been no trace, nothing to say what had taken place there.'

'But nothing has been left.' Sneering condescension returning a smile to his handsome mouth, Theo Vail smoothed a manicured hand across the lapel of his immaculate suit. 'The building went up in flames; a warehouse filled with paint and turpentine would be a positive inferno, one that would leave nothing but ash in its wake.'

'Nothing apart from the remains of a skeleton.'

That has taken the poison from his fangs! Pleasure scything a warm path, Venetia watched the quick flash of alarm whip the sneer away.

'Skeleton? That's impossible!' Fingers still on the smartly cut lapel clenched convulsively before the hand dropped to Vail's side.

'You think so? Then I trust you have not read a certain newspaper cutting.' Handing it to her visitor she waited while he read it.

'...firemen inspecting the site of a fire which destroyed the premises of Johnson paint factory, Station Street, Darlaston, discovered the remains of a body in what had been the office. The Coroner's report is expected within a few days...'

Needing time to re-establish a sharply displaced composure, Theo Vail read the piece through a second time.

'That need cause no concern.' He flung the snippet of paper on to the desk. 'The knife and bowl were brought away, the Pentacle was painted on cloth which would burn easily...'

'More easily than a human body!' Her snide reiteration given, Venetia retrieved the tossed paper and tore it across before consigning it to papers destined for the shredder.

'A down and out.' Vail shrugged, a dismissive, no-need-to-worry movement of his well-cared-for body. 'A kid run away from home ... a vagrant with nowhere to sleep ... an illegal immigrant hiding from the police ... the probabilities are numerous and so long as nothing exists to show the presence of a coven worshipping there – and nothing will still exist – then there is absolutely no cause for anxiety.'

It seemed for a moment that the polished air of refinement that was a trademark of the woman behind one of the most famous cosmetic houses in the world would give way to the scorn smouldering inside her. Then, a brief shake of the head the only clue to her contempt, she replied, 'No cause for anxiety! I wonder, Theo, will the Prince of Darkness hold the same casual attitude?'

7

'Just been havin' a chat in the Staffordshire Knot.' Detective Inspector Bruce Daniels had missed not a single face, though his glance seemed fixed as he crossed to an alcove of the lounge bar of the Frying Pan to join Kate and Torrey. 'Seems our friend Echo has made that his watering hole now the Bird-in-Hand is no longer a retreat for the little toerag. In here earlier, was he?'

'Wouldn't know.' Torrey glanced at Kate. This was becoming a habit, one he didn't particularly care for.

'Hmm.' Daniels sucked on a tablet he had placed on his tongue before leaving his car. 'Don't suppose you know anything of a shindig taking place outside of the Staffordshire Knot last night either?'

Innocence painted a slight frown between coal-dark eyes. 'Shindig...? What would that be then?'

'Oh, just a couple of Walsall's football fans got themselves a hiding, deserved it probably, but we coppers have to go by the book; a complaint is brought and we have to investigate.'

Taking a swallow of best bitter, Torrey suppressed the smile longing to break on his mouth. Neither of those louts had laid a complaint, in fact it was a dead cert they wouldn't go voluntarily within a mile of the nick.

'Can be expected after a local derby.' Torrey set his glass back on the table. 'Their team comes off worst and it leads to a punch-up.'

'Weren't only the team come off worst, and it were no punch-up judging by what was told, least our two football supporters didn't get to land any; one was felled in the first few seconds while the other was frog-marched to the back of a car where his nose was used as a cleaning rag.'

Not his nose. Torrey's look was bland. But he would have a bad taste to his tongue for a day or two.

'So when these men made their complaint did they say who it was had attacked them?'

'Said as it were a taxi driver.' Daniels answered Kate's question. 'Picked 'em up outside of the stadium then got nasty when the pound tip they gave him wasn't enough...' The glance, deceptively guileless to any who were not well enough acquainted with the detective inspector to know better, returned to Torrey. 'Ring any bells?'

It rang the whole Westminster chime! Torrey didn't blink. Let the blues earn their money.

'Thought mebbe you might of heard summat from one of your mates.'

You had to hand it to Daniels, he worked like a ferret down a rabbit hole. Torrey watched the other man's jaw move as he sucked the tablet on his tongue.

'I operate a private hire car, I don't stand in the taxi rank, therefore I get to talk to no other taxi drivers, but you could make enquiries along of–'

'Already have!' Daniels interrupted sourly. 'They are like Sounder, hear all, say nowt, but I'd

84

bet a week's pay the little screw knows very well who duffed them two.'

'Could he not help you either?'

That should get an Oscar! Torrey applauded mentally. When Kate Mallory decided to play innocent she did it all the way.

'He could had he wanted to.' Daniels' eyes narrowed; he had not expected the little turd to answer as he had.

'Echo needs his teeth to chew, he knows if he is found to be whistling the wrong tune he's going to need extensive dental treatment.'

'That be right.' Daniels acknowledged Torrey's reply. 'But then he gets that free if he's banged up in Winson Green.'

'He can't possibly have Echo brought up on a charge of ... of...' Kate floundered, watching the figure of the detective inspector leave, a figure several other pairs of eyes watched.

'Of failing to provide information.' Torrey finished the words Kate's indignation would not allow to come. 'As Echo himself would say, don't lay any odds on that; he knows Daniels could haul him in on a charge of breathing and still make it stick.'

Kate shook her head, lighting from wall lamps sending a shower of amber glints cascading among the sherry-coloured curls. 'Then why not tell? Supposing he knows.'

Torrey watched the miniature display of fireworks dance in her hair. His mother's hair had already shown signs of grey before she was thirty.

'Oh, Sounder knows,' he said, riding the unhappiness thoughts of his mother's hard life generated, 'and you know he gives nothing for nothing. You should also know he values being able to walk on his legs more than he fears a spell in Winson Green.'

'He does get to know things, doesn't he?'

'Sounder?' Torrey finished his drink. 'Nothing passes him by, the man can get where castor oil couldn't!'

Finishing her own drink Kate lifted the bag to her shoulder, then nodding to the bar staff, followed by Torrey, she left the Frying Pan.

Breathing deeply of the cool air of late evening she glanced at the dark silhouettes of surrounding buildings.

The world was full of uncertainty, many countries were torn with internal fighting, but all of what was happening now was insignificant against what could have happened had Echo Sounder not held on to that foreign banknote.

What that scruffy little man didn't know about Darlaston wasn't worth the knowing. The phrase Torrey had once used regarding Echo Sounder whispered in Kate's mind followed closely by another ... maybe he could throw a little light on Annie's old wife's tale.

The discussion with Theo Vail, prior to a business meeting, had not been to the man's liking. Venetia Pascal poured tonic water into a tall crystal flute. Lifting the glass, an elegantly manicured hand holding it to the light, she watched the thousand pin-points of colour dance in its depths; the director of 'Pascal' enjoyed the finer things of life ... and there were even finer yet to be had.

Balancing the fragile glass between long fingers, she nursed it delicately. Vail had been disconcerted. He had made a mistake in not having that body removed and though he had bluffed she had recognised concern ... and she had fed it by asking how the one they both served, the Great Prince of Darkness, would view that blunder.

But she would make no mistake. Vail was not one to take criticism, implied or otherwise, whether in private or in public; and every inch of him had shouted the fact he would not take hers.

Eyes closing she rested the cool glass against expertly painted lips but allowed no liquid to pass between them. She had taken no meal since that meeting and she would take no drink ... not until that which she planned was over and finished.

Behind that veneer of confidence, the swagger with which he had dismissed the idea of incompetence in leaving a dead body in the hope of its burning away completely in the fire he had arranged to be lit as the coven left the paint factory, she had seen reprisal. It had been in his look, his body language; Vail wanted revenge and he would take it at the first opportunity!

Vail was jealous of his position of Magus. Venetia stared at the cream Bokhara carpet, the cost of which would have kept half of the starving of Eritrea in food for a decade. As High Priest of the Coven he wielded authority, but that was not enough; his eyes were set on a higher prize. He wanted that which would give him supreme powers and authority over all other covens, the many hundreds of followers of the Path. Theo

Vail had dreams of attaining the very highest status, that which gave the ability of travel, on the astral plane; he desired to become Ipsissimus, and with that first among the devotees of the Master of Hell.

Given those powers which were encompassed within the Talisman, Vail would be protected, impervious to harm while being able to wreak it upon whomsoever he chose ... and he would choose Venetia Pascal!

Jealous and dangerous. A breath drawn deeply emphasised the knowledge. The self-same attributes held by another of Satan's disciples, Julian Crowley, who had rescued her from one life only to enmesh her in another. He had found her half-conscious from gang rape, by four hooligans who had seen a young woman walking home from Sunday church service. They had grabbed her, the first blow of a balled fist knocking her almost senseless.

Venetia drew another long breath, this laced with hate but also with triumph.

Almost senseless ... but not entirely so. They had dragged her to a derelict building hidden from the road by tall overgrown bushes and trees and it was there, on a filth-laden floor, that they had taken their pleasure. Gagged and helpless, the clothing ripped from her, she had been thrown to the ground, one too eager to await his turn squeezing her breasts while his fellow rapist drove into her. The nightmare had gone on.

She breathed evenly, the remembered events of that night no longer holding any terror.

They had laughed at her naked and spread-

eagled on that dirt-ridden floor, three congratul-
ating the other as each in turn had groaned
satisfaction in reaching climax. But once had not
been enough, their thirst had not been slaked so
they had taken her again ... and then again, and
all the time that laughter.

But that laughter had died abruptly. Even now,
so many years on, she still did not understand
just when, or how, Crowley had appeared; it had
seemed he stepped from the very wall itself, a
shadow on the crumbling brickwork, a shadow
which solidified as the four men stared.

The one who had gagged her, taking a sadistic
delight in tying the foul-smelling rag so tightly it
had bitten into the tender flesh of her mouth, was
the first to recover from surprise.

'You wantin' a fuck?' he had snarled. *'Then go
find your own bitch, this one is ours.'*

Crowley had not answered, neither had he
moved from the pool of shadows.

*'P'raps he don't want to ride, p'raps he's the sort
just likes to watch.'* A second of her attackers had
sniggered.

'Is that right, mate?' The tallest of the four had
stepped forward, a shaved head jutting from a
thick neck. *'You get off by watchin' others do what
you can't?'*

'No...'

Venetia remembered the coldness of the reply,
of black crow-sharp eyes glittering like living
flame as Crowley had emerged from the covering
veil of shadow.

'No,' he had smiled, *'I get off by seeing others
watch me do what they cannot.'*

89

'That bein'?'

Thick lips had parted in a sneer as the bull-necked one pulled up the zip of his jeans.

Cool as the ice in his eyes Crowley had answered, 'That being giving the four of you a much-deserved lesson.'

'Oh yes,' hands dropping from the zip clenched into fists. 'You'll need be a bloody good teacher!'

'Oh, I am,' the return had been quietly filled with confidence, 'believe me I am.'

Shoulders hunching forward, fists rising to chest level, the tall man had laughed. 'Then you'd better start the class, and I'm your first student.'

'If he's as big as his mouth then p'raps he'd like to teach we all at once.'

'Leave out!' The order was barked, halting the three advancing to their friend's assistance. 'I don't be needin' no help to put this cocky bugger's teeth down his throat or his dick up his arse … you tie the woman in the corner over there, we'll each of we be wanting another taste of her tomorrow.'

They had decided that was one instruction could be delayed in its carrying out and stood intent on the promised fight.

'Well, fuck 'ead!' The one who appeared to be the leader barked again. 'Let's see if you've got balls in them there fancy pants, see if they are as big as your mouth? Mebbe's I'll take meself a look after I beat the shit outta you!'

In reply the dark-suited figure had lifted both hands above his head.

'Siras Etar Besonar.' The words whispered against the broken walls.

'What the bloody … he thinks he's Gandalf!'

'Who the hell is Gandalf?'

'You knows, that there magician in Lord of the Rings.'

Behind the one threatening Crowley, the three threw question and answer but it was the one eye to eye with him had the final word.

'Magician!' He had sniggered as they all had. 'He's gonna need more than a magic wand to–'

There had been no more. Venetia smiled as the memories surged on.

'Siras Etar Besonar,' Crowley had repeated, 'open to me the Gates. Hear me, Sammael, great angel of Lucifer, who stands before the Dark Throne, hear the cry of one who worships the Prince of Creation, I conjure and command thee in his name, answer my summons.'

The sound which had been Crowley's softly spoken words was no longer that alone. Like the ripple of waves, gentle at first, it seemed to come from all sides.

Even in the shock of being raped over and over she had been conscious of a new, more terrible fear, one which had her attackers fall silent.

In the dimness of half-hidden moonlight she had seen Crowley, hands still raised and above them a flickering blue light, tiny like the flame of a candle on a child's birthday cake.

But it had been no candle flame!

Almost immediately it had grown and as it spread and widened, bathing the figure stood beneath it in vivid blue light, so the sound had increased, becoming a moan like wind among the leaves of trees surrounding the building; then changing to a slither as though some great reptilian body dragged itself around the walls.

Terrified then, but smiling now, Venetia recalled how she had crawled from where the four had thrown her, seeking refuge in the darkness beyond that rim of light.

'Hear me thou who has passed through the Gates.' Crowley had spoken again. *'Sammael, minister of Satan, do now the will of his servant.'*

Crowley's hands lowered the light which had hovered above his head to become now a shimmering outline about his body. Beyond her hiding place she had heard a man whimper then break into a scream that ended as Crowley pointed. A flash as of blue lightning caught the tallest of the men, lifting him bodily and flinging him like a rag doll across the space of the derelict room to slam him against a wall. As he fell to the ground, the sound of breaking bones crunching the silence, Crowley had directed his hand towards the others. Flash upon flash; cobalt, sapphire, indigo colours blazed and twisted, twining into each other, a chorus of brilliance, beautiful in their promise of death.

But death had not been the lesson Crowley had wished to teach.

In the glow, incandescence shimmering about him, his eyes had been glistening black diamonds, while his face...

Only years later had she fully realised the look Crowley's face had held at that moment.

...his face had worn a look of ecstasy!

As each in his turn had raped her, so each in his turn received punishment. Whiplike, a coil of blue flashed in the darkness. A man screamed fear and pain as it scythed his face to leave a burned-out eye socket in its wake; then the merest flick of Crowley's finger sent it sucking about another's spine, the crack of vertebrae pistol shots of vengeance: and then the fourth man.

The smile which hovered about the perfect mouth deepened. Satisfaction warming like age-old brandy, Venetia watched the last of the mental pictures.

The fourth man had screamed repentance, begged Crowley to let him go. But caught in the throes of power which went beyond himself, Crowley had no desire to show mercy. Instead, he had pointed and a sinuous slender form had issued from the tip of his forefinger, a form which swayed and hissed, a glittering amethyst serpent. The man had screamed again and from her corner she had heard the sound of water trickling on the ground. Then the light-formed creature had moved, undulating through the air, worming along as it might on firm ground, snaking towards the terrified man. Halting a foot from him, its forked tongue sparked its message.

The man had made no more sound, only slipping to the ground as the forked tongue touched his brow, cleaving a scarlet gash across it.

Almost at the same instant the emanation had gone, leaving pallid streams of moonlight to illuminate the figure turned towards her, the man who had asked that she choose between the God who had made no move on her behalf and the one whose powers and protection she had witnessed.

She had chosen!

Leaving the glass where she had placed it,

Venetia walked from the room.

From that moment she had dedicated herself to the service of Satan, and from that same moment had set herself to learning the art of black magic, to acquiring the skills Crowley had so aptly demonstrated.

Skills she was to need if she were to protect herself from the rancour of Theo Vail.

8

Nosing the Sonata through the evening traffic, Torrey smiled to himself. Kate! She wanted so much to write a decent piece for Scottie's latest brainchild ... but Satan's Talisman, the Devil's Seal of Office? That was a tale too far! Of course it wasn't true ... the smile became a repressed chuckle; the devil being chucked out of heaven, having his insignia taken from him only for it to be given to mankind; that didn't just take the biscuit, it took the whole barrel! Man had made mess enough of the world; give him that trinket and he might just blow it away altogether.

Annie believed a piece of jewellery had been carried from Russia and given to the owner of Bentley Hall. Kate had defended her landlady's story. Well, of course. Annie was a sweetheart, she would take as gospel anything told her by her mother or grandmother. Try that with kids of today! Torrey touched a foot to the brake as stop lights flashed on the car in front – the answer you got would constitute a physiological impossibility.

'Traffic is a bit heavy here.' Glancing into the driving mirror he caught the eyes of his passenger and the chuckle still nestling in his throat was suddenly gone. Those eyes were filled with fear. More than fear, terror, the woman sat behind him was terrified! Of what? There had been no tremble in the voice making the telephone booking, no sign of fright or even of apprehension when he had collected her from Shepwell Green; but she was certainly frightened now.

Why? He held his glance to the mirror. There had been reports of women alone in taxis being assaulted by the driver but surely the woman didn't think he–

The sound of metal on metal, a crash of breaking glass, snapped his attention back to the road. The jab of his foot on the brake made the tyres sing on the metalled surface.

'Sorry about that, somebody pushed his luck on the roundabout, you okay?' Torrey glanced behind him.

Christ, she had been thrown out of the seat ... she must be lying on the floor! Torrey's pulse flipped. Lord, that was all he needed, a compensation claim for injury to a passenger! Fingered by the blues for driving without due care and attention! Daniels couldn't bring the charge of assault and battery for that fracas outside the Staffordshire Knot but he would sure as hell bring this one – and it would be hello, Winson Green.

The thought reinforced by the wail of a police siren, he leapt from the car. Snatching open the rear door he directed a silent plea to heaven that he would find his passenger unharmed ... shaken maybe ... he amended the request for clemency ... but unharmed.

'Everythin' all right, mate...?'

A man's head and neck craned from the window of a car behind the Sonata.

'Need any help?'

'Just a box fell off the back seat.'

Closing the passenger door, he pressed against it to give extra clearance to the police motor cycle manoeuvring past. The car was empty. There was no passenger on its back seat!

The uniform had shown more than a passing interest. Once more in the driving seat, Torrey's fingers gripped the wheel. Should he be pulled over, asked why he was checking the rear passenger seats, what would he say? A box had slid from the seat? A good enough answer, except the car carried no box. He could of course tell that constable his passenger had hopped from the car and legged it away to avoid paying. But that would need to be corroborated, cars lined behind would have their occupants questioned and they would say what he himself already knew, no passenger had left his car.

The woman hadn't legged it ... she couldn't possibly have opened the door, climbed from the car and run off without his hearing the slightest sound or feeling the least movement. Add to that the fact the driver in the car behind had made no comment on a woman's leaving the car in the middle of a busy road and the whole thing made no sense.

Yet she was gone!

Torrey's brow showed his confusion.

He had answered a call, made the pick-up from Harrowby Place, Shepwell Green, ascertained the destination as Station Street, Darlaston, seen his passenger into the rear of the car ... so where was she now?

Jaw tightening, Torrey glanced at the ambulance pulling on to the scene. Somebody had been injured ... his passenger? Had she, against the odds, slipped away unseen only to get knocked down at the traffic island? If so she was smarter than Houdini, and Torrey? He'd been well and truly had!

Entering an upstairs room she had unlocked, Venetia Pascal touched a concealed switch which brought curtains across the windows with a soft swish of velvet. A second touch of the console bathed the room with discreet lighting. She closed the door at her back. That contretemps with Theo Vail had shown his colours. He resented her, resented her presence in the coven, but most of all her confidence, her challenging him to call upon the Prince of Darkness, to put his standing as Magus to the test; she was the thorn in his side, but which demon of hell would he call upon to remove it?

He would no doubt do as she now intended; maybe had done so already. But so far the Master had made no move against her ... it was not too late.

The hem of her exquisite designer gown brushing the polished beech wood floor, she crossed to a small table set in an alcove. Its scarlet silk cover gleamed in the muted overhead light. Her own private chapel, her sanctum sanctorum; here she could worship the Master free from the watching eyes of Theo Vail.

Setting a match to candles placed one each side of the table, she watched the flicker of golden flame flare from slender black tips then dance over the ebony cross inverted between them.

She had watched devotions performed by both Crowley and Vail, assisted at the rites celebrating the holy days of the black calendar, but never had she called alone upon the Lord of Hell.

What she planned was hazardous, her life would be a thread which could be snapped with a wrong word. But to do nothing, to take no action at all to protect herself against Vail, that left her open to the same jeopardy.

Touching a second match to sticks of incense and sandalwood in black vases set beside the scarlet-draped table, she held her hands above the pearl-grey drift of smoke, purifying them, cleansing them of the day's activities.

The Master would not refuse her supplication nor would he refuse the gift offered with such devotion. The gift which now lay sleeping beside a bronze bowl and ebony-handled sacrificial knife laid ready.

Satisfied her carefully laid preparations were complete she kicked aside a silk rug to reveal a design set in the wood of the floor, the five-pointed star of a pentagram glimmering in the sheen of candlelight.

Loosing the buttons of the gown, letting it fall in a dark puddle, she stepped naked into the protecting circle. Turning to face the altar, she sank to her knees.

'Great Lord,' she gazed steadily, the candle flames reflecting gold-shot emeralds in her eyes, 'Holder of Eternity, Prince of Darkness, I do homage before you.'

A breath that was not her own spread on the silence, a movement she could not see rippled the stillness.

She was no longer alone!

Breath tight in her chest, she picked up the sleeping bundle. Holding it on outstretched palms she spoke quietly.

'Lord of Wisdom, to whom the earth is subject, accept this the gift of your servant.'

Upon the altar the candle flames flared, drawing together in a golden circle which hovered above the black wooden cross.

Acceptance or denial? Venetia knew she could not question, she could only go on.

With one hand holding the bundle which was now beginning to stir, she reached for the knife with the other.

'Greatest of the Princes of Creation,' her voice rose, 'Lord of the Dark Throne, accept this sacrifice made in your name.'

With the last word, the knife slashed across the throat of the tiny black kitten she held on her palm.

She had done what had long been a dream. Venetia Pascal stood in the shower, letting the hot water play over the body she had marked with the blood of sacrifice.

She had caught the crimson droplets in the

bronze bowl and rising to her feet had dipped a finger into it.

Her face lifted to the jet of water, eyes closed against the warm caress. The words she had whispered while stood within the pentacle murmured afresh in her brain.

'Prince of the Morning, you who witnessed the creation of the world, give wisdom to the mind dedicated to your glory...'

The blood-drenched finger had touched to her brow marking the sign of the upside-down cross.

'...your mighty hand shield the heart pledged in your service.'

Her whole body gripped with a passion she could scarcely control, she traced the sign on her breast; then with one flowing exultant sweep a third touch of her bloodied finger left a crimson line coursing from her throat to the warm moist cleft between her legs. A second line traversing the base of her abdomen completed the inverted cross. She had looked straight into the heart of that glowing, pulsing radiance floating above the altar and in a voice trembling with fervour had breathed the final request.

'Keep in safety the body of this disciple sworn to your name and whose soul is gladly given to your honour and glory.'

Only then, with those final words, had that circle of brilliance moved. Intensifying, blazing aureate gold, it expanded, bathing the alcove in a blinding eye-searing light, but before her eyes had closed against the pain of it she had seen, at its shimmering heart, a face of breathtaking beauty ... a face which had smiled.

There had been several replies to the question posed in the column headed, 'Myths, Legends and Old Wives' Tales'. Kate Mallory leafed through a collection of readers' letters. The article had generated interest as Scottie had said it would and she had been landed with the job of finding answers ... as she had *known* she would.

Exasperated, she threw the sheaves of assorted note-papers down on a desk as cluttered as the huge shoulder bag resting on the ground beside her chair.

Many of the replies had made mention of a story heard from an ancient aunt or grandmother, of something being brought here to Darlaston then taken to Bentley Hall for safe keeping; a thing which, it seemed, incorporated danger. But what had happened to that something? Did someone have it now? And if so, where?

Questions! All she had was questions! Her irritable swipe at the scattered papers sent several fluttering to the floor. She swore as she bent to retrieve them. One day ... one day she would resign this damned go-nowhere job!

'I know the feeling.' Philip Jackson's smile was sympathetic but meeting it seemed only to enhance Kate's irritation.

'Do you!' she snapped. 'Then if you know it why don't you do something about it?'

Freckled face creasing further into the smile, the sports writer pursed his lips in the pretence of thought. 'Is that asking why I don't do something about my job, or yours? Truth to tell, Kate, I'm beggared if I know which would give me most grief right now.'

'Sorry, Phil.' Apology coming on a heavy sigh, Kate tossed the recovered letters with the rest. 'It's just that this is such a waste of time. How many people are interested in crap like this?'

'Judging by those,' Jackson nodded towards the letter-strewn desk, 'I would say quite a few. In fact, Kate, my little North Eastern mate, when you get too cheesed off with journalism you could set yourself up in the fertiliser business.'

'Now why hadn't I thought of that?' Kate's own smile flashed. 'Think I should place an advert in the "For Sale" column?'

'Ye'll both be placing one in the "Situations Wanted" should you waste any more time. This paper is put to bed in an hour, or had your concentration on your work driven that from your mind?'

A gentle word of encouragement ... so refreshing for the soul!

Common sense kept the sarcasm in check. Posts in journalism were not quite two a penny and this, mundane as it was, kept her in bread if not in cake.

Philip Jackson's copper-hued head bent once more over the task in hand, Kate turned uninterestedly to her own. How many more of these letters would her brain take before crashing completely?

'My grandfather always used to say...'

'I remember as a young child...'

One by one she scanned the first few, her eyes seeing while her brain barely registered the words. This was going nowhere! Defeat in every movement she rested the sheaf. One blue-tinted page had slipped from the rest. Kate reached to replace it then paused as her glance took in one line.

'My uncle was footman at Bentley Hall...'

Why had her brain jarred? Pulses jerking as if affected by some electric current, Kate picked up the pale blue paper. Maybe ... just maybe this Old Wife's Tale might prove to have a core!

Letter in hand she was two steps towards the editor's office.

'Just write the answers, that's all I'm wanting.'

Kate paused a few yards from the editor's office. That was the answer Scottie would be bound to give, one which said 'no follow up'.

Between her fingers the thin sheet of paper seemed to burn. There was a story somewhere behind those words, she knew it. She could feel it!

'Kate!'

The call emanated from the glass-partitioned room. No more time for thinking! She slipped the letter into her pocket. She would reason things out later.

'Kate! Oh, there you are.' David Anscott's hair, unruly and prematurely grey, fell over eyes of a remarkably matching colour. Refusing to stay where he'd flicked it, his hair flopped once more over his brow. Standing just inside the doorway Kate smiled to herself. Disagreeable as he found leaving his precious office he would soon have to vacate it for long enough to get a haircut. Either that or get a guide dog!

'Just come in.' His head was already bent again

to the copy he was reading. 'Go see what you can get.'

'Another burglary?' Kate took the slip of paper Scottie was holding like a flag, the diffidence of her reply masking a second surge of electricity singing along her veins.

'Ask your questions when you get there.'

The pen balanced precariously between two fingers suddenly became a weapon of total destruction. Why couldn't Saddam Hussein have bought himself a pen like that ... with that sort of deterrent at his elbow the Bush-Blair alliance would never have dared launch any invasion of Iraq. Seeing the slash of ink rip across the typed sheet, its red trail blazing like that of a scud missile streaking towards its target, Kate winced. Some poor soul was about to regret getting up this morning.

Still balanced over several sheets of typed paper, the editor made no move to look up as Kate turned to leave, but his voice, incisive as a surgeon's scalpel, snicked her spine.

'Copy ... now!'

Two words! Kate's hope of being relieved of having to hand in her 'Replies from the Editor' was stillborn. The man didn't do things by half. David Anscott should have been sent with an early detachment to the Middle East; he would have had Hussein and his cronies surrender in no time!

But, inadvertent though it was, he had just given her the opening she needed. Calling to the office junior, she handed him the finished copy, then grabbing her bag she was gone before the lad tapped the glass door of that Holy of Holies.

Ask your questions when you get there.

Kate's smile was seraphic. She would do just that.

9

Everything had been arranged as he required.

Theo Vail seemed to be listening to the spare-framed man speaking rapid gunfire words but his concentration was on the woman talking with two others.

Every movement of the body beneath the pale green silk Versace dress deliberately modelled to enhance it was smooth and sinuous. Like a cat, feline and graceful. Twisting the stem of an exquisite Royal Brierly crystal champagne flute he watched the nod of the head that sent a myriad darts of light flashing from its satiny auburn depths. Venetia Pascal was beautiful, but like a cat she had claws.

'It was a good meeting, don't you agree?'

'Yes.' Theo took his companion's glass. Getting a refill would give him time to recall himself to the conversation he had barely listened to. Horse racing was not his forte.

Handing back the filled flute he glanced again to where Venetia stood.

'They seem to be having quite a tête-à-tête.'

Laurence Thorold, director of Thorold International, the largest importer-exporter of food products in the UK, followed Vail's glance, the heat in his slate eyes reflecting the flare at the base of his stomach.

'Venetia is a good listener.' Champagne touched against Vail's lips but went no further.

'Makes a man wonder if that's all she's good at.' Thorold gulped from his glass, a heavy swallow that sent his Adam's apple shooting halfway up his neck. 'The man who gets her will be one lucky bastard, the woman's a walking aphrodisiac.'

A walking aphrodisiac, Vail acknowledged silently, she was all of that.

As if sensing the thoughts of the men watching her, Venetia Pascal turned, her sculptured lips parting in a smile sent directly to them.

Meeting the steady gaze was like looking into emerald lakes. Vail felt his own response in the flesh hardening between his legs. But lakes sometimes covered lava waiting to burst through the thin cover of the earth's mantle. Was that same energy lurking inside her? His mind flashed back to the scene in her office, where she had virtually accused him of negligence on the Night of Offering, where she had shown no fear of his powers! Vail felt a tremor of concern. A walking aphrodisiac, or a walking time bomb? A bomb primed and ready to blow!

'Laurence, are you going to spend the whole evening talking with Theo?'

Cool, poised, confident in her beauty with all the hallmarks of a queen, Venetia Pascal came to join them. Thorold's over-effusive greeting filled the moment as Vail set his glass to one side then met the challenge of those green eyes, of their tinted mockery, and the hard demand of desire dropped away. A queen ... or a high priestess? Concern pricked again. Venetia Pascal, First Disciple of the Primary Coven! Would she dare aim so high?

'I was about to ask you, Venetia, are you never going to give a moment to your most ardent admirer?'

Venetia Pascal's glance stayed with Vail though she answered the man whose head was bent over her hand.

'My *most* ardent admirer...?'

Emerald fire stoked with derision blazed their challenge at Vail. 'Really, Laurence, I do not believe that.'

'Believe it.' Laurence Thorold straightened but kept hold of her hand. 'You could be number one with me, you only have to say the word.'

'And dash the hopes of all the other women hoping to occupy that position! I could not be that unkind.' She eased her hand from the possessive hold.

Competently done. A refusal without refusing! Theo Vail silently commended the expertise as he handed her a freshly filled glass.

Accepting it, Venetia watched as he moved to speak with others in the room. Dressed in what was unquestionably Savile Row's finest, fair hair a gleaming contrast against sun-bronzed skin, Theo Vail was indisputably handsome; but then so were snakes! They too were handsome on the outside, a beautiful exterior hiding death: and whose death would that be? Sipping ice-cool champagne she kept the smile fixed to her lips but her brain seethed with thoughts. To those who did not know him, Theo Vail was the very epitome of good manners and charming social graces. But she knew him, knew what lay beneath the façade – a heart blacker than ebony and harder than granite.

'Penny for them.'

'Sorry ... what?'

'I said a penny for them, your thoughts that is... though I'd bet a hundred to one I know them already, you are thinking as I am, that you'd pay a thousand to have that beauty in your bed. Lord, I'd make sure it was well spent.'

'You and just about every other man in this room.' Laurence Thorold answered the man who had come to stand beside him as Venetia Pascal moved away. 'But that is one lady money don't buy.'

'Is that so?' Stuart Fenton watched the exquisitely dressed owner of the House of Pascal smile and speak to several others of the room's occupants. 'Would you lay a hundred on that?'

'Why don't we make it five hundred, might as well make it worthwhile.' Thorold smiled to himself. This was one bet he was more than willing to make; Fenton was about to lose more than his money.

Stuart Fenton's cosmetically perfected teeth challenged the brilliance of the chandeliers. 'Venetia,' he purred as she joined them, 'I was wondering. What would it take to purchase the perfection which is yourself?'

Eyes hard as the emerald glinting on her finger, Venetia flashed a look of undisguised disdain at the man whose own eyes devoured her. The same disdain edged her perfect mouth as she answered, 'Let me just say, whatever it might be, Stuart darling, you just don't have it.'

'Bitch!' Fenton's snarl, vicious as it was soft, followed Venetia Pascal as she walked away. 'Give me one night and I'd have the conceit well and truly fucked out of her!'

'I wouldn't place any bets on that.' Thorold's laugh was short. 'Not that you or I are about to get one minute, let alone one night.'

'Vail's preserve?'

Frowning, Laurence Thorold shot a glance across the room. 'Somehow I think not.'

'Not ... then who?'

Again Thorold hesitated before replying. 'If my guess proves right then the "who" is someone I have no urgent desire to meet.'

Fenton's suave control had slipped. Glancing to where she had left the two men, Venetia's smile remained. She had seen the anger flick swiftly over the face of the shipping magnate. No man liked rejection and Stuart Fenton was no exception. Like Vail, his wealth had bred an arrogance which led to the belief that nothing was beyond its buying, that anything and anyone was his for the asking.

But that would not include Venetia Pascal! Sipping champagne, the cool liquid pleasant against her throat, she played a calm look over the gathering. The smile hovering on her lips echoed a deeper one inside. Fenton was not alone in rejection. For Venetia Pascal no man in this room had it; in fact no man born on earth had it.

So what was it the lady wanted?

Behind the sweep of long curling lashes, eyes as deep and unreadable as the sea masked the answer trembling in her heart.

Venetia Pascal wanted power, absolute power ... the power that only the Lord of Hell could grant.

'Everything is on line?'

Theo Vail glanced at each face in turn. The niceties of greetings over, champagne glasses put aside, the assembled group now sat around a large oval table in the elegant dining room of Vail's beautiful home. Once a manor house complete with its own home farm, it stood secluded among acres of arable land in the heart of Telford.

'We signed a further ten thousand tons of wheat from the USA, seven thousand of rice from Egypt plus soya from Brazil.' Thorold looked up from the document he had been reading. 'That on top of an increased intake of the usual from Afghanistan has the profit margin of Thorold International nicely in the black.'

Heroin from Afghanistan was always a profit leader. The Taliban were creeping back and so was the production of heroin. Theo Vail nodded satisfaction.

'Fenton Mercantile is also healthy.' Stuart Fenton took up the report. 'The Iraq situation ... call our intervention there aiding the country or invading it, it has resulted in boosting our profits significantly, food and equipment has to be taken out there and Fenton Shipping does the taking.'

Nodding briefly, posing a question here and

there, Theo Vail listened to the reports of the several managing directors of companies which owed their affluence to the Prince of Darkness. The Master chose his minions well; the people sat around the table had gladly accepted the lifestyle offered in return for submission of their souls. They would not wish that contract called in a moment earlier than absolutely necessary.

'Miss Pascal?' Deliberately leaving her until last he turned finally to Venetia.

'The House of Pascal is showing a high degree of profit.' Venetia made no reference to the documents she had brought with her. Theo Vail would be very well aware of the state of her business as he undoubtedly would have been with those others. What was happening now was merely a prelude to the real business of the evening, the business that was never discussed in the boardroom of the Vail Corporation, but she would play the man's game. 'However, there is room for expansion. I intend to launch a nationwide search for a girl...' she paused, waiting for the flutter of conversation to end, '...I want a young but pretty teenager ... that is the market to which I shall aim a new range of products. She will become the face of Pascal's teen products.'

'Do we need to expand? Our business is—'

'Our business is to do the work of the Master!' The sharp intervention brought a film of deep red to the face of Theo Vail. The Magus did not favour interruption, Venetia smiled to herself. There were many things to which the Magus took exception ... and if the power of prayer worked then there would be many more!

111

'Widening the market place,' she proceeded smoothly, the recognition that her next words would aggravate the director of Vail Corporation even more affording her a warm feeling of pleasure, 'will be to introduce "Pascal" to a whole new, and younger, generation ... a field where the Master might find many converts. A young mind? Fertile ground! I am sure you are all aware of the vast potential; women both young and old, the rich and not so rich, all derive pleasure in use of cosmetics be it just a touch of powder or the whole works: and one more point well worth considering, in today's world no country bars its female population the wearing of make-up and neither is it excluded by religion. A careful choice of representatives could carry more than the products of "Pascal" to people in this and other countries worldwide, they could also carry the Truth of the Master.'

'Damn good idea.' Stuart Fenton's approval overriding his chagrin of an hour before, he smiled widely. 'A damn good idea!'

'But not the whole idea.' Venetia's slight tilting of the head acknowledged Fenton's verbal applause while her glacial green glance remained on a face barely concealing fury. 'We live in a different climate from our parents and the same goes for today's young people. Yesterday it was considered a form of taboo for men to use any cosmetic preparation other than a touch of bay rum and later a light application of Brylcreem to hold the hair in place. All of that is now changed, men and boys use body lotions, shampoo, conditioners, anti-perspirants and of course an after

112

shave; and, as with women and girls, the list of "must haves" increases week on week; a lucrative market for cosmetics and for the Master: therefore I intend to coincide a search for a young, handsome boy-next-door type who will front a campaign aimed specifically at the male end of the market. Pascal for men will be another door which could open to the Lord of Darkness.'

She had not called for Vail's approval. Venetia climbed into the waiting car. If she could please the Master then perhaps she may never need it again!

Lowe Avenue. Kate Mallory checked the address written at the top of the sheet of blue paper though she now knew every word the letter contained by heart. This was the place, now all she had to do was find the house.

It was at the other end of the street. She had looked at the number of each, sometimes seeing the twitch of a curtain dropped quickly into place as she passed. No doubt whoever was inside would inexplicably be 'out' should she knock on the door. Maybe the person she had come to see would be 'out'. She sniffed ruefully. That would simply be Kate Mallory's habitual luck.

Today her luck must change, if only to protect her sanity! Fingers crossed, Kate lifted a doorknocker as clean and polished as Annie's. Encouraged by the sight she tapped twice.

'I read the piece about summat being took to Bentley 'All.' A face as plain as the furnishings in the small living room smiled as the woman Kate had hoped would be home set a tray of tea and biscuits on a well polished coffee table. 'Set me to thinkin' of a tale my granny used to tell, great one for tales was Granny Spooner ... tek sugar do you, luv? I'd forgot all about it 'til I read that bit in the *Star* askin' did folk know of any legends an' stuff ... 'elp yourself to a biscuit, no need to be shy... well, like I says, set me to thinkin'...'

Choosing a chocolate biscuit her hips would regret, Kate listened attentively.

'It were readin' the name Bentley 'All brought it all back ... lovely house that were, it be a thousand pities it be gone ... pulled it down they did...'

Yes! Kate swallowed the last of her biscuit. But the story ... get to the story!

Pouring tea into Royal Albert rose-patterned china cups that Kate guessed were brought out only for not-so-usual visitors or for funerals, Dora Wilkes handed one across to Kate then, the other in hand, sat herself on a facing chair.

'Were Grandmother's cousin told about it. Albert he were named ... he were under-butler at the time. Said as one evening a young woman come to the 'All asking to see Sir Corben Foley ... he were the owner...'

Kate's pulses beat rapidly as the woman paused to sip tea. Was the whole thing going too well, would the tale – supposing it ever got finished – prove to be of no interest after all? Repulsing the desire to urge her informant on she waited.

'Well,' Dora replaced her cup on its saucer, 'Albert were cleanin' the silver in the butler's pantry when he 'eard the butler and the cook talkin'. Seems the young woman had brought a

114

gift of some kind, Albert said he 'eard a funny-sounding name, Count somebody or other then the word Russia. Nothin' to be wondered at in that, folk with money travelled a lot in them days and no doubt made friends with them as lived in them there foreign countries, so it were to be expected they send each other presents from time to time...'

Time! Kate tried not to fidget. How would she explain to Scottie the time spent here in this house!

'But it were after...' Dora went on, 'Albert said that some few days followin' that wench callin', Sir Corbett said he was going to Lichfield and that he would drive to the railroad station himself. Albert said he had no trust in them horseless carriage things, said they was deathtraps, and it seems he was proved near enough right for there was an accident; the master weren't killed but Albert, he said Sir Corbett weren't never the same after it.'

'What did Albert mean?' She hadn't intended to prompt the woman, but if she should stop now! Lord! Kate drew an impatient breath. If ever she had needed a tab it was now; a cigarette would soothe her nerves.

'Grandmother were gettin' on a bit by the time I were old enough to be tellin' her memories to, and Mother...? Well, it always seemed that her preferred not to talk on the subject. I tried a few times when I were grown and married myself but Mother would say as her couldn't remember aught about it other than Albert would say he never got another job as good as that along of

Bentley 'All.'

'Why did he leave there if the job was good?'

Rose-patterned milk jug in hand, Dora Wilkes glanced at Kate as if to say the answer to that should have been obvious enough.

'Didn't want to leave.' The jug sat gently on the tray. 'But with Sir Corbett dyin' so unexpected like...'

Kate felt her insides tighten. There was something here, she was sure of it, but to push...

'Mother would 'ave none of it, said Gran's mind were not so sharp any more, that her illness were to blame for ramblings which spoke of a love between two cousins. But I watched my grandmother's face as she spoke of Albert and I knowed her were not rambling.'

Returned to her chair, the thumb of one hand absently stroking the delicate china cup, Dora's eyes seemed to be looking on a different place, her mind in another time.

'It were midsummer eve, Albert had come to visit. They walked in the meadow bordering the Foley land, Albert gathered a handful of wild flowers and giving them to her spoke of his love. They dared not kiss or even touch hands for fear of being seen but they vowed themselves to each other. When she became of age they would wed...'

'So Albert was your grandfather?'

Eyes moist from her reverie, Dora shook her head. 'No, wench, he weren't my grandfather, he were killed in the Great War before Gran reached her seventeenth year. But that don't be what you come to ask about. Like I were sayin', Sir Corbett took 'imself off in that there motor car but never

116

reached the railroad station. He crashed into the ditch, unconscious when they found 'im. It were Albert spotted the box, carried it back to the 'All, said his fingers tingled like it were hot. The butler told him to place it in a drawer in Sir Corbett's bedroom but before doing so Albert peeped inside. Told Grandmother it held what appeared to be a necklace; he looked for no more than a moment but in that moment he saw a gold serpent with large red stones for eyes ... they gleamed like the eyes of a living thing. He refused to talk of it after that 'cept to say that as he lifted the lid there were a sound like deep breathing, and a smell ... a smell of death, of evil; he said peering into that box had been like lookin' into the jaws of hell and that the butler was welcome to it.'

'The butler?' Kate frowned.

'Oh, crikey!' Dora's cup rattled on its saucer. 'I shouldn't ought to 'ave said that, should his family read of it in the paper I'd be landed with one of them law suits.'

She couldn't lose it now! Her own cup returned to the tray, Kate leaned towards the other woman, hoping her voice would not betray the anxiety leaping inside her.

'Mrs Wilkes,' she touched a work-worn hand, 'what you tell me will not be printed in any newspaper, you have my word.'

'But that column ... them old wives' tales!'

'I already have more than enough material to cover that, and interest doesn't last very long in that sort of thing ... give it a week or so and it will strike off on another path altogether.'

Why had she said that? True as it might be, it

provided the perfect reason for this woman to say in that case there was no need to finish her tale.

But she wanted it to be told, wanted to hear the whole of what the shadowy Albert had told his sweetheart.

'Please,' Kate's slightly tilted mouth lifted a little further, 'I promise this will be just between us.'

'There ain't no proof!' Dora's head swung slowly from side to side as if convincing herself what she said was true. 'It's only a tale my grandmother 'eard, that's all it be ... a tale!'

'I understand.'

'An' it don't be one for publishin' in no paper.'

'Agreed.' Kate crossed mental fingers.

'Do you be the wench as lodges with Annie Price along of Michael Road?' Entrenched in a patchwork of lines the faded eyes sharpened.

Kate's flush of hope faded. This had been too much to expect, Dora Wilkes would say no more; well! She shrugged internally; as the well-known saying went, 'What will be will be!'

10

'Another one for the collection. This place is getting to look like the National Portrait Gallery.'

'Reckon we might have a tourist problem then?' Sergeant Dave Farnell turned from thumbing a tack into a black and white photograph of a smiling girl.

'Why not?' Detective Inspector Bruce Daniels returned tetchily. 'We get every other kind, Darlaston gets more shit and less money to swill it away with; what we need is a free hand and a bloody great hosepipe!'

'I'll put in a request ... but don't hold your breath.'

Request! Daniels waved a dismissive hand to the chuckle at his back. Wouldn't be worth the ink it took to write. Requests from this crap pile fell on deaf ears ... same as applications for promotion!

Entering the small room that served for an office, he heeled the door with a bang. P'raps if he had taken elocution lessons, if he had learned to talk like he had a bibble in his mouth ... but he hadn't and he didn't ... which meant types such as Quinto got the top chairs while the likes of Daniels got the pat on the back and bugger all besides!

Another few years was all he had left with the Force. Dropping into the chair wedged between desk and wall he stared at the pile of folders awaiting attention. Twenty-five years! He shoved angrily at the folders. Twenty-five years of seeing others go up the ladder while Daniels held it steady ... a few more years! They would go like all the others, no Chief Inspector's chair would cushion Bruce Daniels' arse!

'Tea, sir.'

Grunting his thanks, Daniels looked at the trim figure placing a mug at his elbow. Police women! Some things he could do without and women in the police force was one of them.

'Sergeant Farnell said to tell you the coroner's report is on your desk.'

The wench was too pretty, could take the men's attention from... 'Report?' His hand paused in mid air. 'What report?'

'The coroner's findings on the body found in the factory in Station Street ... the one that burned down.'

'All right, thank you!' Ill humour scorching the reply, Daniels grasped the mug. Female bloody constables. He glared at the retreating girl, grudgingly admiring the spick and span uniform and neatly styled hair. What good would they be in a crowd of boozed-up football fans! But women were already reaching the higher realms of the force ... how long before this one passed Daniels in the race?

Maybe he should have listened to Marjorie. He drank from the mug, hot liquid searing his throat. P'raps he should retire as his wife suggested ... he had grounds of ill health ... he could be out of it all...

And do what? Chair legs which had been tipped off the floor banged noisily into place. What would he do all day? Watch Marjorie plump cushions no one dared sit on, wipe away imagined fingerprints from furniture only polish ever touched? Lord, he'd rather go back on the beat!

Not much to go on. The folder he had opened showed a single sheet of paper. Female, aged probably between twenty and–

'The bastard asked for it!'

A shout followed the crash of a door. Daniels glanced towards the outer office.

'He asked forrit and I give it 'im...'

Interrupted in his reading a second time, Daniels laid the official report aside.

'What's the racket about?' Daniels' enquiring look met the station sergeant as he re-entered the claustrophobic office.

'Domestic.' Dave Farnell looked grim. 'Nasty one this, Bruce, lad beat his old man.'

'How bad?'

'Dunno yet.' Farnell's head swung briefly. 'They've got him up at the Manor, doctors there say they won't know for some time.'

'The lad?'

'I've put him in the interview room, give him a few minutes to get his brain together.'

'Has he said anything ... apart from "he asked forrit"?'

'You heard that?'

'No way I wouldn't,' Daniels grimaced, 'you can hear a fly fart through these walls.'

'True.' Dave Farnell agreed. 'Seems the lad sobbed all the time he was being brought in, said it wasn't the beltings his father give him, he'd had them from the time he could walk, and that it were not the first time he'd seen his mother knocked senseless, but he couldn't stand it any longer and that he had gone for his father with a poker; but being a juvenile we can't charge him until a legal representative is present, that's already being attended to. Do you want to wait for the solicitor before speaking to the lad yourself?'

'Yeah. Thanks, Dave, give me a nod when the curly wig arrives.'

...had them from the time he could walk ... not the first time he'd seen his mother knocked senseless...

Words he could have spoken himself sang in Daniels' brain while images he had long ago buried dredged themselves up from the past.

A lad sixteen years old, a lad who had known the belt for almost every one of those years, falling from a chair while a thin, worn-out woman placed her own body between him and the heavy leather belt, its huge metal buckle singing its song of pain as it swung towards them.

Acid rose, corroding his throat but the fire of it was nothing against the sting of memory.

His mother had pushed him out of the way of another drink-crazed beating ... and he had run from the house. Oh Christ, he had run!

Every particle of his being cried to be released from the trap of memory, but the jaws tightened. He hid his face in his hands.

The evening lecture had finished and he had taken the long route home, unwilling to face the inevitable, his mother's face swollen not with tears, they had long ago dried up, but swollen with bruises, the marks of his father's fists. But his mother had not been in the house. She had been in the hospital morgue.

Fingers tensing over his face, Bruce Daniels trembled as he had on being told his mother had died. That was the moment he had made his decision.

Jack Daniels had been sitting at the table in the kitchen his wife scrubbed daily, his head swinging on his thick neck when told his wife was dead.

122

'An' where was yoh?'

The words stabbed now as they had then, memory showing the drunken bloodshot eyes fill with a new blood lust as his father rose and turned on him.

'Where was yoh?'

Drink-sodden breath had belched fumes in his face and the massive hands had gone to the buckle half hidden by folds of a hanging beer belly.

'Where was yoh when yer mother tumbled over that chair?'

The words rang like machine-gun fire in his head.

'I'll tell yer where yer was, paradin' yer prick in front o' them wenches down along the canal ... that be where yoh was!'

Thirty-odd years and pathetic as the accusation had been, Daniels couldn't, even now, smile at it. There had never been a chance of any wench giving so much as a glance in his direction, jacket and trousers shining brighter than a black-leaded grate had seen to that.

Pain of a young lad laughed at by his peers, mixing with the agony of that same lad hearing his mother had been beaten to death by a drunken brute, had suddenly become a white hot flame, a blinding flare wiping away any thought of himself. He had grabbed the heavy old-fashioned flat iron from the kitchen range, almost throwing it at the hateful face. His father had reeled backwards but the blows had not stopped, they had kept on and on, striking until no flesh was visible beneath the welter of blood.

There had been no remorse, no self-reproach, and in all the years following that night there had never been the tiniest flicker of regret.

Jack Daniels had been big boned, a large heavy man. Behind the shelter of tight fingers and closed eyes, memory persisted in showing its lurid images. Yet somehow a lad a third of his weight had managed to get the inert body to a part of the canal overlooked by heaps of pit waste. He had dragged the still form to the top of a black hill then scooped handfuls of razor-sharp slag and rubbed it into the blood-soaked ruined face. Again and again he had repeated the process then sent the figure rolling into the slime-filled water.

Jack Daniels had been in one of his well-known, drunken stupors, he had slipped while on his way home and slithered face down, ripping away flesh and smashing bone before sliding into the canal.

That had been what he had been told later by the grandparents he had gone to live with and he had never told them differently. He had never told anyone.

Mental strain dragging at his brain, Detective Inspector Bruce Daniels followed the station sergeant towards the interview room. He was about to talk with a lad who had beaten his own father ... and at his back walked the shade of another young lad, one who had committed murder!

'Why tell me you knew nothing of any story regarding Bentley Hall and the death of its owner?'

'D'ain't know no story.'

Should she kick him now or wait until they

were outside on the street! Kate Mallory watched the ferret-faced man in a scruffy jacket scribble a choice of racehorse on a betting slip.

'That's not true.' She decided on the latter. It wouldn't be dignified getting herself thrown out of a betting shop.

'Who says it ain't?' Finished with his scribbling, Echo Sounder pushed slip and money across a steel-grilled counter then took the receipt from an over-painted heavy-breasted blonde.

'I say it isn't,' Kate retorted, watching his grubby fingers slip the receipt into a grease-stained pocket. 'And before we have any more denials let me tell you I have spoken with a relative of yours.'

'Relative?' Eyes sharp as a sewer rat lifted to Kate.

'That is what I said. A cousin, once or twice removed, but none the less blood related. I talked with Dora Wilkes.'

The reaction was profound. In the sallow lighting of the bookies' office, Kate saw the fleeting expression flick across the narrow features. Echo Sounder was already calculating what this could mean for him.

'She told me about...'

'Not in 'ere.' Throwing a swift glance in the direction of the counter, Sounder was through the door quicker than a greyhound leaving the trap.

Not in the bookmakers nor in his favoured public house! Kate followed the rapid footsteps leading along Victoria Road and into the park of the same name. Sounder was being extra cautious ... her journalistic blood warmed ... whatever the little man had hidden up his sleeve he intended nobody to know of it, not until his pocket felt the benefit.

'What did Dora Wilkes tell yer?' From the further end of a park bench, Echo Sounder's question was a whisper on the breeze.

'Quite a lot actually, about a certain Albert and her grandmother, of his being under-butler at Bentley Hall, oh, and a box–'

'Shh!' Head bent to his chest, Sounder's bead-bright eyes surveyed the park, taking in every tree and bush, searching the spaces between. 'Don't want the 'ole world listenin' in!'

Hardly the world, in fact hardly a soul! Kate also glanced around the park. The place was so deserted Darlaston might have been playing for the world cup.

'What did her tell yer about a box?'

This wasn't the usual Sounder, the man who talked money first, second, last and anywhere in between. In her mind Kate saw again the calculating expression which had flashed across his face ... she had thought it one of analysis, that his cagey mind was reckoning just how much money he could get from telling her what it seemed he obviously knew, but watching him now she was no longer so sure. He was never backward when there was the chance of a flyer to be had, but this time...

The confidence she had felt while in the bookies' office took a swift jolt. Kate reached into the shoulder bag set between them on the bench. Perhaps actually seeing a banknote might help things along.

'Dora said a box had been taken to Bentley Hall...'

The folded note rolled between her fingers, Kate related what she had learned at that house in Lowe Avenue and all the time Sounder's ferret eyes darted about the park.

'Yer should tek no notice o' what Dora Wilkes tells yer, her talks a load o' crap!'

He had not even glanced at the money. Kate was bemused. It was this man's practice to at least make a play for what was on offer; why so reticent this time?

'I admit I had the same thoughts to begin with, but when she told me the name of Sir Corbett Foley's butler, and more interestingly, that his family had remained in Darlaston then I changed my mind pretty quickly.'

'So her said a name, that don't mean shit!'

Kate's blood warmed as it had when listening to Dora, but this was the fire of anger. The woman had dealt kindly and honestly with her ... but Kate Mallory would not deal the same way with this man who was basically calling that woman a liar.

Eyes cold as a stream in winter fastened on the hunched figure, she hurled her next words like so many stones. 'This one does. In fact many people in this town hold the view this name is covered in it; I've no doubt when that name appears in the *Star* the result will be a heavy postbag ... how many people have a reason for getting back at Echo Sounder?'

She had promised Dora Wilkes there would be no write-up of what she had divulged, that nothing of it would be published, but Sounder didn't have to know that. Calmly, with as much flourish as possible, Kate unrolled the five-pound note, smoothing it several times before replacing it in her purse. That should have been enough to have him running down the verbal path, seeing five pounds slipping from his grasp. He'd never been known to ignore money. Kate lifted the bag to her shoulder. There was always a first time.

'Yer can't do that!' A hoarse whisper followed Kate as she rose to leave. 'Yer can't print nuthin' in the paper!'

'You think that? Then take a little of your race-track earnings and buy tomorrow's *Star*, or failing that visit the library, you can read it there for free; only do read it, Mr Sounder, I'm sure you ... as well as others ... will find it most interesting.'

The expression she had seen flick across Sounder's face while in the bookmaker's shop, then again in Victoria Park, had been a calculating one. But it had not been financial, he had not been working out how much he might gain from the proceedings but how much he might lose. The look she had mistaken for avarice had not been that at all, it had been one of fear. Echo Sounder had been afraid!

Head bent over her desk, Kate pretended to be absorbed in compiling a report of an attempted robbery. It had been fortunate for her though not for the robber. She had left the park and was making her way along King Street when she had seen a group of people gathered outside a general store. The owner had been eager to tell of the youth the police had taken into custody... it was an event beginning to happen so often Kate could write it in her sleep.

But she was not sleeping now. Kate's teeth nibbled the end of her pencil. Her brain felt more alive than it had in weeks.

Sounder had called her back to the bench. But he had not called for the reappearance of the five-pound note, he had not held out his grubby hand for money up front, in fact he had not demanded anything other than her word. His bargain had been a replica of that struck with Dora Wilkes; he would tell her all he knew but she must promise it would not appear in the *Star*.

Yes, the butler at Bentley Hall had been brother to his grandfather. Following an automobile accident the owner, Sir Corbett Foley, had steadily declined in health and one evening when the butler had gone to his room to enquire would he want supper he had found the man slumped across a table, probably the victim of a heart attack. He had called for help in getting Foley to his bed and as the man was moved he had seen the same box Albert had placed in a drawer of the dresser. It had been hidden by the body lying across it and when the butler had finally left the Hall the box had gone with him.

Along with a few more choice items no doubt. Kate flicked minute particles of pencil from her tongue.

The Hall had been sold and no inventory had shown a missing pendant. Yet that box had held a necklace when Albert had peeped inside, a necklace which gleamed gold and jewels ... so how come a thing so obviously costly was not included in a record of Foley's effects? Kate gnawed the rapidly diminishing pencil. There was one answer ... that box had contained something Corbett Foley hoped to hide from the world.

Evil. Dora had said Albert had used the word *evil*. Looking into that box had been like looking into the jaws of hell.

So what had been inside, and where was it now?

She had asked Echo Sounder those very questions. Kate remembered the look they had produced; it had shouted fear and the grubby fingers had twisted in a display of nerves.

He had never seen any box or anything it was supposed to have contained. Sounder's glance had not once ceased its patrol of the park grounds. His grandfather's brother had died within a few months of leaving Bentley Hall. Nobody had known the cause, not even the parish doctor; it seemed something had slowly sapped the life force from his body while nightmares ate away his mind; then his sons, two of them, had both died, the cholera more'n like, so if either of them had known of the box the knowledge of it died with them.

'Be the all I knows of it...'

The finishing words echoed hollowly. He had sounded so convincing ... so why wasn't she convinced?

'...don't know what become of any box; d'ain't never 'ear no more, Grandad 'elped clear the 'ouse after his brother's widow died...'

Grandad helped clear the house! Kate removed

130

the pencil from her mouth, her lips pursed where it had been. Had Grandad cleared it of Sir Corbett Foley's box, had that somehow found its way into his house ... the house Echo Sounder had been born in?

'...*be the all I knows of it*...'

That was an understatement if ever she had heard one. More likely that was the *all* Echo had been prepared to tell.

'*There be them of the Foley family still livin' in these parts, cousins and the like, I don't want them askin' questions ... ain't as if I could tell them more'n I've told you.*'

Couldn't or wouldn't? Kate's nose twitched. There was more to this than met the eye ... and she wouldn't bet a brass farthing Sounder had told the truth.

'Ready, Kate?'

Nodding at the office junior who had come to collect the finished report, Kate smiled grimly to herself.

Echo Sounder wouldn't recognise truth if it hit him between the eyes!

11

'I'll just lock the door, not that locks be any bar these days... ch! My mother would never believe a body 'ad to lock doors every time they went out ... d'ain't never lock a door in her life did my mother.'

Having carried her suitcase to the car, Torrey watched the thin worried-looking woman lean her weight several times against a maroon-coloured front door. The houses along the street were all of a match; window frames once white clung to remnants of paint flaking away like dirty snow-flakes, doors of the same dark, dismal shade of red stared like open ill-cared-for wounds. These people, like all the rest living in Darlaston, paid a hefty council tax, so what the hell was the council doing with it? As he surveyed the street, a swift rise of anger burned inside him. The gardens were not exactly of Chelsea Flower Show standard but they were neat, the glass of windows gleamed in the daylight and net curtains were clean; folk who lived in these houses obviously had a sense of pride that deserved to be met with pride: but so far as councillors were concerned civic pride meant fancy public buildings like Walsall's new Civic Centre and Art Gallery: of course towns needed a face lift, but cosmetic surgery did little for the people living in surroundings such as he looked at now, a couple fewer civic luncheons or one fewer so-called fact-finding trip abroad would finance a coat of paint...

'I can't say as how I really enjoys bein' away...' The woman had closed the garden gate, her anxious-sounding voice cutting Torrey's thoughts. 'You don't really relax, does you? I mean you worries what you might find when you gets back, there be that many break-ins, don't seem to matter it be somebody's 'ome they be wreckin', nor does they stop at beatin' folk as they finds there ... be a terrible way to go on.'

132

He could tell her that worrying would not deter any toerag bent on robbery or vandalism, he could also tell her the fact of her being in the house was in itself no deterrent as media coverage showed only too regularly, but what would that do except scare the poor woman even more.

'You off for a naughty weekend then?' Torrey's grin as he helped her into the taxi hid the feeling still hot in his chest. What was the world coming to when folk were afraid to leave their houses and many, like his present passenger, just as afraid when staying in them!

'A naughty weekend...!' A tinkling laugh accompanied the reply. 'Now where would you find a man interested in a woman old as meself?'

'You mean you don't have somebody waiting to carry you off ... now that's just my luck, a lovely girl with a free weekend and me booked to the hilt.'

As the laugh tinkled again Torrey glanced into the driving mirror. The ready banter froze on his lips. He had picked up one fare, he had seen one woman into the car ... so how come two faces looked at him?

There had been a plethora of applicants, hundreds of hopefuls responding to the television advert, each aspiring to be the face of Pascal's flower-in-bud.

Sitting at her desk, Venetia Pascal looked at the dozen or so photographs ranged across its surface.

They were each of them pretty, some exceedingly so, but only one of the girls selected could

133

become the face of 'Promise'.

She ran a finger over the smiling faces. Only one ... but the others would not be rejected, they too would be offered propositions they would be unlikely to refuse. A product aimed at younger people needed to be set in a world they recognised, and in so many hearts, longed for. Advertising for 'Promise' must therefore hold an innate quality of glitz and excitement, of the world of models, and film stars; that would be the medium of presentation and these girls would provide the back shots.

But advertising must have the 'fresh young beauty' approach, there could be none of the sophisticated glamour of 'Intrigue', or the seductive overtones of 'Distraction'. 'Promise' called for the breathlessness of standing on the brink, on the edge of emerging into a new and desirable life ... a chrysalis struggling to break free of its cocoon. The teenagers she had interviewed had been all of that and they could have their dream, live what was yet no more than a golden figment of imagination, but in return they must do as she had done, they must vow themselves to the Master, give themselves completely to the service of the Prince of Darkness. But that would come later, let the addiction of wealth and comfort become deeply rooted, then and only then, would they be offered the choice ... take what she offered or return to the life they had left. The finger hovered again, a bronze-painted nail touching the throat of each girl smiling from a carefully posed photograph. The Master would have his neophytes.

'Difficult choice?'

'Very.' Venetia relaxed against the leather of her chair. 'I think I should see each of these again, have them shot in location rather than in a studio. These...' she indicated the photographs lined across her desk, '...are too stilted, the smiles too artificial, they don't have the flavour I'm looking for.'

'I know what you mean, they are lambs striving to look like mutton ... you must admit it makes a change.'

'Admitted.' Venetia smiled at her secretary. A slender blonde, blue-eyed with a face many in Hollywood might envy, Francesca Benson had been with her from the initiation of 'Pascal'. Secretary, Girl Friday, whatever title was preferable, that was the only role she filled. Watching her now collect the photographs, Venetia wondered as she had on many previous occasions, why had she never tried to introduce Francesca Benson into the service of the Master?

'Do you want to go over the male ones now?'

Venetia nodded her head at the question. 'Might as well get it all done at once.'

'You could leave it, I could tell Precious to come back tomorrow.'

Venetia heard the hint of concern in the voice and knew it was genuine. Of all the people working for her, only Francesca Benson gave the feeling of true friendship. Francesca and the Master, they alone had the welfare of Venetia Pascal at heart ... so why had the two not met?

'Never put off ... you know the rest.' She smiled.

'I know you could do with a rest. Why not let

135

me put him off, there's loads of time... All right, all right!' Blue eyes signalled defeat. 'You're the boss, I'll tell him to come up.'

'Give me five minutes, and, Fran ... don't let him hear you call him "precious".'

Francesca touched a hand to her brow in mock salute. 'As I said, you're the boss, boss.'

Yes, she was the boss. Alone, Venetia allowed her head to rest on the back of her chair. Director of 'Pascal' beauty products, ditto 'Venetia', her own jewellery collection, that should be enough.

But it wasn't! She gazed about the beautifully appointed office. Eau-de-nil leather arm chairs, spaced with period walnut tables, sat on deeply piled cream carpet, while plain cream-washed walls were hung with originals of Monet and Constable. All of this had been given by the Master and she was grateful ... grateful but not satisfied.

'You're the boss...'

Words spoken a moment ago echoed in the quiet room. Closing her eyes on the trappings of wealth, she heard the truth beat like a drum. All that she had, all that had been given, still it was not enough! She wanted what Theo Vail had, to take his place as Leader of the Prime Coven, to have the powers that were his.

No! She drew a sharp breath, felt it cut away the half-measures to leave her mind clear of anything except the pure unadulterated truth.

She did not simply want what Vail *had*, nor even that which Julian Crowley had enjoyed; she wanted what neither of those men were capable of even dreaming of. She desired the ultimate ...

the Devil's own gift!

But then came an infinitely more disturbing admission.

The Prince of Darkness would require acknowledgement of so high a gift ... the tribute offered must be the finest.

Two faces watching him from the rear of the car ... two pairs of eyes staring back at him! Torrey's fingers tightened on the wheel. This was impossible ... it was downright bloody impossible!

The car jolted as the wheels touched the kerb.

He had seen his fare into the rear seat, a woman ... one woman! Torrey wrestled the weaving car into submission.

He had picked her up from that dowdy street, he had watched her push her weight several times against a flaking front door then glance back at the house before closing the garden gate. He had been amused. It was hardly Buckingham Palace, in fact it was no palace at all, but it was that woman's castle, one she had been afraid to leave and just as afraid to return to.

'Wolverhampton Station.' He had repeated the destination of the booking to ensure there could be no mistake and she had said it after him calling him 'luv' as she did so.

One passenger!

He blinked furiously. Seeing things he knew couldn't be there was hardly his style.

'Watch it, you stupid bastard!'

The cry, angrier and louder than the blare of an accompanying car horn, snatched Torrey's eyes open. The driver of a red Citroën Saxo shook a fist as he sped past glaring daggers, but Torrey's own eyes were seeking his passenger.

'You all right?' Concern edged the words.

'Yes...' Paler than before, the thin worried woman in the rear seat tried to manage a smile but failed. 'Yes, luv, I be all right.'

'Sorry about that.' Torrey's glance flicked back to the road.

'Ain't your fault so don't you go blamin' y'self. Be like I said to you when you come for me, some folk don't seem to care what they does or who might suffer in the doin' of it, and that mad oik be one of 'em!' The woman shuffled in her seat reaching for the faded black handbag which had fallen from her lap with the sudden stamp of brakes.

Christ, that had been a near thing! Torrey released breath slowly from tight lungs. It hadn't been the other bloke's fault; thank God there hadn't been a copper about. It would have been a dangerous driving charge and no messing! And telling the magistrate that seeing a face that wasn't there wouldn't put penalty points on his driving licence, it would bring him the big prize... a long holiday in a psychiatric unit!

What was it with him? Having offloaded his fare at Wolverhampton train station, Torrey sat for long moments. This was the second strange occurrence. That pick-up from Shepwell Green a few days ago; that also had been a woman on her own, someone who had seemed afraid. There had been a bit of a smash just ahead of them on the roundabout and thinking his passenger had been thrown from her seat he had jumped out to see if

138

she had been hurt ... but the car had been empty. He had written the episode off, telling himself it had been a runaway fare ... but this one ... this was no runaway and it was no bloody figment of imagination either. He *had* seen two women, two faces *had* looked back at him through the driving mirror, but he had helped only one woman from the car ... the other ... the other had looked with brilliant fear-filled eyes ... looked at him as flames licked around her head!

Sinking back in his seat he stared unseeing at the windscreen. Was he cracking up? Was training with the Territorials, working out in the gym, on top of the taxi driving proving too much?

'Only allowed to drop off or pick up here...'

The rap of pencil on window made Torrey jerk like a bungee jumper reaching the end of a fall.

'I said, you are only allowed to drop off or pick up here.'

A traffic warden repeated the words as Torrey's finger activated the electrically controlled window.

'I've just dropped a passenger.'

Beneath the peaked cap pale brown eyes examined Torrey's face. 'You are only allowed a couple of minutes and you've had those already, I know 'cos I've watched you.' The pale glance stroked Torrey's chest coming to rest significantly at the base of his stomach. 'Mind,' the glance lifted, 'you could have much longer than two minutes with me.'

Christ, he was being propositioned! Was this a take-me-or-take-a-traffic-ticket set up? The proverbial catch twenty-two! He looked at the face bent too close to the window, at the smile he was supposed to find provocative. Bringing his own mouth that much closer to the one now graphically parted in obvious invitation, he smiled straight into the pallid eyes.

'Nice try, but you're not my type. I like mine good looking.'

A squeak or a snarl? Not sure which and caring even less, Torrey watched the mouth snap shut and the pencil poise over a ticket.

'You might try using that pencil another way,' his finger rested on the button of the console, 'it's not as thick as the treat you'd hoped to get pushed up your arse but at least you won't have to pay for it, though one thing you will have to pay for is cosmetic surgery; I tell you now mate, you try hanging a ticket on me and the next thing to go up that arse of yours will be a tyre iron, and as for the rest of what you think of as your stock in trade...'

A doubled fist rose to the level of the window.

'... like Humpty Dumpty, nobody will put that together again.'

Could they have everything ready in time? Whisky glass in hand, Theo Vail sat in the drawing room of his beautiful home. The reports had been good. Thorold had procured extra wheat from the USA, plus rice and soya from Egypt and Brazil, and that on top of an increased intake of heroin; Fenton had also reported an increase of business as had each of the several others coming beneath the umbrella of the Vail Corporation; they had all given satisfaction ... except for

140

Venetia Pascal, though her profit too was healthy.

Taking a long draught, he held the whisky in his mouth. The business she ran was not part of Vail Corporation, it belonged solely to her and that was not to his taste!

Allowing the alcohol to glide slowly past his throat, he tightened long expressive fingers about the heavy crystal.

He had attempted to incorporate her holdings with those of Vail, tried to merge her business with his but each time she had refused. She was doing well enough on her own, she did not need Vail Corporation, was her usual rebuff.

Theo took another drink, this time swallowing immediately, relishing the flame of whisky against his throat.

She had smiled as she had answered ... each time she had smiled ... but behind it, in the depths of ice-bound green eyes he had seen the truth – she did not need him!

And with that other business, the worship of the Master? She had not openly challenged his leadership, but insinuation became less veiled at each meeting. Could it be her intention to make a take-over bid, one which would see her as First of the Coven?

The thought jarred and he rose quickly, refilling his tumbler from a matching Stuart crystal decanter.

Savouring the reassurance of the whisky, he smiled coldly. First of the Coven? She was not far enough along the Path, she was a distance from the stage yet of Magus and that was far below Ipsissimus ... and one more thing, the Great Lord of the Dark Throne, Prince of Hades, would never suffer a woman to occupy that highest of earthly positions, to serve at his altar as prime disciple, to make sacrifice in his name.

Carrying the drink to his chair he relaxed, his glance deep in the dancing flames of a log fire. Sooner or later the lovely Venetia would overstep the mark, and Theo Vail would revel in her fall.

12

What the hell was happening to him? Christ, he didn't know whether he was on this earth or 'Fuller's'. Despite himself, Torrey smiled at the phrase his mother had often murmured. Tired after a hard day cleaning, she would sit at the scrubbed table in that poky kitchen of their home in Dangerfield Lane, nursing the cup of tea he had made for her and breathe softly, 'Eh! I don't know if I be on this earth or Fuller's!' But why Fuller's?

He had put that question to her. At seven years old he could not fathom the reason for himself. She had laughed at that, her tired listless eyes brightening for a moment, then from a cupboard on the wall had taken a small cardboard carton on which were printed the words 'Fuller's Earth', smiling as she told him it was a powder used in the wash to remove grease and stubborn stains.

But his earth had been no box of powder, his mind had not been so tired he didn't know 't'other from which'. He had picked up one fare from Shepwell Green only to have the woman disappear from the car before reaching her destination; then he had picked up today's fare, another woman travelling alone, only to see two women sitting in the rear seats, two faces looking back at him from the driver's mirror.

It hadn't been imagination ... yet how could he call it reality? He could tell himself he hadn't seen a second woman sitting in his taxi, a woman whose face had become wreathed in flame, but that would alter nothing. He had seen what he had seen!

'Torrey, which planet are you on?'

Kate Mallory's sharp exasperation reached the mind wrapped in thought.

'Fuller's.' Torrey managed a grin only for it to fade when, having given the demanded explanation of this reply, Kate sniffed tartly.

'If you are not interested...'

'I am, Kate, I am.' It was a lie but he couldn't hurt her feelings. Kate Mallory was great company... but tonight...

'No, you are not,' Kate Mallory's tilted mouth grimaced wryly, 'and I can't really blame you; this business of a trinket being brought from Russia to Bentley Hall, a necklace supposedly endowed with the power of evil, is a load of–'

'Old Wives' Tales?'

That had got him off the hook. Torrey watched brown eyes twinkle, the slightly off-centre mouth curve in a smile. Fetch the lady a drink from the bar and he might just recall enough of what she had been talking about to keep him off it.

Sounder had to be in there somewhere, Torrey was prepared to gamble. Setting both glasses on the iron-legged table he cast his die.

'So what song was our tuneful little canary singing? I've no doubt it was off key if not definitely flat.'

'Sounder! That man lies so often I swear he doesn't know when he's doing it!' Kate sniffed.

Sipping his pint of Best afforded him the opportunity of hiding a smile he knew would result in Kate again accusing him of not being interested. The guess she had met with Echo Sounder had proved a good one, but what to follow it up with?

'He refused a fiver.'

She hadn't waited for any follow-up. Torrey rested his glass. He was still off that hook.

'Five pounds I offered yet he made no attempt to take it, in fact he didn't even look at it.'

Sounder *was* a liar, he trotted them out as often as he saw horses being trotted around a race-track, which was all day every day with action replay on television in the evenings, but to have refused a backhander ... it was either a seizure of the brain or the little toerag was terminally ill.

'Doesn't sound like him.' Torrey's brow creased.

'Didn't look like him either ... well, what I mean is...' Kate saw the crease develop into a frown, '...what I meant to say was he didn't seem his usual "money-up-front" self, in fact he seemed scared, then *very* scared when I told him he could read what I had learned from Dora Wilkes in tomorrow's edition of the *Star*, so much so he offered to spill every last bean if I promised

144

not to publish.'

'And did he?' Torrey asked. 'Did he spill every bean or could he have kept back a few? A reserve against the fiver he let slip from his fingers?'

From the bar room loud whoops of exultation echoed across into the lounge of the Frying Pan. The local darts team had made a lucky strike. Torrey watched Kate's hand wander on its subconscious search of the leather bag then reappear without the sought-after cigarette. Had she hit on a similar stroke of luck?

'He more or less agreed with all that Dora Wilkes told me. Well, he did when I said she was an old friend of Annie's and I would check with her...'

Her straying hand coming to rest beside her glass reinforced Torrey's guess that the search through the bag had been entirely devoid of conscious thought.

'He went on to say his grandfather's brother had been butler to Sir Corbett Foley, that he had seen a necklace in a box in the master's bedroom and...'

'And?'

'You'll never believe it!'

The muted lighting of the pub lounge sprinkled a thousand miniature lights among the sherry-coloured hair as Kate gave a brief shake of her head. Torrey's inward grin spread. What had the girl swallowed now?

'There've been a lot of things in my life I would never have believed, one more won't do any harm; so tell the rest of the ditty our little friend sang to you.'

145

'I...' she paused, a tinge of colour creeping into her cheeks, '...I don't say I believed him myself but...'

'Kate,' he allowed a modified version of the grin to appear on his mouth, 'the Frying Pan is not a twenty-four-hour establishment, the landlord likes his bed and when he's ready for it we get chucked out of here, and I don't fancy standing in the rain just to hear what Echo Sounder drivelled out; so if you are going to tell it you best do it now, I'll think about your disbelieving later.'

'Haad yor whisht!' Irascibility had Kate slip back to her Geordie roots. 'Give a lass time for the tellin'!'

'Mother always said I was too sharp to catch cold, a failing I don't seem to have grown out of ... sorry, Kate, I won't interrupt again.'

He would not interrupt but the landlord might. Torrey glanced towards the bar. Get a move on, Kate, or the confessions of a racetrack junkie would have to wait for another day.

'Dora had already told me of Albert, her grandmother's boyfriend, being under-butler at that Hall and that he had described the contents of a certain box, one which mysteriously made no appearance in the inventory of the house when the furnishings came to be sold, a box that was never seen after Sir Corben Foley's death, and more to the point, after the butler's employment was terminated.'

'Don't tell me...' Torrey's interruption reneged on his promise but Kate made no objection, just a slow nodding of her head marking agreement as he finished.

'...the butler's name was Sounder.'

'Brother to Echo's grandfather, the brother who helped clear the contents of a house after a widow died.' Kate's smile was sheer triumph. 'I thought there was a story somewhere and when I saw Echo's reaction, the fear on his face, the way his hands twisted together, I was certain of it.'

'So his grandad's brother might have nicked something from his employer, but where is the mind-blowing bit in that? It happens all the time.'

'Dora said Albert told her grandmother that box held evil, that looking into it was like looking into the jaws of hell and I got the feeling Echo felt much the same way.'

'Evil!' Torrey laughed. 'C'mon, Kate, you can't seriously say you believe that?'

'I do say it.' Bright and steady, her stare rested on Torrey's amused face. 'I believe something terrible was brought to Bentley Hall all those years ago, and what's more I believe Echo knows it too.'

'Tell you what I believe.' Torrey swallowed a mouthful of beer then smiled. 'I believe that if this box of yours held anything worth anything then it was sold long since, if not by his grandfather or his father then certainly by Echo; he'd sell his soul for the chance of betting the horses. I say forget it, Kate, that box became firewood before you, or even before Echo was born.'

'He claimed he didn't know what became of it,' Kate's lower lip twisted thoughtfully, 'then he said there were others of the Foleys still living hereabouts and he didn't want them asking questions ... but I think there is more behind his display of fright than that.'

This old wives' business had got under her skin! Torrey watched the lip caught now between her teeth. She was usually so sensible, why couldn't she see this was one wild goose chase?

'Sounder doesn't only know how to play the horses, Kate,' he had to say something while she still had a lip left, 'he knows how to play people too.'

'You mean gullible people – like me!' The teeth ceased their worrying, but now her eyes flashed like a warning beacon.

Across the table Torrey caught the signal. Kate really had got a bug in her blood.

'I didn't mean that at all,' he said quietly.

'Then what did you mean?' The beacon flashed again.

Diplomacy wasn't going to work. Torrey met the accusation bluntly. 'I mean that you are being fed a line, you are being conned; this Dora woman fancied seeing her name in the *Star* and Sounder, that little weasel, jumped on the band wagon.'

'And did what? Lose himself a fiver?' Kate's retort was cynical, her glance more so.

'He'll only lose it if you let him. C'mon, I'll give you a ride home.'

Standing in the small car park fronting the Frying Pan, Kate breathed air freshened by rain. The downpour over, the sky now boasted a huge white-gold moon. A witches' moon! She shivered involuntarily. How much evil had taken place beneath a moon just like this one?

'What did you mean by saying Echo could only lose that five pounds if I let him?' The question had burned the tip of her tongue but she had held it until they were free of the confines of the car park.

The woman was like a bloody terrier! Torrey shoved the gears impatiently. Got the rat between her teeth and wasn't going to let go!

'I would have thought you would have caught on to that one for yourself.' He glanced to his right before sending the car round the traffic island then on towards the traffic lights at the Bull Stake. 'Sounder is nobody's fool. He would see your nose twitching a mile away; act like he was shit scared, follow that up by refusing a fiver and he's got you dangling on the hook; play you long enough and he'll get a lot more than that.'

It sounded feasible. Kate stared at the half-demolished buildings of Pinfold Street. Like rotted teeth their broken walls rose black and jagged against the dark background of night. Echo Sounder was devious, that brooked no argument, but refusing money in the hope of making money? That was not part of his agenda! Speculate to accumulate? Only at the racetrack, and then only if it was a dead certainty.

A dead certainty! Kate's breath stilled. Sir Corbett Foley, Albert, the butler and his sons ... so many deaths, and each man connected to that box; was Sounder's real reason for saying he had no knowledge of what had become of it a fear of the reprisal of Foley relatives, or the reprisal of evil? Did that box still hold a threat of death?

'Take it from me, Kate, that toerag will take you

for all he can get and then be back for more. Paint a picture of the devil and his works and Sounder thinks himself onto a winner; evil in a box! What some folk will come up with just to see their name in print.' Torrey swung the car to the right, leaving Wolverhampton Street to drive along Michael Road.

'Dora Wilkes specifically asked me not to publish what she told me, she was afraid...'

'Of the so-called evil, or the Foley relatives?' Bringing the car to a halt outside Annie's neat little house, Torrey turned to look at Kate.

'You don't believe her?' Kate watched the leaves of a wide-branched tree dance in the night breeze, showering the ground beneath with shimmering drops of moonlight.

Sensitive to the mood but more sensitive to the thought of Sounder milking her of hard-earned cash, his answer was straightforward. 'No, I don't, Kate, and neither should you. This is the twenty-first century, we don't believe in bogey men any more, and as for the devil and his evil...'

'You are going to tell me that too is a thing of the past.' Kate continued to watch the ballet of moonlight.

'Evil is only what folk make for themselves!'

The retort had been sharp, meant to snap her into seeing things his way, to bring her to his more logical conclusion. The shadowed interior of the car hid the line setting over Kate's mouth.

'Did you make the evil that was Anna?' she asked quietly. 'Was it something *you* did caused her ghost to drive men to their deaths, was it *you* made that same ghost try to draw you back to hell with it? And what of Penny Smith, of Fred Baker ... did *you* conjure the evil which took their lives? You of all people should know better than to say evil is only what folk make for themselves, you of all people, Torrey, should know that is not always the truth.'

Watching the house door close behind Kate, Torrey leaned his head against the back of the seat. He could not have argued with that even had she waited. Anna! Behind closed eyelids, a lovely face smiled at him, hyacinth-blue eyes sparkling like priceless gems, shoulder-length hair a cloud of blonde silk. Anna, the woman he had loved ... the ghost which had haunted him. Maybe that had been due to him; as Martha Sim had said, he could have called Anna's spirit back ... but Penny Smith, that could not be laid at his door, he had never known the girl ... yet her ghost too had haunted him.

But that was all over, the ghosts were gone.

Turning the key in the ignition Torrey felt the heartbeat of the car throb beneath him. Checking the wing mirror for traffic from the rear, he released the handbrake. Then, as his glance touched the driving mirror, the breath froze in his throat.

'Christ!' he choked. 'Christ, not again!'

The showing of her jewellery collection had been a total success. Venetia Pascal watched the faces of the remaining buyers. The price tags had fazed none of these, but then they expected the price to include more than the baubles ordered for their shops and judging by the smiles they were not due for a disappointing evening.

These models ... men as well as women ... were not those who would be used to launch her range of beauty products for the younger person; these were more mature in the ways of the modelling world. They knew that money could be made off the platform as well as on it.

'You really should model that piece yourself, it would look positively precious against that fabulous complexion of yours ... as for the hair, that gorgeous auburn ... I tell you that would be just divine spread across a pillow of white satin ... precious, darling ... simply precious.'

Remembering the words of the photographer during the pre-exhibition shoot, she smiled into her flute of champagne.

Maybe he had been right about the jewellery, but she had not fallen for his effusive praise nor taken his advice. Instead, the piece, diamonds and rubies set in heavy antique gold, had been worn by one of her regular models.

'You are to be congratulated.'

Venetia turned towards the voice, her smile fixed and automatic. This was the part of the proceedings she liked least. Talking to clients on the business of jewellery sales was one thing, but this was another ... and it sometimes damaged a man's ego to find the object of his attentions was most definitely not for sale.

Teeth brilliant against a deeply tanned skin flashed in the light of the chandeliers. It was well he hadn't smiled during the modelling of the diamonds, they would have seemed like paste in comparison. Venetia kept the bitchy thought

152

beneath her smile, asking instead, 'You liked the collection, Mr Winter?'

'Very much so, Miss Pascal.' Zachary St John Winter maintained the distance of formality, aware of watching eyes and listening ears. As a member of Her Majesty's Foreign Office he was fair game for anyone ready to attack the government.

'Might I ask if anything particular caught your eye?' Venetia glanced at the jewellery greedily sucking the room's lighting.

'Everything is very beautiful, it would be difficult to choose one piece over another.'

Taking his fences carefully! Venetia sipped the regulatory flute of champagne.

'I am sure,' he went on, his voice lifting slightly for the benefit of any interested observer, 'tonight's showing will be a great boost for the jewellery trade in general, and that can only be good for the economy of the country.'

A show jumper in action! Venetia's smile did not move. He cleared his hurdles with expertise. But then Zachary St John Winter was well versed in the art of diplomatic flattery, especially when that flattery was designed to bring its own reward.

'There will of course be a modified version of the collection for the high street, copies for the cheaper market; these, however,' she waved a hand and her emerald ring darted green fire, 'are the real thing and as such exclusive to the purchaser.' Venetia paused while her guest accepted a fresh glass of champagne from a waiter.

'That can be understood.' St John Winter took up the conversation. 'Everything you have shown is exquisite, and a purchaser expects exclusivity, that surely is a tenet of good business.'

Green as fresh sprung grass, Venetia's gaze lifted to his sweeping the smaller of the hotel's banqueting rooms engaged for the private viewing of her collection.

'Agreed,' she answered quietly. 'But the House of Pascal holds a tenet that is of even more importance to many clients, that of privacy. *That* is the guarantee of Pascal.'

It needed no spelling out. Venetia saw the tiny pull of Zachary St John Winter's mouth. He had read between the lines.

'Delivery?'

The question was there, the lips hardly moving, the eyes not at all; they were fastened on a slender long-limbed brunette. Wearing a Valentino gown of dusky-red chiffon with a neckline that dipped between high tight breasts to milk-cream flesh tantalisingly close to the navel, the model was as arresting as the diamond and ruby pendant gleaming at her throat.

As if on cue the dark head turned, a full-lipped mouth breaking into a smile as long-lashed eyes proffered their invitation. Her own glance still on the face of her guest, Venetia silently congratulated herself. She had chosen her models well.

'Pascal undertakes to deliver a client's purchase to any address at any time.'

The barely visible tension in the Minister's mouth lessened. Venetia watched the tip of a tongue slide over the lips. He would make his purchase before leaving.

'Of course,' she smiled, allowing her glance to

154

flick over the room, 'we realise some clients would prefer to view a prospective purchase more closely than a public showing permits ... perhaps to get the feel of it.' The seemingly careless glance caught the fingers tightening about the stem of his champagne glass and almost felt the jerk of flesh hardening beneath the expensive bespoke tailored trousers ... and like a spider hovering above a fly Venetia continued, '...But that might not fit a client's requirements ... a gift delivered to the home would of course ruin the surprise were a client's wife or daughter to take delivery...'

The pause, deliberate and perfectly timed, carried the rest. Across from them the svelte body moved a little closer to its companion; the studied movement sinuous, overtly suggestive, left little to the imagination. St John Winter's tongue slid the length of his lips.

'For any client wanting a discreet viewing tonight, Pascal has reserved private rooms.' Venetia spoke above her smile, 'One has only to make the request.'

Watching him leave the room, followed minutes later by the brunette, Venetia breathed her satisfaction. A member of the government ... especially the Foreign Office ... would surely prove a valuable asset in executing the work of the Master.

13

Like icebergs in a polar sea, Theo Vail's grey eyes showed only the tips of his true feelings as they fastened on Venetia Pascal. She was beautiful, more so than the models she employed, but the look he so quickly banished indicated he was aware of a quality much more potent, one that did not stop at wanting a man's body. She would take his soul as well.

Nodding a second goodnight to people he had spoken with moments before, the smile he turned back to her was as cold as the crystal he held between expensively manicured fingers. He'd like to fuck the brains out of this arrogant bitch, then chuck her back where she came from! But where had she come from? Like all other questions put to her, that one was fielded with a touch that would be the envy of the MCC; and the arrogance! It couldn't be called anything else, that cold 'hands off' aura she wore like a second skin. He had not witnessed that in any newcomer to the Coven, that lack of awe and respect acolytes showed to a Magus; it was almost as if she enjoyed some special protection, but what...? And from whom? Not the Master, he would not favour an acolyte over a Magus, a disciple so much higher in his service. An Ipsissimus? Vail's innards coiled; was that the source of this woman's confidence? Was she perhaps the mistress of a man so far along the Path, was that the root of a boldness he knew bordered on contempt? That was a possibility, one he must address sooner rather than later! The Sabbat of Mabon? Yes, he sipped the champagne, yes the Sabbat of Mabon would do very nicely; Venetia Pascal would meet her Master rather earlier than she anticipated.

'Congratulations,' he said as the last of the evening's guests departed and they were alone except for the hotel staff waiting deferentially for them also to leave before beginning the task of clearing the room. 'That was neatly done.'

'The showing of the Collection? Surely you did not expect anything else.'

There it was again, that damned contempt! Capped teeth clenched, Theo Vail held the smile which might have been frozen into place.

'No, I did not expect anything else.' He set the champagne flute down before going on. 'Nor is it the showing of your jewellery I refer to, my congratulation is for the ease with which you drew St John Winter into your little trap ... it is a trap, isn't it, my dear?'

My dear! Her glass following his onto a silver tray Venetia Pascal's long lashes hid the amusement in her eyes before it was banished. She was not dear to Theo Vail, not even in the remotest sense of the word.

'Whatever you say!' The green gaze lifted coolly. 'I am not inclined to discuss it. Goodnight, Theo.'

She had not wanted to discuss the events of the

evening, she did not even want to look at that conceited face any longer than absolutely necessary. But neither did she wish to sleep. Tension playing her nerves, Venetia walked to the hotel lounge. A drink would help to soothe her. Requesting a vodka Russian she sat at a corner table. The warmth of green ginger would salve the bitterness of talking to Vail.

He was so sure of himself, so certain of his standing with the Master, as sure as Crowley had been. Head of Satel Aeronautics, he also had been leader of a High Coven and like Vail his eyes too had been on the main prize. Julian Crowley had also entertained the same conceit, that unfailing belief in himself as the Chosen and it was that very assuredness that led to the conflict with Richard Torrey. Perhaps none among Crowley's influential colleagues could have foretold the outcome of their clash and certainly none would have believed a man like Torrey – an ex-commando with nothing to his name other than a potential for beating up local yobs – would refuse the wealth each of them had been given, turn his back on the power which went with money; but Torrey had done just that, he had chosen his path – and it had not been that of the Left Hand.

How Julian Crowley must have rejoiced at that decision. Her glance deep in the glass now balanced between her hands, her mind wandered unhindered into a secret past.

She had talked with others of the Coven. Alex Davion of Davion International and Mercury Airlines, Stephen Geddes of Coton Pharmaceuticals, both men rich enough to pay for information. Crowley had suffered a severe mental breakdown, doctors had told them, 'In the strictest confidentiality, of course'.

Of course! Venetia's half-smile was scathing. It appeared he thought he had been attacked by some demon, some creature from hell. The doctor had shaken his head. But apart from a mark similar to a burn on his brow there was nothing to suggest an attack by anyone or anything, real or imagined.

A mark on his brow! She drank, feeling the alcohol sting her throat. The Seal of Asmodai, the mark placed upon each sacrifice; the mark Crowley had believed would never be placed upon himself. He had become aware that his scheme to undermine the financial stability of the Middle East, the plan designed to have those countries at each other's throats, had been discovered by Torrey and Kate Mallory, a journalist with the local newspaper. He had followed them to a cellar beneath the print room of Darlaston Printers. There he had called forth the Keeper of the Great Seal, conjured that terrible messenger to take Torrey and the woman into hell. But Crowley, in his self-assurance, had overlooked one thing. As well as being Keeper of the Seal, Asmodai was also Archangel of Vengeance and when Torrey had defied Crowley, when he had rejected the Lord of Darkness by calling on the powers of heaven, then Asmodai, greatest of all dark angels, had turned that vengeance on Crowley, leaving him with the mark of the Seal burned on to his brow and a mind blown into insanity.

Despite the warmth of the room, Venetia felt a trickle of ice along her spine.

Would Theo Vail follow in those footsteps? Summon the Messenger to take the life she knew he intended to sacrifice ... her own!

Crowley's internment in the medical wing of a secure asylum had resulted in the disbanding of the coven he had headed, the members being absorbed into others around the country, and Nicole Jarreau, whose exquisite gowns adorned the bodies of the rich and famous, had become Venetia Pascal, creator of 'Pascal', now an international name in perfumes, cosmetics and jewellery.

And she was still beautiful.

Plastic surgery had provided a new face, money a new identity, but service to the Lord of Darkness had continued; she had been witness to his displeasure, she would not risk the same happening to her.

'It would have been a great deal to give up, wouldn't it, Nicole?'

Breath caught in her throat, her fingers became rigid, the deeply cut crystal of the tumbler biting into them, but somehow she remained calm.

He did not know, he could not possibly know – yet he had called her Nicole! Beneath the turmoil of thought she clung to the outward indifference. Not looking up, she answered frostily, 'The company I prefer is my own, but should I wish to be picked up then I would make my own choice. Please, go away.'

'Those were not the words you spoke to Julian Crowley when he offered to rescue you from a life you thought hopeless. I am correct, am I not, Nicole?'

No one of that coven had known of her plans, yet if somebody had found out why wait until now to blackmail her? If that was his game it would not go on for long.

'I asked you to go away,' she pushed the words through set teeth, 'but perhaps you would rather I have hotel security throw you out!'

'And risk a scene, Miss Jarreau?'

He was not going to go away. Well, the consequence of that would be upon his own head. Resting her tumbler on the ornate marble-topped table, yet keeping it between both hands, she lifted a coldly disparaging look.

'I am afraid you have me mistaken for someone else.'

Tall, dark haired, he smiled, his eyes seeming to glow like black fire.

'I do not make mistakes. Surgery gave you a new face, you adopted a new line of business, but all of what you had, of what you still have, is through the beneficence of the Master. Oh, yes,' he nodded as breath caught again in her throat, 'I know about that also. The wealth of the "House of Jarreau" and that of "Pascal" are as nothing compared to what you can have, and the powers once held by Julian Crowley...' he paused, the mesmerising gleam of his eyes holding her in chains of ebony, 'they will pale into insignificance beside those now offered to you.'

A slight movement of the hand stilled the question rising to Venetia's lips and when he spoke again his voice was husky, reaching tendrils

161

of pleasure deep into her stomach.

'No.' He smiled again, her mind reeling under its force. 'You have not seen me before, but trust what I say ... take the offer which is made.'

How had he known her name, known of Julian Crowley?

She had asked neither of those questions. At her home in Telford, Venetia stood gazing at the ebony cross inverted on a table in the room devoted to her own private worship of the Lord of Darkness. They had been questions left unasked. Instead she had gone with him to the room she had previously booked for an overnight stay. That had been a week ago yet thoughts of what had taken place there had her insides writhe, flames of desire burn through every part of her.

He had taken her into his arms, the dark music of his voice tightening the bonds set by those coal-dark eyes. He had murmured her name as his hands gently removed her clothing, before stroking like velvet down her back and across her buttocks.

How had it happened? She hadn't known and she hadn't cared, wanting only to be in his arms. Then, without seeming to release her, he too had been naked. The flesh of him was like fire against her own, heating hers with a boiling passion; then, his lips on hers, he had lifted her into his arms and carried her to the bed. For a moment only he had stood looking down at her but that moment had been enough for her to drink in every muscular line of that splendid body, enough for it to be emblazoned on her heart. She had lifted her arms to him and with a slowness that agonised in its torment he had lowered himself into her. Memory of that wonderful contact spewed rivers of desire along every vein, bringing a swift catch to her throat. She had spread her legs wide, exulting in the hardness that drove into her, revelling in the vigorous potency that had her beg for more each time he withdrew. And those pleas had been answered.

Gazing at the makeshift altar, Venetia let the tide of memory flood over her, washing the rapture of those hours spent with that dark-haired stranger deep into her soul.

Twice he had made love to her, the sensuous passion of it awakening desires she never knew she had and in the brief lull between he had covered her body with kisses, taken her nipples into his mouth, his hands stroking her thighs, his fingers touching the warm wet cavern between until greed for him had her cry out, the need burning away all thought except of him driving into her.

He had looked at her with those dark fire-filled eyes, touched her mouth with the sweet wine of his own, then again a heart-stopping jolt of her veins had brought a strangled gasp as that hard column of flesh pushed with new, almost savage appetite, her senses leaping with every thrust.

He had lifted from her to lie quietly at her side.

Hands clasped tight together she fought the desire rising in the depths of her.

She had thought him sleeping and not yet satiated she had touched her lips to that flat stomach, kissing a line past the navel to where her fingers played among the dark pubic hair. It had been like touching sable silk, the separate strands trickling over her fingers like black water ... water which to that moment had hidden the mark.

Venetia's eyes closed but the pressure of her lids could not erase the sight playing across her mental vision.

Crimson as blood it had nestled close to the flaccid penis.

Inhaling deeply she tried to still the pounding in her chest.

Fascinated, she had held the silken cover free of the scarlet stain, had stared, and as she did so it seemed suddenly to deepen in colour; a living flame within its dark cover it had blazed beneath her hand.

A birthmark ... a tattoo?

Venetia's eyelids pressed harder but memory was stronger.

She had touched it, tracing a fingertip over the intricate, convoluted marking. A design within a design, a circle within a circle, and at its centre, spines touching together, gleamed what appeared to be...

She had wanted to pull away, breath snatched in her throat, but the mark burned against her eyes, her hand losing the power to draw free.

Numbers!

She swallowed hard against the restriction holding her chest now as it had held it in that moment.

The mark she had touched, the design blazing

like living fire beneath its silken shroud, had incorporated three numbers, 6 6 6. The symbol of Satan!

There had been a short deep-throated laugh, a hand closing over her wrist burning like acid. Then, still grasping her, he had risen bodily from the bed; that beautifully formed body and herself floating high above the floor!

Terrified she had stared at the space below her feet ... he had released her yet she had not fallen; she had stood in midair! The face watching her changed slowly. Fear threatening to choke her, she had stared at the gradual transformation; the dark, almost black hair becoming a mass first of violet-tipped gold veined with scarlet, then leaping, curling carmine flames, flames which wreathed about the whole of him until it seemed he must perish. But he had not. The face had smiled from the centre of that noiseless inferno, the same face which had smiled at her gift of a kitten! Then he had spoken. Soft, melodic it had pulled at the very core of her, a music such as she had never heard before.

'I am the Keeper of Eternity...'

Velvet thunder, it had rolled in her brain.

'I am the One...'

A song of angels had seemed to fill the room, an exquisite sound echoing vibrant on the stillness, removing the fear of floating weightless in the air, removing fear of him. He had smiled at her, that glorious figure bathed in living fire, and she had no longer been afraid.

'I am The First of Creation...'

It had been an exultation, an elated, jubilant

triumph, a Te Deum of praise and with it the very room had seemed to glow and burn. The unearthly beauty of that music formed a chorale in her mind, the lure of sirens. She had wanted to go to him, to be drawn with him into those scarlet flames, to be held again in those arms, but it seemed her own body was bound by cords she could not break.

'I am He to Whom the World Belongs...'

With those words the flames had died, leaving the beautiful gilded body gleaming at the centre of a circle of light which was both ebony in its blackness and blinding in its brilliance, and all the while the soundless music resonated until it seemed it must fill the universe.

Enraptured, her own breath seeming to have no impact on her lungs, she had listened to words coming not from that glistening mouth but from the very air itself and she had gazed entranced into those eyes.

Those eyes! Venetia pressed fingers against her own. They had scorched into her, consumed her senses in their smouldering heat, burned a desire into her which she knew would never die.

'I am Holder of Earth, Lord of the Dark Regions...'

The golden face had smiled but the eyes had remained pools of negrescent, threatening fire, luminous and molten as black lava and from beneath the soles of his feet, edges rippling red-gold, spurts of flame had curled upwards to encompass the glowing figure again in an aura of fire.

She had tried once more to move, to reach for

that beautiful gilded body, a yearning to feel the hardness of that flesh drive deep into her drowning all else in a flood of desire, but as she had cried out an arm that was living, pulsing flame had lifted, an incandescent hand pointing a finger of shimmering light. It had touched her face, burning yet wonderfully cool and soft as a feather. She had lowered to the bed while the voice in her head swelled in a great symphony of sound.

'I am Lucifer, Prince of the Morning...'

Above her the dark eyes had gleamed, darts of scarlet issuing from still lips, each syllable of those next unspoken words blazing white lightning in her brain, the message they carried leaving her stunned.

'To you is given the Word, to you the Promise. Through you is my will accomplished.'

To her had been given the Word, the Promise ... to her the favour of the great Lord of Darkness!

Eyes still closed, she sank to her knees. Making obeisance to the black painted cross, her whisper threaded on the silence, the same whisper that had trickled from her dry throat as that glittering, magnificent figure had faded slowly into nothingness.

'Thy will be done.'

14

Torrey had definitely not been his usual self.

Pencil between her teeth, Kate Mallory stared into space.

He had denied not being interested in what she was trying to discuss but he hadn't quite managed to dismiss that look which said his mind was elsewhere; and even when he *had* listened his answers had been offhand. So what was niggling in his mind?

'Kate, boss says five minutes and no longer.'

'What!' Kate frowned vacantly at the young lad stood at her desk.

'The boss...' the office junior leaned closer, his voice dropping to what he hoped was a confidential whisper, 'he says five minutes or your copy is obsolete and so are you, and Kate...' he glanced sideways to the glass-partitioned office of the editor of the *Star*, 'he's not in the best of moods.'

'So what else is new!' Kate's volatile return was no confidential whisper. 'That item of information is as dated as silent movies and just about as interesting!'

Shoving the finished copy into the lad's hands, she grabbed her bag and heaved it on to her shoulder. If what she had written was not acceptable to his high and mightiness then he could bloody well write it himself!

'Kate,' the junior shot another nervous glance

over one shoulder, 'I wouldn't leave yet.'

'Maybe you wouldn't,' Kate's answer was sheer mutiny, 'but I'm not you and I *am* leaving.'

'Kate...'

The undertone of anxiety had the word falter in its saying and Kate's threatened eruption subsided. A swift wink accompanying her tip-tilted smile she said quietly, 'You can tell our Scots terrier I think I have a lead on that fire along of Station Street, say I've an appointment with Detective Inspector Bruce Daniels, that if I don't turn up on time he won't renew the offer.'

The office junior had smiled, relieved he had some story to tell if questioned by the boss. But that was all it was, a story; one with as much truth as a government promise to abolish all taxes.

And what of Daniels' reaction should he discover her lie? Kate's sensible size fours rapped the pavement. That one could wait, there was no sense in facing trouble before it roared at her.

So why was she risking her job? Quicker than the question had formed, the answer flashed in her mind. She was bored, bored with writing up 'leaked' council proposals and bored most of all with bloody myths, legends and old wives' tales!

But not all of that was true. She passed the bus stop, preferring to walk. The air might blow away some of the confusion clouding her brain. She was bored with her job ... yet she loved journalism. She was fed up with writing for a provincial ... so why had she not taken the offer of a post with the Nationals? She could go freelance... she could also sign on the dole!

Thoughts churning, it was with some surprise she found herself outside the police station in Victoria Road. Maybe she should ask to see Daniels... the public's right to know and all that!

'If you would like to wait, Miss, Inspector Daniels is with the Chief at the moment but he should be free shortly.'

Minutes after smiling the words at Kate, David Farnell delivered the message that a reporter for the *Star* wanted a few words.

'Tell her I'm out!' Daniels caught irritably at the lid of a carton snatched from his jacket pocket.

'Too late.' The desk sergeant shook his head, 'She knows you're not.'

'How many times do I have to say this? Look, watch my lips. I DO NOT WANT THAT WOMAN IN THIS STATION!'

'It could prove awkward if I have to tell her you're not in after all, you know Quinto and his softly, softly approach with the Press.'

He knew Quinto! The antacid tablet in his mouth, Daniels crumpled the packet, throwing it angrily towards a waste paper basket and scoring a perfect miss. He knew the Chief Inspector only too well ... another one who sat on his arse while others did the work then gave 'reluctant' interviews in that lah-di-dah public school voice. Another avid collector of gold braid, Quinto was no more interested in apprehending the local villainry than in sliding bare-arsed down a slag heap.

'Well, do I tell her to come in, or do I tell her to go?'

The question lowering the steam beginning to rise, Daniels looked at his friend of so many years. 'I'll have your balls for this!'

'Too late again,' David Farnell's blue eyes twinkled, 'the missis had them for breakfast.'

Lucky bloody you. Daniels watched the sergeant leave. Marjorie forgot years ago that I've even got balls!

That had lived up to every expectation. Sitting in the park opposite the police station, Kate smiled ruefully to herself. Daniels had been his usual 'polite' self, answering her enquiries with the finesse of emery paper. 'There is nothing to add to the report previously made,' he had growled like a bear with a boil on its bottom, 'the enquiry will remain ongoing.'

Ongoing! Kate snorted over the notebook she was writing in. What he could have said, had total honesty been in his list of suitable responses to the Press, which it very rarely was, would have been they had no more idea of the cause of the fire which had destroyed that paint factory, or of the identity of the body discovered inside it, than the majority of the staff of that station had of nuclear physics.

Not that you have the faintest notion of any science past the elementary stage, Kate! The pencil and notebook returned to the capacious bag, the smile widened with the self-remonstration. It had been a brief and totally fruitless five minutes spent with Daniels but at least the little she had got would lend credence to the story passed to Scottie.

171

'Guessed I'd find you somewheres.'

'Not much of a guess seeing the size of Dar-laston,' Kate answered the man sliding on to the seat beside her. Hunched inside a jacket which might have been old when Queen Victoria was an infant, Echo Sounder needed to be careful ... the kids could be forgiven for thinking him a replica of Guy Fawkes.

'Ain't got time fer the clever talk!' Echo Sounder edged the words from the corner of a tight mouth.

'Nor for pleasantries.' Kate eased a little further along the bench to put space between herself and the jacket.

'Yoh wanted to know about that which were brought to Bentley 'All...'

'The box?' Instantly interested, Kate's reply was louder than intended.

Unimpressed by the swift 'Shh', Kate watched ferret eyes probe every visible inch of the park. Sounder was following his usual reticent behaviour, hoping pretended caution would add to whatever grubby little deal he had planned ... and the price he would ask!

'You said you knew nothing more ... you had no idea what might have happened to it.' Curbing an interest she knew would cut into her budget, Kate lifted the bag to her shoulder though she had no intention of walking away.

'I also said I ain't got time fer no clever chit chat.'

With no perceptible movement a hand had come to within an inch of Kate's coat, the fingers sliding an envelope beneath the folds.

'Find 'er an' yer'll find that box.'

That was all. 'Find 'er an' yer'll find that box.' The words had sidled from his mouth with a skill a ventriloquist would envy and then he was gone. He should apply to the Tipton Harriers; he was a match for any runner they could put on the track. Kate's glance took in the empty park.

But something had brought his kettle to the boil. The way he had slipped that envelope beneath her coat instead of holding it under her nose while he named his price ... the way he had glanced around the park ... it hadn't been his normal shifty way. Sounder had been scared, really scared!

Trying to keep the transferring of the envelope to her bag as imperceptible as Sounder's placing of it beneath her coat, Kate walked from the park as nonchalantly as the sudden pulsing of her veins would allow. She had been intrigued by the story of that box and its contents. Now she was positively fascinated.

Precious was a first-class photographer. Venetia mentally acknowledged the man's meticulous placing of his models. He was as proficient with the camera as Domino had been. Domino! Her mind flashed a picture of a dark-skinned man, two small white dots marking his forehead. He had been as aptly nicknamed as the man she watched now. Domino had been with her during those years as Nicole Jarreau, but he, like that name, was now part of the past. She had toyed with the idea of employing him as photographer for 'Pascal', then rejected it. There likely would have been no recognition on his part of the woman he had once worked for, but any risk was too great and therefore 'Domino' had been assigned to the ranks of the dispensable.

'Palms to the buttocks, darling, hips forward ... *forward* luvvie, show what's in the lunch box. Oh, that's precious, that's absolutely precious...'

Standing in the shadowed circle cast by the brilliant set lighting, Venetia smiled to herself. Photography was not the only thing this man had in common with Domino; they both had a penchant for men, preferably young and good looking, but more importantly, for 'Precious' at least, a generous endowment in the genital department.

'No, not a smile, that's old hat, too seventies Hollywood! Lose the teeth, luvvie, pull the brows down, threaten, darling, threaten; lean into the camera ... like this.'

She might be watching Domino; he had lost no opportunity to do what Precious was doing now, he missed no chance of hands-on contact. Would one of these 'camera happy' arrangings of a photographic pose one day reward him with a punch in the mouth?

'Which one do you think will get the prize?' At Venetia's shoulder, Francesca Benson's giggle was under tight wraps.

'If you mean a contract with "Pascal", then there are several in the running.' Venetia cast a quick eye over the group of young men she had called for a photo shoot. 'But if the prize you speak of is "Precious" then I would say any one of them is acceptable.'

Watching the photographer tweaking and touching, noticing the embarrassed flinch or encouraging smile with which they were accepted, Francesca touched a finger to brow and breast.

The sign of the Cross! Venetia's veins tightened. The girl followed a religion the same way she did; she honoured her God, but that was all they shared; Francesca Benson worshipped the Christian Christ.

'Mother Benedict would have me say twenty Hail Marys if she knew my feelings at this moment.'

'Oh!' Venetia turned to lead the way out of the studio. 'What are your feelings?'

'I really shouldn't own to them.'

Had watching that photo session awakened something in her secretary? Had sight of those virile, near-naked young men aroused a certain urge?

'Trust me.' She threw a smile as together they entered her office. 'I won't tell a soul; which one was it caught your fancy?'

'Caught my fancy!' Francesca Benson laughed. 'None of them, I merely wanted to giggle, I always feel like giggling watching Precious in action.'

None of them had taken the girl's fancy – could it be her grass was greener in the opposite field? Educated in a convent to the age of seventeen then kept virtually locked away by an ageing grandmother until the old woman had died two years ago, it would hardly be surprising if the thought proved true; but Francesca with another woman! Venetia slipped into the chair drawn to her desk ... what a loss for the male population.

'Publicity sent these up for you to look at.'

Venetia's quick glance took in the photo board set out ready for her inspection. A teenage girl smiled back at her from a series of shots in which she was transformed from a mundane school girl, the various 'Pascal' preparations giving the glowing, happy self-assured look of a young woman finding her beauty for the first time.

'Advertising think maybe this to go with it ... I think it has something.'

The slogan. Venetia looked at a separate, larger photo board slipped over the first. The same radiant smile was softer and in the eyes could be discerned something not present before, a look of ... what?

'It's good, isn't it?'

A few seconds of silence following her secretary's enthusiasm, Venetia shook her head. 'No ... no, it's not good, it's *very* good; Precious certainly knows his trade.'

'But?'

'The slogan.' Venetia read the words a second time. 'Do you long to be beautiful?' She brushed a hand over the vividly painted words as if to wipe them away. 'Every woman, young or old, wants to be beautiful, the whole cosmetics world would collapse if that wasn't so. No, the words don't do justice to what is being said.'

'Being said? I'm not with you.'

'The eyes.' Venetia stared at the board. 'Look at the eyes, what are they saying?'

'Try me?'

'I know a lot of men would take you up on that.' Venetia laughed but it was brief, her concentration returning immediately to the job in hand. 'No, nothing so abrasive; that look is sultry, it draws you to it, the eyes hold secrets age old as woman herself ... they hold hidden promise.'

Grabbing a pencil she slashed a line through the printed words. 'I think this might be better.'

Taking the paper from her, Francesca's nod followed her scanning of the rapidly scrawled words. 'A promise made to you, a promise waiting for you.'

'That's it,' Francesca glanced again at the separate board, 'that is exactly what the eyes are saying, they are giving a promise.'

'And "Promise" is what the line will be called.' Venetia handed the boards to the woman beside her. 'Have advertising get to work on it straight away.'

'Promise.'

Her secretary gone from the room, Venetia glanced at the lush furnishings of her office.

She liked the name, it carried the echo of a different world, a different life, it carried dreams, the wishes of a young girl's heart.

But not only the young. She felt the trip surge along every blood vessel, her heart rise to block her throat. Venetia Pascal was no teenager but she also had been given a promise ... a promise that would make her present lifestyle seem that of a pauper!

Torrey woke, a film of perspiration damp on his upper lip. Something had dragged him from sleep. Lying absolutely still he listened. The flat was silent ... the whole world was silent ... yet

177

something had snatched him awake!

A dream? He couldn't remember having one. A burglar? He was bloody good at it if it was for there was no sound at all.

No sound ... then what was that?

Senses instantly razor sharp he lay motionless. Let whoever had entered his home think him asleep, let him think ... cold and deadly as a cobra, Torrey's smile remained hidden ... think was all the bastard would be able to do for a very long time!

Perhaps it wasn't simply a him, perhaps it was a them! More than one! Beneath the covers his fingers flexed. Good, a little light exercise might help him sleep. It was certainly going to help his nocturnal visitor do that.

Eyelids, the only part of him to move, raised a fraction of an inch. Beyond the bedroom door, which he always left slightly ajar, a flicker of light shone. A torch! His uninvited guest had come prepared. Despite himself the cobra smile surfaced. His mother had taught him always to display politeness to people who called; well, he would show politeness, he would say 'excuse me ...' and then break the bastard's skull!

A few seconds, he would give the intruder a few seconds more, let him – or them – feel at home.

At the other side of the door the light moved in a sweeping arc. Torrey remained unmoving. Burglar or burglars, they were welcome to anything they chose but payment would be made – and payment would be high!

The light had returned. Beneath lids almost closed, he watched the light play at the door. His visitor was wondering had he got the balls to enter; but one thing needed no speculation, that visitor would have no balls when he left!

Time's up! Movement silent as the thought, Torrey rolled from the bed. Agile as a panther, and now the predator, he crossed the room shadow on shadow.

Wait, don't rush your fences, let the enemy come to you.

Tactics learned years before came automatically into practice. Choosing his position to one side of the door he touched his back to the wall. Just supposing whoever was on the other side had heard him move then the door would most probably be smashed open with the hope of flattening him in the process. Shades of the spy who came in from the cold! Torrey's smile died. This bugger was going to be very cold after he came in!

But no one came in.

Eyeballs swivelling to his left Torrey waited.

What the hell was the guy playing at? The light was shining just short of the door; if the one holding the torch was going to come why the hell didn't he do it?

Two seconds ... four. Torrey moved. He'd had enough of pussyfooting; he would teach breaking and entering was not socially acceptable. Oh, he would do it politely, only maybe not in the way his mother had meant. He was going to break a few bones, let daylight into some innards and then ask his visitors – politely – to leave; what Daniels and the Blues made of that he'd worry over when *they* came visiting; right now he had business with a burglar.

Hand reaching for the door he paused. That smell, smoke? It was smoke, the bastards had set fire to his flat!

Fury surged but rationality rode its crest. Yes, it was smoke tickled his nostrils, but what kind of fool stayed on the inside to watch the game through? Yet the beam of that torch said he was still there.

It did not move, not so much as waver. Neither had Torrey's anger, it simply settled in every artery. There would be no questions, no why or wherefore; the bastard who had fired his home would spend the rest of his life in a wheelchair!

Cool and completely in control, dispassion for what he intended to do lending ease to every move, his fingers sought the edge of the door.

Smoke! Nostrils dilated he breathed the acrid stench. Smoke meant fire ... but how bad a fire, and had the culprit left the way he had come?

There was only one way of finding out.

Fingers had reached the door, in the next second torch and bearer would hit the other side of that room. Senses sterile of feeling, mind sharp as a surgeon's scalpel, he threw open the door.

'What in God's name?'

Frozen in mid-air the fist remained a promise.

That light, he stared at the vivid cherry glow, it was no torch, neither was it a fire. It gave off no heat, no crackle of sound, no leap of flame spreading to lick at carpet or furniture, just a cloud, a floor-to-ceiling blaze of scarlet, a pool of fire cold as ice and...!

His intake of breath slicing the silence, his fist

lowered slowly to his side.

...and at its centre a figure... a figure that was watching him.

15

'I know what you think, but I have this feeling of something ... something bad.'

'Mine tastes okay.'

'I'm not talking about egg fried rice!' Kate Mallory's answer was peppered with irritation. Torrey might not have actually ridiculed what she had said but he hadn't been complimentary either; in fact she had the distinct impression he wasn't interested ... and that was on the odd occasion she felt he was listening at all. He had been like this on several of their evenings together, p'raps it was time to bring down the curtain.

'I have copy to write up.' Pushing her plate aside she reached for the bag set beside her feet.

'Copy.' Torrey's half-smile touched cool eyes. 'Since when did finishing a piece come before finishing a meal?'

Hoisting the bag to her shoulder, Kate felt the familiar longing which even weeks after giving up cigarettes still pulled at her from time to time and this was one of those times. A tab had always calmed her nerves or taken the edge from her temper; well, she had no tab to curb her annoyance and she damn well wasn't going to draw a veil over it either! Displeasure added chips of ice to the stinging reply.

'Since the one I share a meal with makes it perfectly clear he would rather be some place else!'

'Kate, that's not true.'

Her smile like the touch of an iceberg, she looked at him. 'Don't ever try lying to make a living. You're not very good at it.'

'Kate, wait!' Dropping a banknote on to the table he followed her from the restaurant. Half-way across the car park he caught her arm. 'I'm sorry. I haven't been the most sociable of company this last week or two but it's not because I'm not interested in what you have to say, and I certainly wouldn't rather be some place else ... unless of course that somewhere else was the Bahamas.'

'Then what is it?' Kate refused to be drawn by the quip or the smile with which it was made. 'You've been acting like one o' clock half struck for the past fortnight. Look!' She turned to face him. 'If it's time to move on then say so.'

'Will you stop that!' Sharper than intended, it brought glances from several people passing in the street. 'Look,' he lowered his voice, 'we can't talk here. What do you say to a drink in the Frying Pan?'

She had said nothing. Kate waited in that same stubborn silence while after collecting drinks from the bar Torrey settled into his seat at their alcove table.

'Kate,' he smiled over his alcohol-free lager, 'about this one o'clock half struck, it's true I've been a bit vague–'

'Vague!' Kate sniffed. 'That is quite the under-statement, I'd say...'

'I was first.'

The smile had become a grin and Kate's umbrage submerged beneath it. 'Right,' she acquiesced, 'but that doesn't say you'll keep the lead.'

The air was cleared but what did he say now? Sorry I wasn't listening to you but I was thinking about a woman sitting in the back of the car, a woman who wasn't there. Christ. Kate would really think him ready for a place somewhere else and the hotel wouldn't be in the Bahamas!

'I was telling you...'

Torrey breathed relief. He need not worry about what to say next, and as for being in the lead, Kate was there already.

'...about Sounder,' Kate went on, 'he came to the park, said he guessed that might be where I could be found.'

'Had you been to see Daniels by any chance?'

Lips pursing Kate nodded. 'I see your point, he must have seen me go into that police station.'

Taking a swallow from his glass, Torrey echoed her nod. 'Our friend Sounder isn't a man to bet on a non-starter. It's likely he saw you before ever you reached Victoria Road, that he followed fully expecting you to take a few minutes in the park; Sounder would know from past experience you would need to blow off steam after a session with Daniels.'

'Trust Echo to come up with a winner.' Kate's lips relaxed. 'But I would hardly call that inter-view a session, I was in and out of his office in less time than it takes to tell; I swear the man has a degree in bad temper.'

'So what did you go to see our friendly Detective Inspector about?'

'Nothing new, p'raps that was his reason for being antisocial, he didn't relish repeating information given already.'

'That being?'

Kate's smile appeared over the rim of her glass. 'That being the paint factory fire along of Station Street. I can't really blame him for being shirty, after all I was using speaking with him as cover for my flouncing out of the office.'

'Scottie?'

Overhead chandeliers spilled light from what Torrey had described as two pearly footballs with a pear hanging between them. Glancing at them now Kate found herself agreeing; but the light they gave was soft and she liked the way it caught the gold fleur-de-lis patterning of the dusky red curtains, tiny gleams dancing like fairy lights when people sitting in the red and emerald upholstered alcoves brushed a shoulder against them.

'No ... well, not altogether.' She brought her glance from the prints of the Edwardian Life hung around the walls. The prints she had noted on her first visit showed no sign of poverty, no sign of the wretchedness of Black Country living so many folk had endured in that era.

'Then what had you doing your prima donna impersonation?'

Bronzed by the room's lighting, sherry curls danced with the quick shift of Kate's head. 'Watch it, bonny lad, you're not over big I canna catch ya a skelp across the lug.'

'Ouch!' Torrey touched a hand to one ear, protecting it from the threatened slap while his eyes reflected the laugh in Kate's. 'Better re-phrase that before I get thumped. It wasn't a rehearsal for a stage appearance and it wasn't the Grand Inquisitor, so what had you walk off the job?'

'I didn't walk off the job, not really. I admit wanting to see Daniels was just a salve to a guilty conscience, but I wasn't skiving.'

That catch of her bottom lip between the teeth, the pause that said, 'I want to tell you but how do I say it', had Torrey wait a moment. Give her time, there was something on her mind but try-ing to rush her into revealing it would only have that something remain there. Kate Mallory had a streak of stubbornness wide as the Tyne and if she felt pushed then it could settle deep as that river.

Picking up his glass he spoke more into than over it; a deceptive ploy he hoped she wouldn't catch on to.

'Sounder followed you into the park. Could only be one reason for that, he had something to sell; so how much did our racetrack fanatic screw you for?'

'He didn't.'

'Good for you!'

'He didn't ask.'

A small frown sitting over a look of disbelief, Torrey set his glass back on the table.

Sounder hadn't asked for money, that was like saying it hadn't snowed at the North Pole, and the little creep was no socialite; he talked to nobody if it could be avoided and never ... *never* unless profit was the basis of every single word. So why the confab in the park ... and why no charge?

'He didn't ask for money,' Kate resumed quietly, not wishing her words to carry to ears other than Torrey's. 'He was nervous, glancing around all the time he was there; it seemed he was afraid he might be watched.'

'That wouldn't be unusual, there are a lot of folk like to keep an eye on Sounder, and acting nervous is his way of driving up the price.'

'I've told you he didn't ask for money!' Shades of returning irritation played over Kate's mouth.

'Then why bother to come looking for you? I tell you, Kate, that scruffy little tout is pulling your string.'

'He asked did I want to know about what was brought to Bentley Hall.'

'Like I said, Sounder is winding you up, get the string tight enough and you'll pay, I've never yet known the man do anything without getting paid for it.'

'So he came looking to get paid,' Kate snapped. 'Then why give me this for nothing?' Taking from her bag the envelope Echo Sounder had given her, she held it a moment before handing it across the table.

'Sounder gave you this!' Torrey opened the envelope and slid out a small piece of card.

'Mmm.' Kate nodded. 'He said find her and I would find the box that disappeared from Bentley Hall. Trouble is I haven't got a clue as to who that girl is or where she is to be found.'

'I've seen her.' Cynicism which had been so obvious now drained instantly, Torrey's next words squeezing between lips suddenly as tight as the fingers gripping the photograph.

Excitement sent a flush to Kate's cheeks. Torrey had seen the girl in that photograph, maybe here in Darlaston!

'Where?' She leaned across the table to share the photograph he still clutched. 'Where did you see her … when?'

What the hell was going on? Torrey stared at the slip of card. It was the same face, the same woman … but where the hell did Sounder fit in?

'I've seen her,' he said this time quieter than before, 'I've seen her several times, I … saw her … last night.'

'Last night?' Kate almost squeaked. 'Where last night?'

Fingers released their hold and returned the photograph to Kate.

'Last night she was with me at the flat.'

She had been with Torrey, they had been together at his flat? They had met several times; more than a friend?

Sharp as winter wind the question cut into Kate. This was the reason for his lack of interest, this was what had been in his mind all the time she had been talking to him! But why had he not mentioned this woman, why the secrecy? Torrey had no cause, it wasn't as if they had anything together, anything more than friendship. Kate Mallory had no claim on him, so why did Kate Mallory suddenly feel part of her world had collapsed?

'It isn't what you think.'

'No need to say any more.' The smile Kate forced was bright as a brass sovereign and just as genuine. 'You don't have to tell me, your life is your own.'

'I'm beginning to wonder just how true that is!' He interrupted sharply, the stool wavering with the abrupt push as he rose to his feet. 'Let's get out of here.'

Sitting in the stationary car Kate felt the tension of the man beside her. Torrey could lose his rag, she had seen it happen on occasions, but that scene in the pub, the way he had stared at that photograph, the hoarseness of his voice when saying he had seen the young woman before ... that had not been the Torrey she knew.

'Kate.' Torrey sucked in air. 'I want you to listen, no matter how it sounds, just listen. That photograph you say Sounder gave you, the woman it shows is dead.'

'Dead! But you said–'

'Kate, please... just listen.'

Listen! Kate's fingers clutched painfully together. How could he ask her to just listen? The woman had been in his bedroom and now she was dead! How could he have known that unless... Eyelids clamping hard down Kate tried to hold back the shiver running the length of her spine as the remainder of the thought pushed its way to the front of her brain. Unless he had killed her!

'I know I said I saw her last night, but I believe she has been dead for some time.'

This was going past the ridiculous! Kate's eyes stayed shut. The woman was with him last night

188

yet she had been dead for some time; that would go down a bomb with Daniels!

Daniels! Eyelids sprang open with the force of a Jack-in-the-box. The police! They were bound to find out. Torrey would be accused of murder!

...dead for some time...

It sang like a dirge in her brain.

Torrey had ... it stopped there, Kate almost sobbing as her brain forced other words.

...I believe...

Fingers twisted tighter but the pain of them made no impression on the wonderful dancing relief surging in her chest.

...I believe...

It could only mean Torrey had not killed that woman. To their left the spire of the church of St Lawrence rose tall against the darkness while across from the car park, their shapes squat in the shadows, the Salvation Army building stood close to that of Darlaston Labour Club. Solid and real, they faced Kate, yet they swirled through the tears pricking her eyes.

'I first saw her when I collected a fare from Harrowby Place.'

Quietly Torrey told of the woman he had been driving to Station Street, of her disappearance from the car and how he thought he had been the one taken for a ride, then of the thin worried-looking woman afraid to leave her home because of vandals, one fare helped into the car yet two faces watching him in the driving mirror.

Hardly breathing lest it halted Torrey mid-stream, Kate listened.

'I thought I was seeing things, too many late-night pick-ups or else alcohol-free beer wasn't so free, but it happened again at Wolverhampton train station and a few nights back she was there after I dropped you at Annie's: each time she made an appearance it was in the car ... until last night.'

Kate heard the breath draw deep into his lungs. She had told Torrey never to attempt to make a living by lying ... he wasn't lying now.

'I woke suddenly,' the explanation went on, 'I don't know what but something had the short hairs standing. I thought it had to be someone who'd broken into the flat. I was ready to take him or them on, when I smelled smoke. I wasn't going to wait for the fry-up but whoever had set that fire was going to be the main course...'

But? Kate's mouth compressed, holding back the question her mind finished, there had to be a 'but'.

'...that in mind I flung open the door,' he breathed, the loudness of it pushing at the silence, 'the sitting room was filled with light; I thought the smell, the glow, to be that of fire but what I saw was no fire, it was just a cloud ... a cloud of vivid red light with a figure standing at its centre. I saw the face clearly ... it was the same one I'd seen in the car ... the face in that photograph.'

Curled into the corner of Annie's comfortable settee, Kate stared at the face smiling up from her lap. Was the young woman in this photograph the same person Torrey had seen in his flat or was it a similarity had him think so? Maybe ... but that was all she was uncertain of; Richard Torrey wasn't given to imagination nor to playing the fool.

'There you go, drink that down, it'll 'elp you sleep.'

She would certainly need something to help her sleep. Kate took the mug of cocoa between her hands. Lord, what wouldn't she give for a tab... just one cigarette!

'Photo come from 'ome, did it?'

'No.' Kate shook her head at the enquiry. 'It was given me today in the park.'

Putting the mug aside, she picked up the photograph. The girl in it seemed fairly young, might even be a school snapshot; certainly it was not yet the face of a fully grown woman... yet the figure Torrey had seen in his flat had not been that of a girl.

'Somebody you knows?'

'I wish I did but truth is I don't, neither does Torrey. I would have asked Sounder but he disappeared before I had chance.'

'Sounder? Be you talking of Leonard Sounder?'

'I don't know his Christian name, I only know him as Echo.'

'Echo.' Annie nodded. 'It were always that, even when 'e were a lad the others called 'im that.'

'You know Echo Sounder?'

'Oh, I knows 'im!' The reply was scathing. 'A black sheep if ever there was one. Do anything to avoid a 'ard day's work. Not like 'is father – God rest 'im – William were honest as the day be long and so was Sarah, but that lad of their'n ain't never been much cop; you'd do better to 'ave no truck wi' Len Sounder.'

Annie knew Echo Sounder! Might she know

the girl in this photograph? It was a long shot, a lot of people lived in Darlaston ... but any shot was better than none.

'Would you know this girl?' Hope springing eternal, Kate handed across the photograph, then felt hope die as her landlady looked but made no reply. It had been too much to expect. Kate took comfort in her cocoa. It was going to be as Torrey predicted, Sounder was playing her like a fish on a hook, arouse enough interest and then–

'You says Len Sounder give you this?' The question carried a note of sharpness and the glance Kate met held no smile.

'Today, in the park.' Kate frowned. 'Annie, is something wrong?'

'What did 'e say, wench? What did that no-good tell you?'' She had never known Annie speak this way, never seen her so agitated. First Echo behaving strangely and now her landlady ... and all because of a snapshot of a girl!

Annie's voice was no longer sharp; it held a new and even more unusual note, that of urgency as she glanced again at the smiling portrait. 'Kate, why has Len Sounder given this to you?'

It would be best to start at the beginning. Cradling her half-empty mug, Kate related her conversations with Sounder finishing with the episode of that morning.

'The box!' Annie stared at the photograph still held in her hand. 'I knowed it ... I knowed no sooner Dora told me of the wench 'aving up and left ... that box...' The photograph fell from her fingers as she raised frightened eyes to Kate. 'The Lord and His holy angels protect us!'

192

16

'Bruce.'

Detective Inspector Bruce Daniels glanced up from files he had no liking for and less liking for having to read.

Sergeant David Farnell stepped inside a room which wouldn't allow the swing of a cat unless you opened the window and slung it out. 'Bruce,' he repeated, 'there's been another fire.'

'So what!' Daniels spit the acid blazing in his gut.

'So I thought you should know.'

'Well, now I know, shut the door on your way out.'

Dyspepsia, or Marjorie ticking him off for walking over her carpet without first changing his shoes for house slippers, or for sitting on her precious cushions? David Farnell felt sympathy; Marjorie *and* a peptic ulcer, Christ, how much could one man stand! But ulcer or not the job must go on.

'Do you want to know where?' He winced, waiting for the blast that would come. He didn't wait long.

'No, I don't want to bloody well know where!' A beige-coloured folder skimmed across the littered desk, several swear words following it on its flight to the floor. 'That's the job of the fire brigade!'

'They are there already, the chief phoned us, said we should send somebody.'

'Then send somebody,' an angry hand swiped at the mass of paper and files spilling a small mountain from the desk, 'send Timmins, Baker or any other of the half-dozen sitting on their arses in the canteen!'

He could have done that. Sergeant Farnell watched the last sheet of paper flutter like a startled ballerina. He would have to if Daniels persisted with his refusal.

'I thought of despatching a constable,' his reply was quiet with no more attempt at humour, 'but the chief fireman suggested a senior police officer.'

Acid burned his chest and throat, as Daniels' reaction favoured an explosion.

'The chief fireman suggested...!' He glared, his voice rising several octaves. 'The chief fireman suggested...! Well, here's *my* suggestion...!'

'Bruce!' Sharp, the hint of 'this isn't for everybody's ears' strongly purveying its message, Sergeant Farnell closed the door before continuing. 'Before you go off half cocked maybe you should hear the rest.'

Another bloody bonfire! The work of kids with nothing to do and less of a brain. So why ask for him, why not a constable?

'We had to hose the fire ... too close to those houses, not to mention the church; having no rain for nigh on a month has the whole area tinder dry.' Removing a white safety helmet emblazoned with the title 'Chief' in bold black lettering, the

194

fire officer wiped a hand across his brow. 'We know you lot don't like anything touched before you've given the scene a thorough going-over but the blaze had to be brought under control.'

He'd take ten to one there would have been nothing to find even if there hadn't been a drop of water played over those sticks. It was a bet even Sounder would lay money on. Daniels glanced at the heap of sodden ash, blackened lengths of part-burned boxes and pallets protruding like limbs struggling to escape. Taking a handkerchief from his pocket he coughed into it. Christ, how did these blokes cope with a mess like this! He coughed again, trying to clear his throat of smoke.

'Your blokes,' he asked through the handkerchief, 'they didn't move anything?'

'Only themselves,' the fireman answered, glancing at the remains of the fire. 'There isn't one of them I would call tickle-stomached, but that...' he returned his glance to Daniels, '...they were only too glad to leave that to your lot; we simply cordoned the area, closed it off with a screen then I phoned your place, that's about it so I'll get off back to the station; you know where I am if you have any questions.'

There would be questions all right but he doubted the answers would be so easy. Daniels picked his way over ground pulped by water and firemen's boots. Kids who had set premature light to a bonfire were hardly likely to come tell him about it. Bloody kids ... a good strong boot up the arse would take the old buck out of 'em...

'Christ! Oh Christ...!'

Walking around the protective screen Daniels felt his stomach come into his throat while at his shoulder the young detective sergeant accompanying him retched.

'Christ!' This time the word was almost a soundless whisper. Daniels looked at the ground just beyond his feet.

'Get back around the other side, take a few deep breaths.'

The detective sergeant trying hard not to spew his guts needed no second bidding.

Young coppers shouldn't have to see scenes like this. Daniels glanced at the younger man, lips clamped tighter than a vice as he whipped beyond the screen. Neither should older coppers but somebody had to do the dirty work and with the Darlaston force that copper was Detective Inspector Bruce Daniels ... or put more accurately, Daniels, the shithole cleaner! He was good at that job, all the gold braid agreed on that point, but when it came to promotion, to the post of Chief, they sang a different tune.

What if he took Marjorie's song and sang it to the braid, opted for retirement on health grounds, who would they send to clean this pile up? Quinto? He couldn't wipe his own arse clean!

'Sorry about that, guv.'

Daniels winced at the term. Like all the sprouts the force recruited these days this one watched too much television.

'Sir will do!' No sooner was the retort past his lips than he regretted it. Bruce Daniels had seen as many Passovers as the Jews in these last twenty-five years but not one was down to the man come to stand beside him and he shouldn't be the one to feel the stick.

'Forget that, lad,' he almost smiled, 'this sort of thing has us all on edge. Get through to the station, tell 'em to get Forensics down here.'

'You reckon it's murder, sir ... guv?'

Where did they get coppers from these days ... the local bloody nursery school? 'Do I think it's murder?' Sympathy that had brought him to the verge of a smile vanished faster than a fiver into Echo Sounder's pocket. 'Well, I don't think that poor sod volunteered, do you?'

Embarrassed, the other man fumbled for the mobile phone in his pocket. It had been a daft question to ask, but then Bruce Daniels could make any question sound daft ... why had *he* pulled today's short straw, why not one of the others?

'Tell 'em we'll need a tent to cover the site an' all,' Daniels added to his first requirement, 'this is gonna take more than a quick once-over.'

A lot more! Listening to his words being repeated into the phone Bruce Daniels looked again at the scene almost touching his boots. Ash, thick and blackened with water, spread along the timbers forming a T-bar, but not so thick they hid what lay beneath.

Vomit thickening his throat, he stared at the remains of the fire, black glistening silver beneath the lingering rain drops of the firemen's hose. Twenty-five years on the force had presented him with some pretty weird sights, but this ... his guts heaved disgust.

Did he reckon it was murder? Christ, what else

did you call a half-cooked body tied hands and feet to a cross!

'Put a red ribbon on a child who has been ill, this will stop the fever returning.'

'Sweep a room after dark, bring sorrow to the heart.'

'If you drop a knife tread on the blade before picking it up or a man you do not like will call.'

Lord, where did people get this rubbish from! Kate Mallory glared at the small mountain of envelopes the morning post had dropped on her desk. How had she let herself in for this?

Myths, Legends and Old Wives' Tales, it was nothing but a space filler, words on pages! Irritation which had been steadily mounting all morning reached saturation level. Scottie wanted a column then let Scottie write a column, she was done with it.

'Kate!'

Already steps away from her desk Kate Mallory halted in mid-stride. Another sermon on the mount! Well, this time she would tell he who was without fault exactly how she felt. Mr David Anscott could take this job and use it as a suppository!

'Kate ... where the hell are you?'

Not where *you* should be! The thought churned rebellion already in Kate's mind, thickening it until it sat like cream on her tongue.

'Ka–'

'What!'

The sharp reply cut the name in half, bringing David Anscott's glance to the figure standing squarely in the doorway of his office. Letters and envelopes screwed to a heap in one hand, mouth trapped in a tight line, brown eyes flashing 'danger do not cross', Kate Mallory's whole frame screamed dissatisfaction. How long before that dissatisfaction carried her off in search of the big time? She had been offered it once, maybe that offer was still on hold. Get pissed off enough and she would take it.

Dropping his pencil on to a desk whose surface had not seen daylight from the day of being installed in the glass box so gloriously and jaundicedly labelled an office, he ran his fingers through prematurely grey hair. Kate Mallory was a good journalist, she had already shown her worth and to lose her would be a blow to the *Star*, but he couldn't create situations, he couldn't call them in off the streets. This was the West Midlands not the East End, one big story in a lifetime was as much as could be hoped for and they had already had that. An international counterfeiting scam! He picked the pencil up again, rolling it between ink-stained fingers. Designed to have the entire Middle East at each other's throats, had it come off it would have made Saddam Hussein's throw look like a game of Ring, a Ring of Roses! And Kate Mallory had picked it up and brought it home. As a man he admired her for her tenacity, as an editor he applauded her judgement while secretly thanking his God for her loyalty ... but how much longer could he keep her writing crap?

Yes, he knew that was the source of the blaze burning in those eyes, the fount of anger holding that mouth, but until something turned up...

'Well!' A missile heralding war, the word shot across the desk.

It was make or break time. David Anscott breathed evenly. Judging by the expression on her face Kate Mallory was ready to wish him au revoir, though possibly in not so polite a term; but then again he could not let her see that her turning her back on the *Star* would have him the slightest bit perturbed.

'This is good, Kate.' He was judging his fences carefully, take one too high and he would be interviewing a replacement journalist and, Christ, good ones didn't often turn up in the Black Country. 'Sales have gone up since we started to run the Old Wives' Tales.' He touched the pencil to the copy sat beside his hand.

'Good!' A second volley hurled across the desk. 'Let's hope it goes on that way.'

'Yes, but for the moment it will need be let lie...' The interruption stalled the barrage, halted the words he knew were poised to follow, *because I've had enough.*

'Had a call come in from Darlaston,' he went on smoothly, ignoring all signs of threatened explosion, 'seems a bonfire has been set alight...'

This was all she needed. Kate's patience twanged. It wanted two days to November Fifth, the traditional time of year for bonfires many of which were set prematurely alight by kids looking for kicks no matter whose fun was spoiled.

'A bonfire has been lit!' Pity I didn't have a tab or we could all have enjoyed the smoke. A sarcasm sandwich Kate chewed hard on every bite.

'I know what you're thinking and yes I know it happens every year but this wee fire has the makings of being different.'

'How different?'

She hadn't thrown the clutch of letters across his desk and followed them up with her resignation. But he hadn't cleared the woods yet! David Anscott read the frustration in the face watching him. Despite herself Kate Mallory was interested. Now was the time to throw his dice.

'It has a police cordon around the site and a certain Inspector growling "keep off". Different enough?'

A bloody barbecue! It had been a bloody barbecue! Some bastards had fastened the poor sod to a stake and roasted him alive. Inspector Bruce Daniels watched the doctor peel off latex gloves.

'Can't be certain at this stage.' Gloves disposed of, the medic picked up a black bag before leaving the tent Daniels had called to be erected. 'But at a guess ... and it is only a guess ... I would say our friend there has been dead ... mmm.'

Our friend. Acid rose in Daniels' throat. Christ, these blokes were cold, but then they had to be to do the sort of job they were called on to perform.

Outside the canvas cover the doctor buttoned his dark jacket. 'I would put it at about ten hours.'

Ten hours! That would be enough time to burn a whole bloody timber yard! But them stakes, they were nowhere near burned through, and the body ... burn that for ten hours and there'd be nothing but a pile of ash to say where it had been!

This was doing wonders for his gut ... a few more sessions like this and *he'd* be the one ready for the slab. Daniels fished in his pocket for the Bi-So-Dol tablets. Marjorie always ensured he had a spare pack; that was one of her finicky ways he *could* be grateful for.

'But you said ten hours.' Daniels walked with the doctor to his car.

'Correct again.'

Tablet on his tongue, Daniels sucked hard but there was no relief for the blaze in his throat. 'Then if the man's body burned for ten hours...'

'I did not say the body burned for ten hours, Inspector.' Easing himself into his car the doctor rested both hands on the steering wheel, his tone disparaging as he added, 'Nor did I say the victim was a man. I believe that I said the *body* had been dead some ten hours, not that it had burned for that length of time; really, it would save a great deal of both your and my time if you listened to what is being said to you and especially to what I say to you now: you should have a doctor look at you or it might well be *your* stomach I'll be poking into next. Good day, Inspector.'

Smart arse! Daniels watched the car drive away. But he was right about consulting a doctor, this burning in his gut got no better. 'You'll be sorry when it kills you!' Marjorie's words. He sucked harder on the tablet. But would he? Could be he'd get promotion in the next world for it seemed a red-hot certainty he wouldn't get it in this.

'They want to know if you're finished here, guv.'

'What? Oh, yes. Tell 'em to bag up, get the remains to the mortuary and, Williams...'

'Guv?'

'You wait here, make sure they do things carefully; if we wanted the job shovelled up we could have it done by a couple of navvies.'

There had been no need to leave the man behind, the others knew what they were doing... or at least enough to know Detective Inspector Bruce Daniels would have their balls for breakfast should they cock anything up. Switching on the ignition he frowned as the engine coughed. Mebbe he should take retirement after all, buy himself a new car with the payout; mebbe ... but first there was a murder to be solved.

17

The idea had been his...

Sitting at her desk, expensive double glazing masking the sounds of traffic jostling for supremacy on the busy city streets, Venetia Pascal stared at the papers spread in front of her.

Theo Vail had given the ordering of it, his had been the decision.

Exquisite lips touched with the merest trace of lipstick drew into a faint smile.

'*I am Magus...*'

The words sounded in her mind while inner eyes watched the arrogant features, the brilliance of ice-grey eyes sweeping the assembled worshippers.

'*High in the service of the Dark Lord, to him have*

I made sacrifice. He has been given the soul, fire will devour the body and we his followers shall be blessed with his favour and protection.'

Favour? Yes. Protection? That also, but only up to a point! The mental picture faded but Venetia Pascal's smile remained. The Prince of the Earth, that greatest of Beings whom they served, rewarded with favour those who pleased; and those who displeased? The instruction Vail had given, having the body of the girl sacrificed on that altar tied to a cross, the whole replacing the Guy Fawkes set atop a bonfire. Should it be discovered before the fire was lit, should it not burn away completely, what then? Would the Master give protection – or had the point of rejection been reached?

It was taking too much of a chance. The smile leaving her mouth, Venetia breathed through nostrils sharply flared with anger. She had tried to tell Vail so, to caution him of the risk he was taking, the risk to the entire coven ... and what had been *her* reward? Contempt cold and deliberate, a sneer no attempt had been made to disguise: Vail had turned icebound eyes towards her and for fully a minute had made no answer, allowing the crash of silence to echo about that black-draped room. She had felt the steel-tight tension, the fear yet at the same time the excitement of the Followers, excitement of seeing the envoy of the Master return to collect one more soul, the soul of Venetia Pascal!

But Belial had not been recalled. Vail had not repeated the ceremony that had brought that messenger from the regions of hell. Instead Vail had laughed, a short hard snigger of total disdain.

'*I am Magus!*'

The repeated words had been a trumpet voluntary, a paean of self-pride. But pride went before a fall and should that body be found before flame could do its work then maybe Theo Vail could find himself falling into a very deep pit indeed. The Master did not look with patience upon mistakes ... and placing that body on a bonfire had, she felt instinctively, been a mistake.

And if the body were discovered ... traced back?

A stab of alarm released the anger.

The girl had been one of the dozens who had applied for an interview, one of the young hopefuls praying they be chosen to present the new line of cosmetics to the public, and she had been one of those politely rejected, presented with a complimentary gift of a box of the, as yet, unmarketed products, then sent home.

A few photographs taken by 'Precious' had been all she, Venetia Pascal, had seen of the applicant; she had not even spoken with the girl.

The thought brought relief to the tension which had gripped her and she slowly eased breath between parted lips.

She had not spoken with the girl, not during or immediately following that photo shoot. That could be attested by her secretary, it was Francesca who had overseen that part of the business; but Francesca had not been party to what had followed.

Breathing normally now, perfectly manicured hands held papers steady though attention played in an area totally divorced of them.

She had stayed over at the office. Telling Francesca there were a few things she wished to catch up on, she had refused her secretary's offer to stay on to help. But she had wanted no help nor had she wanted any witness to what she had in mind.

It had been discreetly done.

Venetia smiled to herself. More discreet than the subsequent actions of Theo Vail.

Alone in the building except for office cleaners and night security staff, she had taken the sheaf of photographs from a filing cabinet and leafed quickly through them until she found what she was looking for. She had paused then, almost afraid the eyes had played tricks that first time of looking, that she had imagined something that was not really there at all.

But she had to be sure. She had twisted the desk-top lamp, angling it so the beam fell full on that young face.

Pretty, holding all the potential of true beauty, it had smiled up at her. Francesca was no fool. Venetia remembered the thoughts which had filled her mind while staring at the photograph. Her secretary must have realised the potential of this particular applicant, must have recognised the girl was the epitome of all the new line advocated, wondered at the reason for rejection of a girl whose face was perfect for launching the campaign.

But the face had not been the reason Venetia Pascal had stayed behind one evening in her office. Yes, it was ideal for launching 'Promise'.

She had held the photograph nearer the source of light but it had not been the face she had smiled back at.

There had been no comment passed on the rejection. Francesca, as with all other employees of 'Pascal', did not question the decisions of the boss. She had simply placed the photograph with others to await the ultimate selection of a winner before being discarded finally.

The particulars of each applicant had been carefully recorded and kept along with the relevant photograph. Name, address, telephone number, they had all been there and she had made a note of them before feeding the rest through the paper shredder.

No one else would see what she had seen.

'I've told you once, do I have to bloody well write it down for you?'

Sergeant Dave Farnell winced at the words no closed door could silence. Daniels was having a rough day with his stomach and his visitor would no doubt suffer an equally rough ten minutes – should the interview last that long.

'There be nothing more to add.'

Except an ear-bashing for himself once that woman was gone. Reaching his desk, Sergeant Farnell shook his head before picking up a file. It might be undeserved but that would make no difference; it would still be dished out. Inspector Bruce Daniels was a bloody good copper but that being said he had no time for the press ... and would have little thanks for a sergeant who let a reporter past the front desk.

'Can you say if the incident you are currently investigating is in any way connected to the fire which destroyed the paint factory in Station Street a week or so back?'

Would he explode, burst like a pricked balloon? Sitting in the small room which served Daniels as an office, Kate Mallory watched the battle between acid and anger. Whichever became the victor it would not be to her advantage, Daniels would still have her chucked out. She had known the reception she could expect but Scottie's Will Be Done!

Shifting a tablet from one side of his mouth to the other, Bruce Daniels glared at the girl standing on the opposite side of a room that would cause a mouse to suffer from claustrophobia. Reporters! They were all cast from the same mould. Hear a word, one bloody word, and they swarmed like rats nibbling and scratching until they got a story; well, this reporter needn't sharpen her pencil!

'I can say what I've already said,' he growled, 'that pending the outcome of a full investigation no connection with or to any other incident can be made.'

'But you do connect it with the other acts of vandalism, the school set ablaze three months ago?'

'I don't connect it with other incidents, and that includes school, factory, kids' bonfire or a match lighting a bloody cigarette. Now if that ain't clear enough for you I'll have it printed out so you can hang it over that desk you should be sitting at instead of being here making a nuisance of yourself!'

Kate's most syrupy smile met the tirade, 'I just thought ... it is my job to enquire, to inform the public.'

'And it's part of my job to see the public isn't fed what hasn't been said. *There can be no positive statement at this time*, that is what you've heard and that you can print! Now before you leave there is one more thing you should hear and I advise you listen careful like ... there are several cells in this station can accommodate you for wasting police time and I won't need more than one of the twenty-four hours I can legally hold you for to think up something that will see you banged up for a month or two. You just ask Echo Sounder if you have any doubts on that one!'

He hadn't exploded or burst, but he had come within inches of it. Kate settled on her usual bench in Victoria Park. Was that disappointment niggling inside?

Despite her none-too-gentle dismissal from the office of Darlaston's irascible detective inspector, Kate Mallory smiled to herself. His 'push off' had been just hard enough to have those inbuilt signals in her brain flash 'go'. There was more to that bonfire episode than its simply being set alight by hooligans days before it was due to be lit ... more than Daniels was willing to divulge. It would serve no end asking him for any more; in any case she could not be certain the threat he had just issued was an empty one. Detective Inspector Bruce Daniels was not the easiest person to question; he could be sour without the help of an acid stomach!

'*...no connection with or to any other incident.*'

From a bush at the farther side of a flower-edged expanse of grass a yellow-breasted tit swooped after an exact copy of itself.

'*...no connection...*'

Kate watched the birds quarrel, wings beating furiously as they each claimed best spot on a branch.

Maybe Daniels truly believed that but she did not. She had felt the tingle in that office, the feeling that told her there was more in the pot than had come out of it!

Lifting her bag to her shoulder Kate got to her feet.

Daniels was hiding something, why else would he come the heavy hand? Maybe she should wait ... let the police finish their enquiry then take what she was given as to the cause of that second fire, but then had her mother not always said her daughter had a nose keener than that of a bloodhound? That nose was twitching now.

Shoulders drawn forward, head dropped low onto his chest, Echo Sounder stared at the glass held between his hands. The television mounted on the wall of the public house was for once being ignored. That feeling in his gut, that something which said one horse was a winner while another was not; that tightening of the bowels telling him which dog would be first to the rabbit. It had never led him wrong. But this time...!

Across from him a field of horses raced across the television screen, the excited babble of the commentator keeping rapid pace with them.

This time it had to be wrong! Yet it had been with him for days, sitting hard in the pit of his stomach, refusing to be shifted; and at night ... at night it was worse; with no racetrack open and no dog or horse races on television the night hours left his mind open to the thoughts which he could not prevent coming or then dismiss. They wormed their way into his brain, wriggling in his mind until it was filled with them.

'...and it's Poacher's Lad leading by a head, it's Poacher's Lad...'

The rising note of the voice from the television transmitted the fever of the race.

He had been to see Dora, asked had there been word from the wench and though the woman had tried to hide it he had seen the worry in her eyes, heard the fear tremble each time she spoke. Yet for all that she had remained convinced her daughter would come back, that she had simply gone away for a week or two, '...see what the rest o' the world be offerin'... 'Er thinks it to be more'n 'er'll get from Darlaston.'

The words repeating in his mind made his stomach lurch like when he rode the Big Dipper he had been taken to as a child on a day trip to Blackpool, and the resulting sickness rose to his throat as it had then.

'...more'n 'er'll get from Darlaston.'

Those were the key words, those that had his gut twist and heave, they that returned again and again as if trying to tell him something. But what? What was it about them, more than anything else Dora had said, that drummed persistently in his brain?

211

'...there's a challenge coming up on the inside, it's Amber Beauty coming fast...'

The television blared but Echo Sounder's head did not lift.

He did not need to ask himself that question; he knew the answer, it had been the one given him years ago. He had loved Dora Wilkes' daughter from her being a girl at school, had waited for her to grow to a young woman, seeing the eight years of difference in their ages being no objection to his asking her to marry him. But she had refused, she wanted no life in a run-down little town, she would see what the world had to offer.

And what had it offered her?

'...can Poacher's Lad fight off the challenge? Can he keep the lead? No ... no it's Amber Beauty ... Amber Beauty wins by a nose!'

Oblivious to the noise around him, Echo Sounder tightened his fingers painfully about the empty glass.

Had she found what she hoped for, had the world beyond Darlaston lived up to her dreams? Or had it ended them?

Low in his stomach his innards knotted. The signal he knew so well. It had never let him down. Pray God it was letting him down now.

18

'It is extremely generous, the PM was most impressed, a shipment of such an amount will certainly make the rest of the UN sit up and take notice.' Near enough six foot in height with a frame an athlete could well envy, Zachary St John Winter ran a glance around the huge well-stocked warehouse, then turned to the man standing beside him. 'You are sure of your figures?' The well-modulated voice became edged with concern. 'I have already conveyed to the PM those you stated, he would not be overly pleased to hear differently now.'

Nor would he be overly pleased to hear of the 'purchase' you made at that jewellery launch! Theo Vail kept the thought to himself, answering instead, 'What was promised will be given. You have no need of concern, what you see here is merely a fraction of the total consignment; of course should the PM wish to see for himself...'

'That will not be necessary!'

Abrupt and defensive, the words brought an inner smile to Theo Vail. St John Winter's autocratic manner was still there, the ways of old money evident in speech; but the money was gone, only a position in the government and the perks it brought were left. That must be protected and to guard it well it was best the PM thought that all of this, the largest gift of foodstuffs yet to be donated to the third world, had been brought about solely due to the initiative of Winter himself.

'I will be seeing the PM this evening at number ten and of course I will pass on to him your invitation to see for himself should he so wish.'

Smooth as the balls on his grandfather's coronet! The smile now allowed to show on Theo Vail's handsome mouth revealed none of the cynicism giving rise to it. Zachary St John Winter would climb on any man's shoulders to reach the top then kick him away once he got there. But there would be no kicking away of Theo Vail, the only fall to take place would be that of Her Majesty's government ... thanks to its Foreign Secretary.

'About transport!' St John Winter blinked against the strong sunlight as they emerged from the warehouse. 'I can request the RAF do the honours.'

As they had today no doubt! Vail glanced at the waiting helicopter, its rotor blades gleaming silver. Being a Minister of the Crown had its advantages.

'I had thought of that.' He smiled again. 'The cost to the public purse would be quite significant, almost what the government would have had to spend had they bought the foodstuffs; having the RAF deliver it is to halve the gain.'

A gleam of sunshine caught the calculation evident in dark brown eyes. Half the gain would bring half the PM's gratitude! Zachary St John Winter was sniffing the bait; flavour it a little more and he would swallow it.

'If I might make a suggestion.' Nearing the

waiting helicopter Theo halted. His next words must be heard by none but Winter.

'Suggestion?' The visit to the Midlands had already palled; the fact that the Foreign Secretary was more than anxious to leave was apparent in his tone.

Making no effort to walk on, Vail refused to let the other man's obvious disinterest put him off. Injecting a note of deference into his voice he said, 'It is merely a suggestion, one you may not think worth mentioning to the PM.'

'I can hardly mention it unless I hear it!'

Let him have his head, let his irritation with those not of his aristocratic class show. Theo Vail swallowed the burn of anger beginning to flare in his chest. The man could claim breeding but could he claim common sense? So far the answer was in the negative, he had not seen the line thrown out by Venetia Pascal, did not recognise the hook which dangled from it, the hook which if taken would drag him and the government down. The final bit of bait, the final lure, must be offered carefully.

'Of course,' he went on quietly, 'the decision must rest with you, I can only make the offer.'

Offer! Vail almost laughed. The word was like a magnet to the man.

'It is simply this. Fenton Mercantile is a subsidiary of the Vail Corporation, it has land, sea and air transport, any of which can be placed at the government's disposal for the delivering of the materials donated by the Corporation.'

He had taken the bait! Watching the aircraft rise

215

into the sunlight Theo Vail congratulated himself. The work of the Master had taken one more step forward. The Prince of Darkness would reward his servant. The helicopter was now a speck in the distance. Theo felt satisfaction course through him. On the night of the Great Sabbat, that most holy of holy nights in the Dark calendar, Theo Vail would become Ipsissimus, High Servant of the Lord of Ten Wisdoms.

Adrian Conway walked slowly along the tastefully decorated corridor of Fairview Hospice, one hand clutched too tightly about a bunch of deep-red roses. The management tried to keep the place welcoming by the use of light delicate shades of paint and framed prints; the nursing staff were of the finest and their care of patients beyond question, but not even their devotion could save those condemned by illness that no medicine could yet cure, those dying as Neal was dying.

There was no real hope ... it was just a matter of time. The pain he had felt on hearing that diagnosis lanced afresh, a searing red-hot stab of agony striking to his very soul.

Neal had taken it calmly. That had been the really strange part. He had not seemed to wonder why, on being pronounced perfectly healthy at the half-yearly medical examination all the laboratory staff were required to take, only a couple of months later he had been found to have so terrible an illness. It had been almost as if Neal had expected it. And time had proved that to be so. Neal had not spoken until yesterday. Even then he had not meant to, only the ramblings of his disturbed sleep revealing what had occurred one evening in the lab, how vanity turned to spite, spite which had resulted in an unknown and terminal illness. Raw with the memory, Adrian Conway sank into one of several comfortably upholstered seats set at intervals in the wide airy corridor.

They had tried to carry on as before, to live life as though nothing had changed, each trying to shield the other from the horror of the inevitable. And now that inevitable was so very near. Tears blurring his vision, he looked at the flowers his nerveless fingers had allowed to fall to the floor. How would he live without Neal? How to go on without his only love?

'By remembering that love.' Neal's deep blue eyes had smiled when he had said that. 'By remembering what we had together, what we were to each other.'

How could he not remember? How to forget when what they had was constantly in his mind? But he would not allow himself to forget, not before a debt had been repaid.

'Mr Conway?'

A hand pressed firmly to his shoulder made Adrian look up. Beside him the sister in charge of the ward Neal was in was not wearing her usual smile.

'Mr Conway, I think perhaps you should come into the ward.'

'Neal, has he...? He isn't...?'

'No, Mr Conway, he is not.' Understanding filling her kind eyes, the woman refrained from using the word time would soon force her to speak. 'Mr Brady asked me to come to see whether or not you had arrived. I told him you would come, that you never missed an evening but he would have none of it ... I must do as he asked.'

'He ... he isn't any worse, is he?'

'A little tired.' She picked up the flowers and handed them to the man unable to hide his fears; the emotions she saw were tearing him apart. Walking beside him into the ward she forgave herself for not answering with the whole truth. Neal Brady was tired, too tired to fight any more.

'Adrian.' Neal Brady's head sank back against the pillow, his face drawn, his skin paled almost to transparency. 'Adrian, listen to me, you...' he paused, a laboured breath rattling in his chest, 'you must listen! The medics have increased the level of morphine ... no, don't interrupt, we have both been in the business long enough to know what that means, so I have to say what I must while chance permits. What I told you...' he paused again, vein-threaded eyelids closing a moment their lifting it seemed only with massive effort, '...what I said happened in the lab, you ... you must put it out of your mind, leave it in the past.'

A hand showing bones clear beneath parchment skin reached to another resting limply on the bed and closed weakly over it. 'Adrian,' it was no more than a whisper, a rustle of breath among dried leaves, 'Adrian, there is nothing you can do, nothing anyone can do. I ... I want you to promise you will leave that laboratory, find employment elsewhere, another ... another town, another country, only leave, Adrian ... please!'

The eyes had closed and this time they did not lift. Adrian Conway stared at the wasted figure of the man he loved so passionately. The drug-induced sleep that had claimed him before any promise could be given would not release him for hours. There would be no chance of saying what he had wanted so much to tell him, but the flowers ... he glanced at them now stood in a clear glass vase ... red roses, they would tell Neal Brady all that needed to be said.

The victim had been murdered. Standing in the mouse-hole that was his office, Detective Inspector Bruce Daniels almost allowed his mouth to smile. He had snapped at that young copper for asking had murder been responsible for that body found fastened to a cross ... now who was the smart arse? Whoever it was who had been 'crucified' hadn't begged for the privilege, but then it was safe to say the wench hadn't begged to be stabbed neither. He had read the pathologist's report. Staring through the window he looked over the postage-stamp yard, its several police vehicles lined up as in a parade, then lifted his gaze to take in the rooftops, a scene he had known for twenty-five years. Everything was the same. Across the street, so close he could spit the distance, was the park he had played in as a lad, everything was as it had always been.

But it wasn't! Teeth clenching 'til they hurt he turned back to the desk, his stare fixing on a blue folder lying open on a pile of others. Nothing was the same, the world had changed, and the

219

people...? Christ, what had happened to the people?

'Doesn't make good reading, eh, Bruce?'

'Well, I wouldn't give it to Marjorie to read in bed,' Daniels answered the man who had just entered the office. 'Christ, Dave, what drives folk to do a thing like this?'

'Who knows!' Sergeant Dave Farnell shrugged his shoulders. 'Some medics say they are sick in the mind and therefore not responsible for their actions, other folk put it down to drugs, kids get so stoned they don't care what they do so long as it gives them a buzz.'

'And you, Dave? Do you think it's kids be behind this?' Daniels nodded in the direction of the open file.

Dave Farnell's usual smile had not appeared once since entering the tight room nor did it break now. 'You want the truth, Bruce?' he asked quietly. 'You want to know what I really think of all this?'

'I could do with a bit of input.'

'No guarantee you'll like it.'

'Hmm.' Daniels blew through teeth still aching from the tension of moments ago. 'Since when did our bloody job come with guarantees!'

'Well, first off I don't think it was kids, they pull some tricks but this ain't one of 'em; sure they deal in arson but their bag is settin' fire to buildings, schools and the like, and yes even that bonfire ... but I don't hold the idea they put a body on top for a Guy Fawkes.'

'An organisation?' The back of Daniels' throat began to burn but he didn't reach into his pocket for the tablets he carried wherever he went.

For several seconds Dave Farnell made no reply. Bruce Daniels was a good friend, one he did not want to appear to be taking a rise out of.

'Is that what you think?' Daniels spoke again. 'This is the handiwork of an organisation?'

They had served together a long time. Daniels must surely know he would never take the piss.

'Not the sort you might be thinking of,' he said, a wry smile paving the way of apology for what was to come next, 'that murder wasn't the work of the local mafia, it don't carry their trademark, a shattered kneecap, a bullet through the head, a quick clean in and out job that's their line, but what turned up on that bonfire ... that wasn't quick and it certainly wasn't clean. Judging on what is there in that report I'd be more like to say that body on the cross was a ritual killing ... a sacrifice.'

'Ah, Daniels! A word if you please.'

I don't bloody please! Bruce Daniels felt the acid surge higher in his throat. This was all he needed, Quinto putting his oar in.

'Will you be wanting DS Williams?'

Christ, not him *and* Quinto! Daniels shook his head as Dave Farnell made to leave. 'No ... no, better have one of the women come along.'

'Right. I'll have WPC Rogers stand by, just say when you're ready.'

He was ready right now! Daniels wanted to call the words after the rapidly retreating sergeant. Five minutes with plum-in-the-mouth Chief Inspector bloody Quinto and there would be one more murder on the books and that one would need no spade work to find out who had done it!

'About this body on a bonfire ... nasty business ... any results yet?' Quinto glanced at the untidy desk, one eyebrow rising.

'Not yet, sir.' Daniels reached into his pocket, suddenly aware of his own small bonfire smouldering in his throat.

'What do you mean, not yet! You have received the report from the pathology bods, that must have given you some idea.'

A tablet extricated from a nearly full carton, Daniels slipped it into his mouth. Oh, he had ideas all right, such as shoving that desk phone so far up this man's arse it would fill the space where a brain should be.

The thought still a pleasure in his mind, he returned the blue and yellow flatpack of Bi-So-Dol to his pocket. 'The report arrived this morning.'

Martin Quinto's expression spoke volumes all easily read by Daniels. There was no love lost between them. Was it all down to Quinto having been promoted over him? Or was it simply the man was an arsehole at the job? Rolling the tablet on his tongue, Daniels knew he had decided on the second reason minutes after the new Detective Chief Inspector had arrived at Victoria Road.

'And!' Above his ultra-white collar the Chief Inspector's face took on a dull shade of red.

Innocence a total fabrication, Daniels' brow quirked. 'And what, sir?'

'Don't try any smart arse games with me, Daniels.' Quinto's hand came down on the desk.

'I know them all!'

The arse games, yes you probably have a whole bloody compendium of them, you've climbed up more than a few. Daniels swallowed hard but the acid in his throat revived by contempt refused to be quenched. Those were games his commanding officer knew well, games practised regularly on the golf course and if the grapevine were anything to go by then the oh-so-cultured Quinto's handicap matched the one he had in solving crime; he was as crap at one as he was crap at the other.

'So,' Quinto continued, 'the report arrived this morning. What have you done?'

This could get interesting! Apoplexy for Quinto or an appearance before a Police Enquiry Board for a certain Detective Inspector? His tone as bland as his glance, Daniels answered, 'I've read it ... sir.'

It would have been worth being hauled up for insubordination. As he crossed the yard towards his car, Daniels' smile came dangerously close to his mouth. Quinto's face had flushed to a decidedly unhealthy glow contrasting sharply against cosmetically whitened teeth until it seemed he must lose a diligently practised control.

'*Good.*' It had been strained, swallowed and regurgitated until it came out like syrup. '*Well, keep me informed as to further progress ... and, Daniels, remember our motto quick and clean. I want nothing the Press can have a birthday with ... clean is the way I like things ... you understand, Daniels, clean!*'

Bruce Daniels eased his frame into his car. He

could have taken what he'd heard nicknamed a wedge of gorgonzola; the term was apt, the squad car colours of yellow and blue did look like mouldy cheese, and the extra elbow room they allowed would have been welcome, but then again it made for recognition and that wasn't always to the good. If the local talent spotted one of those they did a disappearing act that would leave David Copperfield looking like a total amateur.

'Clean...' The words echoed in his mind. 'Clean is the way I like things...'

Daniels turned the ignition key savagely. Quinto was an expert in covering his own back, at making quite sure that whatever the investigation or their results he would come out smelling of roses.

Quinto! Accelerator pedal kicked hard, the small car lurched, protesting at the abuse. Quinto! Daniels' teeth clamped. The man was so bloody clean even his shit didn't stink. Driving the Ford past PictureDrome Way then turning right to cross the Bull Stake and on along Pinfold Street, Daniels relaxed his jaw to give way to an inward smile.

That 'innocent' reply, 'I've read it ... sir', had been like driving a ball straight down the fairway to score a hole in one. Not that he knew anything about golf except the odd times he caught ten minutes or so of a televised match ... and those had been few and far between, what with Marjorie dusting the screen, tutting at him to move his hand, lift his feet. It was a sure cert the job Saint Peter would find for her once she got to heaven. Char lady to the Top Office ... that would be Marjorie's Paradise. And his? No sense in deciding that, Bruce Daniels was destined for hotter climes!

'You've lived in this town most of your life so they say at the station.'

'They say right.' His thoughts interrupted, Daniels glanced briefly at the woman police constable sitting in the front passenger seat. How old was she, twenty-five ... twenty-six?

'Then you probably know most of the people.'

'There are a good few folk living in Darlaston,' he returned his eyes to the road, 'but, yes, you could say I know a fair number.'

There was something else she wanted to ask, another question in her mind; the fidgeting with the cap held on her lap was a dead giveaway. Turning the car on to Wolverhampton Street Daniels waited for it to come.

'Sir...'

There had been a pause, a pause long enough to set him doubting he had been correct in his thinking but now he knew he hadn't.

'Sir,' the woman beside him lifted the cap then set it down again nerves wedging it firmly on her lap. 'Do you ... do you know the woman we are going to see now?'

One more turn bringing the car on to Lowe Avenue, Bruce Daniels looked at the neat windows, the well-polished door of the house in front of which he came to a halt.

Yes. He felt the push of sympathy against his chest.

Yes, he knew the woman living here.

19

Of all the people in the town, Dora had asked him to accompany her, to go with her to the mortuary, asked him to be with her when identifying the woman the cops had thought might be her daughter.

Why him? What had God got against him that He gave such a sentence? God! Echo Sounder stared at the drink he hadn't touched. There was no God, how could there be when things like this happened?

The blues had picked him up in the betting shop; said that Dora Wilkes had asked for him to go to Lowe Avenue. But they hadn't said what for. Christ, they hadn't said what for!

He had refused, thinking it was their way of getting him out of the betting shop without causing a rumpus, that once outside he would be taken in for something he hadn't done; but when they had turned to leave, when they hadn't come the heavy he had wondered. In the end he had gone with them.

Dora had clutched his hands all during that car ride and the trembling of her body had echoed through his own. But he was worrying over nothing ... the blues never got anything right and they hadn't this time, the body in the mortuary wouldn't be Sheryl's.

There had been only one flaw in his thinking.

The police had got it right and the body – the body with a face ruined by fire – the body *had* been that of Sheryl.

He had felt Dora slump against him, felt the weight lift as a policewoman led her away from that glass-sided dais; but he had not heard her cries nor the voice of Daniels saying quietly that he should leave, not felt the touch against his arm reinforcing the advice; all he had heard, all he had felt, was the silence in his head, the screaming, isolating, deafening silence of loss.

The one woman he had loved, the woman he had loved since childhood, she was gone. Sheryl was gone!

Somebody had murdered her, stabbed her through the heart then tried to burn her. But who ... and why?

There were people who had the answers. Echo Sounder's hands gripped the glass so hard that the blood had drained from his fingers; they stood out white against the dark brown of the untouched beer. Someone knew why and they knew who and Echo Sounder too would find out and when he did ... when he did they would scream a long time before they burned!

Immaculate grey suit partially hidden beneath a white lab coat, Theo Vail glanced at the varied array of test tubes and equipment set out on a stainless-steel table that ran the entire length of one wall of the sizeable room. Setting up this laboratory, keeping it separate from any other chemical process the Corporation was involved in, had been a not inconsiderable undertaking but the reward when the work was finished would be inestimable.

'The full amount.' He glanced at the rather slight figure stood beside him. 'I hope I made myself clear on that, Conway, I do not accept any half-measures.'

'There will be no half-measures, I do not make mistakes.'

Had there been a slight emphasis on the 'I'? Theo Vail's eyes narrowed imperceptibly. Conway was a good scientist but he was not irreplaceable and the man knew that. What he did not know was that once his present task was accomplished he would be needing no other employment – for Adrian Conway would be dead.

'Then the client can expect delivery on the agreed date, which means the consignment being ready for despatch the first week of October. And on the subject of despatch, I want no one but you involved in the packing and labelling. The customer insists on absolute security, therefore the fewer people who know what is being made here the less chance there is of ... shall we say ... industrial espionage. I'm sorry that requirement meant we could not replace your colleague. By the way, how is Mr Brady? Recovering I hope. Please give him my regards the next time you see him.'

'Eh, I tell you, wench, poor Dora be beside 'erself, I popped in on me way to Bingo. Well, I couldn't go after seein' the state Dora were in.'

Annie had not played Bingo! She had missed her treasured weekly afternoon at the Monday and Tuesday club held at the Leys Hall on St Lawrence Way. The next earth-shattering news must surely be, 'Heaven is pleased to announce the Second Coming.'

Kate Mallory stabbed irritably at the note pad lying on her knee. Even that wouldn't satisfy Scottie. *'You shouldna let him chase you.'* That had been his reply on hearing she had virtually been the recipient of the bums' rush from the police station. But then David Anscott was like so many other folk she had met, full of advice on how to do something they had never tried themselves; well, next time let the clever little Scot do his own enquiring!

'I said as 'ow I would call in again after I'd seen to you 'avin' your tea, p'raps I'll stay the night, that be if'n you don't mind bein' in the 'ouse on your own. Do you mind, wench?'

'What sorry, what was that?'

The slightly louder pitch of Annie's last sentence made Kate look up. A blue 'halo' hat straight out of the 'Forties' half perched on her head her landlady was watching her with an enquiring look.

'I was sayin' would you be objectional to bein' on your own all night?'

'No.' Kate tried not to smile at the woman's misuse of language. 'No, I have no objection. Are you having a clandestine meeting somewhere exotic?'

'A what meetin'?' Hat secured to hair recently rescued from steel curling pins Annie's look of enquiry became one of bewilderment.

'A secret rendezvous, a stolen night with a

229

passionate admirer, making love under the stars.'

'Eh, the things you young 'uns do say!' Annie laughed. 'The only time I'll get to see love under the stars will be on that.' She nodded towards the wide-screen television which had been a Christmas gift from Richard Torrey and was her pride and delight. 'Though that there cland … cland … that what you just said … I wouldn't go turnin' me nose up should chance present itself.'

'Why, Annie Price … you flighty piece!' Kate laughed.

Concerned that the cement-tight curls might have been disturbed by the merriment, Annie touched a hand to the hair showing beneath her blue 'halo'.

'Ar, Kate,' she said as her hand lowered, 'jokin' aside, I says that from now on I teks any pleasure life might offer and enjoy it afore life be snatched away as it be snatched from that wench.'

'Wench?'

'You knows.' Annie reached for the coat she had laid ready across a chair. 'Ain't I just been tellin' you 'ow Dora be beside 'erself? That girl of her'n was the light of her life and now that light be gone out; meks me wonder at 'ow folk can be so wicked.'

What had she missed? Too wrapped up in your own grievances, Kate Mallory! Kate reproached herself silently. The woman Annie referred to could only be the Dora Wilkes she had interviewed in regard to old wives' tales, and her daughter, the girl Annie said had 'up and left', the girl in the snapshot Echo Sounder had given her in Victoria Park. Was she the one whose life had been snatched away?

'You be sure you don't mind my leavin' you, I'll come back if you wants me to, like as not Len Sounder will spend the night at Dora's if 'e be asked, though if it were meself doing the askin' I'd want 'im fumigated first.'

Echo Sounder! Kate murmured the name into the silence left by the landlady's departure. That name kept cropping up. He had known Dora Wilkes ... known of the affair of Bentley Hall ... and he had given her that snapshot of a girl! But where exactly did Sounder fit into this latest happening?

'*...Find 'er and you'll find the box.*'

Those had been his words on giving her the photograph. And Annie's reaction upon hearing of his mention of that box?

The notepad slid from Kate's knee.

'*...The Lord and His holy angels protect us!*'

Christ, he was losing it! Sat in the car park of Fairview Hospice, Richard Torrey gripped the steering wheel of the car with clenched hands. He was seeing faces where none existed! A woman where there was no woman! Picking up a fare from Harrowby Place, beside that paint factory in Station Street, after dropping a fare at Wolverhampton train station, then in his own flat, his own bloody flat, for God's sake! And now again here. Disbelieving his own eyes he stared at the face reflected in the driving mirror. It was the same damned face!

'What the hell do you want?'

Anger more than fear had him twist his head

231

but the rear passenger seats were empty. What had he expected? He climbed from the car and leaned against the door, breathing in long settling draughts of air spiced with the fading scents of autumn flowers. Had he thought to see an actual woman, a real live person?

'Are you the cab called for Henderson, booked for Moxley?'

Torrey straightened at the quiet question. A yard or so from him, visible in the security lights set about the low-slung building and spilling over the car park, a middle-aged man stood with one arm supporting a sobbing woman.

'My wife.' The man caught Torrey's glance which had slid to the woman. 'It's her mother ... we were warned to expect the worst but when it comes...' he half smiled, 'well, when it comes it's painful.'

Just as the death of his own mother had been painful. Torrey felt the sharp stab that always came with thoughts of the mother he had adored, the mother who had slaved to keep and feed a son whose bastard of a father had walked out on them, a mother who had died before that son could make her life easier. Oh, he had tried, he had joined the Army as soon as he reached the required age; enlisted for two reasons. Not having him at home would mean less work for his mother, while the pay he sent home would buy the little extras she had not enjoyed in the years of his growing up. Torrey stared at the weeping woman, his mind showing instead the sight of his mother sobbing after his father had left. He had so wanted to make up for all his mother had suffered, for all she had done by bringing him up. But he had not been given the time. His mother had died twelve months after his joining the Army.

'The staff in there, very kind they are, they've advised I take her home and put her to bed.'

The half-apologetic words cleared Torrey's head of his yesterdays. The fare he had brought here, a Mr Conway, p'raps one of the nurses could find him, tell him he would need to call another taxi. He was about to say this to the couple when he was halted by the arrival of a black cab that pulled into the car park. Its driver called from an open window if there was a fare for Moxley.

He hadn't been reluctant to sit in the car. Opening the door for his original passenger, Torrey slid into the driver's seat, his glance avoiding the rear mirror. He had been standing in the open the half hour or so waiting for his fare to emerge from that hospice, simply out of need to stretch his legs, not because of any aversion. The self-told lie lay sour inside.

Was lying to himself a newly discovered skill or had he always used it to cover what he didn't want to see?

Behind him a stifled sob murmured into the warm darkness but tangled in the disturbance of his own thoughts Torrey did not hear it.

He hadn't been reluctant, just a little apprehensive maybe. That didn't taste any better! The traffic signals ahead flicked from green to amber. Tell the truth, Torrey! Recrimination adding pressure to the touch nursing the accelerator had the powerful V6 engine surge racing the car forward to clear the red signal by a whisker. Admit it. You were scared.

What a laugh that would give the blokes at the T.A. Centre. Richard Torrey, shit scared of a shadow!

Sourness giving way to a grin he drove into Birmingham Street and brought the car to a halt before a pair of detached late-Victorian houses.

Thanking his fare for the note shoved at him through the open window he watched the slightly built figure almost run the couple of yards to a front door. That character looked to be in the same condition he had been in the hospice car park.

The original exit that had linked the street to the main Walsall Road was blocked by stout iron bollards, so Torrey executed a three-point turn. The Hyundai face about, he glanced left towards the block of maisonette buildings. Butcroft Gardens. Torrey snorted sardonically. The name was the only attractive thing about them. His glance took in a woman he had not previously noticed standing beneath a street lamp. Did she want a taxi? The engine idling, he waited. Give a few moments and he just might have himself another fare.

Beneath the harsh concentrated pool of electric light the woman's hair gleamed. Blonde or silver? Torrey couldn't decide but the figure needed no deciding; that was slender, the dress fitting as close as a second skin.

Dress! Admiration stopped short. It might not be winter yet but the nights could still carry a nip. If this woman were off out somewhere she would surely be wearing a coat. But she wasn't, that meant she was simply going to another house close by. Yet her glance had stayed with the car and she made no attempt to walk away.

Best not wait any longer, might give any curtain-twitcher the wrong idea. Fingers cradling the gear stick he made to drive off but then a movement caught the corner of his eye. The woman had stepped sidewards. Now in the very centre of the lamplight the long hair became molten gold. A light breeze lifted strands, fanning them so they darted like newborn flame ... flame which touched a face he recognised.

Stomach muscles twisted to a Gordian Knot. It was the face he had seen in his flat!

It couldn't be. Torrey swallowed hard. Pull yourself together, Torrey. You're letting imagination run away with you!

As if reinforcing the thought, the figure moved again. No! Torrey stared. She had not moved, what he had caught was a second figure that came to stand beside the first. That was the reason for the woman standing in the street, she had been waiting for a friend. A short laugh rising in his throat, he pushed the gear lever into first. Christ, next he'd be imagining little green men with antennae on their heads!

He moved off, dipping the car's main beam when a light appeared ahead. Sod it! He swore quietly, the laugh already evaporated. This short stretch of road was narrow, with nowhere to pull in. If the vehicle ahead were a lorry then one of them might have to run onto the footpath – one of them being him!

The headlights glaring challengingly in the darkness came no nearer. Torrey cursed again, louder this time. Had the dick-head parked and not bothered to switch off his lights? Inching the car forward he hit the horn. If that bloke was treating himself to a bit of the other then that would take the stiffness out!

It wasn't a lorry! Seatbelt biting across his chest at the snatch of his foot on the brake, Torrey caught the next expletive behind his teeth. The light he looked at came from no vehicle, no street lamp, yet its brightness illuminated the road bathing two figures at its centre.

How the hell had they got there? He had driven away while they stood outside those maisonettes, yet here they were, standing in the road some thirty yards ahead.

But were they standing? A trickle of ice slid the length of his spine. Get a grip, Torrey! He breathed, it's a trick of the light, no more than that, just a trick of the light. Torrey's fingers tightened. It was an illusion, it had to be, yet he could see their feet, he could see the road, and there was a clear half-metre between!

This was the kind of treat you got from reading a James Herbert or from a night on the sauce, except he didn't read Herbert nor had he been on the booze. Moisture clammy on his brow, he watched the glow shimmering a few yards away and knew he must face the truth: he was not imagining it!

A second lung-filling breath cementing the admission, he adopted the tactics he had learned in the Army. Stay calm, be vigilant, let the enemy come to you. Forcing his hands to release their grip, letting them rest on each knee, he waited. Whatever he was looking at, whatever it was out there on the road, it would soon realise it had the wrong guy. He didn't know either woman, so far as he could recall he had never set eyes on them ... but as Kate Mallory had reminded him, he hadn't known Penny Smith, yet her ghost had haunted him.

But whether ghost or fragment of the mind, that business had ended in benefit for everybody – except Julian Crowley – but where the hell was the benefit in what was happening now? If they truly were spirits–

If! God Almighty, how could he ask himself *If!* Body suddenly taut as a whipcord, Torrey stared at a rapidly approaching car – a car that passed straight through the shimmering figures!

It was as if nothing stood in its path. There was no sound of the horn, the vehicle did not brake or swerve but drove on as though nobody–

Christ! He blinked against the glow that now grew brighter. Christ, that driver had seen nobody because those bodies were not real!

Not real. Despite his Army training, Torrey's nerves buzzed, the hairs on the back of his neck rising. Those women were not real, not mortal, so how was it *he* could see them?

But he didn't want to bloody see them! Sudden anger sweeping away the tension of strung nerves, he was out of the car. Forget waiting for the enemy, he would tackle this bugger head on!

'What the hell do you want?' The shout was harsh. 'What the bloody hell do you want?'

Beyond him on the roadway a slender figure in a blue dress, blonde hair gleaming like newly minted gold, stared at Torrey.

'What do you want!' He made to step forward then halted sharply. The figures were suddenly enveloped in flame! They were burning before his eyes!

20

Neal was dead. Neal, his love, his life was dead!

Closing the front door behind him, Adrian Conway sank to his knees. The sobs he had struggled to stifle riding home in that taxi now tore through him in great wracking waves.

Neal, the person he loved most, the only one he had ever truly loved, the man who had loved him in return, was gone.

'Neal!' The cry was pure anguish. 'How can I live ... how can I go on without my heart?'

Somewhere among the empty fields of desolation a cuckoo called. Spent of tears, cramped from crouching so long, Adrian lifted his head, the lilting sounds of the clock pulling at him. They had bought that silly clock while on their first holiday together. Switzerland. Neal had suggested Switzerland saying beach holidays on the Med were sometimes a little overcrowded. They had stayed in a picture-postcard chalet perched high on the side of a mountain, the chimes of cow bells waking them each morning. They had been days of long walks along mountain paths, of yodelling and laughing – and nights of making love, deep passionate love neither of them had ever known before – and he would never know again!

The last sound of the clock faded into silence. This was how it would be from now on. The silence of death for Neal Brady, the silence of an empty heart for Adrian Conway. He would never hear that beloved voice again, never feel the touch which thrilled to the core. It was all gone and he was alone as he had never been before. Neal Brady had been his very life.

'*Leave it in the past...*'

Clearly as they had sounded the evening Neal had said them the words murmured again in his mind.

'*Leave it in the past ... I want you to promise...*'

'But I didn't promise!' The passion of grief giving way to cold hard hatred, Adrian Conway rose to his feet. 'I did not promise,' he said again, 'nor will I forget.'

He had known the Wilkeses for years, a quiet couple never causing anyone grief, never harming a soul. He had stood beside her when her husband had been laid to rest, seen the heartache on her face, and it had been he who had stood beside her while she identified a daughter somebody had used for a Guy Fawkes.

'Christ! How sick can life get?'

'You can always jack it in.'

'Eh?' A hand resting on the report Detective Sergeant Williams had written and which had been handed in to him before being sent to Quinto, Bruce Daniels looked sharply at the man in the doorway of the poky room so grandly termed an office.

'I said you can always jack it in. The job, Bruce.'

'Oh, ar!' Daniels' snort stayed in his throat. 'Pack the job in, sit about the house all day, you know what you can do with that idea.'

'You never know, Bruce,' Dave Farnell's grin broke, 'you could come to like it.'

'I could always come to like jumpin' off church spires except I ain't about to try.'

'Well, you can't say I didn't offer advice.'

'I'd prefer a cigarette.'

'Didn't you always. But seriously, Bruce, you should ease up, let Williams do a bit more.'

Daniels' hand delved into a jacket that several dry-cleanings had not fully relieved of the aroma of tobacco, his brows drawing into a frown when his fingers made no connection with a pack of cigarettes. Smoking was another pleasure this bloody stomach of his had forced him to give up. Add that to every day spent watching Marjorie polish where she had polished ten minutes previously, listen to her telling him to wipe his feet, to be sure and put the seat down after using the lavatory... A month of that and he *would* be jumping off church spires.

'Williams!' The frustrated desire for a cigarette caused him to snap. 'Williams is something else I can do without. Just one more pain in the arse!'

Coming further into the tight room, Sergeant Dave Farnell closed the door. Complaints were for his ears first, the rest – and that included

Quinto – could hear later should he deem it necessary.

'Is Williams giving cause for complaint?'

The frown on Daniels' face hardened. 'Complaint? Against Williams? Who the bloody hell is doing that?'

'I thought you were,' Farnell answered quietly. 'You said he is a pain in the arse; is that to do with the carrying out of his duties?'

'In a way, yes.'

Daniels picked up the folder from the desk but did not hand it across. 'You know me, Dave, I like working on my own, I can't do with having somebody else at my shoulder all the time.'

'That's your only complaint?'

'Gripe might be a better word.' The frown gone Daniels gave a self-deprecatory shake of the head. 'I realise a good cop when I see one and Williams has all the makings; could be I'm jealous.'

'Could be.' Farnell nodded. 'Same as it was jealousy had you help all those other lads climb the ladder?'

'Those who deserved it – and don't count the late unlamented Superintendent James Connor among them!'

That business of a counterfeiting strike still rankled. Dave Farnell saw the slight tightening of fingers holding the folder. But so it would with any detective who had busted it then seen the resulting promotion go to another man.

'Seems I can shunt anybody up the ladder except you and me.' Daniels' tight mouth came precariously near a smile. 'Ain't quite cracked how to do that, eh, Dave?'

241

'Speaking for myself, I never did have a head for heights, the rung I'm on is far enough up for me.'

That was crap! Resentment danced a tango in Daniels' mind. Dave Farnell had been passed over for promotion for one reason only, division following the creed of 'keep the best for yourself and your cronies and push the shit onto somebody else's pile'. That was the doctrine had brought Quinto to Darlaston.

'So, what's to be done with Williams? I mean, will you ask he be reassigned?' Farnell glanced at the file still held in Daniels' hand.

That wouldn't solve anything, and remember ... Bruce Daniels cautioned himself ... shit can travel in both directions and you could finish up with the bigger load! His shrug attesting to the truth of his thoughts he answered, 'No ... no, the lad's all right. He just needs time!'

'And time is what you ain't got much of if you want to keep Quinto off your neck. He keeps asking for your report on that bonfire case.'

'All done.' Daniels thrust the folder into the other man's hands. 'Do the honours for me, Dave, tell Quinto ... just tell him something came up.'

'While you slip out the back way?'

Tapping a hand to the pocket of his worn tweed jacket in the habit of checking for car keys, Bruce Daniels answered the other man's quick grin.

'You've got it, Dave. Reckon with a bit of practice you'd make a pretty good criminal.'

'The things I do for you,' Sergeant Dave Farnell watched the rapidly exiting Daniels, 'I reckon

242

I'm that already!'

Dead between eighteen and twenty-four hours. Stomach contents showed the victim had eaten shortly before death. Blood contained traces of GHB and bruising to the body was consistent with being roughly treated.

As he eased the car out of the station yard, Daniels' mind ran over the details of the forensic report on the body recovered from the bonfire.

Had Sheryl Wilkes been slapped around by a man intent on sex? Was that where those bruises had come from? Had the girl refused then been fed that rape drug so she could put up no more resistance? It seemed the logical conclusion.

Halted by red traffic lights at the intersection of the Bull Stake, Daniels tapped the wheel with impatient fingers. The logical conclusion! But was it logical to stab a woman through the heart then set the body ablaze on a kids' bonfire in order to cover up a rape?

Traffic signal flicking to green, he drove on. Rape was a serious crime in any man's book, it carried a sentence of months, but murder? That put a man away for life and who in his right mind would risk life in order to get his end away?

That most certainly wasn't logical!

Another thing that didn't quite fit. The stab to the heart. No evidence of that having been done anywhere near that fire. So why stab a woman in one place: then move the body to another? There were more questions than he had answers. Yet there was one more to be asked.

And he would ask it now!

Branching to the right at the junction of Catherine's Cross he swept into the car park of the Staffordshire Knot.

And the answer had better be good!

'I don't see what it 'as to do with anythin'.'

'You won't see my banging you up in Winson Green has to do with anything neither, but tek it from me, Sounder, that's the hotel you'll be spending the next couple of years in unless you answer my questions.'

'You ain't got nothin' on me.'

'True.' Detective Inspector Bruce Daniels nodded with all the appearance of genial agreement. 'But that don't mean I can't come up with something. It's your choice. Sounder, talk to me or accept the offer of a free holiday, though I warn you the food leaves a lot to be wary of, not to speak of the holiday-makers you'll share a room with.'

The man was a shit! Echo Sounder's narrow shoulders hunched over his chest. But the shit carried a warrant card and didn't care who he hit over the head with it.

'Take your time, or is that a bad choice of word?' Daniels sipped the drink he knew would kindle the acid in his gut.

'Piss off!' No more than a hiss, Sounder's reply slipped into his own half-empty glass. Why the hell was Daniels on his back, why wasn't he looking for the swine who had killed Sheryl?

Daniels returned his glass to the table, wincing as a familiar blaze trailed the way of the beer. He would suffer for drinking it but then his gut had him suffer for everything he put in it. Get this case cleaned up and he'd let the medics loose on this bloody stomach ulcer, see it ended once and for all.

Head lowered almost to his chest, Echo Sounder caught the movement which brought a blue and yellow carton from a pocket. Daniels could be a nasty bugger when his gut wasn't playin' up. When the tablets were brought out he could be a downright bastard.

'Dora asked would I go with her, d'ain't want to go to that mortuary on her own.'

'We'd sorted that already, what I want to know is why you, why Echo Sounder?'

No use in beating about the bush, Daniels would dig until he dragged the last worm up. Anyway, what did it matter now? Taking a deep swallow, then wiping his mouth with his sleeve Sounder lifted his head.

'This is gonna give you summat you ain't 'ad in a long time,' he growled, 'a bloody good laugh! You asked why me? Why did Dora Wilkes ask me to go with her? Well, I'll tell yer. It were because her knowed I loved her daughter, that I'd loved her from bein' a young 'un, that I'd see the Sheryl that was not some 'alf-roasted corpse, an' Dora also knowed I'd put no blame where I knowed none should lie. Yes, Sheryl left 'ome but her were no tart an' no whore, all her looked for were a better life than her got in Darlaston, but instead her got...'

He had loved the woman they had recovered from that fire. Daniels felt a tug of sympathy as the untidy head lowered once more to the chest. This

245

man was feeling the pain a young lad had once felt on running to a hospital only to find the mother he loved was dead. He should leave Sounder, leave him to grieve in peace, but if murderers were to be caught then questions had to be asked.

Divided off from the large bar room by the original narrow passage that still served as access to the pub, a raised alcove hosted a team of darts players. Attention momentarily caught by a shout of 'One 'undred an' eighty, bloody brilliant, that'll see the Willenhall team off' Daniels glanced in the direction of the noise. There were one or two up there might prove interesting to talk to; there were more muck in Darlaston that got swept up by council hygiene vehicles. Maybe he should put Williams onto one or two of the local heroes, keep the lad busy.

'Why would somebody do that to 'er, why burn 'er?'

The mutterings into a now almost empty glass recalled Daniels to the moment. Why? That was something they both wanted to know.

'Sounder,' he kept his voice low, aware of nearby ears, 'did Sheryl tell you where she was going once she left Darlaston?'

'No, nor 'er d'ain't tell 'er mother neither 'cos 'er knowed we would try talkin' 'er out of it.'

Ditto Dora! Daniels checked his mental notebook. The woman had given an identical answer.

'Was there ever a mention of friends, someone she may have–'

'Look!' Sounder's head snapped up. 'I don't know who Sheryl might 'ave been with or who it was could 'ave done what they 'ave, but I'll find out, by God I'll find out!'

If anybody could sniff the culprits out then this man might, what he didn't know about the local sleaze hadn't yet happened.

Daniels pushed to his feet, his glance missing none of the heads turning away, finding a sudden interest on the further side of the room. He could empty the place in less time than it took to order a pint, the good following the bad and the ugly.

'One word,' he resisted the temptation, 'if you find out you let me have them.'

'Oh, you can 'ave 'em.' Pressed hard about the glass Echo Sounder's fingers whitened more than they ever did when washed. 'You can 'ave what be left of 'em!'

Not the local mafia. Standing in the small car park, Bruce Daniels watched the stream of traffic pass along Pinfold Street. A ritual killing, a sacrifice, was what Dave Farnell had called that murder. It was macabre, no doubt about that – but ritual sacrifice? Not here in Darlaston; there had to be some other explanation.

There had to be. He fingered the keys in his pocket, oblivious to the jingle. But what was it and where did he find it? He had gleaned less than nothing from Dora and the same from Echo Sounder! The tug of sympathy he had felt a few minutes before twisted again. Who would have credited him with loving anybody? But he had loved the daughter of Dora Wilkes, *did* love her if the look on his face were anything to judge by, but it had also been a look that indicated yet another imminent murder.

A blare of car horns ripped along the street followed in seconds by two cars racing neck and neck in the direction of Catherine's Cross.

Bloody hooligans! Daniels watched twin tail-lights disappear in the distance, his mind as quickly returning to his fruitless conversation inside the pub.

Sounder had been down more holes than a rabbit and it was a sure bet he would go down a few more; it had to be hoped he didn't find a fox waiting when he came out! The killing of Sheryl Wilkes had been a particularly vicious act and whoever was responsible wouldn't hesitate to do the same again should Sounder get too inquisitive.

Ritual ... sacrifice...

Was Dave Farnell's theory so crackpotical? After all, there had been that business a couple of years back, when gravestones in Bentley churchyard were daubed with upside-down crucifixes and weird symbols. Black magic had been some of the mutterings heard in the town, but that was ridiculous, the marking of those stones had been no more than the daubings of kids bent on mischief ... but this wasn't simply paint on stones and it certainly wasn't teenagers playin' silly buggers. So what did he tell Quinto when he asked? What to say when the gold braid was flashed in his face? His irritation was added to by the sound of horns and the throb of racing engines. Where the bloody hell was uniform when they were needed? Not behind this aspiring Schumacher ... he was driving that car like he had a rocket up the exhaust!

Zipping across both lanes of dual carriageway, a famous 'V' sign acknowledging the protests of several drivers forced to swerve, a low-slung BMW streaked over Catherine's Cross, tyres screaming as it launched itself into the narrow Mill Street, bounced from one side of the road to the other as it turned about, roaring like a crazed panther.

What the hell was this stupid bugger about! Daniels watched the car. Like a red streak it hurled itself into the car park, missing him by a fraction before being spun about in a hand-brake turn.

What else did Wonderboy have for Christmas? Keep that up and his next present would be a well-polished coffin!

Yards from him the car's engine roared again. The driver grinned, while his foot tap-danced on the accelerator revving the engine and letting it throb like a drum.

'Shift it, arsehole!' The car lurched against the grip of brakes. 'I said shift it!' The vehicle lurched again, a threat on wheels, the grin of its driver already changed to a snarl.

Polite, very polite! Daniels stood his ground, a stream of abuse reaching him as the car whipped around him to shoot into the one remaining space; the grate of metal on metal almost bringing a smile to Daniels' lips. Skilful as well as polite, pity the man was no expert in either.

Beside the car as it sighed into silence, Daniels rested a hand on the frame of the open window.

'Bit dicey wasn't it crossing a dual carriageway like you just did? Not to mention that little exhibition in Mill Street, then there's this...'

Daniels glanced at the damaged vehicle along-side, 'somebody in there isn't going to appreciate what you've done to his motor; you are going to inform the owner? Exchange insurance details?'

'Piss off!'

Thrusting his weight against the car door, Daniels nodded once. 'I'll take that as a "no". Does it also mean you are going to foot the bill for repairs to your own vehicle? This *is* your vehicle?'

'Who invited you to the party!' Like bullets fired at close range the words were spat out, the now-furious driver shoving his way from the car. 'Well, I 'ope you enjoyed it 'cos it's over fer you, I'm gonna break yer fuckin' neck!'

'Mine was a royal invitation.' Daniels flashed his warrant card. 'Dangerous driving; you're nicked, sweetheart. Try fucking that!'

21

Torrey would say she was crazy, Scottie would sack her on the spot... so what was she doing here? Smiling a thank you to the library assistant who had handed her a large heavy book, Kate carried it to a table near the window. Perhaps she was crazy; like Torrey she should have dismissed Annie Price's story of the Devil's Talisman as a myth, an invention of someone's mind – but she hadn't.

Taking notebook and pencil from her over-packed shoulder bag she set them beside the book

Darlaston library staff had requested especially for her. 'It may only be used in the reference section.' The restriction had carried a reminder from the woman handing the book across the counter. That was just as well. Kate smiled to herself. Should Annie see this in her house she really would throw a wobbly.

Maybe she might have put the story on the backburner of her mind and would have except for what Sounder had said.

One end of the pencil in her mouth, Kate nibbled contemplatively. She had gone to the Staffordshire Knot, the pub he had made his new haunt. He had welcomed her in the usual offensive manner requesting nowhere near politely she leave. Instead she had sat herself at the beer-stained table and said quietly, *'The girl whose photograph you gave me, she was Dora Wilkes' daughter.'*

There had been a harsh intake of breath but no answer.

'A bonfire!' He had hit the table with his fist rattling several empty glasses. *'...Say what you mean, her were dumped on a bloody bonfire!'*

She had been unsure as to the outcome of staying. Agony had shown clear on the man's face and the fierce grip of hands clenched together had said clearly he was near the end of his tether.

'It were that box...'

He had gone on as though she were not there, muttering over gripped hands.

'I knowed what would 'appen, no sooner Dora said, as the box were gone I knowed evil would strike and so it 'as, just as it has many times

251

afore. I said it should 'ave been got rid of, should 'ave been chucked in the canal but Dora wouldn't agree; her said the risk of it being found was too much, her should 'ave listened to me ... her should 'ave listened!'

The box! Mention of it had set her journalistic blood tingling. What did it contain that made Echo Sounder, Dora Wilkes and Annie Price so afraid?

She had risked Sounder's anger, had asked what did he know of the Devil's Talisman. He had remained silent for so long she had thought he would say no more but then he had looked at her, his eyes alight with a gleam she had never seen in them before. It had not been the anger she had expected but then what had it been? Reluctance, warning or downright fear?

Perhaps a mix of all three. Kate wiped a finger tip across her lips, removing fragments of chewed pencil.

He had thrown a glance around the room almost as if he expected to see some spectre looming in the corner then had whispered, 'Leave it ... leave it before it kills you as it killed Sheryl!'

But what exactly was the 'it' Sounder had spoken of? Kate stared at the book lying un-opened on the desk. She had spent hours mulling over that question, discarding first one con-clusion and then another while always returning to Annie's whispered, *'God and His holy angels protect us.'*

But how could an object – any object – arouse so much genuine fear in people who claimed never to have seen the thing they feared? 'Stories of the bogeyman' was what Torrey had answered when she had put that to him. 'As kids we were all scared by tales of what might get us if we didn't do what we were told. This Talisman business is just that. Annie and the others, they were fed that story as young 'uns to ensure they never talked of what was simply a robbery ... some trinket box stolen from Bentley Hall; as for Archangels and devils – they don't exist.'

Kate's teeth clamped firm on the pencil. Those last words, 'Archangels and devils – they don't exist.' Torrey's glance had fallen away when saying them. Why? Because he had known them to be untrue. He had seen what she had seen in that cellar at Darlaston Printers, witnessed for himself the powers of evil; to deny its existence now was merely telling himself a lie.

So if one thing were true, why not another? Why should not a Talisman, the symbol of Satan's position as a heavenly Archangel and cursed by him at his fall, exist? And if it had, could there be some record other than an old wife's tale?

That was the reason for requesting this book. Kate read the title, scarlet letters sprawled like blood across a shiny black cover. *Magick and Wychecraft.* If there was anything to be found it must surely be in here.

'Find what you wanted?'

Kate looked up at a smiling woman who was scooping up books left behind by readers ready to return them to various shelves.

'I know how it feels,' the woman went on as Kate stretched her aching back, 'but still it's worth it when you find what you're looking for.'

But she hadn't found what she looked for! Kate watched the woman return to the reception point with its semicircular counter endowed with twin computers. Maybe she should just have asked if they had anything on the Devil's Talisman? What kind of reaction would that have resulted in? A cold stare and the reply, 'Fiction can be found downstairs.' It might be more fruitful to look there because she had certainly found nothing here!

Kate looked at her watch. Half past five. She had spent two hours reading all sorts of so-called magic that would be better termed crap! Shoulders creaked rebellion and her neck said move and I break. It was a lost cause, no sense in going any further. Closing the book her fingers slipped on the glossy cover and it fell back on to the table. Making to pick it up again Kate's hands paused in mid-air. Was it? Could it be?

An upper case heading stared bold and black against a glossy white ground.

The Devil's Aiguillette.

Kate's fingers tingled. Each of the pages she had turned had carried several illustrations as well as a proliferation of texts. So why give this a page of its own and just one sentence?

She bent closer to peer at the picture. Four figures dressed in medieval robes and close-fitting caps stood grouped about a winged fifth figure. It was portrayed in thick black, obviously naked, winged and horned, with forked tail and three-toed feet – this figure was reaching a hand as if to take something from a man standing before it. What was the illustration meant to symbolise?

Kate read the accompanying sentence then, breath locked in her throat, read it again.

'A fifteenth-century woodcut shows Satan taking back his Aiguillette.'

Taking back! Kate's lungs refused to function.

'Satan would possess it only if it were given voluntarily by a mortal...' The tingle in her fingers spread along every vein.

This picture showed a depiction of Satan and of a man, a man holding something in one hand. Could the story Annie had told have been in circulation over five hundred years ago? It seemed too much to believe. Yet the story of the Devil's expulsion from heaven went back much further than that or so her research would have it.

Breath eased slowly from lungs beginning to sting. Old wives' tales, stories told to scare children, they all had to start somewhere and Annie's was no different.

'Satan taking back his Aiguillette.'

That last word might be understandable to folk of the fifteenth century, but not to her...

Pushing up from her chair Kate made a swift search of the surrounding bookshelves, eventually taking back to the table a dictionary and a copy of Roget's Thesaurus.

'Aiguillette, a gilt cord hung in loops from the shoulder of certain military uniforms.'

The dictionary dealt Kate's elation a major blow. This wasn't what she had hoped for. Give it up now... why bother with the Thesaurus? Looking at the second book she shrugged inwardly, might as well check that, then she would pack the whole charade in!

Finding the word in the index at the rear of the book she turned to section 747.

'Sceptre.' It didn't begin well. Once more Kate harboured the thought of relegating the search to the mental bin marked rubbish then smiled to herself, the words of a famous quiz master echoing in her mind, 'I've started so I'll finish.' What Magnus Magnusson had done Kate Mallory would do, at least so far as section 747 went.

'...regalia ... brassard...' she read on, '...badge ... insignia of authority ... rank ... marks...'

Authority! Rank! Interest piquing, Kate scanned the rest avidly.

'...portfolio ... signet ... seal...'

Yes! She almost shouted.

'Talisman.' It was there on the last line. Aiguillette and talisman, they bore a connected meaning; both were a sign of office – a symbol of authority.

He had accepted no bookings for this evening. Tonight he would relax, do nothing, say nothing ... just switch the world off. Eyes closed, Torrey lay in warm soapy water. A bath, a drink and bed, what more luxury could life offer a tired man? There was one thing. Trying to pull his mind from the edge of the precipice it was about to fall into he pressed his eyelids hard, but the battle was already lost.

Anna! It was without sound, a cry from the heart not the lips, yet it resounded in his head. Those nights with Anna!

'Richard.'

The reply floated softly in his mind, a reply

filled with the same love he felt for her.

'Richard Torrey.'

Somewhere beneath the sudden tumult of desire a dull note rang in his brain. Richard! Richard Torrey! Anna had never used either, she had always called him Ritchie! Were the seeds of forgetfulness at last beginning to take root? Was 'hearing' not Ritchie but Richard Torrey a sign that Anna was at last fading from his memory? But Anna would never fade. Even now, given what he knew of the evil she had tried to do through him, she was not yet gone: sometimes, in the long hours before dawn, he would almost feel the touch of that slender body in his arms, a cloud of silk hair brush his shoulder and hear the whispered 'I love you' as she slid beneath him.

'Richard Torrey.'

That was no echo of old memory. Eyes fully open, his body instantly whipcord, he was out of the bath. He had not imagined the calling of his name, he had heard it and whoever had spoken it was not outside in the street, but here in his flat!

Another intruder ... or the one that had been here before?

Let it be the first! Water dripping from his naked body, Torrey's nerves tingled. Let it be a burglar, he knew how to deal with those. But burglars did not announce themselves by calling the name of the person they were about to rob. Common sense! Torrey smiled grimly. But where was the common sense in what he had seen the last time he had heard someone in his flat?

Surely that couldn't happen again. Ghost, spirit, call it whatever suited, it wouldn't be back.

It had got the message. Richard Torrey was not the one it wanted. This, then, was solid human flesh out there in his sitting room and solid flesh reacted quite satisfactorily to the treatment he was about to give.

Lending no thought to bathrobe or towel, he eased from the bathroom, slipping soundlessly across the tiny landing to pause at the living-room door. There was somebody in there, the short hairs on the back of his neck bore testimony to that. One deep drawn breath and he was once more the commando. Brain tuned to every whisper of sound, every hair's breadth of movement, limbs loose yet ready for attack. Only this time he wouldn't wait for the enemy to come to him; this time he would take the initiative! One kick slamming the door back on its hinges, he was in the room.

It couldn't be happening again! Yet it was!

Part of him had half expected what stood in front of him but faced with it Torrey felt a needle-sharp stab, like electricity, run through every vein.

Richard Torrey.

Anna! Torrey felt the world lose its balance. The blonde hair, the hyacinth eyes, the slender shape; Anna, it had to be Anna. For half of eternity the floating figure regarded him, lovely eyes ... eyes! Torrey brought the world back on to its axis. The eyes were not hyacinth, they were blue-green, almost turquoise and the face – it was not Anna's face.

Realisation released him from the grip of unreality only to immerse him in that of helplessness. How did you fight a ghost? That was what this was. But the ghost of whom ... and why was it haunting him?

'What do you want? Why come to me?' One question followed quietly on the other.

Standing in the centre of a pool of scarlet light a young woman raised one hand.

'You...'

The word whispered across the room though there was no movement of the mouth. Him! Torrey remained motionless. This ghost, this apparition, wanted him!

'...find it...'

Words came again; soft, insistent, like the fluttering wings of a caged bird.

'...find it ... evil ... terrible evil.'

'What ... what is it you want? How can I...?'

'Find it...'

Around the figure the shimmering glow became the leap of flames; scarlet, blue, purple, they danced upward licking at the blue dress, at the pale hair, at the face, an inferno that gave off no heat, no sound, nor stretched its fiery fingers to touch any part of the room.

Burning yet not burning ... a blaze that touched nothing but the figure contained within it.

'What ... what do you want me to find?' He stepped forward.

The hand lifted again, one word escaping the last engulfing flames.

'Evil.'

22

She had shredded the file, destroyed all evidence of the girl having attended that photo shoot, of her having been to the offices of Pascal, nothing could be traced.

Venetia Pascal smiled her own congratulations. No one would ever know she and the girl had met together here in this home.

She had called the number taken from the file, had told the girl she had been one of the finalists put forward to become the 'face' of 'Promise'. But before the final decision could be made each of the chosen three would be required to come that evening to be interviewed one last time. It was also a strict requirement they wore exactly what they had worn to the photo shoot.

The girl had agreed, making no comment about the fact that the interview would not take place at the offices of Pascal but at a private address.

Dressed in a pale blue dress beneath a cheap coat the girl had been excited, but what had excited Venetia Pascal had been the necklace. It had cradled the throat, the chain supple as a golden snake, gems glowing as if they lived and breathed. She had stared at it, felt the lure. Could it be what Julian Crowley had searched for? That which would ensure the everlasting gratitude of the Prince of Darkness?

Sheryl Wilkes, a nobody from a nobody town; how had she come by such a necklace? She had asked herself that while complimenting the girl on her choice of dress. But she had not asked, after all what had it mattered? They had talked and at the end of it the girl had accepted a cup of coffee, coffee to which a tablet of Gamma Hydroxy Butyrate had been added. The so-called rape drug! The smile of congratulation spread wider on the lovely mouth. It had not been for the purpose of rape the drug had been slipped into Sheryl Wilkes' coffee.

It had taken just a few minutes. The girl had complained of feeling light-headed then of feeling tired. There had been no objection to the removing of the necklace, nor to what had followed.

She had timed everything perfectly.

Sleek and sinuous as a beautiful cat, Venetia Pascal opened a spacious wardrobe and surveyed the fabulous gowns hanging inside.

Her part in the whole affair had been perfect. How perfect Theo Vail's?

It had been the Sabbat of Mabon, the Night of Offering, the night when each Follower of the Path, each Watcher of the Way, made offering to their Lord, made sacrifice to Satan.

She had toyed with the idea of offering that necklace, of taking a chance, but the Lord of Darkness had no use for trinkets and Venetia Pascal had no desire to arouse his anger by offering a worthless tribute; so her offering had been the girl. And the necklace removed from her throat? Theo Vail had learned nothing of that.

261

Selecting a gown of dusky silver lamé she slid it over her body, the touch of it a kiss against bare breasts. As *he* had kissed them. Desire as hot and fierce as a desert wind raced along every nerve, the desire she had felt the evening of her jewellery launch. He had made love to her in a way no mortal man ever could; Lucifer, the All High, had chosen her, had given the promise, through her would his Will be fulfilled.

If Theo Vail were to know of that! But he wouldn't; she would hold the secret as she would hold secret that necklace.

Turning from the wardrobe she crossed to where a framed print of Leonardo da Vinci's Mona Lisa hid a small wall safe.

Enigmatic was what art critics called that smile. Venetia paused, her glance resting on the serene face. But what did it truly hide? Could it be the woman posing for that famous painting had also known the touch of Lucifer? Had she too lain with a beautiful golden lover?

Perhaps. She slid the picture aside. But had she given the Lord of the Earth the one thing he desired above all else, that which he had held as Star of the Morning, Archangel of Heaven, that which would restore all he had lost at the Fall? The Talisman ... or did she herself have it here in this safe?

Resting on a bed of black velvet, the stones glittered. Red as fire they burned against the darkness of the cloth, demonic eyes which watched and waited while it seemed the voice of ages whispered to her to lift it from its bed, to place it about her neck, to present it...

No! Venetia closed the safe, pulses beating in her temples. She could not take the risk. Maybe Julian Crowley's talk of an ancient symbol had been no more than that, maybe there was no such thing, that it was a figment born of some man's hopes.

But Julian Crowley had not been a man given to dreaming; he demanded proof.

Coming into a drawing-room furnished with couches of cream suede across which multi-coloured spears of light splashed from drop crystals edging the shades of table lamps, Venetia poured herself a glass of tonic water. She had long ago decided it paid not to put alcohol before business, and given the fact this evening's business would include Theo Vail, tonic water it was.

Theo Vail, Magus longing to become Ipsissimus! The same longing held by that other High Priest, Julian Crowley.

Crowley had been so sure of himself, sure as Vail was now. But Crowley had achieved an enviable position in the service of the Dark Lord, mastering the ten Sephirath, the Forty-Two Paths of Wisdom; he had attained the ancient power and knowledge contained within the Sanctum Reghum, but had wanted more, had desired that divine knowledge given to the Magi. In a short while the High Coven would be gathered, the great sacrifice would be made and Theo Vail would be granted that same power; he would be blessed of Satan, would become Ipsissimus ... unless – she sipped the clear liquid – unless Vail, as had Crowley, became over confident.

Julian Crowley had made a mistake, the

mistake it transpired of allowing Max Gau to live long enough to refute the Lord of the Earth, to ask forgiveness of the Lord of Heaven and for that the Master had condemned him to live his years in an institution for the criminally insane before living eternity in the torment of hell.

But Julian Crowley had not been insane. Green sparks darting from the square-cut emerald adorning the third finger of her right hand, she set the glass aside. He had been highly intelligent, too intelligent to speak of the Seal of Power were he not absolutely convinced of its existence. Yet he had talked of it, described its beauty ... but how had he known? Had he called forth Egyn and Gmayon, keepers of the Hokmah Nistarah, that most-hidden of wisdoms; been told by those Satanic Angels where the precious Seal could be found, perhaps been given a glimpse of it? Was that the reason Crowley, High Priest of Satan, First Chosen of Earth, had operated from Darlaston? Had he thought a town so small, so insignificant, the wiser choice for the home of the Premier Coven, or was Darlaston the hiding place of the Devil's Talisman ... and could it be the Talisman that now lay locked in her safe?

'If I hand this to Scottie, he'll have the white-coat brigade cart me off for a leisurely stay in a luxury apartment complete with room padded floor to ceiling, but there *is* something in all of this, I feel certain.'

'You can be certain of the first part, Kate, the padded room bit, but as for the rest then I'd say you've let that old wives' business carry you a bit

264

too far.'

She had guessed he would say that, Kate Mallory, candidate for the lunatic party. A stubborn anger holding her lips tight, Kate delved into a bag she had not seen the bottom of in weeks. Going a bit too far was she? Letting imagination run away with her! Well, wait until the practical Mr Richard Torrey saw this! Fishing a paper from the depths of her leather bag she handed it across a table holding the remnants of the Chinese take-away which had been the meal Torrey had served up; the man was no gourmet and certainly no chef-de-cuisine.

A warning flare turning her brown eyes to glittering bronze, she watched the slow smile form about that strong mouth. Richard Torrey was a handsome man. He could also be an infuriating one.

'Well?' she asked as he finished reading.

'Well what?' Torrey answered the challenge with a challenge.

'Tchaa!' Kate exploded. 'You can be right sweir sometimes.'

Torrey lowered the paper but the smile was gone. 'I trust I'm being flattered.'

'Huh!' Kate blew down nostrils widened with impatience. 'Trust on, bonny lad! I was saying it like it is ... you are downright obstinate.'

'Obstinate, now if that isn't the kettle calling the pot ... you, Kate, could play that game for England, you stick to a story tighter than an Elastoplast sticks to a cut finger. But this...' he indicated the paper still held in the fingers of one hand, '...this is...'

'Is what?' Indignation hurled the words across the table.

They could sit here and probably have a first-class row or go for a drink with the possibility of Kate cooling down by the time they got to the Frying Pan. Torrey refolded the sheet of paper. On the other hand he could hope to see three wise men on camels waiting outside; the possibilities of both were equal.

'Kate.' He decided upon partial surrender. 'I don't know what you were looking for.'

'Yes, you do!' Kate was accepting no capitulation. 'I told you what Annie said about the contents of that box, that what it held was evil...'

'And you think it was this?' Returning the paper to Kate, Torrey shook his head.

'While you obviously think it isn't!'

She wasn't going to let go. Rising to his feet he set to gathering plates and cutlery. He wanted no part of where this was leading, no part of anything that might bring back memories of last night, memories of a ghost reaching out to him.

'That is what you think, isn't it?'

Kate's second salvo missed the target of his thoughts. They remained beneath his answer. 'Help me wash up and then I'll tell you what I think.'

'You have to agree there is a strong similarity.'

Sitting in a semicircular alcove that faced the lounge bar of the Frying Pan, Kate sipped lager and lime.

'Yes.' Torrey nodded, his dark hair glistening in the gleam of overhead lighting. 'But surely you can see the whole crux of my argument is similarity. What you found in that book was no more than an old wife's tale, they had them in their days as we have them in ours.'

'Old wives ... or just their tales?' Kate's lips tilted in a smile, then seeing no reflection on Torrey's, she let it fade. He was his usual self, obstinate, telling her she was chasing rainbows, yet tonight there was something different; the banter and the teasing were not his usual form while his smile ... where was his smile?

The quip had been meant to lighten the situation. Torrey's fingers held firm to the body of his glass. But Kate was on to more than she knew.

'The wording has changed,' Kate was speaking again, 'but the content is the same; Annie's story and the description written in that book are otherwise identical, both are speaking of one thing, the devil's Seal, his Talisman; then there is the box, the one stolen from Bentley Hall, it was said to hold something evil, so evil it brought death to whoever looked into it. Torrey, do you think—'

'No, Kate!' The snap was that of cracking ice. 'This has gone far enough, drop it now, drop it before it's too late!'

'You do believe it!' Spoken on a quiet breath Kate Mallory's reply almost denied what her mind had told her. The level-headed Torrey believed in the existence of the Talisman of the devil! But what had brought about this change of mind and what was it had him say 'before it's too late'?

'What do you mean by, "before it's too late"?' The thought now in words Kate watched the fingers tighten about the glass, the mouth firm with tension.

'You know I won't give up,' she said when he didn't answer, 'there is a story in all of this and I intend to get it.'

'Kate, listen to me. You don't know what you are getting into.'

'Then I will just have to find out, won't I? And I will, Torrey, with or without help from you.'

It was no empty threat. One sniff of a story had her off like a fox hound and she wouldn't stop until the kill. And that kill could well be Kate Mallory; but telling her that would have no effect, she could be a female Attila the Hun if it meant getting a scoop.

The last bringing a shadow of a smile he looked up. 'Now who is being sweir!'

They were a team again. Kate felt relief sweep to her fingertips. Torrey's friendship meant a great deal in her life, far more than he realised ... or that she could tell him.

'It takes one to know one,' she answered, hiding thoughts which hurt behind a quick smile.

'Kate, I meant it when I said you didn't know what it was that nose of yours was leading you into, and I'd like you to drop it, but since I know you won't...' He had shrugged when saying that and inwardly Kate had followed suit. She had hoped ... she would have welcomed ... but this was her story and she should not try badgering him into following it through with her.

'Torrey.' She sipped again looking to find strength in the lager and lime to say what she had to. 'You don't have to. I mean, there is no need for you to get involved, all it is, is a myth, a legend, and after all legends can't kill.'

'Not of themselves, but they can lead people to kill and I think this one has done just that and not only once.'

Large pearl-like globes hanging from the ceiling of the lounge bar spilled delicate light and threw nuances of shade and colour to tables and curved seating. In their small alcove amber fire played over sherry curls as Kate's head lifted sharply.

'You're not serious!'

Torrey half laughed, 'I wish I wasn't. That's why I asked you to go no further with this but ... just let it go.'

'I told you, you don't have to get involved.'

Taking a drink from his glass Torrey smiled briefly as he set it down. 'That's just it, Kate, I think I already am.'

'This is what you saw!' Kate stared at the sketch Torrey had just drawn on a page taken from her notebook.

'Unbelievable, isn't it? But that, given I'm no artist, is a true representation of what that figure held out to me. When I saw the copy you had made from the book in the library I thought you also had been paid a visit by whatever it is that's haunting me.'

'Not what ... *who*; and you know the identity of the woman haunting you, Sheryl Wilkes; the fact she was holding this proves it to be in some way connected with her murder.'

'It doesn't prove anything, Kate, let's not get carried away.'

'All right then, indicates...' she answered huffily, '...it indicates a link between Sheryl Wilkes' death and the devil's Seal.'

'Tell Daniels that and he won't wait to have you shown out of the station, he'll chuck you out himself.'

'I wouldn't dream of bothering Inspector Daniels,' Kate's eyes gleamed innocence, 'I'm sure he has more than enough to occupy his time without my adding to the burden.'

'I sense a "but" at the end of that.' Torrey frowned. 'Seriously, Kate...'

'I've heard you already.' Kate's interruption brought glances in their direction. Lowering her voice she went on. 'I'm not going to give up, not until we know for certain why Sheryl Wilkes was killed and who placed her body on a bonfire, and I'm willing to bet the box Annie and Sounder talked about proves to play quite a part.'

'You think that sketch is a facsimile of something kept in that box?'

Holding Torrey's quickly drawn sketch beside that on her notepad Kate felt a chill run the length of her. Annie had called the contents evil, Echo Sounder had said death followed its opening. It had been kept in the home of Sheryl Wilkes and now she was dead, but a trinket, a few stones grouped about a medallion ... how in God's name could anyone believe? Yet she believed. Kate felt her eyes drawn to the central disc. Her depiction was less defined than that which Torrey had executed but both had caught a trace of the indefinable, had touched an essence almost ... an essence of evil. Trapped by the thing she looked at, Kate felt it enter into her, felt it lie like a shadow on her soul.

The thought trailed fear in its wake yet still she could not break free from the magnetism of eyes now seeming to blaze from the paper and as she stared, it seemed a voice called her name; 'Kate...' Mellifluous, dulcet, soft as swansdown it caressed her brain. 'Kate...' exquisite, its sound entranced, captivated her will, seducing her into itself.

'Kate ... Kate!'

Strident, demanding, the tone cut through the delightful fog holding her mind. Kate glanced at the man catching at her hand.

'Kate, where the hell were you? I've been talking to you for several minutes but it was as if you were not here.'

'Sorry.' Kate glanced again at the two sheets of paper lying side by side on the wrought-iron-legged table, 'I ... I was thinking.'

'Thinking! If what you were doing was thinking I'd hate to try breaking what you might call concentration.'

It was once again just a sketch, pencil lines on paper, innocuous, harmless, yet Kate was reluctant to draw her hand from Torrey's.

'Look at this.'

She wanted to grab his hand, to place her own inside it, to leave it there, to have him say they would go no further with this search for that box and its contents, yet at the same time she knew she couldn't; the journalist in her blood would drive her until the whole story was in the bag.

'Look here ... and here,' Torrey pointed first to

271

a five-pointed star at the heart of the disc, each tip touching the inner rim of a double circle and then to letters contained within both rims. 'Haven't we seen these somewhere before?'

The Pentacle! Kate cast a swift glance about the well-populated lounge bar. It would not do to say aloud what Torrey referred to, not here, where ears other than his might catch it.

'I say we take this somewhere a little more private.' He gathered together the papers, folding them before slipping them into the inner pocket of his jacket. 'Best be my place, Annie will be back from Bingo by this time.'

Sitting beside him in the comfortable car Kate lost the battle to prevent memories from the past flooding the present. They had seen that design before, once in Martha Sim's tiny sitting room and again in that cellar beneath Darlaston Printers and both times it had been used in ceremonies of black magic, both times their lives had been threatened by demons called from the depths of hell, demons whose names edged that pendant.

Once the terror of that second time had faded, she had researched the symbols and lettering bordering the pentacle. Iblis painted on the left, Sammael on the right while at the lower edge the symbols had denoted Lucifer; but it was that on the crest of the circle she recognised best: Satan. They were all titles given to the Devil and they were present on the sketches in Torrey's pocket. But that was not all that disc portrayed, there was something other than cabalistic symbols and lettering; there was an image, a portrait of a man

272

crowned with horns of flame, his body displaying the breasts of a woman and the genitals of a man. Male and female; it stood above a replica of the earth, dominant, commanding, supreme as if of divine right, Master of the Earth. It exuded each of these qualities yet of all of them it was the eyes made the deepest impression. It was simply a sketch, a copy she had made of a medieval wood carving, but there in the pub it had seemed so vibrant, so alive. Wrapped in the warmth of the car Kate shivered. Only a sketch maybe, but tonight Kate Mallory had looked into the eyes of the Prince of Evil.

23

That was the last of it. Adrian Conway peeled off his latex gloves and threw them into a white disposal bag marked 'For Incineration'. He stared at the words written in large scarlet lettering. Burning might destroy evidence of what had been made here in this lab, but it could not destroy the hatred in his heart.

Yes, it was hatred; black and thick it weighed like stone in his stomach, surged like acid through every vein, a fire that only revenge could extinguish.

And he would take that revenge. Slipping off the white lab coat he pushed it into the disposal bag along with the gloves. A nightly ritual. He smiled grimly. Theo Vail, head of the Vail Corporation, wanted no mishap, no accidental discovery of what was being produced here in this private laboratory. But Adrian Conway knew, just as he knew he would make the swine pay.

Beyond a plate-glass screen Theo Vail watched the slightly built scientist. Quite a looker. He followed the deft, sure movements. Thick brown hair with a touch of unruly curl, eyes the colour of molten bronze, a mouth soft and well shaped. Yes, Adrian Conway had all that many women would want in a man, but Adrian Conway wanted no woman and that had been the lock that kept him securely imprisoned in this lab.

But now the lock that had kept that prison secure was broken. The one who had kept Conway here, the man's live-in lover, was dead and now Conway thought of leaving; no special powers were needed to see that, it was only too clear from the man's attitude, his curt answers that smacked of loss of respect. But he would find that respect again.

Beyond the screen the other man was casting a speculative glance over the well-ordered laboratory, a visual check that everything was as it should be, that nothing remained on view of that so secret work.

Yes... Theo Vail smiled to himself. Conway would find that respect again; only then would he be allowed to leave.

'You have done well, Adrian.' Theo Vail smiled at the man who had grudgingly admitted him into the neat detached house.

'I've done what we were paid to do.'

274

Still talking as if part of a couple! Vail's inner smile widened while his features remained exact.

'Ah, yes, Neal Brady. A good man in the lab. A pity to have lost him, a great pity, but an illness such as his...'

An illness you caused! Adrian Conway bit down hard on the reply springing to his lips.

'He was a great loss to the firm as I am sure he was to you.'

He knew. Conway watched the serpentine smile which served to leave the eyes ice cold. Vail knew Neal and he had been lovers ... but did he know the rest?

'The Corporation is satisfied with the job you have done,' Vail was speaking again, 'the work both you and Mr Brady were engaged to do, and in recognition of that satisfaction we are adding a bonus to the payment originally agreed.' There was no answering smile, no murmur of thanks. The mental note made, Theo Vail went on. 'I hope you do not mind my calling here at your home. Maybe I should wait after all, give it to you in my office.'

He would not be returning to that lab, his time with Vail Corporation was over. Keeping that information to himself, Adrian Conway gave a slight shake of the head. 'It is immaterial to me where payment is made.'

And to me. His own silent comment hidden behind an urbane smile Theo Vail continued, 'We ... the board ... hope you will accept Mr Brady's settlement, perhaps donate it to some good cause. In his name, of course.'

Watching the man for whom he had worked

some twelve months, Adrian Conway nodded. He would settle Neal's affairs ... *all* of Neal's affairs.

'I have the cheque with me.' Taking an envelope from the inner pocket of his expensive pale grey cashmere jacket Vail held it out to Conway. 'We are still hoping you will elect to remain with the Corporation, become one of us. I assure you your work has been highly valued as was that of Mr Brady.'

Taking the cheque Adrian Conway glanced at the six-figure sum. A generous bonus indeed but no amount of money would deter him from that revenge he had whispered over Neal Brady's coffin. Lifting his gaze he looked at the man he had come to detest. Suave, cultured of manner, elegantly dressed, Theo Vail sang of refinement, of wealth – but the chorus sang of evil.

'Let's talk about Neal, shall we?' It was rapid, jerked out from behind Conway's clenched teeth. 'Let's talk about what really happened to him, what really caused his death.'

'I'm afraid I'm not with you.'

'No, you are not with me, you are ahead of me, you stinking bastard! I know what you are and this isn't going to persuade me to forget.' Tearing the cheque to pieces Conway threw them at the urbane smile.

Slivers of paper flicked against his face, carrying Vail's smile with them as they fell away, and the voice which until now had been pleasant became chipped with granite. 'Adrian, I know Brady's death was a blow to you, that the friendship between you was rather special...'

'Oh yes, you knew all right!' Every word a missile, they exploded in the quiet sitting room. 'You knew what Neal and I were to each other, that he could never have those same feelings for you; but what he could or couldn't feel was not of any importance was it, Vail? Just having him join in your little games would have been sufficient for you, wouldn't it?'

The last tiny scrap of paper fluttered like a confused snowflake on to the thick Axminster carpet but neither man's eyes followed its progress.

'Yes, I knew what you had wanted.' Conway breathed hard, the memory of that confession spoken weeks ago still gravel in his heart. 'Neal told me all of it, but you ... you couldn't take no for an answer, you couldn't conceive of anyone saying no to the wealthy Theo Vail.'

Expression revealing none of the anger surging inside him, Vail lowered himself to a chair drawn up beside a mock Adam fireplace. Leaning deep into its leather comfort, his voice conveying nothing of the feelings inside him, he spoke quietly. 'So Neal Brady told you everything. Did he also tell you of the rewards of compliance, rewards only I could give?'

'Wealth, status?' Conway laughed, 'Yes he told me about all of that, but Neal was not interested, not in you or your rewards.'

'Just what else did he tell you?'

Eyes closing, Adrian arched his head backwards on his neck, the pain of remembering marking deep furrows across an otherwise smooth brow. God, what else! He breathed long and slow as if the passage of air burned a path to

277

his lungs. Then eyes opening, he looked at the man he planned vengeance against. 'He told me you propositioned him as you would a common whore; oh, he wouldn't have to leave me, you did not wish him to live with you but only to be there for those times you desired a man. You liked to play both ends of the field, to enjoy the delights both had to offer, that was the gist of it, was it not? Do tell me if I'm wrong.'

Concealed lighting shed a muted glow over the room.

'No.' Vail's soft reply made little inroad on a hush that seemed to tremble. 'You are not wrong, I enjoy relationships with both sexes. Believe me, Adrian, it can be very satisfying. You should try it for yourself, you really don't know what you are missing.'

'I should try it, should I?' Whip-like, the words cracked on the velvet silence. 'If that carries the same invitation you gave Neal, then the answer is maybe I will, but not with you!'

'Then you are missing much more than you could possibly realise.'

'More!' Conway laughed, a strangled sound deep in his throat. 'You mean there is more than sucking that which hangs between your legs or of presenting my backside for you to mount!'

Coarse as it was, the reply brought no change to Vail's expression; he merely nodded.

'Those aspects are, as I said, enjoyable, but there are others far more so. I offered these to Neal Brady, now I offer them to you. You can be wealthy, become recognised as the greatest in your field, have status and position in the world...'

278

'Forget it, I'm not interested!'

The barked intervention released venom which until then had been kept from Vail's modulated voice but now it dripped from every word as he pushed to his feet. 'The answer one could expect of a fool! You are refusing more than you could even envisage; it is not mere earthly wealth and position you are being offered. There is more, much more, and should you accept you will enjoy those privileges for all of eternity. Think carefully, Adrian ... it is not yet too late.'

Outside, the street closed to through traffic resounded to the clash of car doors as residents of the facing maisonettes came and went, but no sound penetrated the costly double glazing; nothing but the breathing of two men countered the stillness of the tastefully furnished room.

'That is where you are wrong,' Conway snapped, 'not only is it too late for you and me to engage in any relationship of the sort you look for, there was never any chance of it from the moment we met!'

Moving from the chair to stand before the window, Theo Vail stared a moment at the small square edged now with the almost compulsory cars. Like the city roads, Birmingham Street was not built to accommodate so many vehicles, but then they would not have to cope much longer.

'I have made my mistake.' He turned to face the man still standing at the centre of the room. 'Now allow me to show you the consequences of yours, the other side of the coin as you might say. You shall see what Brady saw, what anyone refusing to do as I ask also comes to see.'

Had there been a movement of the hand or was the light playing tricks with his eyes? Slightly puzzled, Adrian Conway watched rich velvet close off the window. There was no switch or button to operate an electrical circuit. His glance flicked to either side of the figure now backed by closed drapes. How the hell had he managed that?

'It was not simply Vail Corporation you were offered the chance of joining.' Discreet lighting had Vail's blond hair reflecting glints of gold. 'Nor was, as you so very crudely put it, sucking what hangs between my legs or presenting your backside for me to mount, any condition of the proposed association; a man can find that on any street corner in any part of the world. No, my dear Adrian, that was not the proposition.'

'Don't bother going any further,' Conway pulled his gaze from the curtains, 'as I've already said, I'm not interested.'

'Oh, but I insist.' Vail smiled beneath the venom. 'I could not possibly take my leave, or allow you to leave Vail Corporation without fulfilling my word, that would be most ungracious.'

'*Allowing* me to leave!' Derision soaked Conway's reply. 'Allow! Do you think you can stop me?'

Soft, humourless, the answering laugh hung between them. 'Not myself,' Vail replied after several seconds, 'but then I was not thinking of attempting to do so; after all why engage in something unpleasant when others can do it for you.'

He had torn up that cheque, thrown the pieces in Vail's face, told him what he thought about

280

him and expecting him to leave, not become embroiled in a slanging match; so now was the time to tell the man to go before he was tempted to throw a punch at that sickly smile. Contempt darkening his bronze-brown eyes, Conway gave a tight shake of his head. 'Even now, after all your crowing, you have to get someone else to do your dirty work! And you ask me to join you–'

'Not ask. Asked.' Vail cut the reply. 'Two letters different in the spelling, Adrian, but an eternity of difference in the consequence. As I told you, it was not simply myself or even Vail Corporation you were invited to align yourself with but with the Master... Ah!' He paused, 'I see our friend Brady did not after all tell you the whole thing. Did he make you believe it was some foreign substance in a drink he and I shared one evening that caused his illness? No...' blond hair glinted a negative movement, 'nothing so paltry; but that is in the past, now let me introduce you to –'

'The Master!' Conway sneered. 'I thought you were the boss.'

'I never made such claim.'

'Then pardon my ignorance, but you or your superior, I've no inclination to spend another minute with either.'

'But you have no choice.'

'We'll see about that!'

The lunge never really got started. No more than a notion, it died as Conway found himself grappling with limbs refusing to obey.

'As I said, Adrian,' Vail's smile returned, 'you have no choice. You, as did your lover, will make the acquaintance of another servant of the Master.

Or as you would have him termed ... the devil.'

Conway tugged at invisible bonds, shackles that held like forged steel. Vail had not touched him, had not made the slightest move towards him, yet his limbs felt as if they were encased in iron. What the hell was going on?

'A few moments only to make the introduction and then we will both bid you au revoir.'

Both! Conway swore softly as bonds he could not see refused to be broken. Being boss of Vail Corporation had obviously gone to the man's head, he was suffering from delusions; but whatever was holding his own arms and legs, was that a delusion? Was Theo Vail alone in his fantasy or had Adrian Conway picked up the bug along the way?

'Hear me, Messenger of the Dark Regions...'

Christ, what was Vail doing now? Conway watched the other man's hands lift above his head, the cold ice eyes disappear beneath closed lids. Had he fallen completely out of his tree?

'Hear me, First among Angels of the Throne...'

Soft, sibilant, the sound of silk on silk, Vail's voice stroked the quiet room.

'Greatest of the malakhe Khabala.'

Conway stared at the figure standing with head tilted back and arms raised. He knew the phrase 'power corrupts' and no doubt Vail had his fair share of both, but this! Did the man really believe in the existence of hell and its angels? More to the point, did he truly imagine he could call forth demons? Believe that, Conway, and you'll finish up as mad as he is! The last was meant to bolster but as his limbs once again refused his com-

282

mands, Adrian Conway felt the first tremors of fear.

'Iblis, Apostate Angel of Hell...'

It was like some quiet hymn of praise and from its first uttering, from behind and around, from every corner of the room, a sound as of a sigh whispered. At its coming Vail straightened, his eyelids once more lifting to reveal eyes carved of grey ice, eyes which held inexorably those of Conway.

'Servant of the Lord of Darkness, in the name of him you must obey, I call you forth.'

The sound which had been a sigh increased to the rustle of a breeze.

His voice strengthening on every word, his face seeming to gleam triumph, Theo Vail called again.

'Belial.' He breathed long and deliberate. 'Great One who kneels before the Dark Throne, answer to my will. Reveal the power of the Lord Satan, him we both worship. Take that which his servant on earth offers, the life of Adrian Conway.'

He was mad! Adrian Conway watched the slow spread of the lips, the affected sweep of arms as they lowered to the other man's sides. Vail was not only a complete fruitcake, he was the whole bloody dessert trolley!

'Belial...'

He was almost singing! Christ, the man was definitely earmarked for the nut house ... and what of himself? He must be three parts along the same road in believing he could not move. Conway tugged again at invisible bonds. He didn't go along with mumbo jumbo, with the existence of the devil and all his works... so why then was he trussed like some bloody oven-ready turkey?

'In the name of the Greatest of Princes, before whom Asmodai, Ashtaroth and all the Angels of Hell must kneel, in the name of the Great Lord Satan, I command you pass beyond the Gates, come forth from the Dark Regions and do my bidding.'

Instantly the rustle became a roar. A mind-splitting scream ripped about the room, tearing into Conway, pulling at his mind and draining the will which even now had him trying to break free of the hypnotic bonds that held him.

'See, Adrian, see that which Neal Brady saw, that which kissed away his life – as it will take yours.'

Raising one hand, Vail pointed a finger at the ground between them and as suddenly as it had come the screaming died into silence.

Denied the last freedom of will, Adrian Conway's eyes followed the direction of the pointing finger and deep within him a surge of panic erupted. It couldn't be ... things like this didn't happen! But it *was* happening, and it was happening to *him!* Caught by his own fear, a rabbit snared by a trap, he stared. Colours! He blinked. The colours of the carpet ... they were moving. But that was ridiculous, the woven threads of a carpet could not move! The thought was sane enough but the reality ... that was insane; yet the colours, delicate, pale, almost translucent they twisted and turned, blues, mauve, water-green, they rolled and fused until they were one, one huge glistening serpentine coil of colour.

'Belial...'

Vail's finger lifted again, this time to point at Conway.

'Great among the servants of the Prince of Earth, present the gift you bring.'

Glistening, beautiful in its radiance, the coil rose, a gleaming spiral twisting and turning in the air.

'Taker of life...'

Vail's soft exhortation lost in the storm of fear already racing along his arteries, blocking his lungs and closing off his throat, Conway could only stare as the quiet chant went on.

'Belial who stands at the Black Throne, who followed the Great One to earth; Belial, minister of the Lord of Evil, deliver that which you carry, bestow upon Adrian Conway that which you are called forth to give.'

Spinning as if to unheard music, the shining coil gathered momentum, a kaleidoscope of colour reaching floor to ceiling, then at the moment it appeared it must breakthrough, the wild circling stopped. Vibrating gently, a rise and fall of luminous colour echoing the breathing of some massive serpent, it held for a moment and then contracted, withdrawing into itself until of a height with Adrian Conway, and within appeared a face, a gleaming reptilian face whose ruby eyes never left that of a terrified Conway.

'Bringer of Death,' the quiet intonation went on, 'Collector of Souls, take the offering.'

Within the iridescent breathing cylinder, a face of pure evil smiled, the mouth opening to display a forked tongue. Slowly, an act of infinite menace, the tongue emerged, passing lips which had become flame. Darting, flicking, brushing first forehead and then cheek, each touch burned Conway's skin with the sting of a red-hot brand.

'Dear God...'

Robbed of movement, aware only of the sheer terror beginning to numb his mind, Adrian Conway tried to pray; words unused since boyhood stumbling on his tongue.

'Lord Jesus Christ...'

The rest, stopped on his mouth by the flick of a forked tongue, became a screaming in his brain. Helpless, he watched the vibrating column once more become a spiral, a twisting, turning corkscrew of colour, transmuting, merging, assimilating until all was one; one crimson whole that was living fire, fire that wrapped itself around him, licking at body, at face, at head, until he was contained, still screaming, within a flaming vortex.

24

Richard Torrey's eyes flicked open, the transition from sleep to wakefulness instant.

It had been no dream! The sixth sense which never yet had proved false said there was no falsehood now.

Sight already attuned to the near blackness of the bedroom, ears honed to the slightest sound, he allowed his head to roll naturally on the pillow and a slight puff of breath to riffle across his lips.

If there was an intruder it would seem he was still asleep, while the movement of his head gave him a sweep of the room.

Make no other move. Remain immobile but listen hard. Let the enemy come to you. These tactics had saved his arse many times; there were men in Northern Ireland would attest to that, not to mention more than a few here in Darlaston. He didn't invite trouble, yet that commodity had a strange way of finding him – and it seemed a repeat performance was just about to play.

Well, so was he!

The bedroom held no body other than his own. Satisfied the evidence of his eyes held true, he eased from the bed. Sure footed, cat-like in his tread, every muscle completely in tune, his naked body adopted the well-learned tactic of relaxed tension, that deliberate holding in check while being totally ready for the first sign of attack.

There had been a spate of robberies in the area, a series of quick 'ins and outs', the culprits grabbing whatever came to hand.

'Daddies.' He had heard the term. Drug addicts ready to steal your eyeballs just so they could buy their next fix. Each to his own! That was the motto of his life and he tried to live by it, but when it came to the mugging of old folk, of breaking into another man's house – especially when that other man was Richard Torrey – that was where tolerance ended.

Daddies. He almost whispered the word aloud.

In less than two minutes that term would be obsolete for the bastard in his sitting room. Whoever might now be dipping his fingers into

Richard Torrey's belongings would never again be able to associate himself in any shape or form with that descriptive term; for from this night on, not only would his balls be ripped off, but the craving of narcotics would also be over for good, the only drugs this light-fingered little shit would need in the future would be pain killers – very strong pain killers.

Four soundless steps bringing him to a door partly opened on to the sitting room, he paused. This was not the first time he had been snapped awake, his brain singing the overture to danger.

Wait! Instinct born of commando training kicked in. Take stock of your ground, familiarise yourself with the situation, read your opponent!

Read your opponent! How had that fitted in with the time he had thought the flat to have been torched? He had been ready then to break some bastard's neck, to rip him apart and leave the remains to cremate in the fire of his own making. Only there had been no body to rip apart and no fire to cremate it.

Could it be the same thing again? Poised on the balls of his feet, Torrey hesitated. There was no smell of smoke. He glanced at the floor then back to the space left where the door was not closed against the jamb. There was no glow to indicate fire, nor any moving beam of a torch. Then this was not the ghostly visitor which had twice invited itself into his home. Despite the hardness born of active warfare, of seeing men die, Torrey felt a tremor of relief flip like wind around the heart. Men, living men he could deal with, but women, especially dead women ... that took him

288

some way out of his league.

He had thought it was Anna. Captured by memory, the hand he reached towards the door remained in mid-air. That first time his ghostly visitor had called he had thought he looked at Anna; the blonde hair, the hyacinth-blue eyes. Had it been desire had him place those as belonging to the woman he had loved, a woman whose spirit had returned to claim the lives of men who had first raped then arranged her murder? But then he had realised the eyes were not blue but turquoise, the hair though blonde fell over the shoulders instead of curling into the neck, that the figure stood at the heart of flame which did not burn was not Anna but a stranger, a stranger who returned days later to ask that he find something it called 'evil'.

No smoke, no glow of fire! This meant his visitor was of the human kind. Torrey pushed away the thoughts holding his hand from touching the living-room door. That type he could entertain, only they may not appreciate the agenda he was ready to provide.

One breath drawn through nostrils which closed sealing the air into his lungs, he lashed a foot against the door, arms in defensive mode before it slammed against the wall.

There was no movement! Eyes accustomed to night vision made a rapid scan of the room. The whack of wood against brick should have been enough to cause the shithead of a burglar to at least make a try for the window.

But there was no movement.

Arms drawn protectively in front of his chest,

hands ready to strike, darkness no obstacle to his movements, Torrey moved to block a second doorway. To escape that way this candidate for a wheelchair would first have to go through him, and that would be his second wrong move. The window? Torrey's glance creamed across to the expanse of plate glass rarely blocked by drawn blinds.

The window was closed!

Shadow hid the frown but could not obliterate the tremor that returned to sing along Torrey's veins. The window was not open ... but what sort of intruder closed off what might prove his only avenue of escape?

The sort that needed no avenue ... an intruder not of this world?

That was crap! The mental slap dismissed the tremor. Whoever had been fool enough to enter this flat had also been fool enough to think himself able to leave undetected, perhaps shit stupid enough to try that via the front door. Well, as the movies of his boyhood had said, this was showdown at the OK Corral.

Gingerly, every sense alert, he reached for the switch set just beside the door he guarded. That movement alone should have been detected by anyone half smart enough to call himself a cat burglar, yet the room remained perfectly still. No one made for the window, there was no rush for the door. Torrey half smiled. This little toerag was good at his game; he wasn't going to let nerves flush him out.

Good. The half-smile reached maturity. A little night exercise helped a man sleep.

With the last syllable of thought, light flooded the room. Torrey's hand dropped. His fingers hadn't yet touched the switch! He stared into the centre of the room, into what should have been a well of darkness but was now a spiralling cloud of crimson, its edges tiny spears of blue-tipped gold. Fire! The warning rang yet at the same time his brain told him this was no true fire, not in the physical sense.

'Find...'

Had the sound come from behind ... from above? There had been a sound, of that at least he was certain; but it could be no sound made by the living, not if it came from the centre of those flames. Torrey released air slowly from his lungs, then snatched it back as the murmur came again.

'Find ... find.'

Every segment of his brain told him to snap on the electric light, but Torrey's arms lowered. He had no control of his movements; arms, legs, even his eyes refused to obey his mental commands. This was how a rabbit caught in the glare of headlights must feel, but this was no vehicle and that glow was no headlight.

'What the hell do you want?'

Christ, he was talking to a bloody light! Torrey almost laughed. At least he could still speak.

As if caught by those half-shouted words, the gold-tipped spears drew together, merging, coalescing into a shimmering whole.

Unable to turn away, strangely not wanting to turn away, he watched the transition from flame to figure. Blue drained into blue becoming a dress, gold ran into gold forming long straight

291

blonde hair, and from a pretty face turquoise eyes stared back at him. Despite his convictions that this was madness, that no man in his right mind talked to a ghost, he asked, 'Why, why me?'

Did ghosts hear? Again the ludicrousness of the entire situation made him want to laugh ... or was that just nerves? He would be lying should he deny they were anything but normal; Army combat training had prepared him to meet anything with a cool, clear mind, except they had somehow missed out the bit on handling ghosts.

Yards from him the translucent figure hovered in mid air.

'Find.'

The mouth had not moved! Somewhere in the deep recesses of his brain that fact registered. The word had been spoken but the lips of that sad-looking face had remained closed.

'Find what?' Ludicrous or not, he had to ask, had to find out what the hell this ghost, spectre, spirit, call it by any name, wanted of him.

Flickering like a guttering candle, the figure floated on empty air, that same word issuing from an unmoving mouth.

'Find what!' Torrey felt exasperation kick in. 'Look, you've got the wrong guy, I don't – didn't – know you and I don't know what it is you have lost, so how can I find it? I'm sorry...' he paused. Did you apologise to a ghost? What the hell, in for a penny! 'I'm sorry but you've got the wrong guy.'

That should have done the trick, should have had the thing reconsider, take a fresh look at its co-ordinates, in other words put its light out, yet it still floated, its beautiful sad eyes fixed on him. Now what? His brain threw a dozen answers he could not comply with; how did you punch a ghost on the jaw, how did you kick its teeth in, how did you get a woman that was no woman to realise she had her sights set wrongly? That was one more thing commando training had overlooked. Torrey drew another slow breath. This was down to him and if he wanted to keep his sanity he had better get it right.

'Look.' He began more slowly, marshalling his thoughts. 'I really would help you but–'

'Not me...'

No more than a sigh it wafted like breath brushing his senses.

'Too late...'

This was getting more bizarre by the minute. First his spectral visitor tells him to find something only to then tell him it was too late. Just like a woman, couldn't make up her mind one way or the other.

It might have heard the words he had not spoken for a small smile touched the corners of the pretty mouth, while once more words formed themselves on the silence.

'Too late for me.'

'Then if it's too late, why? Why come?'

He could have couched that in stronger terms, tell whatever it was to piss off out of his life, but those were terms he wouldn't use to a lady, or even the ghost of one.

'Find...'

Draped in blue now tinged with crimson, an arm lifted and from its hand hung a chain of glittering stones, at their centre a jewelled pendant.

'Evil ... find.'

It was beginning to fade; the figure which somehow had managed to appear in a locked flat, which had just as unrealistically spoken with him, was beginning to evanesce, colours were losing their identity; blue and gold they intertwined, impregnating each other with parts of themselves.

'Wait!' Torrey disregarded every sense which told him he spoke to empty air, to a figment of his own imagining. 'What's evil? Tell me!'

Though the only move of that mouth was the losing of its faint smile, words emanated from the flames beginning to lick about the blonde head.

'Find...'

The hand lifted higher, holding the jewelled pendant clear of the reaching flame.

'Evil, destroy ... destroy...'

The last was swallowed by fire surging around the blue-clad figure. Red, gold, purple, the flames surged and danced themselves into scarlet chaos, blistering, blackening, charring skin, but out of it all a pair of turquoise eyes pleaded. Then it was gone.

Life flowed back into stiffened limbs, but Torrey made no effort to move. Once more in darkness, the last words echoing in his mind, he tried to argue the reality of those past few minutes. There were no such things as spirits, good or otherwise. Demons were the things of childhood nightmares, and the dead? They definitely did not return to haunt the living; but then, as Kate Mallory had replied to that same reasoning, how did that correspond to the happenings in the village of Monkswell or those which had taken shape in the cellar of Darlaston Printers?

There was nothing to connect what had occurred in either of those places with what was happening now. He had known the people at Monkswell, Martha Sim, her daughter Hilda, the Harpers, Hartley and Anna, yes, he had known the ghost of Anna. But Penny Smith, the girl Fred Baker had told him of, who had been secretary to Max Gau, manager of Darlaston Printers, and Crowley, a black magician; she had not been known to him in life yet she had called to him for help.

But this one! There was no Fred to fill in the blanks this time, no one to say how or what might have happened; just a figure wreathed in flame – a figure holding a pendant.

'There was no one there? No one had broken into your flat?'

Torrey looked at the meal he had no appetite for. Coming here had been a mistake. Maybe being with Kate at all was the wrong thing at the moment. He should have stayed at home or even run up to West Bromwich; with the Albion Baggies at home there would have been plenty of fares looking for a taxi to bring them from the stadium. But he had scarcely been in the mood for half-boozed football fans ... yet on second thoughts maybe a good punch up might have chased the remnants of last night away; the exercise might have cleared his mind. Would it though! He stared at the fried eggs he had fancied and which now his stomach rejected. An hour and a half in the gym had done nothing to help.

'You did say there was nobody in your flat?'

Kate's repeated question had him push the plate aside.

'Nobody!' His own repetition was curt. 'I went to snap on the light fully expecting to find myself teaching a well-earned lesson only there was no pupil.'

Kate looked at her own steak and chips. God, she would swap the lot for a tab, just one cigarette.

'But,' she heaved aside the longing, stabbing her fork into a chip instead, 'there is a "but" there somewhere.'

He ought never to have mentioned the episode of a burglar. She would not let go now. Yet he needed to talk with somebody and who but Kate Mallory would listen without having him down as a red-hot cert for the funny house.

'There was no ... body.' He watched her poke about her plate, selecting the fattest chip.

Kate picked up on the slight pause. If Torrey was still of the opinion he could not be the subject of a haunting, why the hesitation? Why talk around the problem instead of admitting one existed? But there was a problem and sooner or later he would have to recognise the fact or choke on it.

'It was...'

Christ, he would sooner face up to a bevy of hooligans than have to say this!

Kate didn't need to look at him to feel his uncertainty. She swallowed the chip. If ground was to be dug it was she must use the spade. Concentration still on her plate, she finished the sentence for him.

'It was the two women, those you saw in Birmingham Street.'

'No! 'Torrey shook his head. 'Well ... yes.'

Kate's tilted lips firmed. This beating about the bush wasn't suiting her at all. Hazel eyes more than hinting at her displeasure she came back sharply. 'I thought it was women who weren't supposed to be able to make up their minds. Seems that club is no longer quite so exclusive!'

'Sorry.' Torrey had the grace to smile. 'It *was* the same as Birmingham Street except this time there was only one figure, the girl in the blue dress.'

'And?'

'Lord, Kate, you're going to think...'

'Before you tell me what I think, it might be helpful to tell me the rest of what happened.'

'More or less a repeat performance. I thought someone had broken in...'

Forcing herself to concentrate on her meal was difficult, Torrey could leave so much out, but to interrupt might have him leave off altogether. This wisdom in mind, Kate held her silence, but the second he was through, her questions tumbled out.

'She said destroy? Destroy what? Did she mean the thing she held in her hand?'

He hadn't felt much like smiling all day but now the semblance of one hovered in his mind. If that was the way her talk with Daniels had gone today, then it was no wonder the bloke had virtually told her to sod off. The smile wisely kept under wraps,

297

along with any reference to her speaking with the blues, he shrugged. 'She ... it ... didn't specify, all it said was what I have told you.'

'Anything wrong with your meal?' Having come to collect the used dishes, the barmaid-cum-waitress looked at Torrey. 'I'll get you summat else if you wants.'

'The meal is excellent as always,' he answered, the smile he had withheld from Kate now breaking the surface, 'it's me, luv, I think I'm pregnant.'

'You think!' Brown curls bobbing, the woman laughed. 'All I can say is if you ain't certain then it couldn't 'ave been much of a night. But I tell you what, you 'ave me as godmother an' we'll 'ave the christening "do" here in the Frying Pan and no charge to y'self.'

'And if it isn't what I think, if it turns out to be no more than wind?'

The woman laughed. 'Then you best not give it rein in my pub or it's more'n a babby you can be expecting.'

The woman turned away towards the kitchen. Following her, Kate's glance caught the pale veil of cigarette smoke rising from the furthest end of the room where two tables were partly partitioned from the wider area of the lounge bar. Lord, she would kiss the man's bottom for a tab!

'Kate, stop drooling over that man's cigarette!' Torrey followed Kate's line of sight. 'Any second now and you'll charm it out of his hand.'

'If only I could!' Kate breathed hard as if the action would bring the pale lavender veil to her nostrils. 'If only I could!'

'Well, I'm glad you can't, one example of paranormal activity is all I can take in any twenty-four hours.'

Desire for a cigarette abandoned but not forgotten, Kate returned to their previous conversation. 'So, is it that thing she was holding that she wants destroyed? And if so, how did she come by it?'

Facing her across the table, Richard Torrey shook his head slowly and deliberately. 'You know, Kate, you really should concentrate instead of dreaming of a cigarette; I've already told you exactly the words I heard and they did not include what needed to be destroyed ... who wanted it done ... nor how or where the thing was to be found; all I heard–'

'I know ... I know!' Petulance, withdrawal symptoms or just plain bad temper? Kate wasn't sure which gave the cutting edge to her reply and right then didn't care anyway. Torrey was as bad as the rest of society's do-gooders, he only saw things from his own side of the fence. Repentance following hard on the heels of exasperation, a smile offered a truce.

'The girl, it's obvious she is trying to tell you something.'

'But why me? I never knew her, why not–'

'You didn't know Penny Smith but you helped her.' Kate's swift return cut Torrey's disgruntled reply. 'There is no difference between Penny and the girl in the photograph Echo Sounder gave. They were both murdered and I think I have an idea why.'

Should he say, 'so let's hear your idea', or

should he say, 'here we go, you and your creepy notions'? To say either would ruffle her feathers again and that was best avoided when Kate Mallory's nicotine drive was in full throttle; Torrey decided upon diplomatic silence.

'Penny Smith's arm bore a tattoo, didn't it? The Seal of Asmodai, put there by Crowley,' Kate mused on, needing no affirmation, 'Sheryl Wilkes carries a pendant which it seems is the devil's Talisman. Is she trying to show us that Crowley's being put away by the law was not the end of black magic in Darlaston? Is she trying to warn against something equally as evil as that man had planned?'

'Hold on, Kate!' Torrey threw aside his decision of a moment before. 'Let's not get carried away. There's nothing to support that line of reasoning.'

'Nothing to support!' Kate's snort brought several glances their way. 'You heard what Annie and Echo said about that necklace brought to Bentley Hall from Russia, you saw the copy I made of the woodcut found in that library book, you even drew the very same thing yourself! Lord, Torrey, how much more do you need; the thing Sheryl Wilkes' ghost holds out to you *is* the devil's Talisman, there can be no other explanation, just as there can be none that she is warning, "find it, destroy it before"...' She paused not knowing what it was the ghost of that girl was forewarning, but every nerve, every fibre tingled with the same dread – evil.

25

What the hell was going on in this town? Bruce Daniels glanced at the blackened heap lying in the centre of a neat sitting room. A woman burned to death in a paint factory, another used as a Guy Fawkes on a bonfire – and now this. The paint-factory job was no doubt accidental, at least that had been the Coroner's finding, but he couldn't say that of the second. The woman had been barbecued, tied to a cross and set afire, that was murder in any copper's book; and this one? He looked again at the charred figure being zipped into a body bag. Accident? Maybe, yet that theory somehow didn't sit right. Suicide? Pretty bloody gory method of doing away with yourself, a bloke needed some balls to do a thing like that. Murder? That was one more possibility, but how could it have been done without the fire spreading at least to the carpet?

'What d'you reckon, sir?'

It was an innocent enough remark, yet it chaffed Daniels' nerves.

'About what?'

'About *that*, sir.' Detective Sergeant Sam Williams' glance followed the corpse being carried from the room.

'I reckon he's dead!' Daniels knew the answer was churlish but, Christ, he felt churlish! The bonfire case wasn't cleared yet and here was

301

another. What would Quinto have to say about this? 'Results, Daniels!' The words rang in his brain, that was what Quinto would say. 'I want results.' Christ, but so did he! Reaching into his pocket for the ever-present antacid tablet, he threw it into his mouth with an angry, savage movement. *He* wanted results, but the one he wanted most was the one that would take Quinto off his back.

'Very good!' Williams' mouth tightened. 'I can see why you are Detective Inspector... sir.'

Good for the lad! Despite his chagrin Daniels inwardly applauded the younger man. He was learning how to give an answer. This one would climb on his own and hopefully not become a 'Quinto' on the way.

'What I haven't worked out is how,' Williams went on, 'I mean he ... the victim ... is roasted to a crisp yet there is no other evidence of fire, how come? I mean how can a body burn without leaving so much as a singe on the carpet beneath it?'

Daniels sucked on the tablet. The doctor had said something about spontaneous combustion, a body somehow setting itself alight, but that didn't account for the rest of the room showing not even a trace of smoke.

'We'll let forensics worry over "how",' he answered, leading the way into the narrow hall separating sitting room from dining room and kitchen. 'Right now we need to find out if there are relatives or dependents to be informed. Though it's a safe enough bet to say three quarters of Darlaston have already been informed, you can't fart in this town without the whole population hearing it; see what I mean?'

'Yes, sir.' Following into the street, Williams played a quick glance over the group of people who had gathered the moment the ambulance and police car had pulled up. 'Should I take statements?'

He had learned how to reply to sarcasm but he had not yet learned everything. Take one step towards those onlookers and they would disappear before he took a second. For a brief moment Daniels was tempted to say yes but then shook his head.

'Do no good.' He decided on a kindlier answer. 'Apart from the cleaning woman who found him, everybody would deny knowing him, much less what killed him. For now we'll follow up what leads we have. You take over here and, WPC Rogers, you stay with the woman, learn what you can but don't frighten her off by stickin' a notebook under her nose ... let her take her time.'

'Where will you be, sir?'

What was he... a bloody school boy who had to account for his whereabouts? For a moment dislike of having another officer with him rose thickly in Daniels' throat. What had become of the old days where a man could do a job without havin' another one glued to his arse?

'Where will I be?' He forced the answer to come smoothly. 'I, Williams, will be in the Staffordshire Knot.'

'Piss off!' Echo Sounder clutched a near-empty pint glass as if it was a weapon. 'Like I told Daniels earlier, I don't know nuthin'!'

303

'I wouldn't say that.' Kate smiled sweetly. 'I think you are a quite intelligent man.'

Intelligent enough to know when a woman is fishing! Coming to the table just in time to hear the exchange, Torrey set fresh drinks on the beer-stained surface.

'I don't gie a bugger what you thinks!' Sounder snapped. 'Neither do I be givin' any answers, so you can tek your questions an' use 'em for suppositories.'

A polite way of putting it! Torrey handed Kate her lime and lemon. Normally the little man would have said to stuff her questions up her arse. Could his improved terminology have anything to do with Kate's companion, namely Richard Torrey? Seeing the sideways squint darted towards his face, Torrey decided the answer to that question would be a definite yes.

'So what was Daniels asking after? And don't tell me it was nothing.'

There was no 'if or but' about that. Sounder heard the warning behind the words. Torrey had demonstrated his skills on several of the town's yobbos and would be quite ready to give another should something upset him. Sounder knew an ultimatum when it stared him in the face.

'He was askin' same as you.' The little man sent a shifty glance to where several people stood watching the game being played at the pool table.

'Which was?'

'I don't 'ave to tell you nuthin'!'

Leaning slightly nearer the head drawn almost inside the scruffy jacket, Torrey answered quietly, 'You have balls, I'll give you that, but if you don't want them ripped off and served up for your supper you will answer nicely. Now, what was Daniels talking to you about?'

Across the smoke-hazed bar room the television screen showed a string of horses racing neck and neck. Sounder stared at the picture, his thoughts moving as rapidly as the horses. Daniels could bang him up, get him a few months' free stay in Winson Green prison; trumping up a charge would present no difficulty. But at least when the stretch was done he would be able to walk. Cross Torrey and there was an even chance of never walking again. Never one to bet on odds so obviously against him, Sounder took the sensible course. 'He asked did I know anythin' about some 'ouse fire. I told him I gets my buzz outta playin' the 'orses, not playin' with fire.'

'A house fire, where?'

Kate watched the tension behind the question. Torrey had told her of that ghostly episode in his flat but what was it he had *not* told her about?

'Birmingham Street.' Sounder answered quickly. 'Look, Torrey, I ain't no bloody arsonist, I d'ain't set no fire an' I don't know who did. I told Daniels an' now I be tellin' you, it don't 'ave nuthin' to do wi' me!'

'But you did know who it was lived in that house.' Now he was the one placing a bet. His features bland, Torrey waited. Would the bet pay off or would it prove a non-starter?

A few yards from the table a new set of players racked the pool balls then removed the frame, leaving them set in a perfect triangle. Why the hell hadn't he gone to Monmore Green instead

305

of coming here? At the greyhound stadium he wouldn't have had folk breathing down his neck. But Daniels and Torrey would both have been here when he got back. Facing the indisputable, Echo Sounder accepted it.

'Ar,' he nodded, his mouth almost resting on the rim of his glass. 'I knowed 'im, I knowed 'em both.'

'Both?'

Sounder nodded again, his next words those of self-defence. 'It ain't like sayin' summat as don't already be knowed, ask anybody an' chance be they'll tell you the same; the two who lived in that 'ouse though they weren't man and wife still that was the way they carried on.'

'So they were not married.' Kate intervened. 'That doesn't bother anyone very much these days.'

'Mebbe's it don't, an' mebbe's two men livin' as man an' wife don't much bother folk up along where you comes from but there be some in Darlaston that kind of thing be best hid from, there still be them as don't cotton to a man fuc– sleepin' wi' another man, try tellin' them it don't be against nature an' like enough you'll feel a boot against your teeth.'

The man had his principles. Torrey nudged a full glass nearer to fingers still clasped about an almost empty one. Sounder also had sense enough to keep any opinions to himself.

'There was no one else in the house, only one body was recovered, so Inspector Daniels told me when I spoke to him.' That was all the acid-tongued man had told her. Kate's mind slipped back over the few terse words he had spat before saying there would be no more until after the Coroner delivered his findings. That said he had banged away into his office leaving the desk sergeant to the task of seeing her gone from the station.

'Ain't no surprise seein' as out of the two as lived in the 'ouse one was in 'ospital.'

'Which hospital?' It was Kate's question.

'Ain't sayin'.' Sounder snatched the full glass, taking no chances his next words would see it taken from him. 'Why should I provide for the *Star* an' get nowt forrit!'

Things were back to normal. Echo Sounder had given her that photograph and no payment asked. Seemed his brain was recovered; he wouldn't make that mistake again.

Taking a purse from the shoulder bag, she drew out a banknote. Holding it partly covered in her palm she repeated the question.

Sounder's ferret eyes flicked from glass to palm then back to glass. Ten pounds would provide him a day at the race track. 'Don't know the name but it's one o' them places looks after folk with just a few months to live.'

'A hospice?'

'That's it. Can't be more'n one or two o' them in Wolverhampton, but won't be much use in you goin' to any of 'em seein' Brady be dead.'

The fare he had driven back to Birmingham Street the night he had seen that apparition! Torrey's mind flashed to replay. The man had sobbed and now he knew why, he had lost the love of his life. Nobody realised the pain of that until they felt it for themselves, as he himself had felt it the day he had seen Anna's body in the morgue, his beautiful Anna whose face had been half shot away.

'Brady and Conway.' He shut away the thought. 'How well did you know them?'

Torrey's question brought a stab of ferret eyes. 'I d'ain't know 'em as well as you might be thinkin'... I ain't no pansy, a man's arse 'olds no delights for me!'

The flash of memory showing him the destruction of Anna's face, of Anna's own destroying of the love they had shared, spewed vitriol into Torrey's tight reply. 'That makes one thing you won't do for money, now here's the next! You are going to tell everything you know about those men ... and, Sounder ... don't make any bets on what will happen should you try refusing!'

What had suddenly got under Torrey's skin? Kate glanced over the rim of her glass. His conversations with Sounder were often laced with sarcasm and veiled warnings but this one had the veil drawn back; the threat was visible and it was meant.

Echo too had heard the inexorability, recognised the choice and the fact that he had none.

'I knowed Adrian Conway from bein' a kid.' Resentful, the muttered words pushed between clamped teeth. 'We was at the same schools, Rough Hay Junior and then Joseph Leckie Comprehensive. Conway was bright, went for biology an' chemistry, that sort o' stuff...' Sounder swallowed a mouthful of beer before continuing, '...then he went on to university. His mother

308

thought the sun shone out of his arse, God knows what it would 'ave done had her known what was pushed into it. But 'er were spared that, 'er died just a few weeks after Conway come 'ome. Look, I ain't sayin' no more, a lot o' folk reads the *Star* an' I wants none of 'em come knockin' on my door.'

'This isn't for the *Star* ... is it, Kate?'

What did Torrey think he was playing at? She had got almost nothing from Daniels concerning that house fire in Birmingham Street and now Torrey was saying she should not use Echo Sounder's input. What did that leave her with? Sweet sod all! Well, not exactly all, she would have a bawling out from Scottie, not that that was anything new.

'You say it ain't for the *Star*, Torrey, but I don't hear 'er sayin' the same.'

Could she face the responsibility of Sounder losing several teeth or Torrey serving a prison sentence for aggravated assault? Kate stared face on at the challenge, then resignedly stepped back.

'My report for the newspaper is already written.'

She could almost hear the words her mother had always said when catching her in a lie. 'Eh, lass, they divn't pull bigger cod from the sea!' Well, this lie had been told in a good cause. Kate's consolation was a sham but it was all she had.

'That good enough for you?'

Torrey's tone told it all! Echo Sounder's neck contracted into his shoulders, lowering his head on to the collar of his scruffy jacket. He could say

309

no it wasn't good enough; that would result in a smack and a smack from Richard Torrey was not top of his list of Must Haves. And the ten-pound note? That hadn't come past the starting gate.

'Were he and Brady friends from childhood?'

Hair in want of a good shampooing reflected no gleam of light as Sounder shook his head.

'Not so far as I knows. Brady certainly d'ain't go to the same schools as Conway an' meself so it be my bet them two met at university.'

'Do you know what subjects Conway studied?'

When the hell was this going to finish? Echo Sounder's glance appeared not to have shifted from his glass yet nothing in the room had escaped it; and certainly not the looks coming from the men assembled around the pool table. They knew Torrey, knew his usual watering hole was the Frying Pan, so it was odds-on favourite they would be asking themselves what was Torrey and his bitch doing here? For a moment a deeply hidden smile lurked in the pit of Sounder's stomach. Lord, he wished they would ask now, he would take no bets on any of them leaving on their own two legs. But, like himself, the pool players and their audience were well aware of that. No, they wouldn't ask Torrey, but once the man was gone they would ask Echo Sounder!

'Talked to him once or twice after he come back to Darlaston.' Sounder's lips barely moved. 'Seems he'd carried on wi' the chemistry an' such. Said he'd teken a job wi' some sort o' corporation... Vail I thinks it were, ar, that was the name. Vail Corporation.'

Kate lowered her glass at the precise same

310

moment Torrey's fingers whitened around his. What had brought that reaction? Her glance flicked to his face. It was closed tight. Maybe he thought it didn't show, yet she could see that something was definitely rattling his cage.

Heaving her bag to her shoulder as Torrey rose to leave, she dropped the banknote as near Sounder's hand as she cared to touch.

'Fair's fair,' she said as shifty eyes lifted to her own. 'You told us what we asked.' Beside which, she said to herself, to make an enemy of Echo Sounder was to cut off a valuable supply of local gossip.

'Wait?'

'It's okay.' Kate smiled. 'There will be nothing but the bare essentials.'

'Ain't that.' Sounder's head lifted. What he had to say now, the world could hear. 'It be about Sheryl; 'ave you 'eard any more, I mean as to who done it?'

Sympathy welled deep in Kate. Sounder had really loved the girl, the fact was written in his face.

'No.' She answered quietly. 'But if and when...' she paused as the tousled head dropped again, 'well, then I'll let you know.'

The reply was half drowned in a beer glass but Kate heard it. 'I prays you don't 'ave to, I prays it be me finds the bastard first!'

26

'What was all that about?' Standing in the car park of the Staffordshire Knot, Kate threw the question.

'All what about?'

'Look, Torrey, I might be from Tyneside, but I didn't come on any onion boat so don't try treating me as though I'm short weight on brain cells!' Sharp and indignant it rang above the sound of traffic passing along Pinfold Street. 'You were sharp with Sounder – no, don't deny it – you almost cut the man in half with your sarcasm, that's no way to get answers.'

'It got me mine!'

'Oh ... and that gives you a kick!'

Now who was being sarcastic? Torrey released the lock on the doors of the car. But Kate was right, he had behaved like a bear with a boil on its arse.

'So, what gave rise to that performance ... or am I to be treated to a second "showing"?'

His door half closed, Torrey twisted in the seat. 'If it'll make you feel any the less sore I'll go back inside and apologise, that should make Sounder feel better.'

'I doubt that!' Kate snorted. 'You apologising won't make him feel better, it's more likely to kill him with the shock.'

Fastening his seat belt, Torrey seemed to be

312

thinking that over. Her own safety belt secure, Kate clutched her shoulder bag on her knees.

A slight shrug showing that contemplation was over, he turned the key in the ignition. 'In that case perhaps I shouldn't. We don't have too many song birds in this country, it would be a shame to kill another.'

Should she skelp him now? A sharp slap might bring some sense out of him! Kate bridled but remained silent, watching the buildings of Wolverhampton Street flash past. Perhaps there had been more to that visitation in his flat than he had told her of. Kate's irritation began to melt. Lord, if such a thing had happened to her she would be a gibbering idiot by now; given the times Torrey had had experience of ghostly happenings it was no wonder he was snappy. Would it help if she suggested they ask Annie give him a room for a few nights? Her landlady was fond of him and would agree ... but that would prove no deterrent to a ghost that appeared in his flat, in the street and even in this very car. The last thought striking home, Kate glanced nervously over her shoulder.

As Torrey drew to the kerb the last dregs of irritation mixed with apprehension of what might decide to show itself in the rear seat showed in Kate's quick movement in immediately releasing her seat belt.

'Kate, I'm sorry.' Interpreting her rapid reach to open her door to be from the same annoyance that had flared a few minutes before, Torrey was apologetic. 'I didn't mean to upset you or Echo, it's...' he thumped a closed fist against the

313

steering wheel, 'Christ, I don't *know* what it is!'

Instantly regretting her own display of vexation, Kate fought the tiny tremors of fear flickering low in her stomach. She glanced at the glow of Annie's curtained window. Torrey wouldn't talk in there. Yet it was obvious he needed to talk and spook or no spook she had to give him the opportunity.

'Has...' she swallowed hard against the tightness suddenly banded about her throat, 'has she been again, the ghost, I mean?'

A couple of shakes of his dark head gave his answer. Kate tried again. 'You don't have to... Look, you've no need to pretend with me, I believe you.'

'Thanks.' He smiled briefly. 'But it's true, I haven't seen any more of my friendly phantom.'

'Then what is it? And, as you said to Echo, "don't tell me it's nothing".'

Allowing his head to rest against the back of his seat, Torrey breathed out slowly. Maybe he wasn't quite an open book but the lady could certainly read between the lines.

'Kate.' He hesitated. Was he making too much of what he had learned? Kate Mallory believed what he said of those hauntings, but she could still believe him a little mad – but then perhaps he was.

'Kate,' he began again. 'Do you remember Fred Baker?'

'Of course, he was the Joey, the jack of all trades at Darlaston Printers.'

'I mean, do you remember how he was found in his home, the look on his face? Daniels said it

314

was almost as though he had been frightened to death.'

'Crowley?' Kate caught her breath. 'You think Crowley is behind what's happening?'

'No, not Crowley, but another of the same ilk. I think the same thing is happening all over again.'

He had expected her to laugh, to tell him he was all kinds of a fool, and maybe he was. Torrey stared at the shadowed ceiling above his bed. But Kate Mallory hadn't laughed, she had listened while he told of finding that small package in his taxi. Shoved beneath the driving seat he had not discovered it until giving the car its weekly thorough going-over. It had borne no address but simply a name, a name he knew from several bookings. Adrian Conway. He had gone to Birmingham Street thinking to return it but the 'uniform' at the gate had had him change his mind. Let Daniels get wind of his calling and he'd throw questions like rice at a wedding. Then he had heard Conway was dead, burned to death in his own living room. He ought to have gone to Victoria Road then, handed the package over to the blues – but he hadn't.

Christ, he was no bloody thief! One arm covering his face, he tried to reason with his actions. Whatever that packet held he had no desire to keep it. That at least was what he had told himself, yet something stronger had held him from taking the package to the station, something that urged him to open it.

He could re-wrap the thing, say it had become

torn open while lodged under the driving seat of the taxi. His brain had supplied all the answers, common sense failing beneath their barrage.

It had proved to be a small cardboard box, on its lid one simple word, Vail, its contents a small clear plastic bag holding white powder.

Heroin, cocaine? A list of drugs had whipped like snakes in his mind. Had Conway been one of the 'Daddies', the drug addicts he had heard talked of? It had seemed the most logical explanation, unless the man was making his own form of Viagra. The thought had not amused him then and it didn't now. So why hadn't he flushed it down the toilet, burned it? After all, Conway had no further need of it.

Such sensible self-advice. So why hadn't he taken it? Ask me another! Torrey laughed to himself, a cynical, you-bloody-fool type of laugh. But he hadn't done that. Oh no, not Torrey, instead he had taken a tiny amount of the stuff along to a man he trained with at the T.A. barracks. A chemist who owed him a favour for Torrey carrying him halfway back from a ten-mile field exercise yet not disclosing it. He'd analysed the stuff.

It was not heroin, not cocaine and not Viagra.

'So what the hell is it?' he had asked.

The answer had come in one word.

Armageddon!

Kate Mallory's reaction had been the same as his. She hadn't known whether to laugh or choke. He had chosen the latter when he heard the rest of that report. It was a poison so strong that less than a quarter of a milligram would be enough to kill a man; this stuff could wipe out the world. Thank God he'd warned the man to take the strictest precautions when testing the powder.

Armageddon!

It seemed to ring aloud on the silence, to bear down upon him from the shadows of the ceiling.

The war of wars! Satan's war!

No, this was not the work of Crowley, but of someone just as evil.

And that someone felt very close at hand.

'It is good of you to come, I know how valuable time is for you.' Theo Vail shook hands with his tall distinguished-looking visitor. Savile Row suit, Turnbull and Asser shirt, gold engraved signet ring and cufflinks, not to mention custom-made Lobb shoes costing many hundreds of pounds a pair. Zachary St John Winter enjoyed the advantages of new money as well as the benefit of the old.

Leading the way into a drawing room quietly but expensively furnished, Theo Vail's smile hid darker thoughts. The St John Winter family fortune had long since evaporated, leaving its last child to make his own way in life and the man intended it to be of the luxury always enjoyed by his forebears, the who or what of achieving that lifestyle affording him no headache. That suited Theo Vail very well indeed.

'The Prime Minister asked me to tell you that the government thanks the Corporation for its generosity both in the donating of foodstuffs and in the offer of transporting the same; however,' he paused, 'the Prime Minister also feels it would look better in the eyes of the world should it appear Her Majesty's government were the sole donor.'

They wanted to have their cake as well as eating it!

Pouring brandy into Brierly Crystal goblets, Theo Vail handed one to his visitor before taking the other to a chair opposite.

'Forgive me.' Grey eyes smiled deceptively. 'I thought I had made myself quite clear on our previous meeting. What is being given is given to the government to do with as they see fit; the Corporation neither asks for nor requires payment.' Not quite true! Vail held the goblet at mouth level, breathing the aroma released by the warmth of his hand. The Corporation ... or namely its head ... would require very special payment!

Lifting his own glass, St John Winter took a moment to appreciate the bouquet of brandy aged in casks years before he had been born. How to put the next query delicately? The solution had been his to find; mess it up and he would be very quickly out of office. That would dent his lifestyle in more ways than just the loss of a Ministerial salary.

'However, we...' Vail smiled over the brandy, 'that is, the Corporation, do have one question.' He recognised the delay of response. The Foreign Secretary was nervous of a last-minute hitch, of having to return to Downing Street and tell his boss the deal was off. So nice to watch! Vail sipped the century-old liquor, feeling the glow of it against his throat, a glow he would feel much more intensely if things took the shape he planned.

'Which is?' Winter's question displayed no perturbation.

You had to hand it to the man, he hid his nerves well. Vail sipped once more before answering. 'The containers, how would the government prefer them? Without logo or perhaps marked "gift of the United Kingdom"?'

Christ, was that all! St John Winter's lungs relaxed. 'I'm sure the PM would view the word "gift" as patronising; let's just have them stamped UK, far less ostentatious, don't you agree? After all, it wouldn't do to alienate feeling among our international colleagues.'

No, it wouldn't do at all, especially not for someone who entertained the aspirations Zachary St John Winter did.

'That's settled then.' Vail's superficial smile hid contempt. 'Everything is on target, as they say, we have the necessary transport laid on, all we need now is the go ahead.'

'Ah, yes, transport. Your offer was something else the PM was pleased about, cutting costs to the Nation and all that; don't let on to anybody but it might well turn out you have a mention in the New Year's Honours List, could even be a Knighthood in it, old chap.'

Swirling amber-gold liquid around the crystal goblet, Vail forced back the laugh rising inside. A Knighthood ... for one who would be a prince! An honour bestowed by a Queen for a man who would be honoured by the All High Lord of Hell, Ruler of the Earth!

'That would be most gracious.' His steady

glance travelled across the room. 'But I would not wish to be singled out, so many others have helped in putting this operation together.'

'Commendable.' Winter laid aside his empty glass. 'Can't say I would have done the same thing myself, a Knighthood can be influential, *very* influential.'

He would be influential! Vail held the thought to himself. More influential than any Knight of the Realm, or any minister of any government; he would be Ipsissimus, First Prince of Satan on earth; to him would be given greater honour, greater powers than this offspring of the aristocracy could ever dream possible.

'Perhaps Fenton or Thorold, they deserve the honour as much as myself,' Vail answered, putting his glass aside.

'I thought to see them here this evening, a word of gratitude to them also.'

'My colleagues *are* here.' Vail rose with the other man. 'I asked them to wait in the library in the event of your not wishing to be detained.'

'Nothing on in London ... nor in Essex.'

Was the latter a reference to Mrs St John Winter being at home? No doubt of it, seeing the look settling across the suntanned features, but why nothing in London? Could it be the man had tired of the lovely model picked up at Venetia Pascal's jewellery launch?

'Can be one hell of a bore being in the Cabinet.' St John Winter's reply echoed the feeling. 'The eye of the public, not to say its nose, is always trained on you, gets so a man can't call his soul his own.'

Many a true word! Theo Vail's grey eyes glinted. They may have been spoken in jest, but soon they would become fact. After tonight Zachary St John Winter would never again be able to call his soul his own!

27

He hadn't taken a deal of persuading. Perhaps it was the thought of what might transpire from another meeting with the beautiful Venetia Pascal that had been responsible for that. And the woman was beautiful, there was no contesting the fact. Theo Vail watched her now smiling at something St John Winter was whispering close to her ear. The man should be warned, Venetia Pascal was enchanting to look at but appearances could be deceptive; like a snake her beauty could mesmerise and like that creature she was dangerous.

'He seems more than a little taken with our lovely colleague.'

Come to stand at Vail's side, Laurence Thorold too had watched St John Winter make a beeline for Venetia. 'Wonder what happened to the piece he acquired at the jewellery launch?'

'Old news.' Vail's smile was pure cynicism. 'The man likes variety.'

Helping himself to more champagne, Thorold glanced again at the man and woman standing close together at the farther side of the room.

'Don't we all.' He lifted the delicate crystal flute. 'Perhaps a noble lineage will succeed, money certainly hasn't!'

So Thorold had tried his hand, and the bruised ego still smarted. What had Venetia Pascal replied to a man stupid enough to offer money to a woman who doubtless was as wealthy, if not more so, than Thorold was himself? Vail hid his contempt behind a quick reply. 'Venetia will do whatever service the Master requires, as we all must.'

'And the reward for that service, what does the delectable Miss Pascal ask of the Prince of Darkness? She already controls an international cosmetics business, also a very lucrative line in jewellery and as you say, she has all the money she might ever need; so ask yourself, Vail, just what more does the beautiful goddess aspire to, what has she set her lovely eyes on?'

The question, though voiced by another, was not new to Theo Vail, he had asked himself the same more than once and each time the reply worried him more; but of all the answers burning in his mind one remained dominant, returning again and again until it forced recognition. Venetia Pascal wanted power! That was the desire behind her every action, the only lust felt by that exquisite body. She would never be satisfied to be a mere subordinate, an insignificant player in the service of the Lord of the Earth; playing second fiddle to anyone formed no part of the woman's mentality. That became more obvious with every meeting of the coven; it was she who questioned, she who challenged his decisions. How long before she challenged his leadership? He could not afford for things to go that far. Risk was not in his vocabulary. Watching her now he felt a tingle travel his spine, but it was not the twist of desire he had experienced in the early days of their meeting, no hot surge of passion, but the cold electricity of warning. Venetia Pascal must be put out of the running – permanently!

'I don't want to appear to be interfering but it might be prudent to start the entertainment before our guest gets too drunk to enjoy it.'

He was right. Vail nodded agreement to Thorold's remark. A Foreign Secretary too inebriated to know what he took part in was not the purpose of the evening.

As though acting on a pre-arranged signal, Venetia Pascal led the man in question to join the others.

'Ah.' Vail's smile was that of a cobra, masking venom. 'Whenever you are ready.'

'If the entertainment you have planned is anywhere near as enjoyable as that of the past few minutes then I am more than ready.' St John Winter's leering smile lingered on Venetia. 'I have just been telling our so delightful companion that she is the real jewel in her whole collection ... a man would be willing to part with his soul in exchange for her.'

It might just come to that! The thought no more than a smile in his mind, Vail chose to ignore the comment saying, 'From time to time those of our small company wishing to do so engage in a little charade, they plan out some personal fantasy; some would say they are acting out their

323

particular fetish. It will no doubt be very different to the social engagements your duties have you attend; however, should you so wish it will be instantly discontinued. We would not want to offend...'

'Each to their own.' St John Winter shook an expertly groomed head. 'As for myself, I welcome any diversion from the boring routine we ministers find ourselves subjected to, so let the party commence!'

'Tonight we are invited to share the consummation of Fenton's rather quixotic fancy.'

'You will excuse me, there is something I must attend to.' This part of the proceedings had never appealed to Venetia Pascal and she would make no exception now, regardless of the status of Vail's guest.

'You are not leaving, my dear? That would spoil the entire evening.'

'No.' Venetia treated the Foreign Secretary to a dazzling smile. 'I am not leaving altogether, merely withdrawing. I promise to return in a little while.'

'The promise of a beautiful woman is like wine to the soul. I shall drink liberally of it until it is fulfilled.'

Lord, the man was a creep! Venetia almost shuddered as he touched her hand. But then so was Vail, the two were well matched, they both looked on her as a tool, something with which to satisfy their own needs; but both were mistaken in their thinking. Venetia Pascal walked in no man's shadow and she would serve none but the one who had made such passionate love to her in that hotel bedroom; her beautiful golden lover.

It had been so wonderful, the feel of arms she knew could crush her out of existence, the touch of lips so soft yet so demanding; but pleasurable as that had been, true bliss had come with his entering her: the thrust of his body, that hard flesh driving into her; it had been ecstasy, a soul freeing unalloyed rapture she had never known before. But she would know it again. As she closed the door on Vail and the others, a tiny smile edged her perfect mouth. Yes, she would know it again!

'Christ Almighty!' Zachary St John Winter blew through his cosmetically perfected teeth. His glance held as if with rivets followed the line of crimson trickling across the cheek of a young girl bound hand and foot with finc-linked silver chain. Brought into the room by the short balding Stuart Fenton leading her by a matching chain fastened to a neck collar of glistening white stones the girl had whimpered in fear as, arms and legs spread wide, she was manacled wrist and ankle to the wall, a whimper which became a cry as the point of a knife traced across her face.

Sitting next to the Foreign Secretary Theo Vail smiled inwardly. The man had been aroused by the sight of the flimsy dress being ripped from the girl; his indrawn breath at the sight of small firm breasts and the hairless vee between slim legs had been clearly audible.

Long blond hair tumbling to her shoulders caught in the crimson line, whipping spots of it onto Fenton's face as the girl threw her head sidewards in an effort to avoid the knife, her pleas to be released serving only to enhance Fenton's obvious pleasure.

'Christ, Vail, he'll finish up killing the girl!'

'Would you prefer it ended?' Vail glanced at the man beside him. A fine sheen of moisture painted the skin between nose and mouth, but the eyes were bright with the gleam of lust.

The pause between question and a second indrawn breath providing its own answer, Theo Vail felt satisfaction thicken. The show would not end until it was finished; Zachary St John Winter was living his own fantasy.

Across from them Stuart Fenton seemed lost to all except himself and the girl he had enchained. Above them, suspended from the high ceiling, a crystal chandelier spilled a central pool of light, the gleam catching the blade of a knife, dancing along its length like tiny fireflies.

'No! Please!'

The girl's cry of terror was drowned beneath Stuart Fenton's strangled laugh.

'No ... no, please...'

The girl screamed as the knife rose. Now was the moment for Winter to move, to call a halt, but lips parted, breath sucked in short excited gasps the Foreign Secretary remained still, only his eyes following the glittering path of a slim blade tracing the same scarlet trail across each breast.

It was as he had suspected. Vail sat relaxed in his own chair. His illustrious guest had no intention of foregoing the rest of the performance.

The stone-encrusted collar restricting much of the movement of her neck, the girl could not evade the slender finger of steel coming once more close to her face. Her head was pressed back as far as it would go against the wall; the overhead light reflected on tears sparkling like sun on ice crystals.

'Christ, look at the man!' The exclamation no more than a hiss of excited breath, Zachary St John Winter edged forward in his chair, his stare glued to the scene being played yards from him.

Stuart Fenton had touched the tip of the knife to the wet streak sliding down a tight breast, then painted it across her mouth. As the girl cried out, he bent his head so that his own open mouth caught the tiny glistening droplets dripping from taut nipples, his tongue smearing it in a wide arc across the pale mounds. Above his balding head the silver blade touched the girl's chest and as she screamed it was drawn down to her navel.

Theo Vail's sideward glance caught the excitement displayed in the quick, almost agitated, twisting of St John Winter's manicured hands. The stimulation of Fenton's activity had the man ready to shed his load. But inconvenient as the moment was and uncomfortable as the outcome would prove for the Foreign Secretary, it would create no obstacle to what was yet to come; what happened once could always be made to happen a second time.

'Lord!' St John Winter's breath rasped against his teeth.

A hidden smile setting the seal to confidence, Vail returned his attention to the spectacle absorbing his guest.

Risen to his feet, the knife thrown aside, Fenton was staring at the vivid red streak travelling wetly to the girl's navel and downwards to lose itself in the cleft between her parted legs. For several moments he stared before stripping away trousers and jockey shorts then, each breath short and laboured, he took the column of hard flesh jerking at the base of his abdomen, brushing the throbbing head into the scarlet stream before thrusting it savagely into the glistening vee, an almost animal snarl witness to the shuddering climax.

'You certainly had me fooled, Hollywood couldn't have produced anything more convincing.' Zachary St John Winter's disbelief had been evident when with a twist of wrists and ankles the silver chains had dropped from the girl, a flick of her fingers releasing the diamanté collar. Smiling brilliantly she had picked up the flimsy gown and used it to wipe away the scarlet streaks, revealing the fact that no cut or wound marked her shapely body.

'Simply an illusion, the brain believed what the eye would have it believe.' Vail's smile was open as he answered.

'Illusion or not, it had me going ... almost as far as Fenton, but how? The knife I mean.'

Having retrieved the object, Vail handed it to the other man. 'Hollow.' He touched the blade. 'The whole thing is hollow. It acts rather like a syringe. A slight pressure to the top of the handle and liquid is released through the tip of the blade; fill the thing with red paint and you can produce a very convincing injury.'

'Clever.' Winter pressed a finger to a tiny button

set in the knife's handle, shaking his head as a slim spurt of ruby liquid issued from the blade tip. 'Damn clever and, like I said, it had me fooled, I really thought Fenton was slicing the girl.'

'But he was not. As you saw, the girl could have freed herself at any time, her participation in the proceedings was entirely of her own free will.'

'Helped no doubt by an adequate fee.'

'Adequate as that paid for the services of any of Venetia Pascal's models.'

The barb had found its mark. Vail saw the alarm cloud the man's eyes.

'But then fees of that nature ensure complete privacy. That way each of us can enjoy his entertainment with complete peace of mind.'

Was that exhalation a breath of relief? Vail watched the alarm fade and the smile return to the handsome face.

'And that certainly was some entertainment, there can be no topping that.'

'Perhaps not.' Vail took back the knife, cradling it in his hand. 'But what you watched just now was merely the prelude.'

St John Winter's laugh gurgled in his throat.

'Prelude! Christ, if that was the prelude then I'd certainly like to see the sequel!'

It was done! Exultation flushed warmly through Vail. He had cast his line and the fish had taken the bait; now to reel it in. Triumph sheathed, he answered quietly, 'Then stay a little longer and you shall.'

28

These guys certainly knew how to play. He had held his breath for the last fifteen minutes but this, this was something else again! Zachary St John Winter glanced about the room he had been led into. Draped in black silk, walls and windows were shrouded out of existence while the soft purr of unseen machinery drew the pale carpet back from the centre to reveal a design inlaid in the wood of the floor, sections of which gleamed golden in the light, the source of which was cleverly concealed. Hadn't he seen that design somewhere before, that or something very like it? St John Winter stepped closer and memory kicked in. At Eton, he'd seen that design at Eton! Carswood ... yes it had been Carswood ... had found an old book in one of the antique shops and taken it back to his rooms. The book had contained an illustration, an illustration of a pentacle. Black magic! Carswood and a few others had been intrigued by thoughts of what they could do if they drew that same design on the floor, then had the proverbial scared out of them when the lights had suddenly gone off. It had been nothing but a failure of the electricity supply but it had been sufficient to see that book chucked into a rubbish bin. But this was no chalk drawing, this was a permanent feature.

'I see you are familiar with the pentacle.'

Vail's shrewd observation had missed none of the other man's recognition.

'Not familiar, though I have seen it before.' Winter laughed. 'But I did not expect to see grown men still playing such games.'

'When does the man lose the boy ... or the boy leave the man?' Vail shrugged. 'Indulge us, Minister, we still like our games and this one you may share if you wish.'

'I do wish if our delightful companions are also to be players.' Winter's brilliant practised smile played over the two women entering the room. The same model who had performed with Fenton was now dressed in white floor-length chiffon, folds of the soft cloth cupping tight breasts and the same silver chains in place about wrist and throat. She was beautiful but the woman who led her was even more so. Auburn hair tumbling to the shoulders shone rouge-gold, eyes soft and mysterious as a summer evening smiled behind thick dark lashes while a dress of emerald silk jersey followed every delightful contour of a body it caressed rather than simply covering. And what a body! Beneath his own expensive clothing flesh grew tumescent. Christ, what wouldn't he give to be pushing into her right now! The thought jerked his stiff penis. Lord, just the look of the woman could bring him off!

'You kept your promise to return.' He smiled, conscious of an ever-hardening erection.

'I always keep my promise.'

The reply had been for Winter but taking the chain from her hand, Theo Vail sensed a deeper meaning when emerald eyes flicked to him and once more the sharp prick of warning brushed his spine. Was she, as he had thought weeks ago, involved with someone else? With a man higher in the service of the Master than he himself? But then would he not have been told by the Master? The Great Lord of Darkness would not allow his devoted servant to be duped, and especially not by a woman. They could not become high in the service of Lucifer, their role was one of Follower of the Way, theirs was to serve but never to officiate; powers such as he held now, and those he hoped to be his very soon, would never be granted to a woman.

'Then might I ask another promise,' Winter was speaking again, 'that in this game you partner me?'

Outside in the Street a man could find himself arrested for leering at a woman the way Winter was leering at Venetia Pascal. But being arrested would be far less of a danger to a political career than the game he was soon to be playing. Excusing himself, Vail led the other girl towards the centre of the room. But this next part of the evening's entertainment was to be no game and, wish it or not, the Foreign Secretary would be its key player.

'Lead on, my beautiful partner in crime!'

Winter's laugh was halted by Venetia's shake of the head and the touch of a slender finger to her lips. He was displaying bad manners. Sobered by the unspoken admonition he smiled a silent apology. To make waves now would only lead to sinking his own boat and he hoped to sail that through to morning with the delicious Miss

Pascal as first and only mate.

Holding thought and accompanying smile inside, St John Winter returned his attention to the scene before him.

The girl now lay on the draped table, her white gown contrasting vividly against the black silk drape, the silver chains that bound her hands, throat and ankles throwing off light in long glistening spears. Standing to each side of her, Stuart Fenton and Laurence Thorold watched as Vail came to stand beside the mock altar, his ice-cold eyes spearing into the girl, before turning to direct the same cutting stare at Winter.

'You expressed a desire to join in our little charade, do you still wish it?'

The question so quietly put was as deceptive as frost on water. The man beside her would accept regardless of any wish on his part, but it would be easier were he to do so of his own free will. Slipping her hand into that of Winter, Venetia Pascal smiled into the handsome face. 'Come,' she said, 'let us both join in.'

'So what do I do?'

'Take the knife when it is offered.' She nodded towards a slender long-bladed instrument resting on a scarlet velvet cushion held by Laurence Thorold. 'It operates in a similar way to the one you saw Stuart use, except with this one the blade retracts into the handle when pressed against anything, so you see it will cause no harm to our lovely friend.'

'So I pretend to cut?'

'No!' Theo Vail intercepted sharply. 'When I give the sign you will drive the blade as if into her chest, that is all you must do. As Venetia assures, the girl will come to no harm.'

'If you say so.' Allowing himself to be drawn by Venetia, St John Winter joined the others about the makeshift altar, Vail moving to the diagram inlaid in the floor.

Standing in the centre of the pentacle, its black and gold double circle banding a pentagram, the five-pointed star which Winter knew to be the most potent symbol of magic, the apex of each point touching beneath letters deeply etched in gold, Vail bowed – his words carrying clearly.

'Hail to the Benei Elohim.'

'All hail.'

Beside Zachary St John Winter, Venetia Pascal's quiet response joined with those of Fenton and Thorold.

'Hail to the Malakhe Khabala, Angels of Satan.'

'All hail.' The quiet return echoed.

Presenting his face to the topmost point of the star, Vail bowed deeply before the gilded name.

'Hail to you, Asmodai, Messenger of Lucifer, High Prince of the Dark Throne.'

'All hail.'

With the hushed reply the star glowed brilliant black and from the direction of its point a rustle of sound whispered.

Should he laugh or walk away? St John Winter made to speak to Venetia but her sharp 'Shhh!' and flash of green eyes had him do neither. Like Vail, it seemed the lady got her buzz from this mumbo jumbo and, since the reward of the evening was to be having her, then he too could play along. Following her gaze back to Vail the laugh that had been so near became a submerged smile. All Vail needed was a long black cloak, a pointed hat and a stick with a star on one end and the man would make the perfect pantomime wizard.

'Hail to you, Azazel, Bringer of Chaos, Author of Destruction.'

'All hail.'

The second star began to glow, its brilliance that of a diamond and from its point also a breath of an answer like the murmur of dried leaves brushed by a breeze.

Within the pentacle Vail had not missed Venetia's crisp whisper and guessed its reason. Obviously the Foreign Secretary thought him all kinds of a fool but then this minister along with the rest of her Majesty's government was soon to learn they were the fools. Proceeding to turn in an anti-clockwise direction he bowed to the third name.

'Hail to you, Shemhazai, Deceiver of Mankind.'

'All hail.'

Little more than a whisper, sound murmured, the star suddenly erupting light of brilliant jet.

'Hail to you, Iblis, Apostate Angel of the Dark Region.'

'All hail.'

Sound that was without sound throbbed on the silence of a pause; the room glowed with the intensity of black light emanating from the circle enclosing the pentacle. Beneath lowered lids, Venetia caught the nervous movements of Thorold and Fenton. Both men knew the danger they were in should Vail leave the circle incomplete, should

335

he fail to honour the last name. Her own breath locked in her throat, she stared at Vail. At last he bowed.

'Hail to you, Belial, Great Devourer, Gatherer of Souls.'

'All hail.'

The last salutation completed, sound joined with sound, rustle with rustle, growing into a howl that screamed around the room like the death cries of some tortured animal.

He'd said these guys were good! Zachary St John Winter glanced at the men stood with heads bowed. Top marks, they played the part like pros.

'Sammael...'

Vail's arms lifted, his head tipping so he looked towards the ceiling and instantly the glittering stars lost their light and the scream of sound became that of silence.

'Sammael...'

He called again.

'Praise be given to you, First of the Seraphim, Greatest of The Created, Lord of the Earth. Permit your servant to do your honour, acknowledge his devotion.'

With the last word, silk lining the walls billowed and lifted like sails before a great wind and the room was plunged into total blackness.

Christ! Despite himself, St John Winter shivered. If he didn't know it was impossible, he would swear the walls had answered.

'Diabolus, Prince of Darkness...'

Within the velvet midnight, Vail's voice called softly. 'Bornless One, All High Prince of Creation, Lord of All That Is and All That Will Be, your servants here gathered ask the grace of your blessing.'

'Great Lucifer bless your servants.'

From the same encompassing blackness the voices of Thorold and Fenton joined with that of Venetia Pascal while the girl chained to the table stifled a giggle.

The girl's laughter died away as the room dropped into silence, silence which throbbed and pulsed like the beat of some great heart.

What now? Zachary St John Winter asked silently. With what other trick did Vail plan to frighten the natives? Patience thinning, he was on the point of giving vent to his sarcasm when within the impenetrable darkness a point of light appeared. Dull and faint as a sleeping fire it hung over Vail, its faint illumination showing him with arms still raised.

'Great Lucifer...'

Said on a breath, the words hovered on the pulsing silence. With head bowed, Venetia Pascal felt her own heart leap as Vail continued.

'Prince of Evil, Holder of Eternity, we praise and magnify you, our one true lord.'

With the last syllable the pulsing throb increased, beating its way around the room, the sound of it like great wings threshing the air, louder and louder, the race of it becoming a scream that ripped the brain; then as suddenly it was gone, returning the silence it had stolen.

Beneath the dull red glow, Vail lowered his arms then sank to his knees calling in that same low voice, 'Lord of the Throne, he that kneels before you asks the Gates be thrown wide, let pass Belial that he may take the offering we make.'

For long seconds nothing happened. Vail remained on his knees, the others making no move. Was the party over? About to break the numbness of the paralysing silence, Zachary St John Winter felt the hairs on the back of his neck rise. What the hell was happening now? Vail had said tonight's entertainment could be somewhat out of the norm, slightly more unusual than that offered on more formal occasions. Seeing the dull red spot spread into a pool of purple-fringed scarlet, a great vibrating orb brilliant as a setting sun, he swallowed his former sarcasm. Slightly! That was one hell of an understatement!

Beyond the rim of brilliance, dark shadows slid along the silk-sheathed walls, feeling their way, moving, slithering towards each other, coiling, twisting, joining to become a column, only to separate again into fronds of black mist, mist that became torso, arms, legs and lastly a head. It had become a figure.

A figure which lived and breathed!

Beside the altar, St John Winter stared only partially believing what he saw. Of course it was a trick, an illusion, but it was a damn good one.

'Not yet ... don't move yet.' Venetia Pascal caught his sleeve as he made to move.

The movement, slight though it was, had the head of the figure turn their way and again St John Winter's spine tingled. The eyes fastened now on him were like molten lava burning into him, scorching into his brain. Then the wide mouth parted in a smile. A smile of utter menace!

The girl lying on that table must have done this

before or she would surely have bottled out on seeing the thing which floated above her. He glanced at her now, the incandescent light revealing that her eyes were tightly shut, fingers curled into her palms. Maybe that was part of the act she was being paid to perform, but what if it wasn't? What if the girl were truly terrified, too much so to cry out? It had never been part of his nature to play the dashing hero but perhaps he should call a halt to this whole fiasco, let the girl up, tell her to leave.

How would the delectable Miss Pascal take that? If she were getting the same kick out of this melodramatic divertissement as Vail seemed to be getting, then having it snatched away would not sit kindly with her... and that would scupper his hopes for the rest of the night.

Self-interest, always a first with Winter, was reinforced by Vail rising to his feet.

'Sar ha-Olam, Prince of the World...'

Did they all join in the singing or was this a solo? Whichever, the whole bloody thing was becoming farcical. Next time he and Venetia Pascal met he would do the inviting and it wouldn't include Vail or any other, and certainly the amusement would not feature any magic tricks. D.B.S. would be the order of the night, dinner, bed and sex ... with the emphasis on sex!

'To you is given all honour...'

Laurence Thorold had stepped forward at Vail's words and now held the cushion with its knife for Vail to take.

Why didn't he? St John Winter felt the kick of boredom. Why didn't he take the bloody knife, finish his little charade and get it over; then perhaps others too could have some fun!

But Vail did not reach for the knife, instead he turned to look directly at Winter. 'Time to fulfil your wish, Minister.'

Why the hell had he agreed to this? But he had and to renege now...!

Held by his own promise, Zachary St John Winter joined Vail at the altar.

'First the gown.' Vail smiled, then with one snatch ripped the flimsy white dress from throat to hem.

This was more like it! Winter's reaction was immediate. Penis hard and jerking above tight swollen testicles pushed against clothing, as his gaze drank in the sight spread for his enjoyment. Beneath the aura of scarlet light the girl's body was tinted warm and pink; taut nipples set like tiny half-opened rosebuds topped small firm breasts, and between widely spread legs, glistening moistly, beckoned the entrance to pleasure.

'She is yours.' Vail smiled again.

His! St John Winter's veins jolted, the hard column between his own legs jerking violently. Two for the price of one, the evening had its bargains. He could ride this one now, let the first flush of passion run with the tide and later ... later he would take his time, slower would be better with the lovely Venetia.

Clearing the obstacle of zipped trousers he looked at the girl. Her eyes were open now, smiling their special invitation. Christ, he didn't need a second one!

Hands clutching the slim waist, lust the only

guidance needed rock hard flesh drove deep and savage. Thrust upon thrust, flesh slapping against flesh, St John Winter was oblivious of the deepening intensity of scarlet above him and the smile on the mouth of the face at its heart.

'Now the knife.'

He'd forgotten that. Trousers refastened, St John Winter glanced at the instrument glinting on its cushion. Oh well ... you have the goodies, then you pay the price!

'Repeat the words I say then strike the blade between her breasts.' Vail gave the instruction, Thorold stepping back to his place.

'You are sure it ... I mean...'

'Again I remind you, the knife you hold is similar to the one used a short while ago, it will do no harm.' Having interrupted the query Vail began again. Carefully defined so as to give St John Winter no cause for mistake when repeating them, the words broke the vacuum of silence.

'In Nomine Satanum ... hear me, Belial, who kneels before the Dark Throne, hear me, Gatherer of Souls. In the name of Lucifer, Lord of the Infernal Regions...'

Overhead the mist-formed figure floated, its molten eyes gleaming like twin braziers while wisps of blue flame flickered at the corners of the grinning mouth.

A nod from Vail had St John Winter raise the knife. Venetia watched it lift, watched the crimson glow surrounding the floating figure reflect on the metal, watched it glide over the black handle engraved with golden symbols then touch the expertly damascened blade, caressing beautifully embossed lettering with reverence, with blessing.

The Athame! The breath of devotion locked in her throat. Vail was using the Athame ... the ritual knife of sacrifice!

'In the name of Diabolus, Lord of Earth and of Hell, I charge you, take the gift his servant offers.'

The last word repeated, the knife drove downward, burying itself to the haft in the girl's chest; at the same instant of her gasp, the figure of mist lowered to hover directly over the knife from which carmine streaks ran in bright rivulets across a twitching stomach, then as St John Winter released his grasp of the handle mist-formed fingers became flame. Scarlet tipped with purple-blue, they flicked about the knife, endowing each golden symbol with the kiss of fire.

Startled, Zachary St John Winter took a step back but Vail didn't move an eyelid. This was what he had planned for, what he had prayed for; tonight his goal of becoming Ipsissimus, First Disciple of the Devil, would be guaranteed. Satisfaction dancing along every vein, he glanced at the woman whose gaze was locked on the misty figure. Venetia Pascal would kneel at his feet!

'God Almighty!'

Zachary St John Winter's exclamation whipped attention back to the altar. Theo Vail watched feathers of flame brush against the girl's chest then seem to harden into blue steel before driving beneath the left breast. Then as they withdrew, the mouth of the figure opened in a scream as from souls in torment; a great rush as of wind screeched about the room, ripping at the silk drape on the altar, tearing at curtains. For long seconds the howling beat against walls and furniture, then as though with the touch of a switch it was gone, leaving only an echo in the brain.

The minion of the devil had done its work. Softer, mellower wall lighting hid Vail's smile. The soul of the girl had been delivered to the Master... and Zachary St John Winter? The God Almighty, the Christ he called upon, could not save him.

29

'You admit you knew Conway, that he took a post with Vail Corporation, a chemist in their laboratory, so what else do you know about him?'

There was no doubt the little man in the scruffy-looking jacket had heard Torrey's question; he gave no indication so he thought, but Kate saw the fingers tighten about his half-empty pint glass.

'You have to tell us, it's very important.'

'No, Kate, he doesn't have to tell us anything.' Torrey glared at the man. 'All he will need to tell is his name and blood group when they get what's left of him to hospital ... that is supposing he's able to talk.'

In the bar room of the Staffordshire Knot, Echo Sounder tried to draw his body even closer into itself. There were eyes and ears in this place, folk only too interested in what was going down at his table, folk he would rather not have to play with.

'Well! What's it to be? The choice is yours, Sounder.'

The tone warned that Torrey's patience would not stretch much further. Sounder assessed his chances. Play shtum and the *Star* might find it had a few spare pounds in its pocket; after all, the wench would be getting paid, therefore if he were supplying information then he too should get paid; that was a two to one bet: but say nothing and Torrey was likely to make cats meat out of him... and that was a hundred to one odds-on certainty. Some bloody choice! Sounder's thin lips folded in on themselves. A trip to Walsall Manor to have bones set and a couple of hundred stitches courtesy of the NHS followed by a more than probable session with Daniels enquiring into a case of GBH which, if truth were told, he would have no interest in.

'Look.' Kate tried again, anxious to avoid what could turn into a rumpus with Sounder being dragged outside by an irate Torrey. 'Whatever you tell us you have my promise it will not be repeated.'

'I tells ya, I don't know any more'n I've told already.'

'Right! Here or outside!'

Torrey's chair scraped threateningly and with it Sounder's decision was made. Answer and stay in one piece.

'Conway, 'e weren't the same once 'e got to that there University, got a bob on hisself, d'ain't want to know old mates, thought 'e were better'n the

344

rest o' we; then when 'e brought the boyfriend to live with 'im 'e kept well clear of the Staffordshire Knot an' I don't drink nowheres else.'

Was he telling the truth or was he deliberately keeping something to himself? Kate sipped her own lager and lime. Should she tell him of Torrey being haunted by Sheryl Wilkes? No, that would be breaking confidence, and anyway Sounder would never believe it, he would think it a ploy on her part to get him to talk.

'We could give what we have to Inspector Daniels, let him ask the questions.' She put the glass down.

Sharp with anger and pain, the ferret eyes caught hers. 'Oh, ar, yoh do that, an' if Daniels tries as 'ard to find what it is yoh be after as 'e does looking for the bastards who killed my Sheryl, then yoh will be pickin' up a pension long afore yoh sees any result!'

I know the pain you're in! Torrey's anger melted as he watched the other man's face. Sounder couldn't be blamed for accusing Daniels of neglect in that murder case; when he himself had endured the same pain with Anna's murder, hadn't he blamed the world and its brother?

'Wait.' Sounder's head drooped once more. 'There does be summat. The laboratory Conway an' his boyfriend worked in ... it weren't the big one.'

'Big one?' Kate's brow furrowed.

'That be what I said ... and afore I says any more I wants...'

Money! The thought had Kate's hand reach for the voluminous shoulder bag but left it to lie as the little man went on.

'...you to promise me solemn that none o' it goes into the *Star*, leastways not 'til Sheryl's killer be found; after that yoh prints what yoh likes for it'll mek no difference to me.'

He couldn't be saying he intended to live only until the murder of his cousin was solved... could he? Kate's thoughts showed in the glance she shot to Torrey, his own warning her to keep them to herself.

'Them two, they d'ain't work in the big lab,' Sounder continued as his demand was met, 'there were another one, a small place back of Vail's private office, though the way Bradshaw telled it the place were more like a private prison...'

'Bradshaw?' Torrey frowned.

'Bill Bradshaw an' 'im goes back a long way. He were the one picked up stuff from that there lab, said as Vail hisself watched like a hawk all the time 'e were there an' then followed the van in his own car.'

'Followed it to where?'

'Look!' Sounder gripped his glass irritably. 'We could get this over much quicker if yoh listened to the tellin' instead o' buttin' in every fart's end!'

Beneath the pretence of sipping yet again, Kate Mallory fought the smile reaching for her lips. Torrey wouldn't like being chastened but then if Torrey wanted the rest of what Sounder knew then the ex-commando would just have to grin and bear it ... well, bear it anyway!

Aggrieved, Sounder took a deep swallow of beer before wiping his mouth on the back of his hand. 'Like I was a tryin' to say, Bill Bradshaw picked up boxes on a couple of occasions, wrapped an' sealed tighter'n a Jew's money bag they was an' no letter nor word on 'em to say what was inside. Well, Bradshaw delivered the lot to the same warehouse...'

'Whe–?'

Torrey's involuntary question was cut off by Kate's shake of the head.

'...out along of the tradin' estate close by Salisbury Street. Vail paid 'andsome but said should Bradshaw talk of what 'e was collectin' or where it was delivered to then the contract would be broke. Bradshaw said for that kind o' money 'e would 'ave his mouth taped up.'

'Yet he told you!' Torrey's frown emphasised a certain disbelief.

'Ar, 'e told me.' Quick and almost vicious, Echo Sounder's reply was hurled into Torrey's face. 'An' mebbes that be why 'e were found dead, his van crashed into a ditch. Verdict were heart attack while drivin' but I ain't never believed that, be my reckonin' Vail be somewheres at back o' it.'

'Vail was the cause of your friend's accident?'

Chin dropped once more on to his chest, Echo Sounder did not look up at Kate's question. 'I'd lay a 'undred to one on it! Bloke payin' five 'undred a run to 'ave a few boxes carried less than a couple o' miles from Station Street to that warehouse wouldn't think twice about tekin' one more step to guard whatever were in them.'

I'd lay a 'undred to one on it! The words echoed in Torrey's brain. Sounder never laid a bet unless he was absolutely certain it was a winner! And Station Street, that had been the destination of the fare he had picked up from Harrowby Place and Station Street was where he had seen that first apparition!

Tingles ran the length of his spine like electricity along telegraph cables. Were the two somehow connected? The death of a young woman in a paint factory and a man in a crashed van ... police enquiries had certified that the woman had been an employee of the Vail Corporation; now Sounder was claiming the same for Bill Bradshaw.

'Mebbe you should tell me what it is you are here for, Miss, the Inspector ... well let's say he's quite busy right now.'

Kate Mallory smiled deceptive charm before turning to sit on a chair facing the lobby desk of Darlaston's small police station. 'Let's say I will wait until he is less busy.'

'That might be some time.'

'That's okay.' Kate lowered the overfull shoulder bag to the floor beside her then crossed her legs. 'I'm not in any hurry.'

What did he do now! Sergeant Dave Farnell heaved an inward sigh. He could hardly throw the woman out, but then neither would it do anything other than set off an explosion to match that of Mount Etna if he showed her into Daniels' office; he had been simmering ever since the finding of that body on a bonfire and this latest avenue of investigation proving negative had his fuse dangerously short.

'Look,' he tried again, 'if it's about the young woman found...'

'It isn't!' Kate's smile sugared the curt reply.

348

'Then…'

'Sergeant, I wish to see Detective Inspector Daniels, no one else … only him, and you know me well enough to realise I will not leave before doing so … unless of course you get a couple of your constables to carry me from the premises.'

Oh yes, he knew her. Dave Farnell looked across to where Kate sat. Obstinate was not a word he would choose to describe this one. She was like a needle probing a splinter from a finger, she would prick and prick until everything was out, or at least enough to provide a column for the *Star*.

Watching from her seat, Kate could almost read the thoughts furrowing the station sergeant's brow. David Farnell was a nice chap, too polite to tell her to bugger off; perhaps she could give him a break. She took pen and note pad from the bag and scribbled a few quick words. It was a repeat strategy; hopefully it would work as well as the last time she had used it.

The paper creased into several folds she slipped it into an envelope then handed it to Farnell.

'In case Inspector Daniels decides to work through the night…'

The honey sweet smile had not quite reached her eyes. Farnell recognised this was not capitulation.

'…please give him this before you tuck him in.'

He could have her chucked out, there had to be some ordinance … but how would that read in to-morrow's edition… Despite himself, the sergeant smiled. If it was to be a choice between doing as she asked or doing as Daniels asked – namely to leave him alone – then the winning card came down for the girl; at least he could tell Bruce Daniels to go fuck himself, then trust in their long friendship not to see him chucked out of a job.

'I told you...'

No whisper, no mild shout, but a blast of sheer bad temper greeted the opening of the door leading into Daniels' office. Space was ever a premium in the red brick Victorian building and this room with its eternal clutter of papers strewn across every available inch of one of its two desks, as well as several on the floor across from it, was particularly tight. Having to install a second desk for Detective Sergeant Williams' use had not gone down very well with Daniels, that had been made very plain. But then they all had to make sacrifices. Dave Farnell shoved his way inside. Hopefully this would not be his.

'Thought you might like a cuppa.'

The mug of tea he had diplomatically chosen to bring along found a spot to rest after Daniels swept yet one more file to the floor. The desk sergeant hesitated. Should he keep the note in his pocket, say he had given it to Daniels and there was no reply? The woman waiting in the lobby would never know the lie.

I wouldn't tek no odds on that! The reply he knew Echo Sounder would have given brought a wry smile which was stifled instantly.

'Christ, Dave,' Daniels dropped a heavy hand to the desk, 'where the hell do we try next!'

Might be the only place you would get an answer. Once again the thought stayed silent.

350

'I'm runnin' round and around like a dog with its arse on fire!'

Ripples danced on the surface of the tea as Daniels' foot hurled a blow against a leg of the desk.

'But every time we seem to be getting anywhere we come up with the same answers... nobody knows anything; but somebody does, somebody knows the bastard who killed that wench then put her body on to that bonfire, they know who and they know why.'

'You talked with Sounder again?'

'Huh!' Daniels' grunt reflected the acid of his temper as well as that refusing to be calmed in his stomach. 'I talked, Sounder never said a word, his mouth is closed so tight it meks a duck's arse look like the Titanic! But so sure I find out the little nark is hiding something, I swear they'll be racing horses on the moon before he gets out of the Green.'

Sounder must also realise that threat was not an empty one and having already done a stretch in Winson Green prison would he risk a second term by withholding information? Dave Farnell decided against voicing his thoughts, saying instead, 'Sounder would have talked by this time, after all the girl was a relative.'

'Which is why our little canary has lost his whistle. It's my bet he's hoping to find whoever done Sheryl Wilkes in then repeat the process; I think Echo Sounder is bent on a revenge killing.'

'Sounder!' Dave Farnell shook his head. 'The man is a racetrack fanatic, Bruce, but he's no murderer.'

Daniels looked at the man he liked and whose opinions he respected. 'Take a tip, Dave, don't place any bet on that.'

'You really think Sounder would...?'

He had seen the look on Echo Sounder's face as he had questioned him, that same look of anger turning to hatred, seen it and recognised it. Daniels' mind leaped the chasm of years to show a face twisted with pain and fury, the face of a young lad attacking and killing his own father ... the face of Bruce Daniels. 'Yes, Dave,' he said quietly, 'I really think he would.'

The shrill ring of a telephone submerged somewhere beneath the avalanche of papers on the desk chased the memory which never truly left; like the films Marjorie watched again and again it would be back.

'If that's Quinto, then tell him I'm out.'

'I'll tell him,' Dave Farnell smiled, 'but I don't promise to hold him in my arms to prevent him coming in here.'

'And here's me thinkin' you were a true friend.'

'Even the best of friendships has its boundaries.' And this one might just have crossed its point of no return! Dropping Kate Mallory's note on to the desk, Dave Farnell made a rapid exit.

30

'There has been a significant amelioration in the crime rate of the town over the past year, a most definite and satisfactory emendation which you may all be assured has not gone unnoticed by the chief constabulary.'

Sitting at the wheel of the small Ford estate car his wife's legacy had paid for, Daniels snorted heavily. Quinto and his smart-arsed speech! Traffic lights flicking to green, he shoved his foot hard against the accelerator, ignoring the squeak of protest from the tyres and the startled looks of several pedestrians.

'Emendation,' he snarled, 'amelioration, my arse...!'

Why couldn't the stupid git say improvement, or would that have been a word his audience would have understood!

Significantly less crime ... of course the figures showed that when you deleted those break-ins where no serious theft or damage took place, when fires to property were classified 'accidental' when it was obvious to a blind man somebody had set it going ... but dirt got swept under the carpet so Quinto could have a clean sheet, and of course the top brass would notice. Quinto would make bloody sure of that just as he made bloody sure he himself was engaged in some meeting or another whenever something shitty was going down. Like that damn barbecue, a young wench killed then set to roast on a bloody bonfire. Christ, he wished he could lay hands on the swine who'd done that... Quinto's clean sheet could be used for arse paper after that!

But there had been no break-through on that case, no lead that gave anything definite; even Echo hadn't come up with anything ... or was the little songbird suffering a sudden dose of laryngitis? Let that prove to be so and his next pop concert would be performed for the inmates of Winson Green!

The scruffy little turd did know something. Eyes narrowing against the uncertain light as he turned off the traffic island, Daniels swung the car into the pocket-sized car park of the Frying Pan. Sounder knew something, every instinct said as much but getting him to spit it out ... that was not following the usual pattern; this time the man was not responding to bribe or threat, in fact he wasn't responding at all, but then perhaps Williams would strike lucky.

Locking the car door he stood a moment breathing air laced with motor vehicle exhaust fumes where once it had been heavy with the smoke and soot of steel-making furnaces and heavy industry. Progress! He blew through his nostrils. Like so much more it had passed Darlaston by.

Behind him raised voices preceded the sound of fists finding their target. Gratification sweeping warmly through him, he slipped the keys into his jacket pocket. Banging a couple of heads together just might dilute the anger of frustration building inside him.

'Fuck off!' Red hair spiked across the centre of a head otherwise shaved bald, a thick-set man swung a blow as Daniels intervened. 'Fuck off afore I shoves yer 'ead up yer arse!'

'Better make it quick, Geronimo, 'cos I'm about to shove this so far up *your* arse you'll need a surgeon to stitch your eyeballs back in place.'

Light spilling from the windows of the pub showed the warrant card nestled in Daniels' hand. Fighting cock or red Indian! Daniels looked steadily at the man facing him with balled fists at the ready. Whichever he fancied himself as, just let him swing another blow.

'Mr Daniels?' The spiked head moved a fraction nearer, affording beer bleuried eyes a clearer view of the face of the man stood solidly in front of him. 'Sorry, Mr Daniels, I d'ain't know it was you ... sorry...'

So am I. Daniels watched the figure lumber in the direction of the high-rise flats soaring between the Salvation Army and Labour Club buildings, his opponent having disappeared at the first mumbled mention of the name of Darlaston's well-known Detective Inspector. He hadn't been given the satisfaction of cracking heads together. Touching a hand to the pocket which held keys and dyspepsia tablets, he turned towards the pub. One more negative result!

This had better be no wind-up or it would be gaol for the *Star* reporter and for Torrey as well should it turn out he was in it with her. Entering the lounge bar of the Frying Pan, Daniels was once more aware of change. There had been no carpeted floor, no cushioned seating and no fleur-de-lis gold-patterned red curtains in the original public house; even the name of the place had been different in his young days; but even then the Bradford Arms had been known locally as the 'Frying Pan', and now the nickname had been officially adopted by the brewery.

Inadequate illumination, afforded by two pearlised 'footballs' suspended from the ceiling and which received no help at all from the red-shaded wall lights set at intervals around the room, did not prevent Daniels see the quick turn of several heads, their owners not eager to catch the attention of a Detective Inspector. They would have to be a whole lot quicker than that! The last almost a smile in his mind, he crossed to an alcove containing Torrey and the woman who had left that envelope at the station.

Remember Philip Bartley and the heroin? Remember Julian Crowley and the multi-national counterfeit plates found at Darlaston Printers? Thought kept pace with his step. Neither of those had proved a wind-up, and as for that tiny amount of powder contained in a plastic sachet along with the hand-written note in the envelope she had left with Dave Farnell; that too was no wind-up. Despite the warning stuck on the sachet that the contents were deadly, he had thought it to be heroin, but given the analyst's report that stuff had made that drug seem like mother's milk in comparison! So what was it? The analytical chemist did not know ... and where did it come from? That also was unknown, but he would have an answer before leaving this pub or his name wasn't Bruce Daniels!

'Mine's a pint of Hanson's Mild.' And bugger the consequences. The follow-up remained unsaid. Daniels dropped to a stool, his legs spread comfortably one each side. To those of the clientele who were not so conversant with Detective Inspector Bruce Daniels, it appeared he had simply joined a couple of friends for a drink, but those who knew him if only slightly more intimately, recognised that was a fallacy; in fact there were some would say Daniels had no friends unless one counted his wife ... and then there were a few would doubt even that.

He might have viewed her note as a ruse, a way of gaining an interview, but even had he thought of that tiny sample of powder in the same way, he would not have disregarded that. Watching him take a drink from the glass Torrey set on the table between them, Kate Mallory knew for a certainty that in the four days since she went to Victoria Road police station, Daniels would have had the sample analysed.

'So where did it come from?'

'That was my next question!' He looked squarely at the man opposite. 'And I'll have the truth first time, Torrey. I only tell you that for it to serve your best interest 'cos right now I'm not in a mood for arsing about!'

A raising of a left eyebrow and a cynical twist of lips illuminated the thought in Torrey's mind. He also didn't care for arsing about and he cared even less for threats, those issued by Detective Inspector Bruce Daniels or anybody else the blues could bring in. Already half out of his seat and ready to leave, it took Kate's quick conciliatory intervention to have him sit down again.

'We all of us want what is best ... that's the reason Richard asked would I bring it to the station and give it personally to you; but when it turned out you were occupied with other business I left it with Sergeant Farnell.'

Eeh, lass, wherever did you learn to lie so easily?

Kate heard in her head the words her mother would have uttered. Yes, it was a lie, Torrey hadn't been easy with the idea of her taking that powder to the police, and he certainly had made no stipulation as to handing it personally to Daniels. But the opening salvos of conversation had heralded warfare and that would get them nowhere.

There was a reprimand in that reply. Daniels supped again. Slight, and quietly said, but nevertheless a reprimand.

'Can't always drop things at a minute's notice!'

Can't meaning not intending! Torrey's face once more reflected cynicism.

Not one to be cowed and definitely not to kowtow, Daniels met the look with equal acerbity. 'So, I'll ask it again. Where did that stuff come from?'

'That I can't answer... and I mean *can't!*' Torrey's voice was granite, it brooked no argument. 'I can however tell you how I came by it.' Quietly, with a firmness that left no room for dispute, he related how he had found the box with its contents pushed well under the driver's seat of his taxi.

'It couldn't simply have slid under?'

Torrey shook his head. 'It was wedged fast, otherwise I would have found it earlier.'

'So who do you suppose left it in your car? From what you say it wasn't dropped accidentally.'

'I guessed it had to be the fellow I drove to and from Fairview Hospice. It was my intention to go and see him and ask if the box was his but I found he had died in that house fire in Birmingham Street.'

'Box!' Daniels' glass hit the table with a thud, bringing several glances his way. 'You mean there's *more* of the damned stuff?'

Taking a swallow of his own alcohol-free lager, Torrey waited for the interest of onlookers to die away, taking several minutes before sliding a small white cardboard container from his pocket and handing it across to Daniels. Having it gone from his possession was a weight lifted from his shoulders, but the chill he had felt inside since learning of the qualities of that powder stayed with him.

'This is *all* of it?'

The look on Daniels' face told it all. The man knew what the box, small as it was, held – enough poison to wipe away millions of people! The enormity of the realisation had kept him awake nights, that and the questions it brought. What was it manufactured for? Was there more of it in that lab Echo Sounder had talked of?

'Torrey, is this *all* of it?'

Worry ... fear ... both explicit in the question repeated by Daniels, Torrey could only shake his head. 'It's all of what I found in the car.'

'But that don't mean it's the all of what there is!' His mouth tight, Daniels glanced again at the

359

small box beneath his palm. 'But what can they be making this stuff for? Chemical warfare? Christ, they could wipe out the whole of the world with a few pounds of the stuff that's in this box! What the bloody hell does the government think it's playing at?'

He could say he didn't think the government were involved with or even knew of the production of that powder, he could say he thought it was the brain child of a group of Satanists. He could if he wanted Daniels to piss himself laughing. In the event it was Kate who rescued the situation.

'Have either of you read the evening newspaper?' A negative response had her take a folded copy of the *Star* from the capacious shoulder bag lying beside her feet. Handing it first to Torrey, she caught his glance when, having read the article she had indicated, he passed the newspaper to Daniels. He was thinking as she was!

'What's this got to do with what we were talking about?' Daniels finished reading.

'Maybe nothing.' Kate took the paper back then pointed to a photograph. 'But look at the people in the photo – Theo Vail, head of Vail Corporation, and Zachary St John Winter, Foreign Secretary.'

'So?' Daniels frowned.

'The report speaks of a large consignment of food the government is to donate to third world countries; Vail Corporation has supplied it and is to fly it to the various destinations. Zachary St John Winter has officially accepted it on behalf of the government.'

Daniels was already regretting drinking beer. Flicking a tablet from the ever-present pack of Bi-So-Dol, he tossed it into his mouth before asking, 'What's your point?'

This was the sticky wicket. He could bawl her out, for making stupid accusations, he could run her in for withholding information; Detective Inspector Bruce Daniels could find more reasons than that to show his displeasure if he thought he was being taken for a fool. Each thought grated like a pebble in her mind but Kate could not stop now.

'My point is terrorism. What if that poison is used for that purpose? What if it is to be mixed in with that foodstuff? It would make suicide bombings obsolete, a thing of the past.'

'It would make half the bloody world's population a thing of the past!' Daniels shook his head, scepticism clear on his face.

'Do the fanatics who blow themselves up in order to kill innocent people care about that?'

'But that food is a donation of the British government; are you saying they are mixed up in international terrorism?'

'No,' Kate answered, the firmness of her voice belying the quiver in her stomach. 'Not the government as such, but St John Winter as Foreign Secretary could – should it happen as I suggested a moment ago and that food becomes a weapon of mass destruction as far as human life is concerned – be seen as acting with full governmental knowledge and approval, thus leaving them open to condemnation and reprisal by all other countries.'

Christ! Daniels sucked hard on the tablet but the blaze in his gut flared higher. Vail was the name on that box ... Vail was donating that food! Could he be in the employ of some terrorist organisation, a bloody Al Qaeda bastard right here in Darlaston? If he simply suspected such as that he would have to hand over to the NST, the National Security Team, and if his suspicions proved wrong he would have to hand over his resignation, for blotting Quinto's clean sheet would be totally unforgivable. But the whole idea was unthinkable, a journalist out to build a mountain from a molehill and thinking to use him to do it!

He wasn't going for it. Torrey watched the shades of emotion, a visible track of the thoughts churning Daniels' mind, reflecting on his face. He was hearing what Kate had said as no more than make-believe, so what would he make of being told of hauntings and possible black magicians? But that powder was no make-believe, Daniels couldn't reckon that as a figment of imagination, not on Kate's part nor his. But if he didn't go for it and Kate's supposition turned out to be correct! Torrey knew he had to put his twopennyworth in before Daniels offered them both a suite at Victoria Road.

'Look,' he said, 'whatever you might or might not think regarding the use of that stuff, the fact remains it is absolutely lethal, you can't take the risk...'

'My only risk is gettin' involved with you two!' Daniels was clearly agitated. 'You should have brought that box straight to the station, not

362

played bloody detective!'

'Well, now *you* have it ... let's see how you play detective!' The iron grip of Torrey's mouth showed the tension building in him. Should it become anger then this get-together with Daniels was shortlisted for disaster. Kate threw herself into the deep end.

'Inspector,' she crossed mental fingers, 'surely the first thing is to ascertain whether or not there is more of that powder and, if so, where it's being kept; we can argue the rights and wrongs of mine and Torrey's behaviour afterward.'

Bill Bradshaw had picked up boxes from Station Street and delivered them to a warehouse at the Central Trading Estate and Vail followed close as a bluebottle on a shit pile; but Bradshaw could answer no questions. Daniels found himself suddenly wondering about a certain road accident. If Vail Corporation was bent on brewing international genocide, then perhaps that crashed van had been no accident!

31

'...Leading them down to the gate is My Girl...'

Echo Sounder glanced at the racehorse being led around the track. Sleek and honey-blond just like... But he wouldn't think ... not tonight. Savagely, his brain almost reeling from the effort which felt like a physical blow, he pushed the thought away. Today he would concentrate on the races, for a couple of hours at least he must try to forget.

'...and they are at the gate...'

The tannoy spread its information but Echo Sounder needed no help in learning the names of horses that would run, he knew the field by heart, but even so his eye ran over the list of runners printed in the *Sporting Pink*, the crumpled newspaper he had pulled from his pocket.

'...Confident Lad, a two year old trained by Jos Turner...'

The loudspeaker boomed on. Leaning against the railing edging the track, Echo heard only the empty silence pressing on his brain.

They had done nothing... Daniels and the rest of the blues had done nothing; his Sheryl was dead and all that lot did was swan about in squad cars or sit on their arses in that station. Bitterness burned like acid in his throat. Nobody cared! Grubby fingers blackened further with ink from the newsprint plucked angrily at the paper. But he cared ... *he* cared!

'...and it's My Girl making for the inside...'

Habit had Sounder lift his head as the race began.

'...My Girl as they go into the stretch ... My Girl leading by a length ... and it's My Girl first past the post, the favourite romps home at two to one...'

'Pipped at the post again! Well, at least this time it's not my money being thrown down the drain.'

Behind Sounder the words carried as the loudspeaker stilled.

'But you still got something out of it...' the

364

reply was equally clear. 'That photographer has done a great job on your portfolio.'

'Portfolio! It was the winner's prize I should have got!' A woman's voice shrilled peevishly. 'I thought I had it but at that cocktail party it was that other contestant took the limelight.'

'You mean the blonde ... the one come from Darlaston; what was her name? Something trashy and common ... and her speech, all yoh and doh, imagine how that would come over in commercials.'

'...they are lining up and, Oh ... it's Strawberry Field refusing the gate...'

The loudspeaker blared then paused, the few brief moments allowing a woman's words to come to Sounder, words which rocked his world.

'Wilkes ... the name of that contestant was Sheryl Wilkes.'

'I 'eard 'em, I 'eard 'em plain as I be 'earing you. They said 'er name, they said Sheryl Wilkes.'

'It might not have been your cousin those women were talking of, there has to be more than one Sheryl Wilkes in the world.'

'I grants yoh that.' Echo Sounder's retort echoed around a park devoid of people except for himself and Kate Mallory. 'But there ain't another o' that name lives in Darlaston and it were Darlaston that woman said was where her come from...'

It was a coincidence. Kate rested a hand on the shoulder bag lying on the bench beside her. But it couldn't be more than that, even supposing Echo had heard correctly in the first place, which given his state of mind since his cousin's murder could not be guaranteed.

'They said her had been a contestant in summat or another.'

'You get a look at the women you heard talking?'

'Oh, ar.' Echo Sounder grunted his contempt. 'I think every bloke at Dunstall Park racecourse got a look at them two. Tarts ain't the description I'd put on 'em, showin' more'n they was hidin' with skirts up to their arse and boobs more out than in; wouldn't be many as would miss them: trashy an' common they said my Sheryl was, but it was them was the trash.'

Sound judgement could hardly be based on what a person wore, yet Sounder was doing just that. Kate's glance followed a robin, its brightly coloured breast a sharp contrast to the dark leafless branch it perched on. Her free hand turned up the collar of her grey worsted coat as Kate stifled an involuntary shiver. Winter was coming early this year ... or was there another reason for the chill suddenly attacking her spine?

'It were not just the outfits them wenches was wearin'...'

Sounder might have been answering her criticism, except she had not spoken it. Her eyes still on the bird now chirruping loudly, Kate forced her attention back to Sounder.

'It were what they was sayin' ... about what went on at some party or another an' how they thought the outcome o' that competition had been a foregone conclusion, that the "Promise" girl had been picked from the start...'

'Promise' girl! Kate's mental filing cabinet

flicked open. There had been an article in the magazine she had been reading at the hairdressing salon. C'mon! She urged her brain into gear. C'mon, Kate, think!

'...an' all they got was a free portfolio and a complimentary case of "Promise" cosmetics.'

Cosmetics ... of course! The wheels of Kate's mind spun. Pascal had launched a new range of make-up designed for teenagers and they had run a nationwide competition to find the face to front it.

'I knowed the Sheryl Wilkes they'd talked of were my Sheryl, I just knowed it.' He slammed a fist into the palm of his hand. 'I also knowed should I confront 'em, demand they tell me the rest, they'd 'ave the blues cart me off, so I just followed 'em, followed and listened; it had been a fiasco they said, havin' so many contestants when all the time the winner 'ad been chosen, they 'ad all seen that from the attention Theo Vail paid to 'er; but what they couldn't reckon was the fact that the girl they see now on all the adverts don't be the same. That were when I put two an' two together ... it be Vail done for my Sheryl, Vail as 'ad 'er done in an' put on that bonfire, but the swine is going to pay. I swore before God an' the devil that swine would pay an' I think this might do it.'

As surreptitiously as he had slid that photograph beneath her coat a couple of weeks before he now slid a small parcel into her bag. Wrapped in brown paper and tied with string, its several lengths knotted together, he pressed it into the capacious depths. Lord, he might have washed

367

them before coming here. Kate repressed a shudder of a different sort.

'I don't 'ave the clout to mek anythin' outta that and I ain't givin' it to Daniels, he'll just screw me for gettin' it the way I did so I'm leavin' it wi' you. Do wi' it as you thinks best but do it quick.'

'What is it...?' Kate's question trailed on emptiness. Sounder was gone, but the parcel ... the parcel was still there.

'It won't do, Sounder, either you tell me how you got hold of what you gave Kate Mallory this morning or you tell Daniels.' Richard Torrey's dark eyes glinted steel. 'She said you had been to Dunston Park racetrack but don't try telling me you got that package by betting on a horse.'

He hadn't, nor would he reach home in one piece unless he gave Torrey what he asked. Echo Sounder recognised the position he was in and resigned himself to it. 'No, I d'ain't get it by bettin' on no 'orse.' He squinted nervously at a couple of men entering the bar room. Torrey ought to know he didn't like talking here in the Staffordshire Knot, there were too many ears and all of them eager to listen in on that which didn't concern them ... but how was he to know that what he had now did not concern someone in this room or who they might report to if it did?

'So if it was no gift from a horse's mouth, where did you get it?' Viewing the lack of answer as evasion Torrey let a closed fist rest on the beer-stained table.

Sounder squinted again at the two men, his breath easing audibly as he recognised them. He need have no worries there but that didn't go to say he need have none at all.

'I ain't sayin', not in 'ere.' Each syllable was squeezed between lips which seemed to have forgotten the art of movement. 'Give me an hour, that be the time I usually leaves so my goin' won't cause no eyebrows to raise. Come to where Boynton's butcher shop backs on to Picture-Drome Way. I'll wait five minutes, after that I'll be gone.'

'Forget to turn up and you really will be gone – for good!' Torrey's parting shot got no reply.

He ought not to have trusted the conniving little lout. Torrey glanced at the illuminated dial of the Hyundai's dashboard clock. Sounder had most likely found a hole and crawled into it; if he had... A sudden movement, no more than shadow on shadow, halted the thought. Sounder ... or some yobbo in search of mischief? Opening the door he slid from the seat. There was one sure way of finding out.

'Christ, I never 'eard you comin'!' Torrey's hand on his shoulder ripped a startled gasp from Sounder. ''Ow the 'ell do you manage to move so quiet!'

'Training,' Torrey replied with a touch of asperity. 'You should try it sometime.'

'Ain't my scene.' Sounder shrugged the hand away.

'Neither is telling the truth, but be warned, lie to me, Sounder, and it'll be the last you'll ever tell. Now where did you get that rice?'

'Her d'ain't eat none, did 'er?' A high yellow

moon lent Sounder's eyes a touch of gold so they gleamed like those of a cat.

'Eat any of it? After knowing it came from you!' Torrey snorted deprecatingly. 'Do me a favour.'

'Yoh ain't so choosy when it be information yoh wants, Echo Sounder be all right then, don't 'e?'

One hand catching the shorter man by the lapels of the ancient tweed jacket, Torrey slammed him back against a shop wall. 'If I want conversation I'll find it in more enjoyable sur-roundings and with company of the same; now unless you want a free lift in the meat wagon you best say what it is you couldn't say in the "Knot".'

Jerked forward on to the flat of both feet, Echo Sounder choked against the restriction of Tor-rey's hand. 'I...' he coughed then swallowed hard as Torrey's hand dropped. 'I 'eard the name Vail and at that moment it seemed I 'eard summat else, no doubt you'll 'ave me all buttoned up for the funny farm, but I swears I 'eard Sheryl's voice ... it came clear as a bell. It were so real I turned round to look for 'er ... Christ, it were so real!'

A voice from nowhere, a voice without a body. Torrey's mouth tightened. He knew that too, it had happened to him. Now for a moment it seemed the voice of Anna murmured again in *his* ear, that voice he had loved, his own Anna, the woman who had betrayed him. But at least Sounder wasn't seeing ghosts. Was that particular phenomenon reserved solely for Richard Torrey? Tell Echo of having seen Sheryl Wilkes' ghost and he would be the one calling for the men in white coats! He closed his mind to all but Sounder and

370

the reason for meeting with him.

'Vail,' Sounder continued, a catch in his voice indicating the strength of emotion, the pain which came with remembering a well-loved voice, 'it said "Vail". I thought that was all but then there came another word, "evil". I believe it be Sheryl's way of tellin' me who killed 'er an' that be why I went to the Trading Estate out between of Bill's Street and Salisbury Street.'

'That's where Bill Bradshaw delivered boxes brought from Vail's lab?'

In the shadows thrown by darkened buildings, Torrey saw Sounder's head nod.

'Bill Bradshaw weren't the only mate I goes back a'ways with, Joe Bradley be another, an' Joe be night watchman at Vail's warehouse. I often 'ave a few drinks wi' him, 'elps pass the night.'

'Go on.'

'Well.' Sounder wiped a jacket sleeve beneath his nostrils. 'I done that last night. A few bottles and a tablet...'

'Tablet?' Torrey frowned.

'S'what I said, a win on a hoss ain't the all of what can be got on a racecourse, two pound got me one o' them date rape drugs. I fed that to Bradley, kept him out long enough for me to tek a look inside o' that warehouse. There were overalls an' gloves hung on pegs along one wall, piles of empty sacks alongside of 'em while stretchin' back as far as I could see with just a flashlight were sacks of stuff, rice, soya, flour – Christ only knows what else, for I couldn't see 'em all ... an' there was white cardboard boxes, about the size of a shoe box they was but there were no name as I could see. I were about to leave when I 'ad the same feelin' as on that racecourse, it were like Sheryl were whisperin' to me to do summat but I d'ain't know what, so in the end I grabbed a bag then legged it out o' that warehouse. I don't know what be goin' on there, all I knows is there be summat as ain't right an' that warehouse bein' used to store foodstuff... I reckon that be a cover.'

White cardboard boxes ... the size of a shoe box...

Driving along Victoria Road, Torrey glanced at the red brick Victorian police station. Old fashioned. He smiled grimly as he turned the car along Avenue Road heading for Pinfold Street. So was Daniels – old fashioned, but he could be relied on in a crisis and if what Kate had put forward regarding Vail and his so called charity food aid, then the world was facing just that.

32

The time of The Promise was come. This night the Great Sabbat of Samhain would be celebrated; the holiest night of the Black Calendar would see his dearest wish fulfilled. Theo Vail breathed deeply of the scent of willow wood, charcoal, camphor and incense burning in brass cauldrons set on legs wrought to the shape of intertwining serpents. The aroma stoked the excitement pulling at his insides. Tonight *HE* would come, the Highest of the Most High, Lord of the Dark Regions, Lucifer, Holder of Dominion over all of the earth; and he, Theo Vail, his most devoted servant, would receive the promised reward. He would be granted the highest of accolades, the most coveted powers ... he would become Ipsissimus, High Servant of Satan.

Catwalk slim, deep auburn hair tumbling in careless perfection, almond eyes gleaming emerald against a matchless alabaster skin on which no line or wrinkle seemed ever to have gained a foothold, Venetia Pascal looked at the man who turned to stare openly at her, ill-concealed hostility marking a not unattractive face.

Theo Vail. Venetia's inward smile was pure disdain. The feeling he now kept so carefully under control had not always been so restrained. Their first meeting had shown his failings; arrogance and conceit had been there, an integral part of the man, and so too that overweening sense of his own importance ... and none of those failings had left in the time of their serving together. Watching him now, she remembered those earlier times. He had made the usual overtures consistent with an imagined fatal attraction.

Meeting the stare, which with her rejection had become cold and heavy with threat, her inner smile deepened. Theo Vail had expected the most recent member to join the Prime Coven to be so flattered by the attention of a Magus she would fall into his arms and five minutes later into his bed.

But she had been held in arms more worthy than those of Theo Vail, shared the bed of one whose power he could not even begin to imagine.

'The Master must be shown our gratitude.'

Theo Vail's words were meant for everyone in the room but his stare remained concentrated on Venetia and in it was the warning, 'Defy me and you will regret it'.

'The Master is aware of our gratitude.' Eyes green as summer grass met the challenge. 'He knows the gratitude of each of his disciples, he knows its true depth, Theo, just as he knows the scale of their devotion, whether their service be truly out of love for him or for personal gain. Should it be the latter then he also knows its punishment. For myself I do the work of the Lord of Darkness, his will is my will, involve who or what it may.'

At his sides Theo Vail's expertly manicured hands curled to fists, the carefully modulated expression slipping like a mask from his face but instantly it was back, his velvet voice sardonic. 'And he, the Lord of Darkness ... will he so easily risk that work he has honoured us with, will he venture the wellbeing of the High Coven for a mere acolyte?'

For 'us' read 'me', for 'mere acolyte' read 'woman'. Theo Vail's arrogance threaded his every word. Venetia felt distaste turn to anger. Vail thought women to have no place among the higher order, to him they were subordinate, they could follow but only a man could lead ... and only one man could lead them all! There was no prize for guessing who Theo Vail thought that one man to be.

'Risk?' She said the word quietly but the effect on the listening group was stunning. The intake of breath had been sharp and even as though drawn by one person and now the silence was absolute as if the mouth of each was held by tape. 'Risk?' Venetia allowed a smile to touch her own lips but her calm stare was as glacial as polar ice. 'Risk to whom, Theo? Are your fears for the Coven or are they for yourself? Are you afraid the suggestion of a disciple lower than yourself ... a woman disciple ... will find favour with the Master? That it was a woman who wished to pay him additional honour, a woman who proposed St John Winter sacrifice that girl, my proposal and not that of the Magus?' Pausing only to let the smile give way to dislike and derision in open display, she went on. 'Would you care to put the question to the Master? Summon him, Theo, let us both speak with him face to face. I will do so willingly, I am ready to show the fullness of the respect due to the Lord of the World, to reveal to him the truth of my heart, my absolute devotion; can you say the same?'

Condemned out of her own mouth! Theo Vail's body burned with the heat of anger. It was as he had suspected from the beginning, Venetia Pascal had ambition, a greed for power that matched his own, a greed that could prove dangerous for Theo Vail. But he must hide what every sense was telling him; the others, the Followers of the Way, they must not guess at the threat he felt.

Breath widening his nostrils, he took one more moment, a second only, to gather himself then answered, 'You wish to reveal the truth of your heart, to show your absolute devotion to the Holder of Eternity, then we will accord you that privilege.' He smiled at the watching group then at the woman he secretly feared. 'You will show the Master the respect you owe to him...'

In a hush that crackled with tension Venetia Pascal saw the brilliant glacial eyes flicker and darken as if seeing some inner vision, and when Vail spoke again the silken tone had become a rasp.

'You will show him *absolute* devotion...'

It seemed to Theo Vail the words had smiled in his brain, a serpent's smile that spread to his lips ... the cold smile of death.

'...tonight you will fulfil each of the desires you profess to hold for our Lord Lucifer ... tonight you will die for him!'

The concerted gasp coming from the rest of the room quivered on the ensuing silence like the strings of some invisible orchestra. Venetia Pascal looked into cold, viciously malevolent eyes. The eyes of her executioner.

She had been in a room such as this before. Venetia Pascal glanced about her. It had been part of a lovely old manor house, large and grand, standing in its own acres in the heart of the Worcestershire countryside, the home of Julian Crowley. He too had been a devotee of Satan, a Follower of the Left Hand Path, an Ipsissimuss, most powerful of black magicians. But that had not saved him from the wrath of the Master. His mistake had cost him his powers and his sanity. Vail also had made mistakes, those of allowing sacrificial offerings to be discovered half burned, but the Master had not punished him. There had to be a reason but she had not dared to ask it; he who was Lord of the Earth did not explain his reasons even to his most devoted follower, so what of Venetia Pascal? Would Lucifer accept the sacrifice Theo Vail intended to make, his gift to the god he worshipped, and in return would that god pronounce him the Chosen, the one who would carry forward his work to its ultimate degree of power a mortal could hold? Would Theo Vail become Ipsissimus, High Priest of the Premier Coven, First among the Followers, one who could stand beside his Lord for all eternity?

The Lord of Earth did not explain his reasons. Venetia felt a quiver of nervousness ripple through her. Nor would he need explain if the promise made to her in that hotel room was not to be kept!

Across the room Theo Vail stared at the woman Laurence Thorold and Stuart Fenton had escorted and who now stood between them. Venetia Pascal did indeed possess beauty, a beauty which caught a man by the balls and squeezed 'til he begged for that delicious body to lie naked beneath his own, to give him the sublime relief he gagged for. A jerking at the base of his abdomen, which despite everything began whenever he looked at this woman, throbbed its insistent message. Perhaps he should ... it was not unusual for the High Priest to celebrate the Black Mass by making love to the woman before her sacrifice... To rape the beautiful Venetia, to have her scream for mercy, would be delightful indeed ... but then should the Master want this offering delivered unsoiled ... the penalty of denying him that was not to be contemplated; yet still the demand pulsed as he looked into eyes gleaming like rare emeralds in that perfect face. But beauty could be deceiving and in the case of Venetia Pascal positively dangerous. She could smile with the promise of angels, but instinct told him she would do it while sliding a dagger beneath a man's ribs.

'Be very sure of your actions, Theo.' Venetia spoke quietly. 'You have already made the mistake of a sacrifice in which no blood was drawn by the Athame, nor did the woman voluntarily hand her soul to the devil. Then there are the offerings whose bodies were not completely consumed by fire. Do not compound those mistakes by adding another.'

'Mistakes!' Laced with an acid rising from his rejection as a lover, Vail's smile was condescending. 'The Master has not thought so, but then you have not reached a level where all things are made clear, so I will explain to you ... again! Nothing has given rise to suspicion, the public has been given no cause to suspect what is in their midst; as for a fire in a factory, that is as commonplace as is ... murder. Both fade quickly from people's interest.'

Hard as the stones they resembled, Venetia Pascal's lovely jewel eyes held to those filled with contempt but beneath it lay a shadow of fear.

'I agree, Theo.' Her reply held a note of challenge. 'But not that of the Lord of Darkness. Whose attention would you prefer, that of a public interested only for the moment ... or that of the Master? I advise you consider your answer carefully; remember the Lord we both serve is no fool, it would not be wise to say one thing while meaning another.'

Objection Vail had come more and more to feel against the beautiful adept rose again. A glittering menace in his cold-grey eyes, his answer spewed like venom. 'Is that your threat or do you think it his?'

'Maybe it is both.' Sliding between smiling lips, the reply brought an echo of gasps from the assembled worshippers.

She should be terrified, she should be begging for him not to take her life; but she was not! Vail turned to face a table draped in black silk, tall wooden serpent-twined sconces stood at each of its four corners spilling light from newly lit black candles. Venetia Pascal showed no fear. The thought gave rise to a fear of his own.

'All is prepared?'

'All is prepared.'

The answer given by thirteen members, a full coven, Venetia watched Vail walk to the centre of the Pentacle inlaid on the wood floor, the five-pointed Pentagram glistening gold within the circle of the rim. At five foot eight and of moderate physique, Theo Vail was no Adonis; it was only the contrast of pale blond hair against cold slate-grey eyes that made him noticeable ... by any other than himself. Acid of contempt flavoured the thought. Vail was in love with himself. The powerful Magus of the high coven had believed his looks had rendered him irresistible and his proficiency in the Dark Arts gave him endless protection ... but then Theo Vail was more than one kind of fool.

Standing between two of the devil's disciples she smiled and then deep in her heart began to pray.

What in the name of heaven was he doing! Bruce Daniels stared through the windscreen into darkness lashed by rain. He had told Marjorie he would be late. Marjorie! He sucked hard on the antacid tablet, the third since this shakedown began. Other coppers' wives objected, some may even worry when their man was away half the night, but for Marjorie it simply provided a chance to polish her beloved furniture and plump cushions his arse was never allowed to touch. Day in and day out her routine was the same. Christ, how boring could life get! Yet how different was his own life? Darlaston was not exactly the crime Mecca of the country, his days were nothing if not monotonous. Dull! He glanced at a pale watery moon too weak to fight heavy cloud banking to its left. It looked as washed out as himself. He swallowed bismuth, that too was a losing battle, the bloody ulcer never improved. But losing was something he should be well familiar with; after all that was what came of his promotion bids ... lost to chair-polishers like Quinto. So why was he sitting here now when he could be home in bed? The last of the tablet a sticky coating on his tongue, Bruce Daniels almost smiled at the answer in his brain. Why? 'Cos he was a bloody cop!

In the passenger seat Detective Sergeant Williams eased his position, the movement bringing a terse response from Daniels.

'I said there were no need for you to come, daft

for both o' we to sit here half the night. Get yourself away home to bed.'

'I'll wait, sir, don't fancy walking in this weather.'

'There be squad cars at the corner of Gladstone Street and both ends of Salisbury Street, tell 'em they won't be needed after all, then get one of 'em to give you a lift home.'

'Can't go home, sir, my shift isn't finished.'

He meant he wasn't leaving until Bruce Daniels did. Daniels' glance followed racing cloud as it swallowed what little light was in the sky. Williams too was a bloody cop ... good for the lad.

'You mean you intend to wait to see if the fat lady sings?'

Beneath the cover of darkness, Detective Sergeant Williams smiled. 'Something like that, sir.'

'Hmmph!' Daniels growled. 'Well, let's hope the bloody notes ain't flat!'

He hadn't wanted Williams to take part in this. The lad was sharp; keep a head on his shoulders and he could go up the ladder, not stand with a foot on the bottom rung like he did. Was it knowing he would never get promotion had him doing this, following up what could well be a fool's errand? But Torrey and Kate Mallory hadn't fed him crap on those other occasions; that together with what he had squeezed out of Sounder had him here now. He had known the risk of it going down like a lead balloon and he hadn't wanted Williams jeopardising his chances by being a part of it, but once Williams had realised something was on he refused to back away and Dave Farnell had backed him, saying the only way to learn was to take both paths, the uncertain as well as the certain. Well, this path was by no means certain.

'Did Sounder say any actual time?'

'No.' Daniels shook his head. 'Just that Bradshaw told him the stuff was going out on the tenth.'

'That was yesterday.' Williams squinted at the illuminated dial of his wrist watch.

'P'raps it's all one to Bradshaw, p'raps being night watchman has him runnin' one day into another.' Daniels coughed trying to clear his throat of bismuth. 'Anyway, nothing moved yesterday, the place was under observation all day.'

'You think maybe Bradshaw got it wrong?'

Daniels pursed his lips, his answer one word, 'Maybe', the rest spoken only in his mind. Bradshaw might be a bit half soaked but Sounder ... that scruffy little songbird was sharp as a razor, he twittered only the tune he was positive of, especially where singing to a certain Detective Inspector ... no, Echo Sounder wasn't daft, he wouldn't chance his hand on a bet he couldn't win. The thought was interrupted by the sudden sound of music, Daniels glanced towards Williams.

'Hang on.' Mobile phone in hand, the Detective Sergeant gave a nod. 'Something big coming our way, sir, uniform reports a sixteen-wheel pantechnicon having passed Asda and taking a route south towards the junction of Pinfold Street and Walsall Road. What shall I tell them?'

Brain moving faster than Concorde, Daniels

reproduced the route in his mind. If that lorry took a left into Walsall Road there was a fair chance it could be his man, and if it turned again along Bill's Street then...

'Tell them to stay put in case of a doubling-back.'

'You think it's our bloke?' Williams closed the mobile phone Daniels had insisted all units use; police radio was too often tuned into by the wrong sort. Not legal procedure! Williams smiled, replacing the instrument in his pocket. Since when did that worry Detective Inspector Bruce Daniels?

33

In the centre of the double-banded Pentacle, standing at the heart of the five-pointed Pentagram, Vail lifted both hands towards the ceiling of the black-draped room. His opening salutation was strong and clear.

'Hail to the Benei Elohim...'

'All hail.'

'All hail to the Malakhe Khabala, Angels of Satan.'

'Hail to the Malakhe Khabala, Angels of Satan.'

Between Thorold and Fenton, Venetia Pascal made her own responses with the same quiet veneration as the rest of the coven. The Master would expect her adoration even though she was to be the sacrifice, and whether in this life or the next she knew she must never deny him honour.

'Hail to the Saphrire, and the Tihare, Spirits of the day. Hail to Telane and Lilin, spirits of the night.'

This was the night of Samhain, the night full ritual must be observed, and Vail was taking no chances.

The lesser demons accorded respect, she watched him now bow deeply before each point of the star, his voice firm as he venerated the great names of power. Each of the Archangels of Hell duly addressed, he crossed to the black-draped altar where candle flame flickered specks of gold blood over the ebony inverted cross at its centre. Dropping to the floor he lay with arms stretched outward from his sides.

'Bornless One, You Who Were and Who Will Be, grant your disciples the grace of your blessing, accept their honour and their worship.'

Allowing time for the response of the congregation, he rose then made another deep genuflection before the upside-down cross before he turned, the glance he directed at Venetia glittering with triumph as from the shrouded walls there came a sound ... the quiet sounds of breathing.

Senior members of the Premier Coven were all cognisant of the results of calling upon the Master and their breath-held tension indicated that they knew the call had been answered, that an unseen presence had come into the room.

Vail knew it too; the vicious spite burning in his eyes told it as he signed for her to be brought to the table draped in black. She was not bound as the model girl had been, no silver chains circled her wrists and ankles, no collar banded her throat, yet Venetia Pascal made no attempt to run from the room. Theo Vail was not her captor, she was the prisoner of Satan and only he could spare or take her life. Brushing aside the hands ready to force her on to the table she bowed to the dark cross then ascended to the topmost of three steps fronting a small dais. Her presentation to the Master would not be as those other women, her life would be given here on the steps of his altar.

A shake of the head instructing Thorold and Fenton to step away, Theo Vail looked at the woman who was to ensure his reward from the Master. Auburn hair burnished with the glow of candles lay loose about her shoulders, its silken strands caressing rosebud nipples of taut breasts rising and falling beneath the transparent cloth of a simple white robe. She was so beautiful. Despite himself Vail felt the familiar throb beat in the base of his abdomen, the flesh between his legs harden. He could take her now, drive the pole of manhood into the crevice glistening at the top of those shapely legs. The taking would add the crowning touch to this, his special evening, and it would rob her of that air of superiority she had wrapped herself in. It would wipe away for ever that smugness and he would laugh, he would laugh with every soul-satisfying thrust. But first the pleasure of the Master, then he would take his own.

Fighting the desire beginning to flow like molten lava in every vein, the demand holding his penis rock hard, he intoned softly, 'Sar ha-Olam. Prince of the World and Ruler of Eternity, all praise and honour be yours. To you, Great Lord of the Dark Regions, we give worship.'

'Praise, honour and worship to the Lord of Darkness.'

With the reply the sound that had seemed like a quiet breathing intensified, the breeze of it sighing about the room, fingering the shrouded walls, rippling the silken cover of table and altar.

'All High...'

Vail's voice throbbed with near ecstasy.

'...set wide the Gates of Hell, send forth your Emissary, Belial, Gatherer of Souls, that he might take the Offering we bring.'

The last word was almost a sob of rapture that rested a moment on silence, then the sigh that had become a breeze exploded into a wind that tore around the room, the frenzy of it beating and tearing at the air, its sound a convulsion that seemed to rock the earth, to rip the brain from the head. Wave upon wave, it circled like some great winged beast searching for prey: then settled into stillness, a stillness that crushed against the senses and robbed the lungs of breath.

Standing perfectly still, each disciple of the High Coven waited. This was the moment of ultimate danger, that fraction of time that would see their worship acknowledged, accepted by the Lord of Hell, or all of them swept into oblivion. Only Vail spoke.

'In Nomine Satanum, Belial, High Angel of the Throne, I call you to my will.'

From the ground, directly at the centre of the gold-marked Pentacle, a ribbon of mist began to rise. Slowly, as if lifting from the sleep of death, it stretched and widened.

On the step where she lay still, Venetia turned her head, every sense leaping. Each request the high priest made was being answered, his every plea granted. Soon he would ask her soul be gathered. Once more she began to pray, a silent petition to Satan.

Floating free of the ground, the vapour-like mist moved anti-clockwise, hovering for a few seconds over each name engraved within the Pentacle's double rim, then as though endowed with the powers of each demon it shot upward, a volcanic surge of glittering black mist.

Belial! Venetia's prayer died. The Lord of Darkness had forsaken his devotee.

Worshippers who, apart from Thorold and Fenton, were on their knees, heads bowed in deep respect and fear of the Presence standing high above the Pentacle, did not hear the slight gasp which followed Venetia's realisation of denial, but it reached Vail and his lips curled in a vindictive smile. So much for his lovely rival, the woman who coveted his position, who envied his powers of Magus. She had cast her die and lost.

'Belial.' So great was the feeling of triumph, he almost shouted the name. 'In the name of Him Who was Before Time, I charge you, take to him the soul we offer.'

Space that had been dimmed by the lowering of the artificial lighting snapped sharply into blackness. In less than a breath, walls, floor and ceiling merged into one black void, a total and complete eclipse and from its black heart came pulsing vibration, a steady beat pounding the

387

silence like a drum.

On and on it continued, a threatening warning cadence, a tattoo of terror. Somewhere within the tenebrous darkness, a sob escaped an anguished throat, while several tremulous gasps were caught, their life stifled by fear.

The scent of camphor and incense set on willow and live charcoal drifted to Vail's nostrils but no light of its burning penetrated the all-consuming darkness; he had called upon the Power of Evil and it had answered ... but what was that answer to be? The triumph which moments ago had blazed in his veins became a stream of cold anxiety. Would the Master refuse the homage, the sacrifice? Would he refuse the petition of his supplicant, reject the entreaty he be given the powers of Ipsissimuss? The last brought a stab of sudden fury and he hurled the words of its strength at the pulsing darkness.

'Siras Etar Besanar,' he called, 'First of the Created, Greatest of the Great, regard your servant Theo Vail, show him your benevolence.'

The last word died. The insistent throb crashing against the air subsided and a stunning, paralysing silence returned. Within it Theo Vail's heart stumbled in its rhythm. Had he gone too far?

The thought chilled the stream of anxiety, turning it to ice to block his throat and keep the breath of life from his lungs; then as his senses began to swim, a pinpoint of light appeared and with its coming the constriction suffocating Vail fell away. 'Master,' he breathed, 'your servant magnifies your Great Name, he extols your glory.'

As if in answer, the pinpoint spread, lengthening, widening, bathing the Pentacle in the brilliance of its coming. Barred by the barrier of its gleam, spectral shadows retreated, hiding themselves in the deeper shadow of black-clad walls.

Encompassing the symbols inlaid in the floor, a scarlet pool hovered as if in blessing, then flared, bathing the whole of the room with an eye-searing ferocity of scarlet light tipped and veined with streaks of purple, grey and black. Even as the congregation gasped, these coalesced one into another; writhing, twisting, joining and rejoining, forming then reforming until the whole became one great luminous figure.

Floating in mid-air, it circled the kneeling group then moved to the altar where it rested above the black cross.

'All Hail to the Lord of Darkness, Glorious is his Name!'

Intent on ingratiating himself more firmly, Vail bowed before the glowing shape, the demon he had conjured.

'In Nomine Satanum,' he straightened, 'accept our tribute.' Breathing his own sigh of relief that all had gone well, Stuart Fenton took the brazen bowl that had been placed ready on the table, Laurence Thorold lifting the velvet cushion on which rested the Athame, the knife of sacrifice.

Seeing their movements, Theo Vail raised a hand, waving them back into place. He would collect the first of his rewards; Venetia Pascal would join the Master with the blood of sacrifice streaming from her heart ... and the blood of rape staining the cleft between her legs.

'For the honour and glory of Satan.' He said the

words softly, savouring, enjoying each as he removed his jacket. Then fingers already scrabbling at the buckle of his belt, he mounted the steps, his face taut with the intensity of the drive surging through him and bringing his flesh to a painful throb.

Lying at the base of the altar Venetia recognised the gleam in those slate-hard eyes. She had seen it before ... rape! Now in her abhorrence of the proposed abuse, she looked at the figure hovering motionless above the inverted cross, then closed her eyes.

'Master,' she whispered, 'I rejoice in your decision, have your Archangel bring me to you, but please, Great Lord, let him not deliver one soiled by the blood of rape.'

In the instant of her prayer sound wafted, a gentle wash of music drifting over the room. Soft, exquisite, piquant yet tranquil, soothing yet at the same time provocative, a harmony of such haunting beauty it floated like silk in the mind, whispering to the heart, calling to the soul.

It was music Venetia Pascal had heard before.

Opening her eyes in wonder she looked again at the luminous figure hovering above the cross. The transparency of mist was fading, burned away by flame which of a sudden had wreathed around it, darting violet-tipped spears of crimson lancing around and above, a great aureole of fire – and within its inferno the glorious golden figure of a man.

It was he! Her golden lover. Desire raced sudden and hard gripping her stomach as she looked into the face which so often since the night she had lain with him, since that night of passion, had filled her dreams.

'Master.' She whispered the name, but as she tried to lift her arms towards the flame-wrapped presence she found she could not move.

'I am He Who Was Before Time.'

Smooth as velvet, melodic as water trickling from a fountain, the words came gently. But with the last the flames around the figure flared. Arrow headed, they flicked at the shadows seeking refuge in the darkness of the walls; swords of purple-tipped crimson they slashed, cleaving light with light until the very room seemed one blaze of fire. And then it came.

Jubilant, exultant, a triumphal fanfare blazing above the gentle music, drowning it beneath an imperious arrogance.

'I am Lucifer!'

Hands stilled on the buckle of his trousers, Theo Vail stared at the entity he had called from the depths of hell, stared into eyes of a blackness that whipped the skin, black liquid fire that lanced the brain. Self-assurance that had thrived a moment before drained like water into desert sand, leaving a profound fear such as he had never before felt. He staggered backwards down the steps, falling to his knees at the foot of the dais.

'I am He to Whom the World Belongs.'

The call of a trumpet, the very essence of victory, swept like a blast of wind about a room the cessation of the music had buried in silence.

Kneeling beside the table, Stuart Fenton let his trembling fingers lose their hold on the brazen bowl, the fall of it clattering on the exposed wood of the floor. His breath snatched in short terrified gasps and echoed the fear of his fellow worshippers.

Fear still holding him, Theo Vail touched his forehead to the ground in deep obeisance, then by sheer effort of will rose to his feet, a movement of his hand signalling Laurence Thorold to bring the Athame. Dipping his head in a further sign of reverence to the glittering being, he swallowed against the dryness gagging his throat. He along with the others stood in mortal danger.

'Master.' A tremble in his voice revealed the depth of his fear, but Vail knew it was something he must conquer; the Lord of Darkness would not contemplate a Magus too afraid to speak; he would not grant the powers of Ipsissimus to a man who allowed his fears to overcome him.

'Master,' he said again, lifting his eyes to the Being floating in a sea of living fire, 'Master, Ruler of Eternity, accept the homage of your servant, accept the sacrifice he makes to the glory of your name.'

Eyes averted from the cross and the great golden figure above it, Laurence Thorold stepped forward with the cushion on which rested the sacrificial dagger for Vail to take.

Above the altar, diathermic eyes blazed twin furnaces of black fire. One hand lifted. A finger pointed and from it spurted dark flame, flame which touched the knife and left it a heap of calcinated metal, the cushion it had rested upon bearing not even a singe.

Uttering a cry of pure terror, Laurence Thorold

fell to the floor, pressing his body and face hard against it.

'I shall take my sacrifice.'

The golden lips did not move, the mouth did not open, yet with each word quicksilver darts of flame speared into the room.

A breath of relief eased Vail's closed lungs. The Master would accept! But how to perform the sacrifice, how was he to kill Venetia Pascal if not with the Athame?

'The one you have elected is not the one I will take.'

Soundless yet mind-stunning thunder rolled and vibrated, shaking the walls and floor with a silent fury.

It was then Theo Vail saw the incandescent hand lift once more, a pulsing living scarlet finger of flame point towards him while the words scorched his brain.

'I shall take the one who would seek to deceive, who would become Ipsissimus though his service is unworthy.'

'Unworthy?' Despite the terror dragging at him, Vail cried his desperation. 'Master, I have always sought to serve you well!'

'You sought to serve yourself well!'

The answer crashed from still lips, the air crackling with the intensity of lightning charges.

'You would gain the powers you yearn with fruitless sacrifice, now you shall pay.'

Shooting from eyes that were pools of ebony fire, black flames danced over Vail at the base of the dais, burning, scorching, melting flesh to the bone, then the pointing finger moved, fashioning a glistening thread of scarlet that wound about the throat of the screaming man and, as the others watched in horror, lifted him until his incinerated body dangled lifeless in mid-air.

34

'You risked the name of this station.'

The name of this station meaning the name of Detective Chief Inspector Martin Quinto! Answering retorts burned vitriolic in Daniels' brain. Never mind the fact that by raiding that warehouse millions of people had been saved from death by poisoning, pay no heed to the fact the British Government could have been brought down, accused and condemned for instigating and assisting in mass genocide; all of that was by the way when compared to Quinto's official wellbeing!

'I should have been put in the picture, kept fully aware of what was going on, instead of which you took things into your own hands.'

To do what? Daniels almost smiled. Quinto in the picture? That would have been one sure way to cock things up. By the time he had sorted which way was clean, the whole bloody consignment of contaminated food would have been spread halfway around the world.

'Fortunately I managed to speak with Assistant Chief Constable Perrins and persuade him that the whole episode was under my control from the beginning and consequently he feels that the Chief Constable will be taking no action.'

That makes two of you! Daniels' answer smacked against his teeth. Perrins had most likely forgotten the very short time he served on the beat and Quinto's arse had found a chair two minutes after leaving police training!

'In view of that,' Quinto resumed, 'I am prepared this time – *this* time, Daniels – to overlook your lack of procedure ... but should anything of the sort occur again then I promise you it will go very differently for you; do I make myself clear?'

'And did he make himself clear?' Dave Farnell placed a mug of fresh-brewed tea on Daniels' desk, having first cleared a space.

'Oh, yes.' Detective Inspector Bruce Daniels nodded. 'It's all perfectly clear. Quinto spoke with the Assistant Chief Constable, assured him that everything had been overseen by himself. You know what that means.'

This time it was Dave Farnell who nodded. He knew the job Daniels had pulled off was going to merit praise from the highest circles, and not only praise; though any career advancement arising out of it would not be directed towards the detective inspector. Quinto's so-called protective intervention would have seen to that; he had claimed the organisation that had brought results, so to his shoulder would go the gold braid.

'Same as usual then, eh, Bruce!' He smiled sympathetically.

Daniels picked up the mug and looked over its rim at his long-time friend and colleague. 'Too late for anythin' else ... but the same ain't going to go for Williams. I'm going to make sure his part in that sting is recognised even if it means rubbin' Quinto's eyeballs over every bloody word of my report.'

'Supposing he ever gets your report.'

Daniels sipped the hot sweet tea and as the other man turned to leave the cramped office said, 'He'll get it, Dave. Williams will write it.'

'It's Echo Sounder we all have to thank.' Kate Mallory had listened to Detective Inspector Bruce Daniels explain how thanks to her and Torrey the entire contents of that warehouse had been seized. 'If it hadn't been for him passing that package to me then heaven knows the consequences.'

'It was all he could safely get away with; likely somebody had filled themselves a nice little bag of rice then had to leave without it; lucky fella, I say.'

'Even more lucky you found that box of powder in your car,' Daniels looked at Torrey setting glasses on the table, 'even if you didn't bring it straight round to Victoria Road!'

'You know what Sounder's answer to that would be.' Torrey grinned, imitating the racing enthusiast's voice, 'The time it teks the blues to do anythin' ... they would still be decidin' whether the stuff be flour or babby's arse powder five year from now!'

'Mm.' Daniels nodded. 'Could have been right had a certain cop I could name got hold of it.'

'A certain cop?' Kate's nose twitched.

'I said *could* name, but I won't. You have your promise the scoop will be yours once the National Investigation bods are done with it.'

'Scoop! There'll be precious little left. It'll be a case of "in the national interest" which means the government is covering its tail!' Kate's snort emphasised her resentment.

Daniels sipped the mild ale Torrey had fetched from the bar. He could feel for Kate Mallory; she had played her part but the goodies would not be forthcoming. It was a scenario he was only too familiar with.

The curve of the alcove they had chosen in the lounge bar of the Frying Pan partially shaded Torrey's face but the meaning in his voice was clear. 'Kate will get something. She'd better or I go to the Nationals with the whole shooting match!'

He didn't have to ask himself if Torrey meant what he said. Daniels wiped beer from his top lip. This son of Darlaston played with nothing... not even words.

'Made the same deal as was reached over the do with them counterfeit plates,' he answered. 'Whatever is allowed to be told will be given to nobody until the *Star* has published. I will tell you though – and this isn't for publication – they were pretty sceptical until they were given the results of the laboratory tests done on that rice ... shown proof positive it was contaminated with the same poison as in that box found in the taxi. It was smart on your part, Torrey, getting your mate to move so quick; his report cut out the arguments I would have got from the station and it certainly moved the NITs.'

Kate's mouth tilted further as she gave voice to disgust. 'Nits ... ugh! Where do they come in?'

'Slip of the tongue,' Daniels said.

Kate nodded complacently. That had been no slip of the tongue.

'Not the sort you are thinking of, Kate, he's referring to the National Investigation Team.' Relaxed at the assurance Kate Mallory would be given first bite of the apple once the investigation was finished, Torrey smiled.

Swallowing ale he knew he would regret drinking, Bruce Daniels glanced about the room. The raid that had just gone down, did anybody here have part in it? Could there be a terrorist cell right here on his patch? Christ, it was insane! Those behind it must be bloody lunatics!

Kate watched the nuances play over the tired face; pain, yes, there was pain but there was something more, something deeper. Worry? That description fit the bill more aptly. By taking hers and Torrey's word on what might be stored in that warehouse and acting off his own bat had got him into deep trouble with his superiors, maybe cost him his job?

'Inspector.' The smile she tried to bring was dead before it reached her mouth, and the brown eyes usually so alight were cloudy with anxiety. 'Inspector, if we ... if what we told you... Oh, Lord! Look, if Torrey and I have caused ... if we should have...'

'I know what you are trying to say.' Detective Inspector Bruce Daniels came perilously near to a smile. 'But you can forget it. The stuff you came up with and the information you followed with has saved countless lives.'

Not quite what I was trying to ask. Kate clamped down on the comment, allowing Daniels to continue uninterrupted.

'There's nothing final yet, there's still a lot of material to be tested, but what's already been examined has proven to carry more than enough toxic substance to kill any who eats it, even if the diner's an elephant.'

'I think Kate was trying to ask, has any of this landed you in it with your bosses?'

He was always paddling in the proverbial shit, got used to the stink! Daniels shrugged inwardly. He could be honest and say the Detective Chief Inspector had almost filled his trousers on being told of that raid, he could admit the truth of being hauled on to the carpet and rewarded with the threat of dismissal the very next time opportunity presented itself – but then truth didn't always say what you would have it say.

Emptying his glass he replaced it on the table, centring it exactly on a beer mat emblazoned with the logo of a lion rampant holding an axe in an upraised paw, then reached into his pocket for his car keys. There would be no mess. Quinto had seen to that; the man's record would have a new pin looking rusty!

'No trouble, Kate. Who knows, there might even be a medal in it.' His fingers closed over the keys. Those words were not as empty as they sounded. Finding that poisoned foodstuff had avoided an international catastrophe and so was well in line for recognition; Detective Inspector

Bruce Daniels MBE? Not while there was an arsehole like Quinto in charge!

'What I can't get at is how did they mix that powder with the rest of the stuff?'

'That was easy.' Daniels answered Torrey's question. 'The place they used had been a bakery. Most of the equipment was still in place and among it were several large vats used for mixing dough. They could tip anything into them – wheat flour, soya bean, rice – you name it – add the poison, stir it together then bag it, job done. It only remained to poison half the world.'

'They?' Torrey questioned again. 'Meaning Vail? Or do you think he knows nothing of what was going on?'

'He must have known...' Kate's eyes were suddenly questioning, '...otherwise how do you explain the small lab behind his private office? His following Bill Bradshaw each time he collected material from there?'

'Sounder!' Torrey's mouth tightened. 'Echo is looking for someone to blame for his cousin's death and doesn't really care who he finds; should he think Vail then he'll go for him.'

Pushing to his feet, Daniels tossed the car keys in his hand. 'Won't do no good, came over the wire this morning. Telford police found Theo Vail hanged in the bedroom of his house.'

Richard Torrey snapped awake, every nerve in his body tense with warning. Lie still. Play dead. Evaluate your position. Each instruction instilled by training until it had become natural instinct took over. Concentrating on keeping his breathing measured and regular as if still asleep, his head not moving, he slid a glance around the room.

Insipid moonlight filtered by cloud entered grudgingly through windows whose blinds were raised, then like a frightened child scurried immediately into the comfort of shadow.

There was no sound, no movement other than shadows in moonlight, yet something had woken him. Lying absolutely still he waited for his vision to become accustomed to the semi-darkness of the bedroom; if some unfortunate burglar had chosen his flat as that night's venue, and that same burglar thought him still asleep then he would make his move. In the stillness, Torrey's mouth hardened. It would be the last move the bastard would ever make by himself.

Longer, slower, a second glance circled the room cutting incisively into shadow. He was alone. Yet the frigid tingle, the frostbite pinching every nerve, said he was not.

He had lain like this so many times in early childhood, afraid of the dark, too afraid of what might be lurking in the blackness to go to his mother who he could hear crying in her own room. He had felt such anger then, anger against a man who could walk out on his wife, against a father who could leave a son to fight his fears alone, an anger which had grown alongside him and which remained still potent and alive; but fear of darkness had faded until it no longer existed.

But nature's innate warning signal, that inner silent alarm bell which now had him fully awake ... it had not proved wrong during his stint in

Northern Ireland nor had it done so in the yard of the Bird-in-Hand when those yobbos had thought to take him, and every sense told him it was not playing him false now. Throwing off the duvet, he slid easily to his feet. It was at that precise moment the door separating bedroom and living room erupted in flame.

Christ, the bastards had fire-bombed him! Seconds of paralysis stunning reaction he stared at the leaping tongues of flame then movement returning to his limbs he looked again at the raging mass. Leaving by that way was out of the question... The window? Even as his glance began to slide, the fire changed. The fierce dance of flame subsided to a dull red glow and at its heart – Torrey's breath hissed from his lungs – at its heart, long blonde hair resting on slender shoulders, eyes of blue-green turquoise steadfastly locked on him, stood the figure of a young woman. Sheryl Wilkes! His mind did not argue the fact of what his eyes were showing ... but why? Across from him the glow surrounding the figure remained concentrated, no overspill attacking shadows left untouched by fractious moonbeams.

Why? Hadn't the blues found that stuff in Vail's warehouse, hadn't the danger it posed been avoided? Anger cold and sharp hit his stomach. What the hell else did this ghost of Sounder's cousin want!

'Vail's game – supposing it *was* his game – has been stopped.' The words spat rapid and hard, verbal machine-gun bullets. 'The man is dead, now for Christ's sake leave me alone!'

There was no answer, no whisper in his mind,

only the steady glow through which he could see the door, the door which, despite those flames, was not burning.

'How many more times!' Exasperation hit the back of Torrey's throat and his hands balled into clenched fists. How many more times was this bloody apparition going to make an appearance!

'Can't you see!' The words hurled towards the watching figure. 'It's over, the danger is gone, there is nothing more needs be done!'

'*Evil!*'

Soundless, unspoken it slithered like some cold serpent in his brain.

'*Evil,*' it repeated, setting off those mental alarms Torrey knew so well.

'There is *no* bloody evil!' Anger getting the better of him, one fist raised as if to strike, he took a step forward and in that same instant the flames which had enshrouded the figure flared again and with them appeared a second figure of another woman. A body blackened and charred, a face no more than burned bone, it floated beside the pretty blonde-haired woman; but it was neither of them made Torrey's breath lock in his lungs: it was a third figure, one which appeared as the first lifted a hand from which dangled a necklace, the stones of it glinting in the light of unearthly fire. The figure of Kate Mallory!

35

Theo Vail had tried and lost. He had thought causing the deaths of millions across the world would endear him in the sight of the Master, that by this act Satan would then grant him the powers of Ipsissimus, that great power by which a mortal could transcend linear time, travel at will through the fourth dimension; whereby they could reach the astral plane. But Vail had made the gravest of mistakes; he had read the will of the Master wrongly.

Sitting at her desk, Venetia Pascal smiled with the satisfaction of a cat fed cream.

Vail had been so filled with his own desires he had failed to pay due concern to those of the Lord of Darkness. A laugh sibilant yet triumphant stayed in her throat.

Vail had intended to offer millions of people in sacrifice but they would have been bodies only, a sacrifice useless to the Master. Was not the Prince of Darkness Lord of the Earth? With the flick of one finger could he not destroy a city? Could not one swipe of his hand wipe away a continent and every human being living on it? But Satan did not want just bodies, yet that was what Vail would have given, bodies but not soul, an empty sacrifice. The Magus of the High Coven had forgotten that only souls given willingly to the Lord of Hell could be claimed by him.

She had tried to tell him before, once concerning the sacrifice in that paint factory, then that model killed by Zachary St John Winter, as she had when Sheryl Wilkes had been his chosen victim. True, the girl had been put forward by herself. As a way of getting rid of her it had seemed the perfect solution, but first she should have been brought like others to the Master, to have pledged her soul in return for whatever she desired; true, the Athame, the ritual knife of Sacrifice, had been used on both the model and on Sheryl Wilkes, but neither had willingly given their soul.

Stupid, egotistical Theo Vail! Venetia's satisfaction warmed. He had thought to rise so high, but not to dangle from a fiery cord wrapped around his neck.

Fenton, Thorold and the others had gasped their terror but even as they abased themselves, calling on the mercy of their Master, that beautiful golden face had looked at her, the finger which had pointed at Vail pointing at her. The invisible cord which until then had barred movement dropped away and she had risen to her knees, her head bowed in her own submission. The Prince of the Earth had answered her plea, he had saved her from the degradation of rape; now he would take his servant with him into hell. The thought should have terrified her but as she knelt before that golden figure she felt only elation, a heady, all-encompassing joy. He would take her earthly life but she would live beside him in hell throughout eternity.

But he had not taken her life. The finger which

pointed had not spurted cords of silken flame but had touched the crown of her head, and with it had come that wonderful sensation, the feeling of him covering her, of his entering, driving hard flesh so deep into her she wanted to cry out, to shout her desire; then as that desire had been answered with a surge that had seemed to sweep body and mind, the voice that was pure music had spoken.

Liquid in its softness, velvet silk, it had poured over her, filling her soul with its beauty ... with its promise.

'I am Lucifer, Lord of the Earth...'

Whisper soft yet reaching into every corner of the room, each syllable was a sound so ecstatic it pulled at her heart.

'...to you is given the Word, to you the Promise. Through you is my will accomplished.'

The Master had acknowledged her as his chosen, he had signified her as head of the High Coven, the instrument of his will. Such honour should in turn be acknowledged; it called for a gift on her part. She must present the Dark Lord with something she esteemed, a gift which of itself would show devotion and respect...

'I've gone through the post.'

The mundane words cut through the downy cloud of reverie, bringing Venetia's attention to the slim fair-haired young woman entering the office.

'Good.' Venetia smiled at her private secretary. 'Now how about some coffee?'

Francesca Benson continued to cross the large, expensively furnished room. 'Will do.' She returned the smile. 'Thought I'd bring this to you first; I'll wait and see if you want to answer.'

Taking the letter handed to her, Venetia looked at the scrawled address and the 'for the personal attention' marked across one corner of the good quality envelope. Hand written, therefore not a business letter. It would be quicker to read it herself than give it back to be dealt with by Francesca and its content reported to her later. Slitting the envelope with a stiletto-bladed opener, she ran her eyes quickly over the same scrawled handwriting.

'Any answer?'

At the shake of her head, her secretary moved to leave the office. Watching the slender form, Venetia Pascal smiled to herself.

The answer had been shown. The special gift that would show devotion and respect, it was here with her. She watched the girl move, lithe and graceful, her hair glinting as it caught light from the broad windows. Venetia's blood coursed warmly through her veins.

Here was that special sacrifice with which she would honour the All High, her beloved golden Lucifer.

It couldn't have been Kate's face that looked at him, not Kate standing beside that ghost in his bedroom.

Richard Torrey thumped an impatient fist on the steering wheel as the traffic lights flicked to red.

You had to be dead before you could be a ghost and Kate Mallory certainly wasn't dead. Yet the figures he had seen had not been those of living women; they had all three disappeared in a surge of flame and one face that had watched him from within that crimson hell had been the face of Kate Mallory!

But how? Traffic lights barely reaching green he slammed the accelerator hard down so that the tyres screeched as the Sonata lunged forward, the angry protests of pedestrians inches short of the pavement lost in the roar of the powerful engine. How? The car flashed across Bilston's Mount Pleasant. He had asked himself that same question all day and each time had concluded it was a dream.

'It was no bloody dream!' It snapped from him, releasing what had been a plague of thought the whole day but affording little release from the tension that, despite all of those common-sense answers, had his nerves like bowstrings. Now, after talking with Annie Price, those strings were set to snap.

'Her read same magazine at the hairdresser.' Annie had been happy to see him but surprised at the insistence of his questions.

'...said summat about a picture ... excited about it 'er was, I couldn't see why, weren't no relation o' her'n or so 'er said.'

He had forced himself to be patient with Annie. To lose it, to let her know the feeling growing in him, that something that warned all was not well with Kate Mallory, would only serve to upset this woman he had come to ... what, love?

'...But that were some days back, d'ain't Kate mention it?'

Kate had not. Crossing Bilston's Mount Pleasant, speed flat on the limit allowed, he followed the road into Wolverhampton.

'...seemed it were a posh do...' Annie had continued, happy to have someone to talk to. But it had been her mention of Vail had had him truly listen.

'...Bringin' out a new line in mek-up ... huh ... cosmetics for kids...!' Annie had snorted her contempt. 'Children be 'ardly ourta the womb these days afore they be dolled up like adults ... no childhood ... they 'aves no childhood.'

Vail! Annie had been quite sure of the name. That was what Kate had said, Theo Vail, head of Vail Corporation, and also Zachary St John Winter, the Foreign Secretary, but grab him as that had, it was the next titbit Annie passed on that caught him by the throat.

'...the woman who were launchin' them there, cosmetics ... Venice ... no, no, Venctia ... that were it, Venetia Pascal, 'er were wearin' of a brooch, Kate said it were identical to summat 'er 'ad seen in a book along o' Darlaston library.'

Something Kate had seen in a book! Swinging the car on to the A41 Tettenhall Road, Richard Torrey felt a cold tingle prickle along his veins.

The woodcut! That ancient depiction of the Devil's Talisman, was that what Kate had recognised on Venetia Pascal's lapel?

Venetia Pascal smiled pleasantly at the young woman sat on the gilt chair, the crystals edging the heavy silk shades of several table lamps playing a chorus of multi-coloured light through

409

the bronze of her hair. Kate Mallory had sent a pencil sketch along with a letter requesting an interview, a sketch which had at first startled, then seconds later afforded a deep glow of satisfaction. She would show this woman what she had locked in her wall safe and then she would show her something else. She would show her the road to hell!

'I was quite taken with the similarity.' Kate fished in the leather bag beside her feet, there was a notebook and pen in there somewhere. 'Had you seen that woodcut? Was that the inspiration behind your brooch?'

'I had not seen it. The sketch you sent proved quite a surprise.' Venetia watched the scrabbling in the bag. She would give the journalist her interview. It would be quite amusing, especially as not one word would ever be printed.

Kate found the pen. Returning several crumpled sheets of paper spilled in the process, her cheeks blushing, she looked up. 'Sorry.' She grabbed one more stray paper and shoved it with the others. This beautiful house looked as if it had never seen a sheet of paper, much less half a dozen strewn across its wonderful cream carpet.

'No need for apology.' Venetia Pascal crossed her shapely legs, the rustle of her silk crepe dress almost an intrusion in the quietness of the elegant room.

Lord, why invite her here? Kate touched the tip of her pen absently to her tongue. Why her own home, why not the offices of Pascal? The woman must have her reasons, but her own private house! It had not occurred to her to question the venue when Venetia Pascal had called to confirm her willingness to be interviewed, but now...! Kate felt a twinge of unease. What little she had seen of this house was undeniably tasteful ... expensively so, but for all its handsome furnishings and graceful charm an undercurrent ran through it, a feeling she could not quite identify, but one she could definitely feel. She would be glad to get this meeting over and be on her way back to Annie's little semi in Michael Road.

'The design of your brooch and that portrayed in the woodcut, they are one and the same, yet you say you haven't seen it.' Kate went for the heart of the interview, the rest could follow.

The quick tightening of her veins not showing in her face, Venetia Pascal continued to smile. 'That is what I said and it is the truth; I have never seen any drawing other than the one you sent, though I have seen a necklace, the centre of which bears that very design.'

She had *seen* a necklace with the same design, the Devil's Talisman! Kate made a display of writing though her mind held only one thought. Did Venetia Pascal know what it was she had worn on the lapel of her Versace suit?

'Might–' Kate swallowed, trying to ease the sudden tightness in her throat, 'might I ask where you saw that necklace?'

She had dangled the carrot and like the proverbial donkey the journalist had trotted in its wake. Venetia Pascal rose from her chair, the movement feline in its grace, Eau-de-nil silk crepe complementing without accentuating the figure it sheathed. Green-gold leopard eyes rested on Kate

411

as she smiled again. 'I saw it here in this house. Would *you* care to see it?'

'Looking into that box had been like looking into the jaws of hell...'

Dora Wilkes had trembled when saying the words, terrified of the contents of a box. Were those contents now in this house? Caution whispered in Kate's mind but was devoured by the insatiable appetite of curiosity.

'I can see your answer is yes, but first let me offer you some refreshment, champagne ... a glass of wine?'

Her brain still wrestling with the possibility of the Talisman being under this roof, Kate shook her head.

'Coffee then.' Waiting for no more refusal, Venetia Pascal left the room.

'It appeared to be a necklace ... it seemed the gold chain moved like a serpent ... red stones gleamed like the eyes of a living thing...'

Words spoken in that small house in Lowe Avenue tumbled chaotically in Kate's mind. Dora Wilkes had been afraid, so had Annie Price, and Echo... He had been his usual cagey self but beneath that reticence? He too had been afraid.

But Venetia Pascal showed not a trace of fear; it could only be that the necklace she had, though it bore a similar design, could not be the one which long ago had disappeared from Bentley Hall.

She hadn't wanted coffee. Reluctantly Kate watched Venetia place a silver tray on an elegant Georgian table. Everything about this woman shrieked taste, refined elegance, money. The kind

412

of money that could buy the Devil's seal?

Handing first a cup to Kate, Venetia Pascal took her own. Cradling porcelain delicate as a moth's wing she watched her guest sip the hot aromatic liquid, liquid which gave no indication either in aroma or taste of the drug it contained.

Thank God Annie had kept the slip of paper Kate had left lying beside the phone after making a copy in her note book.

''Ere it be,' Annie had fetched the scrap of paper, 'that be what Kate wrote so I supposes that be where 'er be gone to. Said 'er were surprised that there Venetia Pascal had agreed to give 'er an interview, much less one at 'er own private 'ouse.'

That makes two of us, Annie. The words jangled in Torrey's brain. But it was more than just surprise that had his nerves jumping like raw recruits on a parade ground; it was fear gnawed at him, fear for Kate. Why did the woman always have to jump in with both feet? Okay, so there might be nothing in this, he could be wrong in his feeling, but then again it wasn't only women had intuition.

Eyes skimming the street names, he breathed loud relief as they caught Wergs Road. Swinging the car left he passed between large spacious houses set well back within wide grounds. Unwilling to slow the vehicle, he struggled to read the names flicking rapidly in and out of the headlights but then they touched on one written on the paper Annie had given him. Saxon Place. This was it ... this was the address Venetia Pascal

413

had said for Kate to come to.

As he brought the car to a halt outside the impressive double-fronted house, his nervousness evaporated, leaving Torrey fully in control of all emotion. He had done this same thing a hundred times over, moved into enemy territory, been on top of them before ever they had known he was there. Surprise had proved a vital element of success; hopefully it would prove so this time.

But what if there was no enemy, what if the feelings he had harboured proved wrong and Venetia Pascal posed no threat to Kate? Well, then he would apologise.

Easing from the car, scarcely a sound marking the closure of the door, he stared at the lighted window, one more thought running in his brain. He might be too late.

Venetia Pascal knew the effect of the drugged coffee. Hypnos was not a paralysing drug, it did not render its user unable to move or speak but merely induced a semi-hypnotic state, one which left a person's mind easily controllable by another; and she would control that of Kate Mallory.

'You wished to see the necklace.' She smiled at Kate. 'It is in my bedroom, I will show it to you.'

She had stood here every evening, stared at the serenely smiling face of the Mona Lisa, wanting to take that which lay concealed behind the copy of that beautiful masterpiece, to fasten it about her neck, to feel the touch of those glittering stones about her throat. But each time she had resisted the temptation. A servant should not wear what belonged to the Master; and that

414

necklace did belong to her Master, every instinct, every tingling fibre of her said so. It was the Great Seal of Power, the Talisman of Satan. Now she, his most devoted of disciples, would return it to him along with the soul of Kate Mallory.

But she must not make the mistake Theo Vail had made. Kate Mallory's soul must be freely given, sworn to the Devil by her own tongue. Sliding aside the heavily framed painting, she opened the safe.

She would return the Seal to him, present it to her beautiful golden lover and in return she would be given his love, know again the thrill of him inside her. Venetia looked at the velvet pad she had brought into the sitting room, stones scarlet as blood gleaming against rich ebony velvet. Virgin's blood! Maybe not in the case of the woman sat in her drawing room, but then a sacrificial victim was no longer required to be of unimpeachable virtue and what might be lacking in this offering would most certainly be made up for by the one drugged and tied hand and foot in the bedroom next to her own. A gift of special value, something she esteemed! She relished the smile hovering beneath the thought. Francesca Benson was the secretary she liked and trusted, one woman she esteemed.

'Would you like to hold it, or perhaps you would prefer to try it on?' Her smile, open now, played on Kate Mallory. 'It is so very beautiful, the stones glisten like fire yet they are so cool against the skin.'

'*Evil.*' The frightened voice of Dora Wilkes echoed in Kate's consciousness. '*Albert said it were evil.'*

Perhaps she should have used GHB instead of Hypnos. Venetia Pascal caught the uncertainty weaving a frown between Kate's brows. But having the woman so drugged she could not acknowledge ... no, this way was best, but it needed to be done quickly while the drug was still potent in Kate's veins.

36

Did she wish to hold it, to try it on? Kate stared in awe at the necklace, the superbly worked gold glinting in the light of the table lamps, the wonderful stones gleaming. It was a totally magnificent piece of jewellery, an ornament fit for a queen – or a prince of hell!

'Where did you get this?' It was direct, meant to take the other woman by surprise, but Kate saw only contempt in those lovely cat-like eyes.

'Let us say it was a gift from a friend.'

'That friend being Sheryl Wilkes!' She had no proof the necklace was the one that Echo and Dora Wilkes had spoken of, nor that this woman had ever laid eyes on Dora's daughter, but the quick flash of alarm passing over the flawless face told Kate she had hit the nail on the head. 'You took it from her,' Kate pressed her advantage, 'in exchange for what? Money ... fame? Is that what you promised Sheryl Wilkes?'

'The girl had no idea what she was wearing.'

416

'But *you* did!'

'As you *do!*' Venetia Pascal touched a finger to the black velvet. 'You *know* what this is just as I did when I first saw it around that girl's neck.'

'And you were determined to have it for yourself.' Kate blinked against a heaviness settling in her head.

Looking up from tracing a finger over the silky velvet pad, Venetia Pascal saw the slow movement. The drug was beginning to work.

A slight shake of her head scattering a myriad shimmering darts of gold among the rich auburn folds of her hair, Venetia's voice lost its sharpness, becoming soft and sultry. 'Not for myself, Miss Mallory.'

'Yet you still took it!' Kate snapped. 'Sheryl Wilkes did not trade that necklace, did she? Nor would she ever give it away. Is that why you killed her?'

Venetia could afford to answer truthfully; her words would never be heard by any other than the woman watching her with such obvious dislike, and that woman would very soon be dead. Calm with the assurance of one fully in control, Venetia laughed, a low quiet sound whispering in her throat.

'Again, Miss Mallory, not myself. I did not kill the girl, I merely suggested she become a Follower of the Master; it was Theo Vail who made the offering.'

'Offering?' Kate fought the heaviness clouding her mind. Why the hell was she so tired?

'Theo never could take advice!' Venetia continued. 'Impatience was only one of his many shortcomings. He would not wait for the girl to become an initiate, to take her vow to serve the Master but made the offering immediately...'

Master! Offering! The words pressed against the dullness beginning to grip Kate's brain.

'It was Theo Vail's decision to sacrifice Sheryl Wilkes as it was his to leave her body tied to the cross and placed on some bonfire. Poor Theo, the Master was not impressed, he takes no delight in failure as Theo Vail has subsequently found out.'

Slowly, heavily, as if wading through treacle, Kate struggled to grasp the thoughts lapping the margin of her drowsy mind, trying to drag them fully into consciousness.

Master... Offering... Sacrifice ... the Devil's Talisman!

'I see you understand.' Venetia smiled into eyes glazed by the effects of the drug in the coffee.

'Sheryl Wilkes was sacrificed to Satan; I gave her that honour as I shall give it to you.'

This was breaking and entering in anyone's book. Torrey eased open the French window. When would folk learn the locks on these things were too flimsy to keep a fly from getting in? Burglary! What a kick that would give Daniels supposing he was caught. Torrey, a bloody tealeaf. The Inspector would feast on that for days. At least it wouldn't give him indigestion. This brought a wry smile as he slipped into the darkened room. This was breaking the law, but then what did a cat burglar get by way of punishment these days, especially one who stole nothing? A slap on the wrist from a magistrate and an order not to do it again. Not the punishment he would dish out, not the action he had planned to take when he thought his own flat was being burgled. But if it was an offence when he thought it was happening to him, it was equally an offence for him to do it to another.

Then why break into this house, why not ring the front door bell and ask if Kate Mallory was here?

That was something he couldn't answer, he knew only he had seen an apparition holding a necklace, and beside that ghost another and that other had been Kate Mallory – and Kate had come here to this house!

Soundless as shadow he moved to the door that the moonlight had illuminated opposite. He would make a swift recce, listen for Kate's voice and if he didn't hear it he would leave.

'You ... killed ... Sheryl Wilkes.'

Kate! Torrey stilled instantly, every sense alert. That was Kate's voice but why so hesitant? That wasn't Kate Mallory's style at all!

'Yes ... you see it was the only way. She had to die in order for the Master's secret to be kept.'

A woman's voice answering Kate, a woman who had owned to Sheryl Wilkes' murder! Motionless, his breathing making no impact on the silent darkness, Torrey waited. The woman was probably Venetia Pascal but was she alone with Kate or were there others?

'I could not take the risk.' The voice reached again from somewhere ahead. 'I could not have Vail or any of them see the necklace, maybe realise as I had what it truly was; had that happened then as Magus Theo Vail would have claimed the honour of returning it to its rightful owner. I could not allow that, therefore I gave him the girl.'

Necklace? Rightful owner? The small hairs on Torrey's neck bristled. Dora Wilkes had talked of a necklace, saying it was evil. Echo Sounder had been so scared talking of it he had forgotten his usual fee – and Kate? Kate was convinced the thing was the Great Seal of Power, the Devil's Talisman; did the woman now talking with her believe that same thing?

'I could have made the Offering myself, of course, cutting the girl's throat or stabbing the Athame into her heart would have presented no problem.'

She could have killed! Christ, what sort of woman was in there with Kate? Torrey's hands curled into fists as the voice continued.

'But I could afford to be generous, for my reward will be greater than ever Vail could imagine, mine will be the supreme blessing. It is ordained. The great Lord Lucifer gave me the Word, the Promise; through me shall his will be achieved.'

'Promise ... will?'

Kate's words! They were slow and thick as if her mouth was silted with sludge, but it didn't sound as if she was in pain. Good for Kate, but even better for anyone who might have hurt her.

'His will is that the necklace be returned to him. With the Great Seal of Power once more in his possession, he will take his rightful place, not among the angels but above them. The Lord of the Earth will become Lord of the Universe; everything created, everything born, will be subject to him. Tonight will see that redemption. I will return the Talisman restoring the full glory of the Prince of Darkness and he will fulfil the Promise. I shall become his wife, crowned Queen of Hell to reign beside him for all eternity!'

Queen of Hell, First Lady of Hades! The woman was tenpence short of a shilling, had a few empty rooms in the upper storey, a true candidate for Burntwood lunatic asylum. Torrey's instinct to laugh gave way to the next thought. Fair was fair, some folk believed in a queen of heaven, so why not a queen of hell? Mental debate ceased as more words reached from the room.

'As for the Wilkes girl, you need have no worries of her having suffered, I gave her a much stronger drug than I have given you; she would have felt nothing of being fastened to that cross nor of the sacrificial knife cutting into her heart.'

Stronger drug than I have given you?

Kate was drugged! That explained her slurred speech.

The sacrificial knife... Magus...

Torrey felt the blood slow in his veins. He had heard those terms before, from Max Gau the manager of Darlaston Printers, and his boss Julian Crowley...

Gau had been a Magus and Crowley an Ipsissimus, both had been worshippers of Satan and they had sacrificed Penny Smith. Black magic! He had had a strong feeling that had been behind the happenings of late and it seemed his

421

gut hadn't told him wrong; whoever was in that room with Kate walked the same path as Gau and Crowley!

Vision now attuned to the semi-darkness, ears straining to catch any sound, Torrey's brain clicked into overdrive. There could well be several people in that room, any one of whom could put a knife in Kate's heart before he got the last one of them. Not one of the bastards would escape, but that would be of little solace if Kate was dead and that would certainly be the result of him barging in there Rambo-style.

No house alarm had sounded, no one had heard him enter, no one knew he was here; that was his advantage. If luck held – he breathed slow and easy – if luck held he could be in that room and Kate behind him shielded from attack – if luck held!

Hands relaxed, arms loose at his sides, tread catlike on the balls of his feet, limbs and brain in perfect unison, he made his move.

Kate ... Kate and one other woman! With the stealth of a moving shadow he had slipped into the room, one swift glance showing Kate sat on a small gilt chair while the other... Christ, what was the other woman doing?

Kneeling in the centre of a circle enclosing a star, turned away from him, she was speaking quietly ... praying?

He could have saved himself the effort of the shake of his head meant to warn Kate not to call out. Kate Mallory didn't realise she was on this planet, much less that Richard Torrey was on it with her.

His spine against the door, his fingers turned the key. Anybody coming now would have to smash their way in, he would settle with them after that and parcel up the remains for the nearest morgue.

'Satan, All High Lord, hear your servant.'

She *was* praying. She was praying to the bloody Devil! A familiar prickle sent goosebumps over his arms. The woman was another Julian Crowley, probably with the same powers of that black magician, and Torrey ... what did he have? Nothing but the cloth-wrapped object he had taken from the glove compartment of the car moments before leaving it.

'You who were the Morning Star, Prince of Creation, pass now beyond the Gates, take the offering brought to your glory.'

'If that offering is meant to be Kate then you can forget it!' The words acted like strings jerking a puppet to its feet. Venetia Pascal turned to face Torrey.

'How?'

'Take my advice,' Torrey cut her question short, 'next time you intend to sacrifice to the Devil set your alarm system before you begin. As for the victim you think you have now...'

'Think?' Initial shock lasting only moments, Venetia Pascal now smiled contempt. 'You are the one should think, Mr...?'

'Torrey ... Richard Torrey.'

'You are the one should think, Mr Torrey. Do you imagine what you see here to be play acting? I assure you it is not. I also assure you the Lord Lucifer will not be denied. He will take not only

Miss Mallory but you too.'

The last word a laugh she spun round to face an alcove containing a table draped in crimson silk, in its centre a black inverted cross set between matching candle sticks. Lighted candles of the same blackness spilled tiny flares of gold over the red silk cloth.

'Zazas Nasantanada Zazas...'

Well, she had one thing in common with other women he had known, her attitude could change in less time than it took lightning to strike, and in this case be just as lethal. Where was the humility now, where the praise? There was more command than plea in the voice used now, an authority which seemed to imply there was no question of it being refused. This woman knew her game. Torrey moved to stand beside Kate. Knew it and was possibly a master at it.

'Zazas Nasantanada Zazas, open to me the Gates, set wide the Portals of Hell...'

It rang with the confidence of a bell. Across the room, the flames of the candles began to dim, slowly, fraction by fraction, as if operated by a dimmer switch, until only the merest dot of light remained, then as it seemed they must fade completely leaped back into life, flaring in great beacons towards the ceiling, huge spasms of light coiling and recoiling to form a pale yellow cloud over the scarlet altar.

'Sar ha-Olam, Lord of the Regions of Hell, let your will be done.'

Every corner of the room seemed suddenly filled with a rustling, a creeping of sound, a blindness feeling its way like some great slug.

'...*He will not only take Miss Mallory but you too.*'

The words thrown seconds ago fell like stones in his brain. Right now there was a better than even chance they would prove correct!

Standing in the centre of the Pentacle, the tips of the five-pointed star that was the Pentagram seeming to flare from her feet, Venetia Pascal lifted her hands towards the hovering cloud, the gleam of it turning her auburn hair to red fire.

She was beautiful. Despite recognising the danger he and Kate were in, Torrey could not deny his admiration of the woman now turned to watch him. The pale green crepe she was wearing though not figure-hugging, hid none of that body's perfection, the rich and glossy hair framed a face many women would give their soul for. Was that what she had given hers for? Was physical beauty the price tag she had placed on her immortal soul?

'Master...'

It was as quiet as it had been loud, beseeching as a moment before it had been imperative, the demand once more a request, and as it was spoken a hand dipped into a pocket of the silken gown.

'Prince of the Dark Throne, take that which your servant has recovered, take back your Seal of Power.'

The slither as of some unseen serpent undulating around the room seemed suddenly to collide into itself, becoming a great orchestra of sound beating against the temples, driving into the brain, beating Torrey to his knees, then as his legs buckled it ended, an abrupt cessation of mind-reeling sharpness.

Breath tight in his throat, Torrey forced himself upright, his glance following brilliant spears of new golden light lancing from above the altar to touch the object held in Venetia Pascal's hand; shafts of gold which danced on gold, streaming from stones glittering like living fire.

The necklace! Torrey stared at the fingers of topaz caressing the ornament. Kate must have been right in her belief that the necklace taken so long ago from Bentley Hall was the Devil's Talisman. Now he was about to be re-united with it, and once he had it what happened to Kate and Torrey? It needed no second guess, they would be two more candidates for the post of Guy Fawkes!

Gold withdrawing into gold, the lances of light left the necklace. Trails of gleaming mist, they spiralled towards the altar, combining, blending and absorbing, twisting into each other, ropes of glittering vapour drawn back to coalesce and become one with the whole. As they did so, they reshaped until the figure of a man floated above the altar.

Steady! A hand already protectively upon Kate's shoulder, Torrey cautioned himself. Chicken out now and they were both done for. But what the hell could he do? He'd seen what one of these demons from hell had done to Julian Crowley, what it had tried to do to himself and Kate – and this time he had no holy water stolen from a church to protect them.

37

The shimmering figure was moving ... it was coming towards them and he had no way of fighting it ... unless...

Torrey's hand brushed against his jacket feeling the object he had dropped inside a pocket.

It might prove useless but he had to try and try now before it was hello hell, here we come!

Quick as the thought itself, he had the piece from his pocket in his hand, the cloth it was wrapped in fluttering like a leaf to the floor. He spun on his heel marking a circle in white around himself and Kate; then threw the small cylindrical container which had held salt at the advancing demon.

It wouldn't stop the thing but at least it had given it a kick in the groin! Torrey's satisfaction as the figure halted was evident in the look he flashed at Venetia Pascal. She hadn't expected that!

Watching her now, green-gold eyes glistening passion, hands holding out the fabulous necklace, Torrey changed his assessment of her. The woman was deluded, of that there was no doubt, but it was a madness of the heart; it showed in her face, her whole body language expressed desire. But desire for what? For physical satisfaction or to be queen of hell? Listening as she spoke again, each word soft and seductive, a verbal net of lust, he made another assessment. Venetia Pascal wanted both.

Lifting the head she had bowed, Venetia held the necklace on outstretched palms and softly, seductively, a siren song of a lover, murmured, 'Great one, Lord of the Dark Regions, take back your Talisman.'

Feet resting on flames of scarlet gold, eyes burning like twin braziers, the figure floated at the rim of the Pentacle.

'It cannot be returned by a Follower.'

The devil, whatever the thing he looked at was, had answered; the words had come from it but the lips had not moved. A ventriloquist as well as a demon. Despite tight nerves, Torrey smiled wryly. Clever buggers these beings from hell.

'It cannot be given of your hand nor that of any disciple...'

Dark music, his voice rolled over the silent room.

'To be offered with free will by the hand of mortal man, that was the decree.'

A few feet away, separated by no more than the thin line of salt, Torrey could not resist a jibe. It was the only weapon left to him and he would use it. 'You're mortal, Miss Pascal,' he sneered, 'you're not queen of hell just yet. True, your body is not that of a man but it is flesh and blood, so why won't your friend take the little bauble you offer; could it be he doesn't wish to saddle himself with a wife? Or is it just you he doesn't like!'

'Master...' Venetia began again. 'Master, why?'

The barb had gone home. Torrey enjoyed the moment of triumph. She had ignored his remark but the flush rising beneath the perfect alabaster skin attested to her fury.

'*Enough!*'

Words which had been dark music crashed in black thunder, while jets of purple flame shot from blazing charcoal eyes, threats of fire dancing about Venetia Pascal who had dropped to her knees with the first eruption.

'*The decree will be observed...*'

Peal upon peal, each word a thunderclap, each an ear-splitting, clangorous shell-burst of sound that rocked the room, they spat from a mouth that did not move, from red-gold lips that did not part.

'*My Seal shall be given by one who follows the faith of the false one, a believer in the Christ. With that ultimate betrayal, will I laugh in the face of God. Give the Talisman to the one who watches.*'

'If your demon friend means me then he's wasting his time,' Torrey called, 'I don't believe in God, Christian or otherwise.'

'*Not true!*' Flames scorched across empty space, flicking against Torrey's face with burning darts of pain. '*You were a believer when you called for deliverance in the cellar of a printing works; but that is of no consequence, for it is the woman you so vainly try to guard who will present me with that most precious of gifts.*'

He might be Lucifer, the devil incarnate, but he had that wrong; Kate was out for the count. But the count was finished! Alarm stabbing spikes along his spine, Torrey felt her move, heard the short confused breaths of recovery. What now? Kate had shown no resistance against the spectre that had tempted in that cellar and it was a dead cert she wouldn't be able to resist this one. Try again, Torrey, try before it's too late!

'Why don't you bring it, Venetia? Are you afraid to leave the Pentacle, scared your fiery friend will strike you dead? And you, Prince of Darkness,' he glared defiantly at the glowing figure, 'why not bring it yourself, surely it can't be the salt holding you back?'

He was inviting death but so what, this creature from the black lagoon would take them anyway, but it would find Richard Torrey did not part easily with his soul, nor would he give up on a fight while life remained in his body. Which might not be very long, judging by what was happening now!

Venetia Pascal was not only standing, she was floating! He shouldn't be believing any of this, it was simply an illusion, lies told by a tired brain. But Torrey knew the only lies were those he tried to tell himself now, the lie which said he could beat this thing.

'Kate.'

Venetia Pascal was floating towards them calling softly, coaxingly. The salt... Torrey glanced at the circle enclosing himself and Kate, the spectral gleam of that figure turning the whiteness to anaemic yellow. Would the salt prove a barrier?

Still hovering beside the Pentacle, the figure pointed and the circle of salt disappeared, vanishing into the floor, leaving no trace of itself.

Well done! If he were in a theatre he would applaud! Torrey used virulence to keep himself focused. This wasn't a theatre and the face watching him was not that of your ordinary everyday conjurer and there was no telling what other tricks he had up that golden sleeve.

'Kate.'

At Venetia's second calling of her name Kate rose to her feet, throwing off Torrey's hand as she might brush away a fly.

'Kate, come join the Master, feel the love he has for you.' Venetia held out the necklace. 'Return this to him and know his blessing.'

'The blessing of that thing will be eternity in hell! Kate, don't listen!'

Christ, she wasn't going to listen! Grabbing her as she stepped forward Torrey found himself sprawled on the ground, the gilt chair on top of him. Where the hell had Kate found the strength? In the question was the answer. It came from hell, or at least from the ghoul conjured from that place.

'Return the Talisman,' Venetia Pascal's voice was gentle persuasion, her smile temptation, 'give it freely and join in the Glory of the Prince of the World.'

'Kate, no!' Springing to his feet Torrey reached out, trying to knock the necklace aside, to grab her, to prevent her taking it, but before he could touch her a finger of light licked at him, binding his limbs with invisible cords, the same unearthly power blocking the words in his mouth.

Kate! Kate don't do it! Words ran in his mind but found no outlet. She had almost reached the floating figure, had only to hold the necklace towards it... Kate! The shout remained a silent torment. He had failed her; Kate Mallory was

431

already lost.

But not yet, that bloody demon hadn't taken her yet! Torrey's mind struggled to find a way to help her.

'I don't believe in God...'

Those were words hurled a moment ago but what of the words said to the ghost of Anna, the apparition of the woman he had once loved? It had tried to lure him into hell, only releasing him when—

From some dark corner of his subconscious a tiny throb began to pulse, a flicker of hope among desolation.

'...the power of the Most High God commands you...'

Those words had not only broken the power of the devil's collecting agent but had brought a stronger power, one so blinding in its brilliance he had been forced to shield his eyes, to bury his face in the hair of the old woman held protectively in his arms.

But what were words when the tongue couldn't speak them?

'Always remember, son, the Lord hears not only the words we speak with our mouth, He hears what we speak with our heart.'

The gentle whisper so often heard from his mother sounded now in his head and the tiny flicker of hope surged into a flame. His limbs and tongue were bound but his heart and mind were free!

'I am Lucifer...'

Above Kate's head the red-gold mouth smiled, scarlet brazier eyes burning.

'...*and you, Katherine, shall be my consort, you shall be at my side for all eternity.*'

'No!' Venetia Pascal's scream rang across the room. 'That promise was given to *me*... I am to be queen of hell!'

Caught by the suddenness of the outburst, the floating figure looked at the distraught Venetia its furnace-like eyes deepening to glowing coals, the smile of the beautiful mouth drawing back in an animal snarl while one finger lifted.

'...*what we speak with our heart.*'

The thought danced in Torrey's mind. Would prayer be acceptable from a man who never prayed? But from childhood he had not prayed except that time in the cellar of the printing works ... and that had been accepted.

Our Father, who art in heaven.

Not even a whisper, the words no more than thought between himself and the God he had claimed no belief in, Torrey spoke in the silence of his heart.

Lord God, Creator of heaven and earth, let the light of your mercy shine upon Kate Mallory, the strength of your hand protect her...

Across the room the gleaming hand paused.

Torrey's nerves jumped as the burning luminescent eyes turned their look to him. The creature knew what he was doing! It had heard the silent words!

A flick of an iridescent finger sent Venetia Pascal crashing against the wall. Eyes gleamed hatred, amorphic tendrils broke from the golden form to drift menacingly towards the man whose own eyes stared defiance. Helpless to avoid the touch coiling about his brow, fingering into his ears, pressing against eyes he could not close, Torrey felt the intensity of its malice, a scorching, blistering assault striving to enter his mind.

But it could not! Torrey felt a triumph he could not shout. It could hold his body, keep his limbs imprisoned, but somehow that power could not reach his mind.

'What we speak with our heart.'

His mother's words when she listened to the prayers of a young boy. Prayer! Torrey's senses leaped again. That was a weapon this floating obscenity had no strength against! Fighting the pain burning into his head, every atom of his will concentrated on the words he somehow had to find, Torrey began again, the silent entreaty rising from his heart.

Lord, not for me, but for Kate, accept my prayer, deliver her from evil.

With every unspoken word, the burning coil about his head grew tighter, blinding mists of pain swirled sight from his eyes and his brain rocked until it seemed it would crash through his skull.

He had to hold on; somewhere beyond the pain, Kate Mallory was in mortal danger.

Kate! It seemed to give him strength, the will to fight one last time.

Lord, his heart whispered, *protect Kate, release her from the evil which draws her.*

Maybe Kate would be saved or maybe she would, like himself, finish in hell, he could have no more effect on the outcome. But there was one more thing he could do. Drawing air deep into his lungs, gathering every last ounce of will, he concentrated.

You! He hurled thought into the silence, into the face of the creature he knew watched him. *In the God of Heaven I place my trust. I defy the Devil, and every demon of Hell!*

The last silent syllable thrown, Torrey felt the bands about his limbs fall away, the coil crushing his head snap loose, his vision clear and with it an overriding sense of elation. More than the relief of freedom, it sang along his veins, throbbed like a living thing along every nerve. Whatever the cause or reason, whether the surge flowing in him was fact or imagination, he didn't question, it was real enough to him right now.

'Kate!'

The shout still in his throat he was across the room, dragging Kate away from the gleaming hand stretched towards her, but the golden fingers already held the necklace and as he looked into the face the red-gold mouth opened in a cry of triumph, a great silent boom of jubilation, silent yet ringing around the walls, bouncing against the ceiling, a whirlwind, a revolving swirl of silence upon silence streaming over the room in a great mind-swelling flood.

Then as abruptly it was ended.

The thing was gone, and they were still here, still alive. Held against him, Kate stirred as though waking from sleep. Maybe she would remember nothing of that golden phantom. Opening eyes forced closed by the dinning cacophony of a moment before, Torrey felt the pulse in his throat jerk.

It wasn't gone! That fiend from hell was still in the room ... and it was not alone!

But the other figure, it wasn't golden, it didn't glisten, it was an ordinary man. Still holding on to Kate, Torrey glanced at the door he had locked from the inside; it was still firmly shut yet another man had come in! Frowning, he looked at the newcomer. Not Daniels, not Echo Sounder; he wouldn't have been surprised had Sounder followed him to this house, broken in as he had ... but Sounder facing up to a being that glowed and floated on air? That much he couldn't swallow.

So who was the new guy ... and how come golden boy had backed off?

'Torrey,' Kate's voice shook, 'Torrey, I gave it to him, I gave him the Talisman.'

'Yes, you gave it to him ... you returned the Seal of Power to the Master but it was I who found it for him!'

He had not thought of Venetia Pascal; in the turmoil he had forgotten her. Torrey's glance swung to the woman, her hoarse shriek a warning which had him pull Kate clear of fingers clawed like a tigress about to strike.

'It was I lured that girl to this house,' she screamed again, 'I who stole the Talisman and then delivered her to be sacrificed and it is I and not you who will be taken as consort... Master...'

It died in a shocked silence. Leaning against Torrey, Kate Mallory followed the woman's locked gaze and her own body stiffened.

The Talisman, Satan's Great Seal of Power, the other man was reaching for it!

'*You!*' An animal snarl, silence on silence, it

ripped from the red-gold lips. *'Michael, Sword of Heaven ... but you are too late, the Seal has been returned in the manner decreed, given by a mortal of its own free will.'*

Softly, gentle as sweet music, the chilling words rested on the air.

'Will cannot be judged free when held by a drug, nor can you take what is rightfully mine!'

In response a blast of fury slammed about the walls, ricocheting from floor to ceiling, a tornado of swirling vibrating anger.

'It was given to me before time. Before the world was made, I, Lucifer, First of the Seraphim, the Morning Star, was given the Seal of Power, and with it the earth and all mankind.'

Venomous, heavy with threat, eyes blazing like crucibles of molten lead, the golden head turned towards Torrey and Kate, the hand not holding the necklace reaching for them.

This was it. Torrey gripped the trembling Kate. How did the saying go? It is better to have tried and lost than never to have tried at all. Not quite right but near enough! The smart arse who had dreamed that one up should be standing here right now!

'These are mine...'

The silent thunder of rage crashed again.

'I will take them...'

Brilliant, sinuous as reptiles, the tip of each a forked tongue of blue flame, the glittering fingers slid nearer.

Folding Kate's head to his shoulder to prevent her seeing the malevolence, the sheer maleficent savagery twisting the once handsome gilded fea-

437

tures, Torrey stared into the smouldering hate-filled eyes. They were going to die, but first he would kick this thing straight in the golden mouth.

'Seems that little trinket isn't yours after all.' He smiled, defiance a fire in his blood. 'Tough isn't it ... but that's the way it goes.' Then quietly, a whisper close against the head pressed into his shoulder, 'Sorry, Kate, but one consolation, we will each have one friend when we get to hell.'

The flickering viperish tongues were almost touching his face, in the next moment they would peel the flesh from the bone. Well! He continued to stare, an arrogant insolent rebuttal. As he had said to golden man a moment ago, that's the way it goes ... pity he couldn't have kicked him in the golden balls!

Mankind nor earth belongs to you.

His form insignificant against that of the gleaming phantom, the other man lifted a hand and the one reaching for Torrey and Kate snatched back, the hiss of a thousand snakes pouring from motionless lips.

It didn't like that! The thing from hell didn't relish playing tit for tat. But how long before it struck back? Torrey watched the spectral form return to float above the silk-draped altar.

Tendrils dark as storm clouds broke from a body suddenly becoming the colour of pitch; nebulous spindrifts of charcoal mist curled and spiralled, pivoting together in some macabre dance, separating only to join and rejoin sliding together, twining and intertwining, drift into drift until they enclosed the figure, the pale light of the altar candles playing over the negrescent

438

shining coils.

From where she knelt still in obeisance, Venetia Pascal sobbed, her emerald eyes stretched wide with fear. The cry reached Kate who lifted her head but even as she would have reached to comfort the other woman, a black hissing coil lashed Venetia Pascal across the face. The force of it skimming her like a broken toy against the furthest wall.

'No, Kate!' Torrey drew her back, once more pressing her face to his shoulder. He had seen the molten eyes flick to Kate. The thing wanted vengeance and Kate Mallory might just fit the bill.

But what was that other figure doing, who was he and why wasn't he as scared as they were? Almost in answer the room became suddenly filled with light, a vivid, gleaming radiance, amber, pale gold, colours that were pure light merged together; iridescent, sparkling, they coalesced one into another, saffron and topaz shimmering in a dance of light, a ballet of ivory and pearl whirling together to become a whiteness so intense Torrey felt his eyeballs scorch, yet still he could not look away.

'I am Michael.'

Coming from the centre of that radiance, the words were a symphony, a wondrous blend filling every corner of the room, every reach of space, each atom of the universe.

Still holding Kate tight against him, Torrey stared at the creature hovering above the altar. Its mouth was opened in a scream but no sound came though its eyes spat black fury.

'I am Michael, Archangel of the Throne of Light,

Sword of God.'

Pure music it sang on the silence.

*'In His name I take back the Seal, the Ending has
begun.'*

38

Kate Mallory looked up from the meal Torrey
had served in his flat. Take-away pizza wasn't her
style yet she had enjoyed it. Or was it the chance
to be with Torrey she enjoyed?

'What do you really think happened in that
house?' She asked the question, embarrassed at
the one she had just asked of herself.

'Venetia Pascal must have fallen, caught her
face against the wall.'

'You know that isn't what I asked. I mean, what
really happened?'

'What can I tell you?' Torrey shrugged. 'Annie
told me where you had gone, I decided to come
pick you up and it's lucky I did. The house reeked
of gas ... the cooker tap left on presumably ... you
and the Pascal woman were totally out of it, that
must be how she came to fall. That's all I know,
anything else must be the result of fumes messing
up your mind.'

It was nothing but a lie; but then how could he
tell her that a demon had struck Venetia Pascal,
leaving an inch-wide gap across her face, destroying her beauty for ever? And to say the Archangel
Michael had snatched back the necklace and

440

then in a cloud of brilliance had swept away the creature hovering above that altar, to tell Kate Mallory that would have her call in the white coats.

'Gas.' Kate collected plates and cutlery and took them to the sink. 'Was that what caused the house to go up in flames?'

'So the fire department reckons. Thank God I heard that poor secretary moaning through her gag. She'd have been toast otherwise!'

'But what do *you* reckon?'

'Kate.' He forced a laugh. 'I drive a taxi, I don't fight fires. By the way...' he changed the subject, '...how did your report on the Vail case go down with Scottie?'

'What little I was allowed to report! Inspector Daniels did his best but the big boys in London closed ranks, the public would panic, international confidence in the government would be undermined, so they replaced the Vail stuff with foodstuff brought in from some other place.'

'But you still got your scoop?'

'Call it half a scoop,' Kate grinned. 'Still, we didn't do too badly, in fact I think we were pretty good. I reckon we could start our own detective agency.'

'Oh yes.' It was Torrey's turn to grin. 'And call it what? Myths and Legends or Old Wives' Tales?'

'Not such a good idea? Then try this one, Mr taxi driver. How about giving a friend a free ride home?'

Venetia Pascal had caused the death of Sheryl Wilkes, had the girl sacrificed in a black magic

441

ceremony just so she could steal that necklace.

Having dropped off Kate, Torrey guided the car from Michael Road, picking up speed as he turned on to Wolverhampton Street.

The woman was as evil as the master she had served. Consort of Satan, Queen of Hell. Torrey's hands tightened on the wheel. Venetia Pascal hadn't made it that far, though she was a true daughter of the devil. Thank God she hadn't got her hands on Kate.

Kate! He smiled wryly. Did she truly believe that rigmarole about a gas tap being left switched on? With Kate you never could tell. But she had got her scoop, beating the Nationals yet again. And Daniels? Who could tell? Maybe he might even get promoted. They had all come out on top except for Echo Sounder, that poor sod had lost the love of his life – as he had lost Anna!

For half a second longing surged. He pushed the memory away. He had lived with his pain but then that pain had been taken away ... but Echo ... how could his pain be eased?

Coming to the junction of Pinfold Street he glanced towards a building to his left. The Staffordshire Knot. On impulse he drove into the car park.

'It were the necklace, weren't it?'

Echo Sounder voiced the question as Torrey set two pint glasses of beer on the stained table.

'That be what Sheryl were killed for. Oh, I knows the blues ain't found who it were set 'er body on that bonfire!' He picked up the glass placed beside his hand and drank deeply.

Steadying his nerves! Torrey recognised his own behaviour of years before. He drank to avoid the need for answers.

Daniels had spared the man that. He and Kate had told the Inspector what Venetia Pascal had admitted but it was evidence the police could not use; as Daniels had said, the woman had been pronounced of unsound mind and no court would agree to her being brought before it.

'You can think me daft if you likes.' Echo Sounder wiped his mouth with the back of his hand. 'But I knows what I knows. That necklace were a thing of evil and I 'opes it don't never be found no more.'

He could assure him on that point. But as with Kate, tell Sounder an angel had taken it and Torrey would be the one thought daft. Tell him of Sheryl Wilkes' ghost and the man might well crack that pint glass over his head.

His offer of a second drink refused, Torrey left the pub.

'I thanks you for comin' to talk wi' me.'

Surprised that Sounder had followed him from the smoky bar room, Torrey looked over his shoulder, sympathy finding a new level as light from the pub forecourt glistened on tears edging the man's eyelids.

'Sounder, I...' Lord, how did he say this? 'Don't ask how but I'm sure Sheryl...'

'You don't need to say.' Sounder blinked the tears away. 'I knows 'er be all right for I be lookin' at 'er ... there against the lamp post.'

Glancing to where Sounder pointed Torrey saw the figure. Clothed in a blue dress, long blonde hair gleaming, a pretty face showed clearly in the light of the street lamp. For several seconds it watched them then, a sad smile touching its mouth, came the words, *'Forgive me, Leonard.'*

It was a mere whisper carried on the breeze then, one hand lifting in farewell, it was gone.

From the car Torrey stared at the spot where the figure had been enveloped in a cloud of silver white. The hand she had raised no longer held that necklace. Sheryl Wilkes was free of its evil.

The publishers hope that this book has given you enjoyable reading. Large Print Books are especially designed to be as easy to see and hold as possible. If you wish a complete list of our books please ask at your local library or write directly to:

Magna Large Print Books
Magna House, Long Preston,
Skipton, North Yorkshire.
BD23 4ND

This Large Print Book for the partially sighted, who cannot read normal print, is published under the auspices of

THE ULVERSCROFT FOUNDATION